Death and the Librarian and Other Stories

D0071757

ESTHER FRIESNER

Five Star • Waterville, Maine

Published in 2004 in conjunction with Tekno Books and
Ed Gorman.

Set in 11 pt. Plantin by Christina S. Huff.

Printed in the United States on permanent paper.

Library of Congress Cataloging-in-Publication Data

Friesner, Esther M.
    Death and the librarian and other stories / Esther Friesner.
      p. cm.—(Five Star speculative fiction)
      Contents: All vows—True believer—"White!" said Fred—A
    birthday—A pig's tale—Love, crystal, and stone—In the realm
    of dragons—Jesus at the bat—Chanoyu—Ilion—How to make
    unicorn pie—Death and the librarian.
    ISBN 0-7862-4682-0 (hc : alk. paper)
    ISBN 1-4104-0177-4 (sc : alk. paper)
    1. Fantasy fiction, American. I. Title. II. Series.
PS3556.R5683 D4 2002
813'.54—dc21   2002029724

Death and the Librarian
and Other Stories

This book is dedicated to my husband, Walter Jacob Stutzman, and our kids, Mike and Annie, who are always there for me, always appreciated, always loved.

It is also dedicated to the memory of my parents, David and Beatrice Friesner, who knew a thousand different ways of telling me, "You can do it!"

Table of Contents

Introduction

I'll never forget the first time I encountered a fellow-author who declared, with a straight face, "I hate to write but I love having written." I could believe the second part of what he said, but the first? Impossible. Incredible. How can anyone *not* love to write? Granted that the process can be challenging, even frustrating, but the level of satisfaction I derive from the actual act of writing is something I would not trade for anything.

(Anything except possibly a free round-the-world luxury cruise, First Class all the way, unlimited expense account. For some reason, I don't hear anyone making me the offer, which is just as well because I love to write.)

What I hate is having to write about writing.

I know exactly where to place the blame for this bad attitude of mine: Education. I am a long-time lover of stories, not just writing and telling them but reading them and listening to them. Poetry, too? Oh yeah, bring it on. There are few things as delectable as that moment when the words on the page send a physical thrill through you, giving you a glimpse into something magical, something beautiful. I hereby present my credentials as a card-carrying neo-Victorian sentimentalist and admit that I get the same sensation whenever I hear a bugler playing "Taps." It happened to me while reading "The Piper at the Gates of Dawn" chapter in *The Wind in the Willows*, the conclusion of *The Divine Comedy*, the

9

poems "Little Things" and "The Bells of Heaven," and more. I will spare you from my citing a list of works that are all a matter of personal taste or, to say it in fluent Netspeak, YMMV.

Now imagine how I felt the first time a teacher presented me with a poem—one that gave me the thrill described above—and told me to analyze it. Take it apart to see how it worked. Dismember it. Dissect it. Poke around in the now-lifeless interior with scalpels and probes and pointy sticks. I was aware that this was an important part of my education just as I knew that boiled liver and okra provide us with many essential nutrients, but that did not mean I *liked* it. I could tolerate it when the piece under analysis was not one that evoked a deep emotional response in much the same way that I endured the unit on dissection in ninth-grade Biology because they gave us a frog to cut up and not a baby bunny-rabbit.

Come to think of it, I didn't want to dissect the frog, either. Thank heaven for lab partners! She did the dissection, I took the notes, and everyone was happy except the frog.

Now I'm being asked to write about my own writing, to which all that I can say is: Thank heaven for lab partners! Or, in this case, life partners.

My husband Walter is wonderful in many ways. He gave me much invaluable help in the creation of this book, from making suggestions about the selections contained herein to actual aspects of production. He has always been highly supportive of my career, encouraging me through those dark days when it seemed as if none of my stories would ever see publication, proofreading manuscripts above and beyond the call of duty, even allowing himself to be dragged into co-authoring a story or two (or three) with me. Plus, he can play the bagpipes. Very well. Yes, that *is* possible.

He has also consented to write about my writing, specifically about the stories chosen for this collection. Ladies and gentlemen, my husband:

I have often suggested to Esther that she select her favorite works of short fiction. With over a hundred titles, I was curious to see which she felt were significant. Although she is well-known for her humorous takes on subjects ranging from an elf-versus-human palimony suit to Valley Girl vampires, Esther's awards have recognized her sensitive treatment of those facets of life and death which all of us encounter. It is from these subjects that most of her selections are drawn.

Some of these stories will make you laugh out loud, while in others the wit is gentler. In some, the violence is physical, while in others words and actions injure just as readily. Esther's views ring clear in some stories, while she considered it a great compliment that her opinion on abortion does not leap from the text of "A Birthday."

If there is a single theme linking these stories, I think it is this: Know yourself well enough to find those things of true value and, having found them, don't waste them. True love, in all of its expressions, is precious: recognize it and hold onto it. Knowledge—of self, of others, of the world which all of us share—is likewise precious: use it wisely. And, as I am sure Esther would remind us, a sense of humor is an invaluable aid during our life's journey.

This collection will let you look at the world through Esther's eyes. If you are moved to think more deeply or even to act after having read a particular story, then both you and Esther have helped to make our world a better place for all of us.

Back again; did you miss me?

Even though I believe that writing should speak for itself, I suppose I'd better say a little something about the stories you're about to read, especially the one called "Ilion."

One of the reasons I enjoy writing as much as I do is because it provides me with so many different benefits:

Sometimes it lets me stand in the spotlight, center-stage, and do stand-up comedy about suburbia and other fantasylands.

Sometimes it lets me slap on a black mask, load up on silver bullets, leap onto my white stallion and gallop off to right wrongs, or at least make people aware of them.

Sometimes it lets me make up for the fact that I never had a chemistry set as a child, so now I get to experiment with language itself. (Feel free to view "Love, Crystal and Stone" as either homage to the great Spanish surrealist, Federico García Lorca, or as what happens when you let a child dump a glass of fruit punch onto a lump of sodium.)

Sometimes it just lets me deal with a situation or a cause or an event that I am unable to cope with by any other means.

This brings me to "Ilion":

"Ilion" is the only story in this collection that has not been published previously anywhere else. I wrote it following the events of September 11, 2001. I know that some of us are still unable to read about it, unable to bear a visit to Ground Zero, unable to cope with images of what happened. My husband Walter was there, working in the World Financial Center across from the World Trade Center, so I understand all too well about how difficult it can be to come to terms with the events of that day.

I dealt with September 11 in the idiom of fantasy, but I did not do so to trivialize the horror of what happened. I did it because it was the way this particular story needed to be told, and because at the time it was the only way for me to be able to express my feelings in a satisfactory manner.

If you do choose to read it, thank you. If not, I understand, and I hope you will still enjoy the rest of the stories in this book.

All Vows

I'm cold. I wish it'd stop raining. Granny Teeth never comes when it rains, and I like her, even if Sammy don't.

"What you want any ol' gook ghost-lady to come hanging 'round bothering us?" he asks. Then he smiles at me. I think maybe he likes her, too. Some. Even if the only reason why he likes her's 'cause she keeps me quiet. That's important, keeping quiet, for a kid.

When we're warm, when we're places out of the rain, that's when she comes. Other people don't see her, and Sammy . . . I dunno if he sees her or if he just says he does, for me. Times Sammy gets enough money together to buy the two of us a couple of hamburgers at McDonald's, that's funny, then. We go in, see, and Granny Teeth, she comes in after. Sammy says what we want and puts down the money, all crinkly and dirty like it gets. Times we go in, ain't hardly nobody there 'cept us and the people behind the counter. They act like they're half asleep most times, seeing nothing, almost. Sometimes Sammy's gotta shout and shout to get our order heard, and even then . . .

While the girl's got her back to us—getting our burgers, I guess—Sammy talks to me. He don't say boo to Granny Teeth, though. Could be he don't see her; could be it's a game. I dunno. Sammy, he plays games with me. Anyway, this game he turns away from the counter and Granny Teeth shuffles around him real careful, then she just floats up over

14

the counter and down behind it. Ghosts can do that. Ain't noplace ghosts can't go. Sammy, he don't look, but I see what she does. She grabs us a bag, stuffs it full of burgers, fries, two chocolate shakes, what we wanted, shoves it over the counter at us and takes our money real fast. "Have a nice day!" she says, and her teeth flash gray and gold.

One time I looked back, she swapped our money for her own. I know, even if I never seen her do it. I saw the girl back of the counter pick up what should've been Sammy's money, only all it was was a bunch of brown, dry, dead leaves. Granny Teeth was just standing there, watching the girl, looking all upset. Maybe 'cause the girl's gawping at them leaves, I dunno. Sammy says gooks got fifteen thousand different ways you can insult 'em, and something mean to do back at you for every one of them insults. I hope the girl didn't get in no trouble with Granny Teeth, insulting her dead leaf money. I guess when you're a ghost, money don't matter. I wish Uncle John knew that.

I wish Sammy'd buy me a Happy Meal sometime. I never had one of them. But I don't like asking Sammy for more than he gives me straight out, on account of he'd give me what I asked for and go without himself. So I don't ask. Already he give me more than Uncle John ever did, and I never give him even my last name.

I give that to Granny Teeth, though. I give her my name; hers, too. Sammy tells me, "Corey, thing about these gooks is, see, that they got some names no way a kid like you could pronounce. What are you—six? seven?"

I won't tell. You tell *one* thing, you start telling all of 'em. Anything you say maybe gets back to someone else. Maybe the police, and then I know what *that* means: They'd take me back.

I'm not going back. I'm going to Washington, D.C., with

Sammy, and Granny Teeth, and after we get there and see what Sammy says he's got to see, then I'll try to get him to let me stay with him forever.

If he says no, I'll run away again. I can. I got to. If you can't go back, you got to run away.

It's safe to tell Granny Teeth, though, seeing as how she's a ghost. I talk to her; Sammy don't. You got to name what you talk to, else it's not real. She has these gold teeth, see? Two gold teeth right where a vampire's got fangs, only she ain't no vampire. I call her Granny Teeth, and she smiles.

It's raining now. Seems sometimes like it's been raining forever, the black over me, and the wet, and the cold. We found us a place to sleep 'long by an old road that used to be a pretty important highway. Used to be, people'd stop here. Lotta things used to be. Sammy, he's got us a fire burning in this old oil drum was a trash barrel, but there ain't nowheres near anything like a solid roof over our heads; just only trees. Picnic tables, too; most too bust up to lie under so it'd do any good, though.

Sammy looks up into the rain. He got brown hair color of the dirt back home and green eyes pale as a peeled twig. He smiles up to heaven and his teeth run shining with the falling water.

"This it, Lord?" He's laughing when he talks, so easy with his god. "*This* the thanks a man earns from You for trying to keep a promise?" He taps his wrist like he's got a watch there. He ain't got a wristwatch since I know him, since that night I come on him out of the trees and there he was, like he's waiting for me.

"You can't tell me You don't know what day it is, Lord," he says. "And that means You know what day's coming. When I heard that last blast, I got on the road right away, but ten days isn't all that much when you're going so far on foot.

Now listen: I don't have all that much money; I never did. Anybody wants to tell You any lies about how us Jews got all the money in the world, You send them around to have a word with Sammy Nachman. I'll set 'em straight, You bet. If I had the bread, I'd be sitting in some nice, warm Amtrak train, drinking a cold beer. But it's all on foot, all the way, and the kid—" He looks at me and I don't know what to do with the good feeling it gives me "—the kid can't march as fast as me. So whaddaya say, Lord? You do Your part, I'll do mine. Ease up on the rain, okay? Save it for spring."

I look up at the same spot in the sky I see Sammy do. Nothing but clouds, nothing but rain. I never knowed the Jews to pray like he does, out loud, talking so anyone can understand. I hope his god don't mind English. I thought it was against the rules or something for a praying Jew to talk like that to his god. We need Sammy's god to listen to him now. I'd ask mine, only Jesus don't listen to all the lies a dumbass little kid makes up to tell. Jesus hates liars; he burns 'em in Hell. Anybody knows that. I didn't need Uncle John to tell me something I knew. I don't take off Jesus no more; just only Sammy.

Granny Teeth got her a god? A ghost-god? I wonder. She comes back, I'll ask.

Sammy asked real good. The rain stopped that night, while we lay wrapped up in our old green blankets on the ground by the picnic tables. I brushed the hair out of my eyes, first up. It's pretty cold, and the little bit of grass I see's got frost. Sammy says he could always sleep through anything, even in 'Nam. Home, I got used to waking the minute I hear any noise. Nothing sneaks up on you that way. It's safer.

So I wake now; and the first thing I see is Granny Teeth's feet next to my face. She's sitting on one of them bust-up tables. Ghosts don't mind splinters or the cold. Her toes are curled up, brown and round like a row of acorns. She goes barefoot—what's a ghost got to worry over about where she steps, anyhow?—and her toenails are thick and yellow and gray.

" 'Morning, Granny Teeth," I say. I'm glad she's back.

"Good morning, Corey." I like how she bows her head to me—not much, only a little. It makes me feel grown up and worth something. "Does it go well with you and this man?" she asks.

"Could be better." I smile to let her know I'm joking. Ghosts, they're monster kin. It don't do to get 'em mad. I remember how Granny Teeth looked the time I told her just a bit about Uncle John and how it was. I thought her eyes'd take fire, burn me right up then and there.

"Better? How? You are hungry?" She's wearing an old brown robe, loose, but she's got a cracked blue plastic pockabook hanging off her neck. It snicks open and she roots through it. "You need money, you and Sammy?"

Money? From Granny Teeth? Ghost money. Dead leaves. She scrabbles in that old pockabook of hers, I can hear 'em rustling. I don't laugh, because of what I said about ghosts getting mad. I don't laugh, but I know how it makes me feel full of bubbles inside, holding in the laughter. It feels good, holding in laughter, knowing laughter's all that's in there to hold.

"We be okay, Granny Teeth," I tell her. I know how to talk respectful. I got taught that much, didn't I? Hard taught. "You keep your money." *Your dried-up old dead leaf ghost money.* "Thanks anyhow."

I smile, 'cause it just tickles so to think I'm please-and-thanking this ol' gook-lady ghost for offering us them leaves she totes 'round and swaps for the real dollars we plunk down every time Sammy and me buy food. I smile big—can't help but—and that feels good, too. More right-feeling things are coming into my life these days. I'm some surprised I recognize them after this long.

Granny Teeth clicks that cracked blue pockabook shut; her lips, too. She don't smile. Her whole face folds in at the mouth, all the wrinkles running like fishnets, like roads crisscrossing good brown country earth. "Sammy is a good man," she says, "but he does not know."

"Know what?" I ask. She shakes her head.

"You do not know either, Corey. You are too young to know."

" 'Bout what? The war? I know all 'bout that," I say, proud. "Soldiers an' bombs an' fire-fights an' the jungle-bugs big as cats, rats big as dogs, I know it. Sammy told me."

Granny Teeth sighs. "Sammy is a good man," she says again. "But he can never teach you what he refuses to see for himself. He can not tell you what he will not let *himself* know." And she sits so still it's like I could reach out and scoop a piece of stillness off her, hold it in my hand. Then, any time the hollering started up, and the hitting, I could just uncup my hands, let the silence and the stillness fly high, fly free, soar up to Heaven and drip down over me, wrap me safe in the blanket of the rain.

Sudden I 'magine that was I to come close, lean in, put up my arms to her long, skinny ones like I used to do with my daddy and lay my head against the hard bones bottoming her neck, could be I'd smell the earth smell. New-turned earth, wet with the deep-running water of melted snow. Spring earth, gulping down the seed, pushing up the flowers.

My daddy once give me a little red plastic shovel, let me plant yellow tufty flowers by the big tree out behind the house come spring. After he went and let that tractor roll over on him, stupid like he done, and Uncle John come, I didn't get no more time to do more'n smell the springtime earth. No red plastic shovel any more. No yellow tufty flowers.

What'm I doing? I was only dreaming 'bout doing that, putting my arms 'round Granny Teeth, and here I go, catch myself doing it for real. I yelp loud and push back from her, squirming out of her arms, shaking bad. Oh Jesus, touch a ghost like that, it's cold. *Cold!* Her robe's like fuzzy brown worms all over—I *felt* them, I *did.* Worms that crawl in your skull, eat out your eyeballs when you die. Oh Jesus, I didn't mean what I said before 'bout You. Jesus, You gotta help me now, don't got no one else but You, like my daddy always did used to say. You don't burn up liars when they're only little children, You couldn't do something half so heartless, no, and anyway, no matter what Uncle John says, don't believe him, they was *his* lies, all! Jesus Lord, I'm scared, and Sammy's sleeping, and maybe his god won't pay me no mind 'cause I'm no Jew. Oh Jesus, *cold!*

"Corey!" Granny Teeth stares at me. I see by her eyes how sharp I hurt her, shouting like that, shoving her away. Lord, it wasn't *my* fault, I swear. One minute I'm just thinking 'bout how nice it'd be, smelling home earth, next I'm in her arms. . . .

Magic. Yeah, that's what. Ghosts can do magic, can't they? Witch you any old way they can?

See, I said so. Not my fault at *all.* I don't lie. I don't care what *he* said, or the way that tired-eyed skinny lady with the clipboard looked at me that time she come 'round to ask all those questions. I don't ever lie.

I don't know I'm still shaking 'til Granny Teeth lays one hand on my arm and I feel my flesh twitch and shudder in her grasp. Her face is flat and calm, like the surface of a pond. Almost I dream I'm seeing her eyes through a depth of brown, weed-scummed water. She's got kind eyes. She's not even some mad at me. Not like the *waste-my-time* clipboard lady at all.

"Corey . . ." Hearing my name soft-spoke that way makes the shakes stop. She takes away her hand from my arm. "I did not mean to frighten you. I am only here to help you and Sammy. It is difficult. There are too many walls, but I must try. It is a debt. A vow I made. Do you understand vows, child?"

I nod. Not that I *do* understand or anything, not really. Vows are for when you get married. Who'd marry a ghost, birth a bunch of ghost babies? Debts are what bills mean— too many bills, not enough money; too many mouths, not enough work got in return to make feeding 'em worth a man's while, but only live folks got debts to pay and money to pay 'em. What's she mean to do? Count out stacks of dead leaves into Sammy's hand?

Granny Teeth got the gentlest smile I ever see, even if it does always look half sad. "You are a good boy, Corey." Her hand's cool, full of the spring-earth smell cupped in the palm. "You will help me pay back what I owe Sammy, and there will be enough left to repay all that is owed you, too."

Owed me? What's owed me? 'Cept the farm, and the earth, and I'm not going back for *that*. Uncle John wanted it so bad, let him keep it. Maybe my daddy'd should've left it to *him*, like he was always saying after he drunk too much. Sometimes when he didn't drink a drop. I don't want nobody owing me *nothing*. Just let me alone.

The longer Granny Teeth looks at me, the stiffer her smile gets until there's no softness left at all. Little ghosts get under my skin just looking at her. Stern, she says, "To bury such treasure! This is sin. It shall be repaid! Oh yes, this debt too." Then she's gone.

Well! Sure enough, now I do know what ol' Granny Teeth

meant with all her talk of debts and help and the like. Treasure! Why, sure, I heard the tales, the old ghost stories telling how the dead lead the living to riches hid deep in the walls of abandoned houses, buried at the roots of old trees.

But when it's light and I wake up Sammy to tell him what Granny Teeth's promised us, he just laughs.

"Treasure, Corey? *Her?* Tell me some ol' gook ghost got any money hidden? Sure, maybe a coupla dozen coins buried back in 'Nam, but *here?* Sorry, Champ. No way you and me're gonna go back to 'Nam to dig up that kinda treasure."

He don't say no more about it and I don't say nothing too. I think maybe Granny Teeth's gonna come looking after us, all her talk of paying, but that's the last I see of her for nights and nights.

Sammy and me, we press on. Nights, it gets lonesome. Sammy and me, we make fire, steal fire, borrow fire anyplace we can. When we take another man's fire, Sammy pays with his stories 'bout 'Nam. If they'll hear 'em. Sometimes the men we meet got too many 'Nam stories of their own and don't even want what they got to start with. Then we move on.

Finally the night comes when the dark runs out and all the sky's a light we can't ignore. No more shadow-walking. ("Folks see a raggy man like me with a kid like you, they'll ask questions, and I got no time for answers. Let's try to get there on the quiet, Corey.") There ain't no more shadows. Lights everywhere, every street, every road, and the sky ahead's holding a white dusting of light that makes the shapes of buildings burn black and shiny against my eyes.

City light. Washington, D.C., city lights. Sammy says we're almost there.

We walk in over the hard roads. Nighttime and no rain. Sometimes, beside the highways, there's trees. Days, we sleep there. I like the feel of the bark against my back, the roots twisting down deep into the earth like they're looking for something they lost. I put my ear to the trunk and dream I can hear the old tree's heartwood singing.

Soon there's big buildings, harder roads, and more houses than trees. Sammy says we're in the city itself now. We pass houses where the light inside's all warm and gold. I put out my hands to catch the sweet spill of it, like it was magic that could warm me. Oh, it's cold out here! I stare at the windows, slabs of shining light thick enough to be tombstones, holding back the warm, keeping it away from me. I can't hardly recall how it used to feel, being on the right side of windows, and a roof above, and someone to give me a way to keep warm without a fire to sear my skin.

I look at my arm. The old marks are still there. Little round red blisters all up and down the inside of both my arms from the cigarettes. Some come fat, some come thin. Uncle John rolled his own. *Be a man, Corey! Christ knows, you eat enough for a man!*

I can still smell the soured beer hot on his breath. The sizzle of my own skin clogs my ears so much, sometimes I miss hearing anything else. So, when I try, why can't I re-member more than the sweet spring earth smells, and the little red shovel, and the tufty yellow flowers by my eyes? Where's my mama's face? Where's my daddy's arms to keep me safe, the way he promised when she died? But all I got to wrap 'round me in the dark is Sammy's old green blanket, and that smells burnt some too.

Comes the night we don't got to steal fire no more. There's steam grates to lie on, and that feels nice. The other folk, the ones who tell us to shove over, we got their spot and they'll fight us for it maybe, Sammy knows what to say to 'em:

"Look, I got a kid here." And they kinda blink their eyes

and tilt their heads like sorry old birds to stare at me. But they move over and they let us rest.

This is the night we'll go there. Where's there? I don't know. Only Sammy said it like it was the most important thing in the world, *there.* He puts all the weight of his heart behind a word, you know it's important, even if you don't know nothing else, nor need to be asking.

"Soon as it's dark, Corey," he says. "We're gonna go there. I'm gonna sleep some now, you stand guard, okay? Sentry duty. You can sleep tonight, while I do what I came here to do."

"I don't wanna sleep then," I tell him. "I wanna help you do it."

He smiles at me, and when he reaches out his hand to touch my cheek I don't flinch back. Funny. His hand's hard, got a bitter, sad smell to it, but under the shell there's a kindness makes it softer than anything in my memories. "You don't even know what I'm here to do," he says.

"I don't care," I tell him.

"Yeah, I guess you don't." His smile gets some brighter, and it's so sweet to feel a hand on me that don't got any pain behind it. "Okay, then. But I bet you're gonna be all confused. See, there's a vow I've got to keep—"

"A vow! You getting married, Sammy?" It's the first I hear of it, and my stomach goes to knots.

"Marri—? Nah, not *that* kind of vow, kid!" He laughs, and I can share it with him. "A vow's a *promise,* is all. Just let me do what I gotta, you keep quiet. If you get bored waiting, find something to do with yourself, no questions until after, then I'll explain, deal?"

"Deal." I nod. I'm good at keeping quiet. And a vow's a promise; now I know.

"Okay," he says again, curling up like a fat ol' caterpillar in his green blanket. "Wake me when it's sundown."

While he sleeps, I watch the people. They don't see us. We're camping on a steam grate up against one of the big buildings here. There's plenty of bushes for cover. Sammy told me all 'bout how that's important, cover. There's all kindsa ways a man can hide, he said, and sometimes knowing when to hide will save you. I knew that already; I just wasn't so good at it. I sit real still on guard over Sammy. I find this big branch and I pretend we're in 'Nam together, and I got a gun in my hands. Nobody better try to mess with me now. He tries, I'll shoot him dead.

I watch the feet of the people passing by, see 'em through the roots and low branches of the bushes. It's boring all right, but I stay true to my promise. My vow. Now I got me a vow to keep too, like Granny Teeth, like Sammy. I start off pretending that I'm all there is to stand between him and them who'd stop him from keeping his vow, and I end by believing it's truly so. Like a little nothing kid like me could really do anything to keep off danger! Like I got any kinda power in me at all, that's *so* funny! That's so funny, I forget to laugh.

Then she's there. One minute I'm watching these feet going by, counting the high heels and the polished fancy shoes and the cool high-tops, and then being surprised 'cause there's this one pair of scruffy ol' blue bedroom slippers hustling past, and then all of a sudden the scruffy blue slippers turn the corner of the bushes and come right on in, and it's Granny Teeth herself.

Why's she want to come here like this, in daylight? I thought ghosts don't like the day. Maybe that's just evil ghosts as fear the light. I don't know too much, I guess.

"Corey, does it go well with you and this man?" she asks, like always.

"We're doin' good, Granny Teeth," I tell her. "We're al-

25

most there. Tonight's when we're gonna do it."

Granny Teeth nods. "His vow. He told my daughter of it many times. I often saw them sitting together, speaking. She told me he was a man who carried the burden of many ghosts, although he was guilty of none of their blood. To carry a ghost's weight is a heavy thing, child. No wise man does it willingly. It is done when it can not be helped, for guilt. But sometimes it is done for love."

"Sammy love your daughter?" I ask. Could be he *is* getting married. My stomach hurts around that.

She shakes her head this time. "His promise was made to *all* my family, not just to her alone. No one believed him but me. We were his friends; he told us he would be our shield. That vow was kept. When the soldiers left our village but came back later, running, frightened, all the eyes of the jungle burning cold into their backs, acting as if they did not re-member who we were, friend or foe, he was the only one who stood between us and them—them, his own people!—so that we could flee their fear, the fear that killed first without asking, without thought, without—"

Granny Teeth sighs away the rest. "He did not love my daughter as you would think, child. But yes, he did love her."

I'm confused. "How come you say, no, he didn't love her, then, yes, he did?"

She squats down flatfooted so's we're eye to eye, and the shiny black of her eyes holds me so still I 'most forget to breathe. "Because, Corey, in this world there are as many loves as ghosts, and as many vows as loves." Then she's gone.

When it starts to get dark, I wake Sammy. I'd been thinking on what Granny Teeth said and I still couldn't make heads or tails out of it, so I decide it wasn't worth more trouble. Still, I have to ask:

"Sammy, what's this vow of yours you're gonna keep?"

26

He just says, "You'll see," and he stows his blanket and picks up his pack and takes my hand warm in his.

It wasn't far we had to go. Just a couple city blocks, and into some trees and out again. The moon wasn't up yet that I could see. There's this long stretch of flat ground, and a big lawn all crisp with frosted grass. Sammy says, "Sure did get cold early this year." I been feeling cold so long, it don't make much difference to me, but it seems like it matters to him, so I agree.

There's some signs. There's a pretty domed building near our end of the lawn, lit up white. There's this metal thing like a one-legged table, like the place where the preacher stands up in church and rests his Bible when he gives the sermon. Sammy goes over to it, and I see how weird it is, because instead of being a place you could rest a book on top of, there's this big fat book underneath the glassy top, see, and Sammy has to reach under to turn the pages. The book's chained down. Why'd anyone want to chain a book?

I guess Sammy was right 'bout me getting bored. I watch him turn the pages awhile, but he goes so slow. I look around some more. There's some people strolling in the dusk, but they walk right by us 'cause we're so raggedy-looking. Sammy says being poor's next best to being invisible. I look back at Sammy and I see there's some drops of wet starred out on the glass. I hope it don't start to rain again for real until we're done.

Sammy stands up straight, holding on to the edges of the glassed-in book like he's gonna preach a text. He even cries out, "Oh Lord!" like he's moved by the Spirit. But I remember he's a Jew, and I don't think they do it like that. His hands look mighty white, especially where they're grabbing hold. You can almost see the metal edges and the glass cutting through. I feel my whole chest get tight with fear so's it starts a black burning. I'm afraid.

27

When he lets go, I can draw breath again. He don't say 'nother word to me, just jerks his head so I know I'm to follow. We walk to this statue of three soldiers. That's where he lays down his pack and takes out a funny little thing, like a ladies' pockabook, almost, only it's flatter and smaller and it don't got a strap. It's white with blue stripes, 'cept it's so dirty the white part's just a guess. Sammy unzips it and takes out a book and a shawl.

He puts the shawl on his head. It's clean enough so's you can see it really is white and blue; got all these fringes at the bottom, but not all the way across. He surely does look funny with that thing draped over his head. "I lost my *yarmulke* a long time ago," he says to me, and smiles when he realizes I don't know what the hell he's talkin' about. "Never mind, Corey." The book's a clean blue and he kisses it.

There is a place in the earth and you go down into it slow. I follow Sammy, but it's like he don't see me no more. There's a sliver of black, shiny stone rising at our feet like a wave, and the farther down we go into the earth, the higher up the black stone rises. Sammy looks straight ahead, like he don't know the black wall's rising at his left hand. I follow him, and there's a scary tingling in my bones.

I look down at the gray walk at my feet because I don't want to see the wall. I tell myself *It's rock! It's just rock, what's to be afraid of? Don't be so stupid, Corey!* 'til I sound like Uncle John, so I stop. There's things on the ground propped up against the wall, bright things with some color to them besides black and gray. I see a flag, folded up so just the star part shows, all wrapped in plastic. I see fake flowers bound in little wreaths, bobbing stiff on wire stems. I see real flowers, touched with frost, lying on the stone. There's a wind that comes up and sighs down into the earth behind me, tugging at the little scraps of paper weighted down. One blows away, and something in me makes it important that I run and catch it and put it back by the wall. I can read the words, "We will always love you." Someone once said that to me.

I look up. The wall's taller now. I can just about see over the top to where the grass is growing. I can read the names in the wall, but they're just a lot of names to me. I look to where Sammy's gone ahead, deeper into the earth, his white fringey shawl blowing on the wind like a ghost. I wonder if he's going to go on forever, when he stops.

"*Yit-ga-dal ve-yit-ka-dash she-mei ra-ba—*" Sammy's voice climbs the wind and the wall and the night like a ladder of angels. "*Be-al-ma di-ve-ra chi-re-u-tei—*" All the words he sings, they must be the right way for a Jew to pray, 'cause I don't understand a one. "*Ve-yam-lich mal-chu-tei be-cha-yei-chon—*" It's his voice I understand. I can feel it straining for the sky, crying out, tugging at the one tip of God's sleeve that trails down out of Heaven. *Daddy!* he's crying. *Daddy, why'd you ever go away and leave me here alone? Oh Daddy, Mama, help me, save me, I need you, don't leave me! Mama, I'm so frightened! Daddy, I'm so cold!*

He's touching the wall down there. I shiver in my skin. Cold, too *cold,* the black shiny stone. Even up here, where I can still see over the top, I'm scared to get too near.

But that's Sammy down there. And now he's done with all his wailing prayer. He's looking up here, smiling for me, stretching out his hand. I look over the top of the wall at the grass, all cold-killed and withered. If I look hard, I think I see what's left of living flowers. I look back at Sammy, and then I run into his arms.

"Just one more prayer, Corey," he says to me. He still looks funny under that white shawl. "Just the one I promised them I'd say tonight. Tomorrow I'll see if maybe we can't find a synagogue'll let me in to say the rest of it, ask God to forgive us for all the bad things we've done. That's what this is all about, kid, no big mystery. My people have a special day for telling God we're sorry, that's all. I bet you understand about that, huh? Saying you're sorry, being told it's all right."

I understand. All except the part where you get told it's all right. *I* understand saying I'm sorry without knowing what I done, getting told sorry ain't enough. Getting *worse* than told, even while I'm screaming out I'm sorry, I'm sorry, I'm sorry . . .

"But see," Sammy's saying. "See, when there's people you care about, people you've loved, and they can't stand up for themselves tonight, you've got to stand up for them. Anyhow, I promised them I would, back in 'Nam. This is a good night to keep promises. It's not just my sins I'm carrying tonight, but theirs. That's what we believe, that no man stands alone before God, that all of us carry our sins and our salvation."

He laughs. "Listen to me! Bugging a kid your age with words like salvation, when you probably don't know what I'm talking about."

I look at him very steady. "Jesus is my salvation," I say.

Sammy hugs me tight. "Good for you, kid. Good for you."

Then he's on his feet again and the words are pouring out. The singing's different, sadder than before: pleading, but not like a whipped dog's eyes beg you not to hit him any more. More like knowing you've hurt the one person you love best in all the world and you want to make it be all right again. Like all the pain for what you've done wrong is pain you've given away.

"*Kol ni-dre ve-e-so-re, va-cha-ro-me, v'-ko-no-me . . .*" It's just Sammy and the wall. And the song. And maybe God.

I turn away. We're deep into the earth now, the wall's above my head. There's light behind us, cutting all the names so deep it's like the letters are a blacker black than the wall

30

that's frozen 'round them. If I bring my nose up close to the stone, I can see that the black ain't all black. There's little flecks of light caught there, gold and silver, like it snowed stars.

Black. Black and shiny over me. Black and shiny against my eyes, against my mouth, covering me, making me fight for air, fight for each last, burning breath. Black like the names are cut black, black without the shimmer or speck of a star to light my eyes. Black letters in the wall, black burning my eyes with what they say, black that's wrapping me all 'round so that I can't escape it ever, black and sharp as truth or waking:

SAMUEL NACHMAN

And out of the blackness in the words that spell out what's truly so, Granny Teeth's reaching up to take my hands . . .

She don't talk, just leads me up the rising path. I feel the black wall falling away from me, and I smell the good smell of fresh-turned earth.

There's a man looking down at me. I'm scared, but Granny Teeth's got her hands on my shoulders and she pushes me up forward to meet him, up into the light. He's the same man I seen riding 'round town with Sheriff Randolph; deputy somebody, but I don't know his name.

Why's he looking at me like that? Why's he look and say, "Dear God," and all the color leaves his face?

I hear a voice I never want to hear no more. I hear Uncle John, shouting like he always does, shouting and stomping around and hollering, "I don't give a damn what kinda warrant you got, you get the hell off my land before I—"

Then he sees me, too, and all the color that left the deputy's face seems to want to flood into his. I try to pull back, but Granny Teeth won't let me. Maybe she won't let Uncle

John hurt me no more neither. I try to face him and be brave.

But it's so hard, having to look at Uncle John again, seeing the deputy's face go hard as stone, watching him turn and crack Uncle John across the jaw like Uncle John once did to me. Uncle John falls down and puts his hands on his face. Jesus, don't let him lay the blame for this on me too!

Granny Teeth's whispering in my ear so soft I can hear the gold in her mouth go *tappa-tap*. "This day all vows are fulfilled," she tells me. "This day all debts are paid." And she makes me go stand beside the deputy, over Uncle John, and beside Sheriff Randolph, who's just come out of our house. He don't look too strong either, for such a big man.

Deputy says, "Under the oak tree. Just like she told us. He had him wrapped up in a plastic garbage bag. Like he was trash. Just like that poor little boy wasn't nothing but trash!" Then: "He tripped," meaning Uncle John. I ain't gonna be the one to call it a lie. He's smiling like he's done something good, even if he got no real joy from it.

But Sheriff Randolph says, "You know the woman who called to tell us 'bout—" He don't say what, just jerks his head. I turn in spite of Granny Teeth holding me still and see he's nodding at our old oak. Someone's been messing 'round, digging up by the roots. The smell of home earth blankets me moist and cool.

"Yeah, from New York, that old Vietnamese lady, Mrs. Tran," the deputy says. "I couldn't hardly understand her."

"I don't wonder." The sheriff takes off his hat, wipes his forehead with the back of his hand. "I just called back to tell her what we found. I got her daughter on the line. Mrs. Tran's been six months comatose in the hospital."

"Yeah, but today—"

"Last night she died."

Who died? Who they mean died? I turn around real sharp,

32

but all I see in front of me's the wall. I put out my hands to hold it back, but it rears up above my head and crashes over onto me. I cry out when I feel the blackness fall across my face again, because now I know, I really *know* what's been lies and what's so, and why the blackness won't ever let me go.

"Corey . . ."

In the dark, a voice. He's there. Sammy's there beyond the wall, reaching out his hands to me. And Granny Teeth, she's with him, holding out the edges of dead Sammy's white shawl like they was wings. First I just stare; I'm afraid of ghosts. Then I take me a deep breath and throw myself heart first against the wall, shatter it, plunge through the cold black surface to meet them. The black closes around me, but it's kept away by the circle of their arms. And wings; all around us, wings: Sammy's wings, Granny Teeth's wings, wings of glory, wings of prayer, shining white wings like the sword of God to cut away the blackness and wrap me in the warmth and the love and the light forever.

True Believer

"Aw, *Mommmmm,* do I *haaaaave* to?" Jimmy Hanson screwed his mouth shut and made a prune-face, prunes being the only thing he hated more than medicine. (He had even told his parents that prunes were an alien plot by the Toad-Men of Skraax to take over the minds of Earthlings before the invasion, human minds being just so much Silly Putty to the aforesaid Toad-Men, or so the latest issue of *Captain Hamster and the Frenzies* said. For some reason his parents remained unconvinced.)

Mrs. Hanson stood at her son's bedside, calmly pouring out a dose of thick cola-colored glop into a tablespoon. "Yes, you have to," she said. She placed the open bottle on Jimmy's nightstand and gave him a no-nonsense-now look. The spoon of doom swooped down to the boy's lips. "So open up."

It was the direct approach, and Mrs. Hanson knew it was doomed to fail. Still, every time the hour struck for Jimmy's medication, she went through this little charade for form's sake. It was rather like the way Mr. Hanson suggested a just-the-two-of-us trip to the movies on nights when he wanted a conjugal right or two.

In point of fact, Jimmy not only did not open up, he clamped both hands over his mouth and glared at his mother. Mrs. Hanson shook her head: Why did she even bother? Time for a little bribery. "Jimmy, darling, while I was out I bought you a nice present. You can have it just as soon as you take your medicine."

"Whi'zit?" Jimmy inquired suspiciously from behind his self-imposed gag.

"It's the very newest issue of your favorite comic book, that's what."

Slowly the hands lowered. Jimmy sat up a little straighter in bed and declared, "Huh-uh. Can't be. I already *got* the May issue of *Captain Hamster and the Frenzies*." To prove his point, he snatched up one of the two dozen comic books bestrewing the counterpane and held it so that his mother might see its garish cover and know herself to be caught and shamed in a lie. It was no mere coincidence that he likewise held the book so that it effectively blocked his mouth against any sneak attacks of the maternal spoon.

"Yes dear, I know, but that's not the one I bought for you." Mrs. Hanson was beginning to lose patience. She had not been as gently raised as Jimmy and it was an effort for her to maintain an air of sweet reason when all her instincts clamored to drop negotiations and simply scream *Look, you spoiled little yard ape, I've already missed ten minutes of* General Hospital. *If you don't want to wind up doing a guest shot there, you swallow this stuff now!*

However, Mrs. Hanson's whole experience of marriage and maternity had been the triumph of pop-psych and theory-of-the-moment over instinct and gut-reaction. Therefore when a skeptical Jimmy demanded to see proof that his mother had indeed purchased a newer edition of *Captain Hamster*, she complied without demur. Setting the filled spoon down carefully atop Jimmy's chest of drawers on her way out of the room, she returned in jig time with the comic in question. "See?" she said from the doorway.

"That doesn't look like *Captain Hamster*," Jimmy challenged. "Anyway, Daddy just brought me this issue last night."

"Daddy buys you all your comics at the newsstand across from his office downtown. Maybe they don't have the latest issue."

"Oh yeah? He said he bought this one at CVS in the mall!"

"Darling, it says *Captain Hamster and the Frenzies* right here on the cover, and it says June too. Maybe they changed artists. Besides, I didn't buy this at a newsstand *or* CVS. I bought it at a genuine comic book store."

"The kind you won't let me go in." Jimmy's brow was knit with the pain of past civil wrongs done him in the name of parental judgment calls. At eight years old he couldn't spell *censorship* but he could tell it when he saw it, all right. "The kind *you* don't go in either. How come you did?"

Mrs. Hanson sighed and patiently explained, "When I went out to fill your prescription, my car broke down before I got to the mall. I just barely made it into a service station. You know I don't like leaving you home alone for long when you're sick, so I asked the nice man if there was a pharmacy nearby. Well, there was—a real old-fashioned drug store with a soda fountain and everything—and the comic book store was only a block before it. I got your medicine *and* your present while my car was being fixed. See how Mommy's always thinking of you? Now you just open up for Mommy and—"

"I will if you lemme hold *Captain Hamster*," Jimmy replied. He looked angelic enough to be packing a shiv.

Motherhood works havoc on perception. Mrs. Hanson heard surrender in her baby's voice when what she should have heard was the sound of butter firming up rock-hard in his mouth. She offered him the comic with one hand and closed in with the filled spoon in the other.

In a breathtaking exhibition of speed and dexterity, Jimmy contrived to slap the new issue of *Captain Hamster* into the *Back off, Jack!* position across his mouth while at the same time flinging the old one aside so that it knocked over the open bottle on his nightstand. As the last dribble of medicine oozed its way into the shag carpet, Mrs. Hanson's last drop of patience went the way of the dodo. The neighbors who heard her scream only stopped short of calling 911 because they didn't want to be a bother.

Little Jimmy took the one remaining dose of his wasted medicine without further ado, in rightful fear for his life.

Mrs. Hanson went downstairs to the kitchen to call Jimmy's pediatrician, Dr. Beeman, and ask for a refill on the prescription. She had just hung up the phone when she felt something heavy fall on her shoulder. She turned to find herself staring into a pair of slightly buggy, definitely beady black eyes set in a hairy brown face. A teensy, triangular nose framed by bristling whiskers twitched furiously at her.

"What's this we hear about you yelling at your son?" the giant hamster demanded.

"Yah! Yah! Lemme at 'er! Lemme pound 'er! That'll learn 'er!"

Something vaguely human was bouncing wildly up and down behind the hamster, its mop of untamed hair flying. It beat disproportionately large hands rhythmically on the kitchen walls, the counters, even the ceiling, like hell's (or possibly Bedlam's) answer to Gene Krupa.

"Easy, Bongo." The hamster held up one dainty pink paw. From a great distance away, figuratively speaking, Mrs. Hanson noted that the roly-poly beast was clad in a blue jumpsuit, complete with yellow cape. She'd never known there was that much Spandex in the universe.

"Aw c'mon, Cap, let Bongo do a number on her." A fresh

voice butted in. For some reason it seemed to be coming from the oversized hummingbird zipping around the hamster's head. On second glance, Mrs. Hanson saw that it was no hummingbird but a winged girl in a spangled pink thong leotard. Despite her small size, she flaunted a pair of mammaries that simply had to be an aerodynamic disadvantage. "Do it! Do it!"

"Be silent, Laggi, Girl of the Starways," said a fourth voice. "It is not always Bongo's turn to deal with our foes. Sometimes they belong . . . to *me*." Those warm, sinister, seductive tones put Mrs. Hanson in mind of dark places where unspeakable secrets murmured siren songs, luring the unsuspecting ever closer to a hideous doom. She realized it had been much too long since she'd last cleaned out the bathtub drain.

It just so happened that *drain* was an unfortunate thought to have right then, for the fourth voice belonged to a female whose unnerving smile revealed a formidable pair of fangs. She shunned the Spandex togs of her companions, favoring instead what resembled a full-body covering of black seaweed. Like Laggi (Girl of the Starways) she was a prime candidate for severe lower back pain after the age of thirty.

She took one of Mrs. Hanson's hands in both of her own and with a look only slightly less intense than a coiled cobra's said, "I am Lexa. I walk the night. And I hunger."

Mrs. Hanson couldn't quite make up her mind whether or not to tell this person that it was only three o'clock and that she was walking the mid-afternoon. She decided against it. Some people didn't appreciate having their mistakes pointed out to them by total strangers.

Before Lexa could pursue the conversation, the caped hamster stepped between the two ladies. "First we allow her to explain her shameful treatment of our pal, Jimmy. *Then* we extract the full measure of justice." The tiny eyes, aglow with righteous indignation, fixed themselves on Mrs. Hanson. *"Well?"*

"Thank you very much for the opportunity," said Mrs. Hanson, and fainted.

Mrs. Hanson's belief in the curative powers of fainting spells was based entirely on her experience watching soap operas. In that happy realm, it was generally the case that if the heroine found herself facing the unfaceable, she'd faint, subsequently to come to her senses and be handed the happy information that It Had All Been Just a Horrid Dream. (Unless, of course, faltering ratings demanded that she come out of the faint only to pass into either full amnesia or a coma, depending on the state of contract negotiations at the time.)

Such was not the case for Mrs. Hanson. She revived to find that her uninvited callers were still there, that they had contrived to transport her unconscious form upstairs to her own bed, and that Captain Hamster had rooted through her drawers and soaked her best WonderBra in water to make a cold compress for her forehead.

She rose up squawking inarticulate protests, one black, lace-trimmed B-cup slipping down over her eye. Little Jimmy stood by her bedside, holding Lexa's pallid hand and snickering. "Gee, Mom, you look like a pirate," he declared, delighted.

"A sissy pirate," said Bongo, then added, "Arrrh."

Before Mrs. Hanson could respond, Captain Hamster spoke up: "Mrs. Hanson, we beg your pardon. Our pal Jimmy has explained that you were only trying to make him take his medicine. Although we do not approve of your methods, we are willing to overlook minor maternal thuggery in the interests of the boy's health. We feel quite comfortable leaving him in your capable hands once more."

"Leaving . . . ?" Mrs. Hanson could not believe the sweet words she was hearing. She didn't know whence this gang of refugees from a nightmare had come, but she no longer questioned their reality *vis-à-vis* her sanity. Illusions did not tote full-grown women up an entire flight of stairs, as a rule. And since they *were* real, she didn't so much care where they'd come from as when they were going to get the hell gone.

"Of course, dear lady. The Frenzies never stay where they are not wanted. I promise you, we will be out of your house and your hair anon."

"And my underwear drawer," Mrs. Hanson specified.

Captain Hamster raised one paw and crossed his heart with the other. "Superhero's honor."

One week later, Mrs. Hanson's opinion of superhero's honor was not a thing lawful to be uttered, but at least it was somewhat less incendiary than her opinion of some of the *other* lifeforms infesting her home. Unfortunately, she couldn't call the exterminator to get rid of them either: They came from the government and they were there to *help*. They said so. And they showed their IDs and badges and guns to any who dared disagree.

One of these lifeforms was Dr. Lorenzo Oglethorpe, Ph.D., who had neither badge nor gun, but whose unarmed tongue was a hideous implement of destruction nonetheless. It was a vast and terrible pity that he was off limits to exterminators everywhere, for in his own modest way he embodied their professional Grail: He looked exactly like the world's biggest cockroach.

"There's really a very simple explanation for what's happened to your son," said Dr. Oglethorpe.

"Sure there is," said Mr. Hanson, settling back in his favorite armchair. Although it was a weekday, he was at home, on leave with pay until further notice. His employer had proved to be quite understanding of the extraordinary situation chez Hanson, especially after a visit from the government. Now the lucky man took a pull at his beer and frowned to find the bottle empty. "Be a pal?" he said to the FBI agent at his elbow, brandishing the longneck in his face.

"I'll get that, dear." Mrs. Hanson sprang from her seat, closely followed by the agent assigned to her. She snatched the bottle from her husband's hand and hurried into the kitchen. Behind her, Dr. Oglethorpe was expanding upon Jimmy's condition, although he had yet to examine the subject in person. The government-appointed man of science had arrived at the Hanson household that very morning, just after Jimmy's departure for school, yet his lack of firsthand data did not bother Dr. Oglethorpe for an instant. As he himself had said when accepting the Nobel, "Formulate an elegant enough hypothesis and you can always persuade the facts to fall into line."

In Jimmy's case, Dr. Oglethorpe's hypothesis had something to do with Chaos Theory and cough syrup. Mrs. Hanson didn't need to hear it. She didn't want to hear it. Whenever a professional nerd like Dr. Oglethorpe promised you a "very simple explanation" it was never simple, except to another nerd. Wayne Hanson didn't have the scientific know-how to program the VCR, but at least he could fake interest and comprehension while the good doctor droned on.

"Better him than me," she muttered, flipping the lids off a pair of longnecks.

"You say something, ma'am?" asked Mrs. Hanson's personal G-man.

"I was just wondering if you'd like one too," she replied brightly.

"Thank you, ma'am; not on duty."

"Okay." She shrugged and sucked down half a bottle, then belched and giggled.

"Ma'am, are you all right?" The agent seemed to be sincerely concerned.

"No." Mrs. Hanson absorbed the remainder of the beer with a second gargantuan swallow. "Now I am."

There was a sharp humming in her ears. "Did anyone ever tell you that chug-a-lug contests were what brought down the exquisite galaxy-spanning civilization of the Fnorn?" It was Laggi, Girl of the Starways, and not the abrupt attack of some beer-fueled illusion. The minuscule heroine hovered in front of Mrs. Hanson's eyes, a blur of wings. "Captain Hamster wants me to tell you that there's to be no more alcohol in this house. It sets a bad example for little Jimmy."

"Little Jimmy is in school right now, along with a bodyguard of seven—count 'em, seven—FBI agents, and you can tell Captain Hamster from me that if he'd spend less time running my life and more time eating those pesky Jehovah's Witnesses, he might do some actual good around here," Mrs. Hanson snarled.

"Hmph!" Laggi's weensy lips curled with scorn. "In the first place, Captain Hamster does not eat Jehovah's Witnesses or any other religious proselytes; he only stuffs them in his mighty cheek pouches of steel until they've learned the error of their importunate ways. Besides, he doesn't stuff *all* of them; just the ones who can't take a hint. Second, he says that last batch wasn't Jehovah's Witnesses, they were videojournalists from *Hard Copy*. Third, he wants to know why your house is under constant siege by these people, and fourth—" She zipped over to perch provocatively on the FBI agent's shoulder and croon in his ear, "—has anyone ever told you you look like David Duchovny?"

Mrs. Hanson snatched up the little alien and squeezed her

with enough force to crush a full beer can. The assault had no ill effect, for—as Jimmy could have told his mother in a moment—Laggi's body was strong enough to withstand the whole gamut of cosmic forces from Asteroids to Zeta Rays. (Lucky for Laggi that Mrs. Hanson didn't know her only weakness was a severe allergy to dairy products, or the put-upon housewife would've dunked the Girl of the Starways in moo juice like an alien Oreo.)

"Now you listen to me, you twerp!" she bellowed. "You go back and tell Super Rodent that he's the reason we're combing *paparazzi* out of the privet hedges; him and the rest of you. When you idiots showed up, you could've just left this house and us in peace, but no: *You* had to hang around until the neighbors noticed. *You* had to stay put until the cops came, *and* the press, *and* the government!"

"I don't see how it's any of our doing," Laggi replied in the same tone of voice Mrs. Hanson generally used on Jimmy, five parts condescension to one part long-suffering patience. "Our purpose is to right wrongs and fight crime. How could we do either until we found out where the wrongs and the crimes were happening? So we had to wait for the six o'clock news, except by that time we *were* the six o'clock news. You know, *some* people aren't too cheap to spring for cable so they can get CNN."

"You don't get cable?" The FBI man was appalled.

Just then, there was a loud riff on the door leading from the kitchen to the back yard, then a FLAM! that blew it off its hinges, aided and abetted by the battered body of another federal agent. Bongo stepped into the room, grinning ear to ear.

He was promptly followed by Captain Hamster, who scurried through the ravaged portal and stared down at the bruised and bleeding man. He turned to Bongo and peevishly demanded, "Once, just once, couldn't you simply *knock?*"

"What can I say?" Bongo shrugged. "I got rhythm." His devil-may-care attitude evaporated when he saw what Mrs. Hanson had clutched in her hand. "Hey! Wottcha doin' to Laggi, Girl of the Starways?"

Before Mrs. Hanson could reply, a slender white hand materialized out of thin air, its blood red nails tracing the length of her ribcage, tickling without mercy. Helpless laughter shook her; she released the alien adventuress just as her assailant, Lexa, became fully visible.

"Dear God, how did you do that?" the G-man blurted.

"How?" Lexa echoed in tones favored by better sepulchres everywhere. "Does it truly matter, the *how?* In the vast, shadowed realm that is eternity, so little truly matters. I know this, for I am Lexa. I walk the night. And I hunger." She lowered smoky eyelids and drew nearer, adding as she closed in on him, "Also, do you know you look like David Duchovny?"

He blushed becomingly. "Well, I have been told that I—"

"Shall we find out if you taste like him too?"

"I saw him first, you breathing-impaired bimbo!"

Mr. Hanson, Dr. Oglethorpe, and the spare FBI agents walked in just in time to help break up the catfight between the winged alien and the vampire.

Mr. Hanson quickly decided to leave the peacekeeping violence to the professionals. Taking his wife by the arm, he drew her off into a DMZ corner of the kitchen. "Honey?" he said in his patented just-the-two-of-us-movie-hotcha wheedle. "Darling? Uh . . . Do you think you could maybe remember where that drugstore was where you got Jimmy's prescription filled?"

"I already told you, I don't remember," Mrs. Hanson snarled. "I only went there because I happened to get stuck in the neighborhood. I never intended to go back, so I didn't pay attention to where it was, just like I told you *and* the journalists, and the FBI and that chinless geek Oglethorpe. And I'm getting damned sick and tired of being badgered about this. Dr. Beeman can give you all the copies of Jimmy's prescription you want, so why bug *me?*"

"Because it is not the prescription *per se* which is important," said the aforementioned chinless geek. Dr. Oglethorpe too had opted to retire from the field of battle. He was presently cleansing the left lens of his eyeglasses with a pristine white pocket handkerchief. (Laggi, Girl of the Starways, was a fierce fighter, but not the world's most accurate shot with spit.) "You see, Mrs. Hanson, the original medicine which your son took is a simple compound meant to relieve heavy otolaryngological congestion."

"Well of course it is," said Mrs. Hanson blandly while inside she was screaming *He's going to make me listen to his simple explanation! Damn gun control anyway!* She cast about for the nearest escape hatch, but all exits from the kitchen were blocked by the squabbling forces of Law and Order versus Truth and Justice.

"Ordinarily, it would have done nothing more to your boy than relieve symptoms of stuffy ear, nose, and throat," the doctor went on. "It is a readily available, frequently prescribed, and constantly stocked pediatric medicament. However, it is my theory that at the drug store where you purchased one particular bottle of this elixir, the pharmacist was, er, less than punctilious in the execution of his professional duties and—"

"He stored the stuff wrong and it went funny on him," Mr. Hanson put in.

Dr. Oglethorpe sniffed. "Hmph! I see nothing humorous about a molecular-level change brought on by undetermined environmental factors. Nor the effect it has had on your son."

"Oh no?" Mr. Hanson folded his arms. "Anything that kid

wants to *be* real *gets* real! He wants to see a giant rat in tights, *whammo!*, he gets a giant rat in tights. And as soon as the little woman remembers where she bought the stuff, I'm going over there, buy a bottle, suck it down, and start doing a little wanting of my own. You don't think *that's* funny, just wait'll you hear me laughing on board my own private yacht!"

"Uh, Mr. Hanson, sir?" It was the agent whose resemblance to David Duchovny had set off the Lexa/Laggi donnybrook. Having successfully reduced that brawl to an exchange of nasty personal remarks (with Bongo as the gleeful referee), he was at liberty to turn his professional attention elsewhere. "Sir, it's not that simple."

"I should say not!" Dr. Oglethorpe agreed. "The medicine in question is not sold over-the-counter. You would need a prescription to—"

"Besides," the agent put in, "if your wife does happen to recall the location of the drugstore where she purchased the cough syrup in question, we'll have to confiscate all remaining supplies for reasons of national security."

Mr. Hanson took umbrage and launched into a spirited rant against Big Government. It was one of his standard rants, an old favorite that his wife had heard many times before. While Wayne inveighed against jackbooted thugs (though he couldn't tell jackboots from jack squat) she ignored him with a clear conscience and gave herself up to one surprising thought:

I actually understood *Dr. Oglethorpe's explanation! Wow. And after all those years of Mom telling me that* real *girls can't handle* science.

Yes, it had all come together for her in one vast Unified Geek Theory. However, there were still a few details bothering her. Seeing as how the squabble between Laggi and Lexa had run out of steam, she sidled over to the presently unoccupied cosmic quartet of wrong-righters to double-check her conclusions.

"Let me see if I've got this straight: Jimmy always wanted you to be real, so as soon as he took that screwed-up cough syrup you became real?"

"*Quod erat demostrandum,*" said Captain Hamster.

"Uh-huh," said Mrs. Hanson, as if a Latin-spouting rodent were an everyday occurrence. "Well, that accounts for it."

"For what?"

"For why we've been attracting sects and violence like free gin attracts Republicans. Why our front steps are hip-deep in pamphlets from Buddhists, Bahais, Baptists, Brahmans—"

Captain Hamster raised a staying paw. "I get the picture. I do read the newspapers before I shred them for bedding, you know. I get out of my giant nuclear-powered exercise wheel *sometimes.*"

It was no use: Mrs. Hanson was on a roll, and she didn't even need a giant nuclear-powered exercise wheel to keep going. "—Muslims, Methodists, Manichaeans—" She paused, took a deep breath, and concluded: "—Jews, Jains and heaven-help-us gymnosophists! They're all after Jimmy because if Jimmy wants something, it's so. Including what he wants about God, the universe, and—and—" She spread her hands. "—and the cough syrup did it?"

The hamster nodded. "More or less."

"And if I can remember where I bought the cough syrup, maybe the pharmacist has some more, and then the government can go confiscate it, analyze it, duplicate it; and use it only in the best interests of national security?"

"Um . . ." Captain Hamster never could tell a lie. "It will make the government very happy if you can remember where you bought it, yes."

"And once the government's got it, maybe we can sic these religious noodniks on them, for a change?"

"Well, I *suppose* . . ." The hamster shrugged very expressively for a creature with no shoulders worth the name.

"Oh, well if *that's* all—!" Mrs. Hanson had one of those bell-like laughs singular in its power to annoy. "I charged my car repair on Visa and I gave my husband the receipt. It's got the garage address on it. Find the garage and you'll find the drug store, find the drug store and you'll find the—"

"—boy's been kidnapped!" shouted the bloody and bedraggled FBI agent who lurched into the kitchen and collapsed into Captain Hamster's outstretched paws.

Less than an hour later, the kitchen was virtually deserted. The wounded agent had barely gasped out half his tale before Captain Hamster and the Frenzies as one shouted their copyrighted battle cry, "Duck and cover, here comes Justice!" and charged off. The other G-men did their comrade the courtesy of letting him tell the full story: How a suicidal band of men (and possibly women) in ninja-knockoff black p.j.s and face masks had stormed the P.S. 187 lunchroom; how Jimmy's bodyguards had been unable to use their firearms, for fear of hitting the children; how in the fierce hand-to-hand combat that followed, the masked invaders had defied both the agents' kung-fu and the lunch-ladies' auxiliary attacks with iron ladles, Formica trays, and Swedish meatballs.

A gallant defense, to no avail: The invaders glommed Jimmy and were gone. Luckily—if the word could be applied to such a perilous situation—as they were making their escape, one of their number slipped on a Swedish meatball, fell, and was captured. Under questioning he revealed all, including where his confederates were taking the boy. He even gave the FBI agents a business card with the address of the zealots' hideout on it.

"How did you get so much out of him so fast?" asked the agent who really did look a lot like David Duchovny. "I mean, the *regulations* say we're not allowed to torture suspects, but—"

"I used my fake IRS badge," the battered agent replied. "He sang like Streisand." He then passed around the tattle-tale business card.

That was all the remaining G-men needed. They lit out without a backward glance, leaving Dr. Oglethorpe to accompany their injured comrade to the hospital and the Hansons to stand in the midst of their half-wrecked kitchen looking like idiots.

Mrs. Hanson broke down into wild sobs and clung to her husband while he did his poor best to comfort her. "Look, honey, it's not like they don't know *where* Jimmy is. The worst is over. Now the only thing we've got to do is wait here and—"

"The worst is *over?*" Mrs. Hanson was no superbeing, but she had powers of ridicule and sarcasm far beyond those of mortal men. "And I suppose an armed hostage situation with our son in the middle of it is just a little walk in the park?"

"Depends on the park," Mr. Hanson replied, trying to lighten the mood. "Ow," he added when his bride wordlessly expressed her desire that he stop playing the fool. She would have added a dollop of harsh words to accompany her patented instep-stomp, but tears overcame her once more.

Her husband held her close, whispered soft words that were the usual nonsense most people intone when trying to soothe the distraught. His assurances had as much footing in reality as a politician's promises, and were similarly based on what he thought his audience wanted to hear.

Mrs. Hanson had spent enough years in the company of Mr. Hanson to recognize yet another load of his patented bushwah when she heard it. He meant well this time, but he had snowed her once too often in the past for far less noble reasons, one of them named Donna and the other Tawni. In ordinary circumstances she would have snapped, "Oh, clam it, Wayne. If someone blew up the whole damn world you'd still try telling me that everything was going to be all right. I believe you about as far as I can shotput Newt Gingrich. Grow up, would you?" Then she would have resumed bawling even louder, just to show him who was boss.

These were not ordinary circumstances.

To her own silent astonishment and completely against her will, Mrs. Hanson found herself becoming less hysterical. The longer her husband rattled on about how the SWAT teams would never do anything to endanger Jimmy and how the FBI had the situation under complete control, the more she became convinced that he was right. The sensation was at once comforting and terrifying. One tiny spark of self-determination flared up in the back of her mind, demanding *What the frap is going on here? What's happening to me?*

She caught herself saying, "Yes, darling, of course you're right." Her vision flickered. She realized she was actually *batting her eyelashes* at the goofball she'd married, and that words were escaping her lips bathed in the richest tones of unconditional faith and adoration. The last ort of her former contempt for Mr. Hanson stuck around until it heard her say, "I'm not afraid of anything bad happening so long as *you're* here to protect us." Then it went belly-up beyond hope of resurrection.

"How right you are, my angel," said Mr. Hanson. (Was it a trick of the light, or was his jaw squarer than before? And where had that manly cleft in his chin sprung from?!)

"There's no need to fear so long as I am here to make every-thing all right. And I will. But why do we waste our time, waiting for others, less worthy, to do what only I have the power to accomplish?" He thumped his chest.

"But you were the one who said we should wait here, my beloved," she replied, running her fingers through his flowing locks. The erosions of time had been miraculously reversed—better than reversed, for Mr. Hanson had suddenly sprouted a mane of hair that could only be described as lush and—could it be?—heroic.

"Would I suggest so craven a course of action? Forbid it, almighty God! Our little boy *needs* us. Our place is with Jimmy!" he declaimed, and he swept Mrs. Hanson up in arms gone inexplicably muscular and bore her out to the car.

It was a cow-crap brown Toyota when he popped her into it. By the time he drove through the fifth red light, it had transformed into a sleek, midnight-black vehicle one-third Porsche, one-third Batmobile, and one-third robo-panther. He drove at speeds only seen in Spielberg movies, had no ac-cidents, got no tickets, and wore no safety belt. As for Mrs. Hanson, the only sounds she seemed capable of making were alternately "Eek!" and "Oooh!"

Mr. Hanson finally brought his new vehicle to a shrieking, brake-burning halt in front of a comic book store in a strange section of town. As she climbed shakily out of the car, Mrs. Hanson looked up and down the street, a sense of *déjà vu* heavy upon her. She stared into the comic book shop window; a giant cardboard cutout of Captain Hamster stared back at her, his mighty cheek-pouches of steel crammed with bad guys.

She wanted to exclaim "Holy shit," but for some reason it came out of her mouth as "Oh my goodness me!" One block away, the street was a moil of prowl cars, fire trucks, ambulances, and assorted police transports. Yellow crime-scene tape and sawhorse barricades cluttered up the few feet of space not already occupied by vehicles. All sorts of men with all sorts of guns were swarming everywhere. A dozen bull-horns contended for supremacy.

"Loud, isn't it?" said Captain Hamster.

"Eek!" exclaimed Mrs. Hanson, jumping into her husband's arms. In the past thirty minutes she'd spent more time in his embrace than in the past thirty months.

The caped critter waddled up to the comic shop window and studied his cardboard alter-ego. "They didn't get my good side," he opined. "Are my eyes really that beady?" He made a sound of disgust, then turned to the Hansons. "The hour has struck," he intoned.

Mrs. Hanson said, "Huh?" and checked her wristwatch.

"Not that hour," Captain Hamster told her. He stared Mr. Hanson full in the face, and for a heartbeat the two of them appeared to be the poster children for Significant Pauses everywhere. "*Your* hour," he said.

Mr. Hanson slapped the giant rodent on the back, threw back his head, and gave one of those exultant laughs sacred only to heroes with prior script-approval and a percentage of the gross. "Oh, this won't take an hour," he said, and strode straight for the nearest prowl car, his wife and the mighty marmotoid trailing in his valiant wake.

He was met by a pair of uniformed officers who attempted to persuade him to turn back, go home, move along, and break it up. He chose the lattermost option.

He's not really picking up that car and holding it over his head, Mrs. Hanson told herself as she stared at her husband's new way of dealing with less-than-helpful policemen. *It just* looks *that way.* The prowl car went sailing through the air and landed one intersection down with a crump. It resembled nothing so much as one of the abandoned Concertinas of the Gods. This done, he continued his onward march, heading right for the storefront site where the police and FBI had the kidnappers holed up.

His approach was greeted by a hail of gunfire. He behaved as if the bullets were no more than bumblebees. In fact, he behaved better than that: In the past, Mr. Hanson had been known to run into the house, screaming like a schoolgirl, whenever his stint at the barbecue grill was interrupted by the appearance of anything with a stinger or a nasty bite, from chiggers to chipmunks.

Mrs. Hanson pressed her fists to her mouth and strangled a shriek as she watched her now-beloved husband wade through the firefight. She heard herself gasp out the words, "Bullets won't stop him!" and then something heavy struck her from behind, whomping the breath from her body and sending her sprawling headfirst into the side of one of the other police cars. Pretty stars twinkled before her eyes in a charming selection of decorator shades, but she stubbornly refused to slip into unconsciousness. Something deep within her protested that it was bad enough she was spouting clichés, she was damned if she was going to live them too. She hauled herself hand over hand back into the realm of full awareness and rested over the hood of the prowl car.

"Sorry 'bout that," came a sheepish voice behind her.

She turned her head slightly to see Bongo toeing the ground, his face hot with blushes.

"I told you and *told you*," Captain Hamster chided his redoubtable sidekick. "Some of us were never meant to give others an encouraging pat on the back."

"Well, I *said* I was sorry," Bongo snapped, and slapped his hand down on the car's roof for emphasis. The vehicle doubled up into scrap metal, and its complement of officers broke into prayers of thanksgiving that they had not been inside their ruined car at the time.

Mrs. Hanson shoved herself off the windshield and stood up. (She'd slid down the hood the instant Bongo smacked the car.) She rounded on Bongo and demanded, "What are you waiting for? Why are you just standing there while my poor husband's facing a nest of ninjas single-handed. You're a superhero; go help him!"

Captain Hamster intervened. "I'm afraid he can't do that now, Mrs. Hanson," he said. "None of us can."

"Why the heeee—Why not?" Just in time Mrs. Hanson reminded herself of the Frenzies' dislike for gutter language. She'd taken enough upside-the-head lessons for one day.

"Because little Jimmy believes that his daddy doesn't need any help to save him."

"I don't care what the kid wants, he's got his nerve making Wayne go in there and—"

"I didn't say that this is how Jimmy wants it, Mrs. Hanson," Captain Hamster said softly. "I said this is how he believes it should be."

"Not what he wants but what he . . . ?" Mrs. Hanson spoke as one awakening from a deep and discombobulating dream. Two and two suddenly clicked together on the abacus of her brain, even though the same Mom who'd taught her that girls can't handle science had said similar things about math. In that moment, Mrs. Hanson achieved a conclusion, a decision, and a plan of action all at the same time.

Bullets were still flying, but not so many as before. She shaded her eyes and tried to see what had become of Wayne. He was gone from sight, but the door to the kidnapper's lair was now no more than a tangle of twisted metal and shattered glass.

She knew that door. In happier days it had sported several

lines of gold-trimmed letters informing the general public that Dolan's Drugstore was open from nine to six weekdays, nine to three Saturdays, with extended evening hours Thursday and Closed all day Sunday.

The last gunshot sounded on the air and was stilled. The FBI agents exchanged speculative looks with the police until someone in authority (or with a lot of nerve) announced, "Let's move in, boys!" They plowed forward *en masse,* ready for anything.

Anything but Wayne Hanson, glorious in red-white-and-blue Spandex, his shoulders wider than the mangled doorway. He had little Jimmy perched on one shoulder and in either hand he dragged an unconscious ninja wannabe by the scruff. He sidestepped into the street, then tossed his captives, one by one, through the gaping doors of the waiting paddy wagon. The policemen stared, nonplussed.

"Where the hell did that thing come from?" asked one.

"Looks like something out of an old gangster movie," said another.

"Not like anything we've got in the motor pool."

Mrs. Hanson thought she could tell the nice men just where their newest vehicle had sprung from, but she had other fish to fry, and she was going to do them up brown in magic cough syrup. She dashed through the doorway while SuperWayne fielded the plaudits of the crowd, his rescued son grinning like a beaver at a peg-legged pirates' convention.

Inside the drugstore, all was still and a little sticky. Battered ninjas slumped in puddles of strawberry sauce and slowly cooling hot fudge. Mr. Dolan himself was still tied up and stowed under the soda fountain counter, just below the taps that spouted Coke and Seven-Up and Dr Pepper, a piece of duct tape over his mouth. Mrs. Hanson tore it off without preamble or ceremony, indifferent to the pharmacist's shriek of pain.

"Where do you keep the cough syrup?" she demanded, waggling the tape in his face. It now sported more than half of the gentleman's former mustache and looked like the world's biggest caterpillar.

"What? Why do you want—?" Mr. Dolan winced. His upper lip was an angry red and it obviously hurt to talk. "Look, lady, if you'll just untie me—"

Mrs. Hanson ignored his request. Calmly she glanced about the ruined drugstore until her eyes lit on one of those ornamental glass vessels filled with colored water. She dumped out the water, smashed the glass, selected a good-sized shard, and held it to the still bound pharmacist's throat. "It's a prescription cough syrup for kids, you just dispensed me a bottle of it a couple of days ago, I want some more, I want it now, and I bet you five bucks that if I slit your throat they'll blame it on the ninjas."

Mr. Dolan pursed his lips. "They're not ninjas," he said sullenly. "They're members of the First Church of the Divine Harmony. If you kill me, you won't be able to blame it on them: They don't believe in violence."

Mrs. Hanson surveyed the wreckage. "Pardon me if I die laughing," she said. "They kidnap my son, they beat the crap out of a bunch of FBI agents, they hole up here, they bind and gag you, they hold off all comers in a hail of gunfire, and *you* tell me they don't believe in violence?"

"Except in the best interests of protecting the Church and saving unbelievers from burning in hell for all eternity," the druggist clarified.

"Oh, well that sounds . . ." *Reasonable* didn't strike her as quite the word she was after. ". . . familiar."

The druggist sighed. "You want to talk sons, try talking to

mine. He joined them, which is how they happened to pick my store for their hideout. Even swiped a bunch of my business cards! I tell you, kids today—"

Mrs. Hanson didn't have time for this. Any minute now the FBI and the cops would come pouring in. "Okay, so they won't blame the ninjas for it if I slit your throat, but you'll still be dead, and all because you wouldn't give me one lousy bottle of cough syrup. Does that really seem like something worth dying for?"

"Hell no," said Mr. Dolan, and to quote the worse-for-ninja-wear FBI agent, he sang like Streisand (the Early Years).

Following his directions, Mrs. Hanson looked up Jimmy's old prescription in his files, told him what she found there, and with his continuing help located the large dispenser bottle on the shelves. Her eyes shone as she took it down and unscrewed the cap.

The cap would not unscrew. The cap was covered with a welter of taunting heiroglyphics instructing the would-be opener to turn cap while pressing down, pushing in at the arrows, doing the hokey-pokey, and sacrificing a red yearling bull-calf without blemish to Aesculaepius.

"It's child-safe!" Mrs. Hanson howled. "This miserable cap is child-safe and it's not even on a consumer-sized take-home bottle! Dear God, why?"

"New regulations," said Mr. Dolan. "I could help you get it open if you untied me."

Mrs. Hanson's fingers flew over the knots binding the druggist's wrists and ankles. *Sotto voce* she cursed all Boy Scout leaders everywhere. Didn't they realize that statistics showed that thirty-one percent of all Tenderfeet grew up to be religious loonies-cum-ninjas?

Once free of his bonds, the pharmacist sat there rubbing

the circulation back into his wrists. Mrs. Hanson squatted before him, bouncing on her haunches in an agony of impatience. "Come on, come on, put wheels on it, get that bottle *open*," she whined.

"What's the rush?"

"Don't ask questions, just do it." The glass shard flashed in his face, trimming the hairs in his left nostril.

As she watched the druggist deal with the recalcitrant bottle, Mrs. Hanson's thoughts bubbled in joyful anticipation. *Soon, oh soon! Money, mansions, movie star lovers, my own line of designer clothes at prices most women can afford, a signature fragrance, everything that I always believed should be mine—*

"Hurry up," she snarled, making another feint at Mr. Dolan's face with her pickup dagger.

Just then she heard a gasp from somewhere behind her. "Mom! What're you doing?" came little Jimmy's plaintive cry.

The hand that held the nasty, long, sharp pointy piece of glass went numb at the sound. The shard dropped and shattered. Mrs. Hanson turned to see her only child standing in the doorway, backed by Dr. Oglethorpe and a brace of FBI agents. From outside came the hubbub of SuperWayne fielding a host of questions from the media.

Under Jimmy's horrified stare, Mrs. Hanson sensed a bizarre conversion overtaking her. It was as if somewhere deep inside her a hungry vortex had opened up and was now sucking away all vestiges of ruthless ambition. Every Danielle Steel novel she had ever read, replete with the interlaced sagas of long-legged, orgasm-enriched, strong-minded and iron-thighed career women, dwindled to so much mental dross. They were replaced by the unmistakable urge to bake chocolate chip cookies and a celestial vision of Martha Stew-

art's face illuminated beneath the legend *In hoc bimbo vinces.*
The cavern of her skull, where once she had hosted the un-
slaked desire to be one of the Rich and Famous, now echoed
with the alien thought: *That's not how my Mom's supposed to
be!*

It was a frightful experience, that invasion. For the first
time in her life she was living up to someone else's expecta-
tions, willy-nilly. *What about self-determination?* her ego
wailed. *What about celebrating the abiding power of* me-*ness?*

As if you ever were self-determined, came the sneered response from the one reactionary morsel of her much-
beleaguered spirit. *You got married because every second article
in the women's magazines is about how to nab a man and every
third one's about how to hold him once you've got him. You had
Jimmy right off the bat because your parents kept sending you
newspaper clippings about the rising rate of infertility and the
dangers of late-life pregnancies. You've let everyone else tell you
what you're supposed to want so far, including Danielle Steel.
Why not let your son in on the act too? Trust me, it's easier than
thinking for yourself.* And with a sigh of relief it tied on an
apron and started hanging dimity curtains all over Mrs.
Hanson's soul.

She started toward her son on wobbly legs, hands outstretched. "Oh, baby—" she began.

Before anyone else could move, Dr. Oglethorpe crossed
the wreckage and was there to support Mrs. Hanson, lest she
fall. "There, there, dear lady, you've been under some strain,
but soon everything will be—"

"Who's that guy?" Jimmy wanted to know.

"It's all right, darling," Mrs. Hanson said, smiling weakly.
"This is Dr. Oglethorpe. You never met him. He's a scientist
who—"

"A *scientist?*" Jimmy's voice scaled upwards, aghast.

"Well, yes dear," his mother said, puzzled by her boy's horrified reaction. "What's wrong with—?"

"Hey, lady!" Mr. Dolan called from behind. "You still want this?" He wigwagged the big bottle.

The air crackled. A hollow, hideous evil laugh rang out. "I'll take that!" In the blink of several eyes, Dr. Oglethorpe sprang upon Mr. Dolan like the world's biggest spider and snatched the bottle from the pharmacist's grasp. Madness had transformed his bland, geeky features into a writhing mask of power-hungry ruthlessness seldom seen outside a Jonny Quest cartoon. "Today the cough syrup, tomorrow the world!" He threw back his head and cackled, then drew a bulbous purple raygun from the pocket of his chinos.

One of the FBI agents flanking Jimmy tried to shoot the hideously mutated scientist, but a single blast of Dr. Oglethorpe's raygun turned him into a skink. The second agent was a slow learner, for which fault he too was soon scuttling all over the floor on four scaly legs. Grinning like a shark with lockjaw, Dr. Oglethorpe rounded the gun on Mr. Dolan. The pharmacist raised his hands in the most peaceable of surrenders. Dr. Oglethorpe zapped him just for the hell of it, then filled the drugstore with maniacal tittering.

"Jimmy, get Daddy!" Mrs. Hanson shouted, but to no avail. Jimmy gaped at the three hapless raygun-spawned lizards and flew into an unreasoning panic. He uttered a wail of despair and, in the best of Stupid Sci-Fi Movie traditions, bolted in the wrong direction: Not out the door and off to summon his suddenly super-endowed father, but over the skinks and straight into the arms of his mom. Even as he did so, Dr. Oglethorpe was upon them, the raygun's snout pressed to Mrs. Hanson's temple.

"Don't try anythink . . . *foolish,* my dear," he hissed in her ear. He had acquired a Mittel-European accent, heavily laced with the overtones of the Orient, from the same place he'd gotten that raygun. "It vould be a shame if the boy vere to zee you become a zalamander, ah so?"

Mrs. Hanson moistened her lips. They had gone quite dry, despite a liberal coating of Glossy Melon Surprise. Having a raygun poking you in the side of the head did things like that, the promises of the U.S. cosmetics industry be damned. "Jimmy dear, Mommy thinks this would be a very good time to wish the naughty scientist faaaar, faaaar away," she said quietly.

"He can't wish him away," said the familiar voice of Captain Hamster. The fluffy avenger stood just within the doorway of Dolan's Drugstore, backed by the Frenzies and SuperWayne. Never had Mrs. Hanson seen so grave a look in the colossal creature's eyes. "No more than he can *want* or *will* or *wink* him away. I told you before: Jimmy has the power to change reality not according to what he wants, but according to what he *believes*."

"That's what I thought." Mrs. Hanson nodded as much as Dr. Oglethorpe's raygun would allow. "You know, you might've been more specific about it earlier. You're the one who said that if Jimmy wanted something—"

"No, madam, *you* used the word 'want,' not I; you and the rest of the humans."

"*This* is a fine time to chop logic," the imperiled lady said. "You'd make a great lawyer."

Captain Hamster looked hurt. "I'm only a superhero," he said. "I'm usually too busy advancing the plot to explain it."

"I, on zee ozzer handt, am a zientist," Dr. Oglethorpe purred in her ear. "Ond I humbly beg to assure *Memsahib* Hanson zat zere iss a verry zimple eggsblanation for—"

"Stow it, Frankenstein!" Bongo shouted, bouncing on the balls of his feet and drumming out his frustration on the soda fountain. The marble countertop snapped and crumbled like a piece of Melba toast.

"Let her go, you fiend!" SuperWayne bellowed from the doorway. He flexed his biceps and the concussion alone was enough to dislodge a fresh shower of plaster from the battered ceiling.

"So sorry, please not to come any closer." Dr. Oglethorpe's trigger-finger twitched. Mrs. Hanson heard a distinct click even though she was pretty damn sure that no raygun worth its salt would make a sound like a Colt .45 being cocked.

But that's how Jimmy thinks it should be! she realized. *That's how he believes it is. The same way he believes that his daddy can rescue him from anything and that I'm the perfect housewife and that giant superhero hamsters really exist and that all scientists are mad scientists and—and—and—!*

Her heart sank. She knew how great the difference was between *wanting* and *believing*. It was a gulf of meaning that had swallowed many faiths, marriages, and Federal budgets. No matter how much Jimmy might want to see his mom rescued from this ugly situation (skinkifying raygun to temple), he didn't *believe* it could be done in the existing circumstances (skinkifying raygun to temple). Even though he was only eight years old, he no longer believed in Santa, the Easter bunny, or a *deus ex machina*.

All of a sudden she remembered one more thing that Jimmy did believe.

"Dr. Oglethorpe, why don't you put that nasty ol' raygun down?" she wheedled.

"Vhy?" he echoed. "Ze mad zientist alvays needs zer beautiful hostage to guarantee his ezgape!"

"But it's *soooo* unnecessary. You've got what you came for. Gulp down a big swallow of that cough syrup and none of them will be able to stop you from walking out of here and taking over the world before dinnertime. That *is* what you have in mind, isn't it?"

The doctor stared at her as though she'd turned into a skink of her own free will. "You know, zat's right." He released his hold and scratched his balding pate in thought. "It neffer occurred to me. You know vat zey say: Ven you are a megalomaniac, ze mind iss ze first zing to go, heh, heh. Vell—" He raised the open bottle to his lips "—here's vorld domination in your eye."

"Oh, wait a minute, doctor darling." Mrs. Hanson laid one soft, white hand on the madman's arm. "That stuff does taste icky—just you ask Jimmy if you don't believe me. Let me get you something to wash away the aftertaste, okay?" She used her dimples on him in ways forbidden by the Geneva Conventions. Jimmy rolled his eyes at his mother's kittenish excesses and made loud, pointed gagging sounds, but since he held fast to every eight-year-old boy's belief that all girls are mushy, his powers didn't impede Mrs. Hanson's use of full-bore feminine wiles.

Dr. Oglethorpe regarded her suspiciously. "Ah so, vhy are you beink zo nice to me?"

"You're about to rule the world. Can you blame a girl for wanting to get on your good side? Besides, how could I hurt you?" She brought the eyelashes into play.

"For zat zere iss a very zimple eggsblanation: You could zlip somesink naughty into zat drink."

Mrs. Hanson actually said the words, "Pish-tush, silly man. You're going to be drinking the cough syrup first: Whatever you believe will be real. Do you *believe* that a woman like me could outwit a man like you?"

"*Ha!*" Dr. Oglethorpe's contemptuous response was pure reflex.

"Besides—" Mrs. Hanson suggestively traced the curves of the madman's raygun with one finger "—*don't* you believe that a woman like me could fall for a big, strong, mad scientist like you?"

"You could?" His eyebrows rose to new heights.

In answer, Mrs. Hanson leaned nearer and breathed in his ear, "A very simple explanation of Fermat's last theorem gets me sooooooo *hot.*"

"Ah . . . ah . . . ah . . ." Dr. Oglethorpe's forehead was shiny with sweat which he ineffectually tried to wipe off with the cough syrup bottle. "I zink I *vill* haf zat drink, my little cherry blossom."

"Your wish is my command," Mrs. Hanson murmured, and tripped gaily over to the half-ruined soda fountain to draw him a dark and foaming draught. None of the assembled superheroes made a move to interfere, for the evil Dr. Oglethorpe made sure to keep his raygun trained on little Jimmy the whole time as surety for their good behavior.

"Undt now," he said when she returned to his side, "again a toast: To me!" He guzzled the contents of the cough syrup bottle, then dropped the empty to the floor and made a face.

"I told you it tasted icky, pumpkin," said Mrs. Hanson, passing him the chaser.

He looked good for guzzling that too, but partway through he paused, lowered the glass, and stared into it. "Zis iss not zer pause zat refreshes!" he accused.

"No, it's Dr Pepper," Mrs. Hanson told him.

"Dr Pepper?" Jimmy echoed. "Ewwwwww! Prune soda!"

Calmly and casually, Mrs. Hanson said, "Sweetie, Mommy's told you over and over, Dr Pepper is very nice and very tasty and Daddy likes it and it is *not* made from—"

"It is *too* made from prunes!" Jimmy insisted.

"Do not contradict your *mama-san,* unworthy offspring,"

Dr. Oglethorpe snarled. "If she says it is not made from prunes, zen you vill agree or . . ." He aimed his raygun at the child meaningly.

"But it *is so too!* It *is!*" the boy cried with all the fervor of an early Christian opting for the lions. "It *tastes* like it *is,* so it is, and if you eat prunes or drink 'em then everyone knows what hap—"

"Eat hot skink, miserable worm!" the mad doctor shrieked, and squeezed the trigger.

A large, green, webbed hand knocked the raygun to the floor, deflecting its beam neatly. "Don't move, earthling," said the warty, pop-eyed alien who had suddenly appeared. Yellow squiggles of pure mental energy shot from his eyes to Dr. Oglethorpe's, buzzing like a hive full of asthmatic bees.

Immediately the deranged scientist froze in place, his eyes glazing over. "Yes, Master," he intoned. As Jimmy could have told him in an instant, if he'd been in any state to listen, not even the awesome powers conferred by the mutated cough syrup could stand against the psychic might of the Toad-Men of Skraax.

Two more Toad-Men materialized in a haze of twinkly lights to slap the helpless human into Salvador Dali's idea of a straight-jacket. "Good work, Commander!" said one. "Close study of this specimen will do much to aid, abet, and hasten our inevitable conquest of this puny planet, mwahahaha *croak.*" The lights twinkled all around them again and they vanished, taking Dr. Oglethorpe with them.

Bongo leaped forward. "Pulsing percussion, Captain Hamster, we can't just let them beat it like that! He may have been a power-hungry maniac, but he was also a citizen of Earth."

"We can't let them get away with this," agreed Laggi, Girl of the Starways. "Give the Toad-Men of Skraax an inch and they'll take a parsec."

"He was evil, but he was AB-Negative," Lexa chimed in. "My favorite flavor!"

Captain Hamster sighed. "You're right. The twenty-four hour automated teller window of Justice never sleeps. Laggi, summon the Hamstarship!"

The little alien pressed her fingertips to her temples and assumed that constipated look which indicates mental telepathy (as opposed to the other kind) in action. A loud humming overhead made the drugstore shudder as a circular section of roof melted away to reveal a hovering spacecraft. A hole irised open in its light-encrusted underbelly and two incredibly long ropes dropped to the ground. While Lexa merely dematerialized and Laggi soared into the ship under her own power, Bongo and Captain Hamster shinnied up hand-over-hand and paw-over-paw in less time than it would take to please the most autocratic of seventh-grade gym teachers. Then the ropes were sucked back into the spacecraft like so much spaghetti, the hole closed, and the mighty Hamstarship spun off into the cosmos.

Mrs. Hanson watched Captain Hamster and the Frenzies go, petulance creasing her brow. "Great, just great," she muttered. "*Now* who's going to clean up this mess?" And when she said mess, she wasn't thinking of the wrecked drugstore or the forever-lost cough syrup or the fact that Wayne couldn't possibly sell insurance dressed in a caped leotard and tights. She was thinking of Jimmy.

Jimmy, who in five short years would be a teenager. Jimmy, who would then be ripe for believing any stupid thing his stupid friends told him. Jimmy, who would believe with all his omnipotent heart that his parents were reactionary troglodytes with the brains of cole slaw.

Mrs. Hanson didn't like cole slaw. Something had to be done.

Jimmy was still staring after the vanished Hamstarship when his mother tapped him lightly on the shoulder to reclaim his attention.

"Didja see it, Mom?" he exclaimed, whirling around. "Didja see it? Gee, I wish I could've gone with them."

"You can, darling," Mrs. Hanson said.

"Huh?"

"I said yes, you *can* go with Captain Hamster and the Frenzies to fight the Toad-Men of Skraax."

"I *can?*" This from the woman who wouldn't let him bicycle around the block by himself? That guarded look of juvenile skepticism was back on Jimmy's face full force. Mrs. Hanson smiled inwardly. Perfect.

"Sure, you can," she pressed. "It's all up to you. You see, anything you want to happen *will* happen. Now don't give me *that* look, dear, there's a very simple explanation: It's all because that cough syrup I fed you a couple of days ago gave you the power to—"

"It did?" Jimmy scowled. Mrs. Hanson could almost see his thought processes at work: *Magic cough syrup, yeah, right, what does she think I am, a kid? She's just saying this so next time I'll swallow that yucky gunk without holding out for a new Captain Hamster comic. Well, she can't fool me!* With a smug look of complete triumph Jimmy shouted, "That cough syrup didn't do anything to me! I don't believe it!" And he meant it, too.

The universe went *poik*, a comprehensive sound-effect that included a lot of retroactive reality-adjustments.

"Did you hear that?" asked Wayne, his old self once more.

"Sounded like a backfire," replied one of the restored FBI agents.

"Since when do backfires go *poik*?" a rehumanized Mr. Dolan wanted to know.

"I'm sorry, sir," said the other former skink. "You're not cleared to receive that information."

Mrs. Hanson surveyed the results of her ploy and was satisfied. She breathed a great sigh of relief and turned to her son. "Come along, Jimmy, we're going home now."

"Aw, *Mommmm,* do I *haaaaave* to?" Jimmy dodged her outstretched hand and dashed behind the smashed-up soda fountain. Mrs. Hanson shook her head over her headstrong child and gave chase.

The chase was cut short when she stepped on something round and her ankle twisted out from under her. Cursing merrily, she picked up the offending object and was about to hurl it against the farthest wall when she noticed what it was.

It was the discarded cough syrup bottle. A single drop of the fabulous contents glistened on the rim. Dr. Oglethorpe had done his best to drain it dry, but he was a man, not a vacuum pump. Mrs. Hanson caught the drop on her fingertip before it fell and popped it into her mouth.

The structure of DNA unscrolled before her like a runaway sheet of shelf paper. Differential equations rattled through her mind as easily as nursery rhymes. She never had believed what her mother said about girls and math and science. And that was only the beginning. As for some of those women's magazine articles she'd swallowed whole, and those all-wise parenting gurus she'd obeyed without question, and those three or four or fifty-some-odd gentlemen in Foggy Bottom who kept preaching that equal pay was the first step that inevitably led to devouring your young . . .

For the first time in her life, Mrs. Hanson knew exactly what she believed.

Somewhere in the universe the cry rang out: "Duck and cover, boys, here comes Justice. And man, is she ever *pissed!*"

"White!" Said Fred

Nigel and his chums were giving the unconscious Paki a few last kicks for luck when they heard a voice cry, "Oi!"

"Wossit, Nigel?" Fred asked, leaning back against the alley wall to catch his breath. He was a weedy thing when lined up next to his mates, but he owned the best pair of Doc Martens in the bunch. You couldn't get any real efficient kicking done without a decent pair of DMs on your feet.

"Woss wot?" Nigel replied, still hammering on the Paki's ribcage. "I didn't say nuffin'."

"Me neever," said Bert. He stepped back and added, "Leave off, Nije, 'snot like 'e's feelin' the benefits no more."

"Oi!"

"There it goes again!" Fred made it sound like an accusation. His eyes darted from side to side, rats in a box. "You think it's the cops?"

"Nar," said Bert. " 'Ave a lookabout. Ain't no woodentops come by this way on patrol 'til later. You knows 'at."

"Well, if it ain't you two, and it ain't the cops, and there ain't no one else around as I can see, and it sure as 'ouses ain't 'im—" Fred pointed at the Paki "—then 'oo the fuck said 'oi'?"

"*I* did," said the Paki's back pocket.

Nigel and Bert jumped in their bovver boots and leaped for the relative safety of Fred's chosen alley wall. They felt better with something at their backs, especially when a bloody foreigner who by rights should be half dead and fully unconscious started talking from places decent white folks never did.

The pocket sighed. " 'Ere, don't tell me you lot've scarpered?" Nigel nudged Bert and Bert nudged Fred, but no one responded. The silence seemed to annoy the voice in the pocket. "Oh, *bugger!*" it exploded. "Gone an' run out on a mate again, just 'cos 'e's in a bind. Stupid tadgers!"

" 'Ere!" Nigel objected. " 'Oo're you calling a tadger, you-you-'aberdashery bit!" He left the shelter of the wall and strode back to the prostrate Paki. "Show yourself, if you're 'arf a man!"

The voice chuckled. "If I could show meself, that'd be the battle won, mate. But if it's face-to-face you want, reach in this sooty's pocket and yank the bottle."

Nigel scratched his shorn scalp, perplexed. He prided himself on never taking orders from anyone with a face he could bash. Here was no face, just a voice telling him what to do. He decided to do it and hope for a bashable face to show up later.

The bottle was cold silver, hammered into a pattern of interlaced nubile maidens performing outrageous contortions for their mutual delight. The lads gathered around to examine this *objet d'art* in what little light seeped through to the back of the narrow alley.

" 'Ow's she do *that* wifout them bristols getting inna way?" Bert wanted to know. He reached for the bottle, firmly in Nigel's possession. He got a full-face shoveaway for his answer.

"Let a feller out an' I'll do better'n *tell* you," the bottle said, quivering in Nigel's grip. "Pull the stopper, there's good lads."

Nigel made ready to comply without demur, but Fred clapped his hand over his chief's and asked, "You think you otter? I mean, you don't rightly know woss likely to 'appen if you *do,* do you, now?"

"Cobblers," Nigel sneered, giving Fred a thump on the head with the bottle. "I know woss gonna 'appen right enough! A bloody *genie*'s gonna 'appen, thass wot! Ain't you got no edgy-cayshun? Genie's wot *always* comes otter bottles wot talks to folk. Bloody fuckwit."

He wasted no more time, but yanked the cork—a cork sheathed in silver and capped with a shimmering black opal, true—and stood back, awaiting a stream of strange-colored smoke, a clap of thunder, or any of the many different dramatic effects that always heralded a genie's appearance in the stories.

"Oi," said a voice behind him, and someone tapped him on the shoulder.

Nigel spun around, ready for a fight. He threw the first punch, still clutching the bottle, and found his hand engulfed in a fist as big as a rugby ball and twice as leathery. A sensible man would weigh the situation and back down, but this was Nigel. Instinct took over. He lowered his head, ready to give his unlucky assailant a Glasgow kiss—they weren't in Glasgow and it wasn't a gesture of affection, and it didn't even involve lips (headbutts don't, unless you do them wrong), but the irony of it all was wasted on Nigel. All he knew was one fast clonk of his shaven skull to this yobbo's chin and it would be all over.

Nigel heard voices in a dream.

"Nigel? You awake yet?"

"Arr, 'e'll be orright, Fred. Don't be such a nana. Go on, drink yer pint an' lay off 'im."

71

Nigel blinked. Everything looked and sounded fuzzy and smelled of stale tobacco and beer. He shook his head slowly, still blinking, until things came into focus.

The first thing he really heard was Bert saying, "—so then this Paki stops the bloke an' asks 'im, 'Wossit you mean, walkin' up an' down this bridge singin' "It's twenty-four an' a beautiful day"?' An' the bloke grabs that little wog, tips 'im over the bridge inter the water, an' goes on 'is way singin' 'Oh, it's twenty-*five* an' a beautiful day!' " Nigel's ears rang painfully with the ensuing laughter.

He looked around and recognized where he was. It was the *Crown and Garter* public house, a small establishment not far from his (quite literal) stomping grounds. The lads had somehow dragged him in here and propped him up in a corner seat with a pint of bitter awaiting him on the table.

"Well, well, well, look 'oo's back among the living!"

Nigel saw a blond, bare-chested, blue-eyed man who dwarfed him and Bert put together. (Fred was too big a gonk to enter the equation.) He sat across the table from Nigel, pint in hand, and seemed to take up half the pub, when in truth he only occupied two of its chairs. " 'Oo the fuck are you?" Nigel demanded.

The man laughed, showing off horsey white teeth interspaced with gold fangs. " 'Oo'm *I?* I'm yer bloody fairy godmomma, you great wanker! 'Oo d'you *think* I am?"

" 'E's the genie, Nije," Fred said meekly. "Name of Doug. 'Ere to grant us a wish 'cos 'e's so bloody grateful we got him otter that bottle."

"Wot sort o' name's *Doug* for a genie?" Nigel roared.

"It's the one I *got*," the genie replied affably. He drained his pint, leaned across the table and helped himself to Fred's. Fred gave a muted squawk of outrage. "Shut yer gob, thickie," Doug said, and turned him into a newt. "Now, any more t' say 'bout an honest genie's given name?" he asked the survivors.

Nigel flicked the newt off the table with a snap of his fingers. It hit the wall and turned into Fred again. The other patrons of the *Crown and Garter* observed this transformation with the detachment of the overworked and weary who prefer to mind their own business and get home again in one piece in time to watch "Coronation Street."

"Orright, then, Doug it is." Nigel was pleased to be gracious. "Fer me first wish, I'll 'ave the crown jools delivered to me flat, fer me second I'll 'ave—"

"Ballocks!" said Doug. "Listen, you cack-'anded charlie, I'm not just *any* bloody genie! Take a grolley at me if you don't believe it."

Nigel studied the genie, rubbing his stubbly chin in thought. "Bugger all if you ain't right! T'ones I allus seen in the story books looked like a bunch o' rag-'eads."

"Sambos, the lot of 'em," Doug agreed. "You think it was easy, an honest workin' man like meself lumped in wif *that* lazy crew all these centuries? Passed down through the ages, 'and to 'and, from one wog t' the next, always 'avin' t' grant 'em the same bloody three wishes—" He sighed and grabbed Nigel's untouched pint. "But them's the rules."

"Well," Bert opined, "it must be a mercy to finally 'ave some white folks t' grant them wishes to."

"Codswallop." The genie demolished Nigel's drink at a gulp. "It's three bloody wishes each time I'm set free, is all I can grant! First time in *ages* I've got some decent lads t' serve, 'stead o' them pissin' Pakis, and there's nowt but one wish each I can give the lot of you!"

Nigel was so touched by the poor genie's plight that he didn't even object to losing his drink. He just waited until Fred bought himself another and then nicked it. Fred gave him a look, but that was all Fred had the balls to give anyone, when he wasn't acting with the gang. He went back to buy himself a replacement.

By the time Fred returned, Nigel had had ample opportunity to think. He swallowed the last of his beer, wiped his mouth on the back of a hand hairier than his smooth-trimmed skull, and announced, "Doug, old wodge, it seems t' me you've been sent to us as a sort o' Providence, like. You an' me an' Bert an' even nitty ol' Fred 'ere, wot we is is we're all victims of the *system*."

There was a chorus of agreement from the membership, although in this case it was shouts of *Bloody right!* instead of *Here! Here!*

"It's the fuckin' system woss took decent jobs away from honest men like us an' give 'em to a bunch o' bloody *foreigners* woss thicker'n fleas on a dog's bum," Nigel went on. "And you mark my words, woss done to *us* plain lads is just woss been done to this poor ol' genie, just 'cos 'e's not no bloody groid!"

"Too right." Doug looked hangdog. " 'Snot like any of woss happened's been *your* fault, eh?"

"You said it," Nigel concurred. "When there wasn't no black faces elbowing in on a man in this country, *them* was the days!"

A pall of nostalgia fell over the party. And there it might have remained until Doomsday or closing time had not the genie heaved a sigh like a toddler typhoon and said:

"Cor, *wot* a grateful country this'd be to the bloke woss got the pills t' turn it back *around*, eh, lads?"

Later, Nigel claimed it was his idea, which gave him the right to tell the others exactly how they were going to do it.

"Awwww, Nije, I wanted t' use my wish for a girl woss a real goer," Fred whined.

"Stuff it, you pillock. If we pull this off right, you won't be able t' get no sleep wossever 'counter all the thankful little pieces wot'll gob-job you to death, a'most."

Fred had the big, sad eyes of a horny basset hound. "You really think so?"

"I know so," Nigel reassured him. "Look, it's simple: You makes your wish first, an' you wishes for things to be set right, like, fer all us honest white folks woss made this country wot she is."

" 'At's not fair," Fred protested. " 'Ere I'll go an' spring me one an' only wish on making this a bleedin' pair o' dice for *you* lot, an' then you'll still 'ave *yer* wishes free an' clear!"

"Fred," said Nigel, throwing a chummy arm around his companion's neck. "Fred, Fred, Fred," he said, drawing that arm in tighter, until Fred's Adam's apple was nearly reduced to sauce. "Ain't yer ma never read you no nice little books o' fairy tales, like?"

Fred tried to reply, but lacked the air to do so.

"See, in them stories," Nigel went on, "it's the genie's bounden dooty to grant three wishes, but 'e can't bloody well 'elp it if the wishes wot gets made is *stoopid,* now can 'e?"

"*Khkhkhkhk!*" said Fred.

"Right," Nigel agreed. "See, in this one story, these two old gumbies gets three wishes, only th' 'usband wastes 'is first wishin' up a sossidge fer 'is tea."

"Yeh!" Bert chimed in. "I knows that'n. So 'is missus starts chunterin' on about wot 'e wished for 'til 'e loses 'is temper an' says, 'I wish that sossidge was stuck on the end of yer nose!' "

"So then—" Nigel grabbed the ball for the final goal "—'e 'ad to waste 'is last wish on gettin' that sossidge off 'er nose, an' there they was, up shit creek an' on the dole 'til their dyin' day!"

Fred made a sound that might have been pity for the impoverished old couple. It was hard to tell.

"So *that's* why we're 'avin' you wish first—seein' as 'ow you're even stoopider'n good ol' Bert, 'ere. Ain't I right, Bert?"

Bert nodded enthusiastically.

"That way," Nigel went on in a reasonable tone, "if you fucks up yer wish good an' proper, we've still got us two more chances t' get it right."

"An' if you doesn't fuck it up—" Bert's voice as good as added *Fat chance!* "—you gets all the credit for savin' England from a fate worse'n death! 'Ow's that?"

Nigel removed his armlock in time for his captive to croak, "You mean in case I gets a sossidge stuck on me own nose?" His companions smiled. "Fair enough."

Doug the genie pounded Fred on the back. "There's the spirit! Now wish away, lad, and don't be scared. There's two spare wishes waitin' to save yer hide if you gets it wrong. Ah! But if you gets it *right* . . ."

The genie waved one hand, and a crystal ball appeared in his palm. Inside the glassy sphere a host of naked ladies danced attendance on a hypothetical Fred, enthroned in glory, a pint measure in either hand, a lissome blond wench at his feet doing incredible things. (Although perhaps the single most incredible thing was that the Fred in the tableau didn't spill a drop of beer, no matter how energetic the blond's attentions became.)

"You mean if I gets it right, I gets 'er?" Fred asked.

"Nothing ain't too good for the man wot makes it so's we're livin' wif our *own* kind at last!" Doug declared.

"Our own kind. . . . Yeh, that sounds good t' me. I wish—I wish—" Fred closed his eyes tight, crossed his fingers, and shouted, "Oh, 'ow I *do* wish I was livin' just among white folks!"

"Comin' right up," said Doug.

"Ain't you genies 'sposed t' say somefing like *'Earkening and obedience?*" the educated Nigel asked.

"Wotever gets the job done, mate. Now naff off," said Doug. He snapped his fingers and Fred vanished.

"Oo," said Bert, staring into the crystal ball. "Why don't they got no *noses,* eh?"

Nigel gave him an elbow jab to the ribs. " 'At's 'cos they're bloody lepers, innit?"

"Leopards?" Bert's voice scaled up with wonder.

"Yeah, right enough," Doug averred. "That's a first class leper colony off on a nice little Pacific isle, it is. Don't hardly find 'em like that no more."

Bert scowled. "Wot'd you want to drop poor ol' Fred, wot never done you no 'arm, in the middle of a bunch o' leopards?"

"Stick it, spod. 'E asked to be livin' among white folks an' I *give* it to 'im."

"Mmmmmmm, they *looks* white enough," Bert admitted.

Doug made a helpless gesture. "I only grant wishes, mates, I can't change 'em. Them's the rules. 'Oose fault is it if 'e didn't 'ave the sense to ask for what 'e wanted so's a magical bloke could understand it? Done's done. So which one o' you'll be the one t' save 'im?"

"Wot? An' waste me own wish?" Bert was incensed.

" 'Sides," Nigel put in, " 'snot like we otter bring 'im back after where 'e's been. Could be 'e's contagious, like."

"Fred allus did say as 'ow 'e wanted to travel an' meet new folk," Bert added.

" 'Ave it your own way, lads." The genie blew on the crystal ball and Fred's pathetic face vanished as the lepers swarmed over him.

"That's enough for me," Bert said. "I'm gonna use me wish fer a squillion pounds, or maybe a big motor, or a—"

Nigel gave him a punch in the head. "An' 'ow long you think you're gonna enjoy it if the country goes on like she's *been,* eh? The bloody system'll get it all away from you an' find a way t' give 'em to some Paki prat, you mark my words!"

"It's my wish, innit?" Bert demanded, rubbing the side of his head. "Well, sod the country! Woss the country ever did for *me?*"

Nigel clicked his tongue. "Bert, I'm surpised at you. Where's yer sense o' patriotics?"

"Sod patriotics. I wants a *motor!*"

"Wot, not a woomin?" Nigel asked snidely.

Bert snorted and doled out the received wisdom: "Them wot's got th' good *motors* gets all the best bits o' kilt."

"Look, you prong, we agreed—"

Bert folded his arms. "Changed me mind," he said.

Nigel studied Bert's arms and knew that in a fair fight, the victory could go either way. Not like with poor old Fred. He wrinkled his brow in thought, and the ripples went halfway up the top of his skull.

"Orright," he said. "Pull yer finger out an' *wish* that way, all selfish. But you just remember: *I've still got me own wish left.*"

It was Bert's turn to frown. "Woddyer mean by that?"

"Sossidge," was Nigel's cryptic reply, but it was clue enough for Bert.

"You *wouldn't!*" His face was a study in cold horror.

"Oh, wouldn't I!"

Doug prodded Nigel in the shoulder. "Wouldn't you *wot?*"

"Use me wish to undo '*is,* thass wot!" Nigel wore a smile of triumph. "Maybe *worse'n* undo it. Maybe I'd wish 'e was turned into a Paki hisself. Serve 'im right."

78

"Nije!" Bert was wounded to the heart's core.

"Well, an' why not? If you're so bloody fond o' the black devils that yer willin' to let yer own country stay saddled wif 'em, maybe you'd be 'appier *bein'* one!"

"Arrr, Nije, you know I 'ate's 'em just as much as you."

"*Prove* it, then!" Nigel snapped.

Bert looked down. "I'm afraid."

"Afraid? Afraid o' wot, you great loony?"

"Wot if—wot if I fucks up me wish too, an' ends up like poor ol' Fred?"

"Is that all?" Nigel patted Bert heartily on the back. "You fucks up, I'm right 'ere t' save you."

Bert gave Nigel a suspicious sideways look. "You didn't save Fred."

"Neever did you. But that was only Fred. This is *us*, Bert. You can trust *us*, can't you?"

Bert considered this. "I 'spose," he said.

" 'Ere, listen t' me. The important fing t' keep in mind when wishin' is that ol' Doug 'ere can only give you wot you *asks* for. So long as you're bleedin' careful wif wot you says you wants, it'll all go pimpsy."

"An' if it don't, you'll 'elp me out?" Bert sounded doubtful.

"Don't be a namby! 'Course I will." To prove his sincerity, Nigel bought Bert a pint, and, after this was gone, he urged his mate to wish away. "Arter all, you ain't near so stoopid as was Fred."

"No." It came as a revelation to Bert. "No, I *ain't*, am I? Orright then, 'ere goes: I wish—I wish—"

"Remember, you gets just what you *asks* for!" Nigel cautioned. "It don't 'urt none to be specific, eh? Unless you wants to visit the Pacific, too."

"Not that! I wants t' stay right 'ere in England and I wish—I wish that the only folks as was living 'ere wif me was whi—"

" 'Old it! Best not say 'white,' Bert. Remember wot 'appened to Fred. You otter be *scientific*."

" 'Owzat?"

"Wish as you want everyone living in England otter be *Caucasian*." Nigel was proud of himself for remembering that word.

Bert turned surly. "Bugger that! I don't want no more Asians at all. Trouble with Fred was, he didn't say as 'ow the folks should be 'ealthy. Well, I wish I only 'ad to live wif *'ealthy* white people in England an' that's what I mean!"

"Comin' right up," Doug said, and snapped his fingers for the second time.

"They don't *look* white," Nigel commented as he peered into the genie's crystal.

"Well, under the dirt, they're white enough," Doug said. "Even count as bleedin' *Caucasians*." He turned the last word into sneer enough to make Nigel—for the first time in his life—blush hot with shame over his great burden of education. "An' they're 'ealthy. An' it's England."

"Yeh, but it's England about a million years ago!" Nigel stared into the crystal, watching his old chum slowly approach a group of squat, hairy people. They had been hunkered down around a small campfire up until Bert's sudden appearance. Now they were edging closer to their bewildered visitor, holding an assortment of large sticks and rocks. Their throwing arms looked extremely healthy.

"Bring 'im back, then, shall I?"

"Orright."

"Well?"

"Well wot?"

"Well, *wish* 'im back!" The genie was impatient.

"Wot! An' waste me last *wish?*" Nigel made a rude noise.

"I thought as 'e was your mate."

"Wossat got t' do wif it? If I wishes 'im back, we're back where we *started*, wif England in the shit 'counter all them Pakis! 'Sides—" he cast another glance at the crystal "—I got faith in Bert. 'E can make friends anywheres 'e goes."

Almost anywhere. Bert smiled and raised both hands in the universally accepted gesture that means "I come in peace." The antediluvian Englishmen made a unilateral decision *not* to understand it, based on the premise that the universe was wrong and they were right. (The prehistoric precursor of driving on the left side of the road, perhaps.) Bert was still grinning when the first rock smashed in the front of his head.

The genie sighed. "Too late t' bovver bringin' 'im back *now*. Oh well. No use cryin' over spilled grey matter, I always say." He drew a discreet curtain of mist over the bloody scene in the crystal, then turned to Nigel.

"Ready to make your wish, lad?"

Nigel bobbed his head eagerly. "I'm goin' to wish for a squillion pounds, or a nice little tottie wif big bristols, or a—"

" 'Ere!" Doug drew himself up to his full height. Being a genie, that meant he suddenly swelled from a six-foot-tall specimen of over-muscled manhood to a veritable Aryan Godzilla whose crewcut head brushed the rafters of the *Crown and Garter*. "Wot about all that you lot was goin' t' do to get them darkies otter Blighty?"

"Sod *that*," said Nigel, echoing the late Bert's philosophy. "Wot if I gets it wrong, too? 'Oo's gonter 'elp me out, eh? Not *you*, I wager!"

Doug shrugged. "I can't, like to or not. But if you uses your wish right—"

"An' if I don't? Bert an' Fred, they was stoopid. No *fore-sight*, like, that was their trouble. But me, I likes t' look ahead,

81

an' lookin' ahead I sees that I'd do best to take me wish, make me pile and let th' country take its chances."

"So be it!"

A change came over Doug, a change most awful, most dramatic, most terrifying. The genie's pale skin, blue eyes, and fair hair all darkened. His crewcut sprouted in some places, withdrew into the scalp in others, until his deeply bronzed skull was shaved clean except for a long black topknot. A pointed beard and trailing moustaches spilled from his face in hirsute profusion. His eyes assumed a tilted angle and an unnerving glint of scorn.

"Behold, it is even as the sages decreed!" Doug's voice rumbled through the public house like thunder. A few of the regulars gathered up their jackets and hurried out, to beat the incipient storm home. "These colorless worms are an effete and weakling race, cowards all!"

" 'Oo're you callin' a coward?" Nigel demanded, trying not to shake in his seat. "An' wot've you done wif Doug?"

The genie's laughter made plaster dust fall from the ceiling. "Foolish mortal, I am Doug! My true name is Daoud ibn Khalil, though I doubt your meager linguistic skills will allow you to pronounce such mellifluous syllables."

"Wotcher on about? Talk like a white man, you pissing towel'ead!"

"Bah, why bother to lower myself thus? You milk-faced buffoons are beneath contempt, unworthy swine who only seek the gratification of your own pitiful material desires. Give you a pint, a ten pound note, and a female with pendulous udders, and you count yourself blessed!"

"A piece like wot I wants costs a sight more'n ten pounds," Nigel objected.

The genie spat. The blob of supernatural spittle sizzled into purple smoke on the table between them. "I give thanks to the Providence which placed me in this dissipated land. By the laws of magic I am constrained to grant the wishes of whosoever finds and uncorks my bottle. To grant wishes is labor, and labor I despise. Therefore, I always seek to find some way to turn my master's wishes against him. So has it always been, since the time of Solomon."

"So you don't fancy doin' an honest day's work, eh?" Nigel's lip curled. "Ain't that just like a wog!"

Daoud regarded him with disdain. "Better a wog than a witling. Since I have been here, I have known many masters. Of these, not a single one who so proudly vaunts his *whiteness* has managed to phrase a wish so that I had to give him what he truly wanted! Ho, ho! Fully twenty-three of your great white minds have gone down in defeat before me in the duel of wills between genie and master, most of them paid-up members of the National Front. And yet never have I been able to avoid granting the wishes of those of your countrymen with more wit than whiteness!"

By this time, the genie's spittle was not the only thing that was steaming. "You sayin' as 'ow Bert an' Fred an' the Front lads an' I don't 'ave the brains of a *wog?*" Nigel snarled.

"If the bovver boot fits—"

"Orright, that's it!" Nigel slammed both fists onto the table. "I've 'ad it wif you an' all your sooty kin! I'm gonter wish so's you won't 'ave no choice but to give me wot I wants, an' wot *I* wants is gonter boot the 'ole mess o' you groids otter 'ere on your black arses!"

Daoud showed all his teeth in an impressive smile. "I would like to see you try."

"*See?* I'll give you *see!*" Nigel was on his feet and breathing hard. "I'll give you my wish so's you won't be *able* to twist it! I wish it t' be right 'ere in England, so's there's no plonkin' me down in some godforsaken place like you done

wif Fred; I wish it t' be right *now*, so's there's no funny business wif sendin' me back in time like you done wif Bert; I
wish folks t' keep their general state o' 'ealth as is—"

"Another tribute to poor Fred, I assume," the genie
drawled. Nigel ignored him.

"—an' I wish wiv all that, that I never 'ad to see anovver
one o' your ugly black or brown or yellow faces again as long
as I live!"

"That is your wish?" the genie inquired sweetly.

"Fuckin' *right!*" said Nigel.

"In that case . . . *Hearkening and obedience!*"

And everything went black.

Nigel felt a gentle wind on his face. It brought with it a
strange yet familiar odor, one he could not quite place. All he
did know was that it was a perfume distinctly lacking in yeasty
beer fumes and tobacco smoke, a very un-public-houselike
smell. He turned his head this way and that, but he could see
nothing.

"Where the fuck am I?" he demanded.

The genie's hated voice purred the answer: "As requested,
O Master, you are in England."

"When? Th' soddin' Dark Ages?"

"It is, as requested, neither England past nor future, but
the very hour in which you made your wish."

"Yeh?" Nigel jerked his head back and forth a few more
times and was still unable to place that smell. He also noted
that he no longer heard the clink of glasses and the mumble of
tired voices. Instead he caught the clank of machinery and the
grumble of passing motors. "An' the rest o' wot I wished,
then?"

"Granted. By my powers you will never more see another
black or brown or yellow face all the days of your life."

Nigel grinned into the dark.

"Or another white one," the genie added.

Nigel frowned.

"Hard to do that, blind."

Nigel screamed. From somewhere far below a boat's fog-horn answered.

"But don't worry," the genie concluded. "You only asked it to last as long as you lived. Well wished, O Master!"

Nigel felt a heavily booted foot connect with his backbone. He felt the bones crunch, then cold air rushing past, then the smash of icy water, and then . . . nothing. Eternity lacks impact, but has real staying power.

Simon, Andy, and Bill were shuffling along the nearly deserted bridge when the happily humming Paki bumped into them. They were out of work, out of cash, and out of sorts, but never out of ways to strike up a conversation.

" 'Ey!" said Bill. "Whyn't you watch where yer goin', you bloody monkey?"

Before the man could reply, Simon cut in. " 'E's one monkey don't need no organ. *Singin'*, 'e was!"

"Singin'?" Andy gave his newfound prey a shove against the railing. "Wotcher singin', you wankin' mongrel?"

"Yeh! Sing fer *us*, then!" Simon's shove turned into a punch halfway there.

"Thass right, sing!" Bill's landed hard enough to bloody the man's nose.

Trembling, their victim complied. It was too bad for him that his audience had such stringent taste in music and such forceful ways of expressing their criticisms.

Standing above the Paki's motionless body a short while later, a still-puzzled Simon repeated, " 'It's twenty-four an' a beautiful day'? Wot kinder song was *that?*"

"Oi!"

A Birthday

I wake up knowing that this is a special day. Today is Tessa's birthday. She will be six. That means she will start school and I won't see her during the day at all.

My friends will have a party for Tessa and for me. The invitation sits on my bedside table, propped up against the telephone so I can't possibly forget it. I wish I could.

There are pink pandas tumbling around the borders of the card and inside my friend Paula has written in the details of time and place in her beautiful handwriting. I get up, get dressed, get ready for the day ahead. Before I leave the apartment I make sure that I haven't locked Squeaker in the closet again. Squeaker is my cat. You'd think it would be hard for a cat to hide in a studio apartment, but Squeaker manages. Tessa loves cats and pandas, just like me. She told me so.

I am almost out the door when I remember the invitation. Tessa hasn't seen it yet. Today will be my last chance to show it to her. I keep forgetting to take it with me, not because I want to deprive my daughter of anything but because of what this birthday means to us both. I don't like to think about it. I tuck the invitation into my purse and go to work.

I arrive a little before nine. Mom always said I never plan ahead, but I do now. There are flowers on my desk at work, six pink fairy roses in a cut glass bud vase with a spill of shiny white ribbon tied around its neck. There is a freedom card propped open on the keyboard in front of my terminal, signed by most of the women in the office. I hang up my jacket and check my IN box for work, but there is nothing there, no excuse to turn on my terminal. Still, a good worker finds work to do even when there's none, and I do so want to touch the keys.

I sit down and reach for a sampler sheet to rub over my thumb and slip into the terminal. Damn, the pad's empty! I know I had some left yesterday; what happened? I can't turn on my terminal without giving it a sample of my cell-scrapings so the system knows it's me. Who's been getting at my things? I'll kill her!

No. I mustn't lose my temper like this. I have to set a good example for my girl. It's important for a woman to make peace, to compromise. No one wins a war. Maybe whoever took the last of my sampler sheets needed it more than I do. Maybe she had to stay late, work overtime, and everyone else locked their pads away in their desks so she had to help herself to mine.

"Good morning, Linda." It's my boss, Mr. Beeton. His melon face is shiny with a smile. "I see you've found my little surprise."

"Sir?" I say.

"Now, now, I know what day this is just as well as you do. Do you think the ladies are the only ones who want to wish you the best for the future? Just because there's a door on my office, it doesn't mean I'm sealed inside, ignorant of my girls' lives." He pats me on the back and says, "I'm giving you the day off, with pay. Have fun." And then he is gone, a walrus in a blue-gray suit waddling up the aisle between the rows of terminals.

I don't want to have the day off. What will I do? Where will I go? The party isn't until six o'clock tonight. There is so much I need to say to her before then. I suppose I could go to the bank, but that's only ten seconds' worth of time. It's no-where near enough. Here at work I could keep finding ex-cuses to—

Mr. Beeton is at the end of the aisle, staring at me. He must be wondering why I'm still sitting here, staring at a blank screen. I'd better go. I put on my jacket and walk away from my terminal. It will still be here tomorrow. So will part of me.

I hear the murmurs as I walk to the door. The women are smiling at me as I pass, sad smiles, encouraging smiles, smiles coupled with the fleeting touch of a hand on mine.

"I'm so happy for you," they say.

"You're so strong."

"I've been praying for you."

"Have a good time."

"Have a good life."

"See you tomorrow."

But what will they see? I think about how many sick days I have left. Not enough. I will have to come back tomorrow, and I will have to work as if everything were still the same.

As I walk down the hall to the elevator I have to pass the Ladies' Room. I hear harsh sounds, tearing sounds. Someone is in there, crying. I don't have to work today; I can take the time to go in and see who it is, what's wrong. Maybe I can help. Maybe this will kill some time.

The crying is coming from one of the stalls. "Who's there?" I call. The crying stops. There is silence, broken only by the drip of water from a faucet and a shallow, sudden in-take of breath from the stall.

"What's wrong?" I ask. "Please, I can help you."

"Linda?" The voice is too fragile, too quavery for me to identify. "Is that you? I thought Beeton gave you the day off."

"He did," I tell whoever it is in there. "I was just on my way out."

"Go ahead, then." Now the voice is a little stronger, a little surer when giving a direct command. "Have fun." Another shudder of breath frays the edges of her words.

I think I know who it is in there now. Anyway, it's worth a guess. "Ms. Thayer?" What is she doing in here? The executives have their own bathrooms.

A latch flicks; the stall door swings open. Ms. Thayer is what I dreamed I'd be someday, back when I was a Business major freshman in college: A manager never destined to waste her life in the middle reaches of the company hierarchy, a comer and a climber with diamond-hard drive fit to cut through any glass ceiling her superiors are fool enough to place in her way. Sleekly groomed, tall and graceful in a tailored suit whose modest style still manages to let the world know it cost more than my monthly take-home pay, Ms. Thayer is a paragon. Every plane of expensive fabric lies just so along a body trimmed and toned and tanned to perfection. Only the front of her slim blue skirt seems to have rucked itself a little out of line. It bulges just a bit, as if—as if—

Oh.

"Would you like me to come with you?" I ask her. I don't need to hear confessions. "If it's today, I mean." If I'm wrong, she'll let me know.

She nods her head. Her nose is red and there is a little trace of slime on her upper lip. Her cheeks are streaked with red, her eyes squinched half-shut to hold back more tears. "I called," she tells me. "I have a four o'clock appointment. Upstairs, they think I'm going to the dentist."

"I'll meet you in the lobby, then, at three-thirty," I promise. And I add, because I know this is what she needs to hear more than anything, "It's not so bad." She squeezes my

Esther Friesner

hand and flees back into the shelter of the stall. I hear the tears again, but they are softer this time. She is no longer so afraid.

I could take her sorrow from her as I took her fear by telling her there are ways to make what lies ahead a blessing, but I won't do that. She'd never believe me, anyhow. I know I would never have believed anyone when it was me. Besides, I was in college. I knew it all, better than anyone who'd been there, and the evening news was full of stories to back up my conviction that I'd chosen purgatory over hell. You're supposed to be able to survive purgatory.

I should have known better. Surviving isn't living, it's only breath that doesn't shudder to a stop, a heart that keeps lurching through beat after beat after beat long after it's lost all reason to keep on beating. I was wrong. But I was in college, Mom and Dad had given up so much to provide the difference between my meager scholarship and the actual cost of tuition, books, room and board. They said, "Make us proud."

When I dropped out in junior year and got this job as a secretary, they never said a word.

I think I need a cup of coffee. I know I need a place to sit and think about what I'll do to fill the hours between now and three-thirty, three-thirty and six. There's a nice little coffee shop a block from the office, so I go there and take a booth. The morning rush is over; no one minds.

The waitress knows me. Her name is Caroline. She is twenty-six, just two years older than me. Usually I come here for lunch at the counter, when there's lots of customers, but we still find time to talk. She knows me and I know her. Her pink uniform balloons over a belly that holds her sixth baby. She admires me for the way I can tease her about it. "Isn't that kid here *yet?*" I ask.

90

"Probably a boy," she answers. "Men are never on time."
We both laugh.

"So how far along are you?"

"Almost there. You don't wanna know how close."

"No kidding? So why are you still—?"

"Here? Working?" She laughs. "Like I've got a choice!"
She takes my order and brings me my food. I eat scrambled
eggs and bacon and toast soaked with butter. I drink three
cups of coffee, black. I don't want to live forever. I leave
Caroline a big tip because it's no joke having five—six kids to
raise at today's prices, and a husband who doesn't earn much
more than minimum wage.

I get a good idea while I am smearing strawberry jam over
my last piece of toast: The Woman's Center. I do weekend
volunteer work there, but there's no reason I can't go over
today and see if they can use me. I'm free.

I try to hail a cab but all of them are taken, mostly by busi-
nessmen. Once I see an empty one sail past, but he keeps on
going when I wave. Maybe he is nearsighted and can't see me
through the driver's bulletproof bubble. Maybe he is out of
sampler sheets for his automatic fare-scan and is hurrying to
pick up some more. Maybe he just assumes that because I am
a woman of a certain age I really don't want to ride in a cab at
all.

I walk a block west and take the bus. Busses don't need
fare-scan terminals because it always costs the same for every
ride and you don't need to key in the tip. Tokens are enough.
I ride downtown across the aisle from a woman with two
small children, a boy and a girl. The boy is only two or three
years old and sits in his mother's lap, making *rrrum-rrrum*
noises with his toy truck. The little girl looks about four and
regards her brother scornfully. She sits in her own seat with
her hands folded in the lap of her peach-colored spring coat.

She wants the world to know that she is all grown up and impatient to leave baby things behind. I wonder if she'll like kindergarten as much as Tessa did? She didn't cry at all when it was time to go, even though it meant I couldn't see her in the mornings.

Things are pretty quiet at the Woman's Center. After all, it is a weekday, a workday. You have to work if you want to live. But Oralee is there. Oralee is always there, tall and black and ugly as a dog's dinner, the way my mom would say. She is the Center manager. It doesn't pay much, but it's what she wants to do. She is seated at her desk—an old wooden relic from some long-gone public school—and when she sees me she is surprised.

Then she remembers.

"Linda, happy freedom!" She rises from her chair and rushes across the room to embrace me. Her skin is very soft and smells like lilacs. I don't know what to do or say. Oralee lives with her lover Corinne, so I don't feel right about hugging her back, no matter how much I like her or how grateful I am for all she's done for me over the years. It would be easier if she hadn't told me the truth about herself. A lesbian is a lesbian, I have no trouble hugging Corinne, but what Oralee is scares me. She clings to Corinne not because she loves her, but because it's safe, because she'll never have to risk anything that way, because her body craves touching. Oralee is always telling us we have to be brave, but she is a coward, pretending she's something she's not, out of fear. I can understand, but I can't like her for it.

Oralee leads me back to her desk and motions for me to sit down. She leans forward, her elbows on the blotter, a pen twiddling through her fingers. "So, to what do we owe the honor?" she asks, a grin cutting through the scars that make her face look like a topographical map with mountains

pinched up and valleys gouged in. Today she wears the blue
glass eye that doesn't match her working brown one and that
startles people who don't know her.

"My boss gave me the day off," I tell her. "With pay."

"Well, of course he did. Soul-salving bastard."

"I have to be somewhere at three-thirty, but I thought that
until then you might have something for me to do here."

Oralee pushes her chair a little away from her desk. The
casters squeak and the linoleum floor complains. She runs
her fingers over her shaven skull in thought. "Well, Joan and
Cruz are already handling all the paperwork . . . Our big fund-
raising drive's not on until next week, no need for follow-up
phone calls, the envelopes are all stuffed and in the mail . . ."

My heart sinks as she runs down a list of things that don't
want doing. I try not to think about the empty hours I'll have
to face if Oralee can't use me. To distract myself while I await
her verdict, I look at all the things cluttering up her desktop.
There is an old soup can covered with yellow-flowered
shelving paper, full of paper clips, and another one full of
pens and pencils. Three clay figurines of the Goddess lie like
sunbathers with pendulous breasts and swollen bellies offered up to the shameless sky. Oralee made the biggest one
herself, in a ceramics class. She uses Her for a paperweight.
Oralee says she is a firm believer in making do with what
you've got. Mr. Beeton would laugh out loud if he could see
the antiquated terminal she uses. All you need to access it is a
password that you type in on the keys so just anyone can get
into your files if they discover what it is. At least this way the
Woman's Center saves money on sampler pads, even if that's
not the real reason.

The photo on the desk is framed with silver, real silver.
Oralee has to polish it constantly to keep the tarnish at bay.
The young black woman in the picture is smiling, her eyes

both her own, her face smooth and silky-looking as the inner skin of a shell, her hair a soft, dark cloud that enhances her smile more beautifully than any silver frame.

At the bottom of the frame, under the glass with the photograph, there is a newspaper clipping. It's just the headline and it's not very big. The event it notes was nothing extraordinary enough to merit more prominent placement on the page: ABORTION CLINIC BOMBED. TWO DEAD, THREE INJURED. The clipping came from a special paper, more like a newsletter for the kind of people who would read TWO DEAD, THREE INJURED and smile. Oralee tells us that most of the papers weren't like that; they used to call them birth control clinics or family planning clinics or even just women's clinics. As if we're none of us old enough to remember when it changed! She talks about those days—the times when the bombings were stepped up and the assaults on women trying to reach the clinics got ugly and the doctors and sometimes their families were being threatened, being killed—as if they'd lasted as long as the Dark Ages instead of just four years. Thank goodness everything's settled down. We're civilized people, after all. We can compromise.

"I know!" Oralee snaps her fingers, making me look up. "You can be a runner. That is—" she hesitates.

"Yes, I can do that," I tell her.

"Are you sure?"

"Just give me what I need and tell me where I have to go. It's all right, really. I need to go to the bank myself anyway."

"Are you *sure?*" she asks again. Why does she doubt me? Do I look so fragile? No. I take good care of my body, wash my hair every day, even put on a little lipstick sometimes. It's not like before, that hard time when I first came to the city, when I was such a fool. I almost lost my job, then, because I was letting myself go so badly. I know better, now. It's my duty to set a good example. Children past a certain age start to notice things like how Mommy looks and how Mommy acts. I've read all the books. You get the child you deserve.

Oralee goes into the back room where they keep the refrigerator. She comes back with a compartmentalized cold pack the size of a clutch purse, a factory-fresh sampler pad, and a slip of paper. "You can put this in your pocketbook if you want," she tells me, giving me the cold pack. "Make sure you only keep it open long enough to take out or put in one sample at a time. And for the love of God, don't mix up the samples!"

I smile at how vehement she sounds. "I've done this before, Oralee," I remind her.

"Sure you have; sorry. Here are the names and addresses. Bus tokens are in the clay pot on the table by the front door. You don't have to bring back the pack when you're done; just drop it off next time you're here." She cocks her head. "If you *are* coming back?"

"Of course I am," I say, surprised that she'd think I wouldn't.

"Oh," she says. "Because I thought—you know—after today's over—Well, whatever. Good luck."

There are five names on the list, most of them in the neighborhood close to the Woman's Center, only one of them farther uptown. It's a glorious spring day. Soon it will be Easter. The holiday came late this year, almost the end of April. I think April is a pretty name to give a girl—April, full of hope and promise, full of beauty. Maybe I should have named my daughter April. I laugh away the thought. What's done is done, too late now to change Tessa's name. Too late.

When I get to the first place I'm surprised by how old the woman is who answers the door. I introduce myself and say that the Woman's Center sent me. I show her the cold pack and the sampler pad, telling her what I'll do for her at the bank. She has black hair that is so shot through with silver threads it looks gray, and her fingers are stained with tobacco. She stands in the doorway, stony-eyed, barring me from the dark apartment beyond, making me stand in the hall while I run through my entire explanation.

After I have finished and I'm standing there, holding out one sampler sheet, she speaks: "I'm not Vicky," she says. "I'm her mother. God will judge you people. You go to hell." And she slams the door in my face.

I feel like a fool, but by the time I reach the next address on the list the feeling has faded. It's better here. The woman's name is Maris and she lives alone. She urges me to come in, to have a cup of tea, some cookies, anything I'd like. Her apartment is small but tasteful, a lot of wicker, a lot of sunlight. "God bless you," she says. "I was just about at my wits' end. I thought if I had to go through that one more time I'd go crazy. It's supposed to get easier with time, but it just gets harder. I've got three more years to go before I'm free. Never again, believe me; never again."

She rubs the sampler sheet over her thumb and watches like a hawk as I fumble it into its thin plastic envelope. The envelope goes into the cold pack and the cold pack goes back into my purse. "Are you sure you remember my password?" she asks as she sees me to the door.

"Yes, but please change it after today," I tell her.

The third and fourth women are not as hospitable as Maris, but there is no one there to tell me to go to hell. One of them is an artist, the other lost her job, and Maris, I recall, told me she'd taken a sick day off from work just on the off chance the Woman's Center could find a runner to come help her. It feels very strange to me, sitting in rooms freckled with spring sunshine, to be talking with strange women when I would normally be at work. In the course of these three visitations I drink three cups of tea and also share a little gin with the woman who has lost her job. My head spins with passwords and special instructions, my hands clasp a pile of three plain brown self-addressed stamped envelopes by the time I teeter out the door in search of my final contact.

I take the bus uptown. Out the window I see new leaves unfurl in blurs of green made more heartstoppingly tender by the gin. It was a mistake to drink, but if I looked into the glass I didn't have to look into the woman's eyes. I decide to get off the bus a few blocks away from my stop. A walk will clear my head.

The blue and red and white lights flash, dazzling me. Two police cars and a crowd have gathered outside a restaurant that's trying to be a Paris sidewalk café. A man is clinging to the curlicued iron fence around one of the trees in front of the place, his face a paler green than the leaves above his head. I smell vomit, sour and pungent. I watch where I step as I try to make my way through the crowd.

One of the policemen is holding a shopping bag and trying to make the crowd back away. The bottom of the shopping bag looks wet. Another one is telling the people over and over that there is nothing here for them to see, but they know better.

A third stands with pad in hand, interviewing a waiter. The waiter looks young and frightened. He keeps saying, "I didn't know, I had no idea, she came in and ordered a Caesar salad and a cup of tea, then she paid the bill and started to go. I didn't even notice she'd left that bag under the table until that man grabbed it and started to run after her." He points to the man embracing the iron girdle of the tree. "I didn't know a thing."

The girl is in the fourth policeman's custody. I think she

must be sixteen, although she could be older and small for her age. Her face is flat, vacant. What does she see? The policeman helps her into the back of his squad car and slams the door. "Said she couldn't face it, going to a clinic, having it recorded like a decent woman. Bitch," I hear him mutter. "Murderer."

As I walk past, quickening my step as much as I can without beginning to run, I hear the waiter's fluting voice say, "I don't think it was dead when she got here."

A man answers the door when I ring the bell at my last stop. "Frances Hughes?" I ask nervously. Has a prankster called the Woman's Center, giving a man's name that sounds like a woman's? Oralee says it's happened before. Sometimes a prank call only leads to a wild goose chase, but sometimes when the runner arrives they're waiting for her. Trudy had her wrist broken and they destroyed all the samples she'd collected so far. It was just like those stories about Japanese soldiers lost for years on small islands in the Pacific, still fighting a war that was over decades ago.

The man smiles at me. "No, I'm her husband," he says. "Won't you come in?"

Frances Hughes is waiting for me in the living room. She is one of those women whose face reflects years of breeding and who looks as if she were born to preside over a fine china tea service on a silver tray. If I drink one more cup of tea I think I'll die, but I accept the cup she passes to me because she needs to do this.

"We can't thank you enough," her husband says as he sits down in the Queen Anne armchair across from mine. Frances sit on the sofa, secure behind a castle wall of cups and saucers, sliced lemons and sugar cubes and lacy silver tongs. "I wanted to do it, but Frances insisted we call you."

"You know you couldn't do it, George," says Frances.

"Remember how hard it was for you in the clinic, and after?"

"I *could* do it," he insists stubbornly.

"But you don't have to," she tells him softly. "Spare yourself, for me." She reaches over to stroke his hand. There is an old love between them and I feel it flow in waves of strength from her to him.

I leave their building still carrying just three brown envelopes. They don't want me to mail them any cash, like the others; they only want me to close Frances' personal account and transfer the funds into George's.

I also have a check in my wallet from Mr. George Hughes made out to the Woman's Center. He gave it to me when I was leaving the apartment, while I set my purse aside on a miniature bookcase and rebuttoned my jacket. He said, "We were very wrong." I didn't know what he meant. Then, just as I was picking up my purse, my eye lit on the title of one of the volumes in that bookcase.

"*No Remorse?*"

It is the book that changed things for good, for ill. You can still find it for sale all over. My aunt Lucille gave a copy to my mother. My mother has not spoken to her since. They study it in schools with the same awe they give to *Uncle Tom's Cabin* and *Mein Kampf*. Some say, "It stopped the attacks, the bombings, it saved lives." Others say, "It didn't stop the deaths. So what if they're forced to suffer? It still sanctioned murder." Some reply, "It threw those damned extremists a sop, it truly freed women." And others yet say, "It sold out our true freedom for a false peace, it made us terror's slaves." I say nothing about it at all. All I know is what it did to me.

I looked at Frances' husband and I wanted to believe that the book had come there by accident, left behind by a caller who was now no longer welcome under that roof. But when he looked away from me and his face turned red, I knew the truth. I took the check. "You go to hell," I told him, the same way Vicky's mother said it to me.

I will not use Frances Hughes' password and sample to steal. I could, but I won't. I will not betray as I hope not to be betrayed. But George Hughes doesn't know that. Let him call ahead to his bank, change the password. Let him be the one to come down and face the truth of what he's helped to bring about, this dear-won, bloodyminded peace. Let him twist in the wind.

There is almost no line worth mentioning at the bank. It is a small branch office with only one live employee to handle all transactions past a certain level of complexity. All others can be taken care of through the ATMs. There is only one ATM here. As I said, this is a small branch.

I prefer small banks. Larger ones sometimes have live employees on duty whose only job is to make sure that no one uses the ATMs to perform transactions for a third party. That would be cheating.

I stand behind a man who stands behind a woman. She looks as if she is at least fifty years old, but when it is her turn she does not take one of the sampler sheets from the dispenser. Instead she opens her purse and takes out a cold pack like mine, a little smaller. Her hands are shaking as she extracts the sheet, inserts it, and types in the password.

The child is no more than nine months old. It can coo and gurgle. It can paw at the screen with its plump, brown hands. "Hi, sugar," the woman says, her voice trembling. "It's Nana, darlin', hi. It's your nana. Your mama couldn't come here today; she sick. She'll come see you soon, I promise. I love you, baby. I love—"

The screen is dark. A line of shining letters politely requests that the woman go on with her transaction. She stares at the screen, tight-lipped, and goes on. Bills drop one after another into the tray. She scoops them out without even bothering to look down, crams them into her purse, and walks out, seeing nothing but the door.

The man ahead of me dashes a sampler sheet over his thumb, inserts it, and does his business. He looks young, in his twenties. He is handsome. The girls must have a hard time resisting him, especially if he knows how to turn on the charm. He may have the ability to make them think he is falling in love with them, the passion of novels, spontaneous, intense, rapture by accident.

Accidents happen. Accidents can change your life, but only if you let them. While he is waiting for the ATM to process his transaction, he turns his head so that I can see his profile. He looks like a comic book hero, steadfast and noble, loyal and true. If there were an accident, he would accompany her to the clinic. He would hold her hand and stay with her for as long as the doctors allowed. And then it would all be over for him and he could go home, go about his business. No one would insist on making sure he stayed sorry for what was done.

There is no picture on the screen for him.

I am next. I do the other transactions first. Maris has a little three-year-old boy, like the one I saw on the bus. He can talk quite well for his age. He holds up a blue teddy bear to the screen. "T'ank you, Mommy," he says. "I name him Tadda-boy. Give Mommy a big kiss, Tadda-boy." He presses the bear's snout to the glass.

The artist's little girl is still only a few months old. This is easy. I never had any trouble when Tessa was this young. I could pretend I was watching a commercial for disposable diapers on the t.v. It got harder after Tessa learned to do things, to roll over, to push herself onto hands and knees, to toddle, to talk . . .

The woman who lost her job has a one-year-old with no hair and the bright, round eyes of the blue teddy bear. I can't tell whether this is a boy or a girl, but I know he or she will be blond. Tessa is blond. She looked like a fuzzy-headed little duckling until she was almost two.

I see why Frances Hughes did not let George handle this. The child lies on its back, staring straight up with dull eyes. It must be more than a year old, judging from its size, but it makes no attempt to move, not even to turn its head. I feel sorry for Frances. Then I remember the book in their house and for a moment I am tempted to believe that there is a just God.

Of course I know better.

It's my turn. I glance over my shoulder. A line has formed behind me. Four people are waiting. They look impatient. One of them is a woman in her sixties. She looks angry. I guess they have been standing in line long enough to notice that I am not just doing business for myself.

I leave the ATM and walk to the back of the line. As I pass the others I murmur how sorry I am for making them wait, how there was no one waiting behind me when I began my transactions. The three people who were merely impatient now smile at me. The woman in her sixties is at the end of the line. She waits until I have taken my place behind her, then she turns around and spits in my face.

"Slut!" she shouts. "Murdering bitch! You and all the rest like you, baby killers, damned whores, can't even face up to your sins! Get the hell out of—"

"I'm sorry, ma'am, but I'm going to have to ask you to leave." The bank's sole live employee is standing between us. He is a big man, a tall man. I have yet to see one of these small branches where the only live worker is not built like a bodyguard. That is part of the job too.

"You should toss *her* out, not me!" the woman snaps. She lunges for me, swatting at me with her purse. I take a step backwards, holding the envelopes tight to my chest. I am afraid to drop them. She might get her hands on one and tear it up.

The man restrains her. "Ma'am, I don't want to have to call the police."

This works. She settles down. Bristling, she stalks out of the bank, cursing me loudly. The man looks at me but does not smile. "In the future, please limit yourself to personal transactions," he says.

"Thank you," I say, dabbing the woman's spittle from my cheek with a tissue.

It is my turn again. I want to kiss the sampler sheet before I run it across my thumb, but I know that if I do that, I will not be able to access my account. I wonder how long we will have together? Sometimes it is ten seconds, sometimes fifteen. Maybe they will give us twenty because it's Tessa's birthday. I take a deep breath and insert the sampler sheet, then enter my password.

There she is! Oh my God, there she is, my baby, my daughter, my beautiful little girl! She is smiling, twirling to show off her lovely pink party dress with all the crisp ruffles. Her long blond hair floats over her shoulders like a cloud. "Hi, Mama!" she chirps.

"Hi, baby." My hand reaches out to caress her cheek. I have to hold it back. Touching the screen is not allowed. It either cuts off the alloted seconds entirely, or cuts them short, or extends them for an unpredictable amount of time. Few risk the gamble. I can't; not today.

I take out the invitation and hold it up so that Tessa can see it. "Look, honey," I say. "Pandas!"

"I'm going to school tomorrow," Tessa tells me. "I'm a

big girl now. I'm almost all grown up."

"Baby . . ." My eyes are blinking so fast, so fast! Tessa becomes a sweet pink and gold blur. "Baby, I love you so much. I'm sorry, I'm so sorry for what I did, but I was so young, I couldn't—Oh, my baby!"

And I *will* touch her, I *will!* It's all lies they tell us anyway, about how touching the screen will affect how long we may see our children, about how now we are safe to choose, about how our compromise was enough to stop the clinic bombings and the assassinations of doctors and the fear. I don't believe them! I will hold my child!

Glass, smooth and dark.

"I'm sorry, ma'am, but I'm going to have to ask you to leave."

I go with my own business left undone. The man takes a spray bottle of glass cleaner and a cloth from his desk and wipes away the prints of my hands, the image of my lips.

There is another small bank that I like on the east side. I think I'll go there. I start to walk. It's getting late. Paula must be making all kinds of last-minute phone calls, settling the details of my party. They call it freedom. I call it nothing.

At first I hated her, you know. I hated my own child. She was there, always there, on every CRT device I chose to use in college, in public, at home. After the procedure, the college clinic forwarded the developmental information that the central programming unit needed to establish her birthdate. The tissue was sent along, too, so that they could project a genetically accurate image of my child. She wasn't there until her birthdate, but then—!

Then there was no escaping her. Not if I wanted to use a computer, or an ATM, or even turn on any but the most antiquated model of a television set. I hated her. I hated her the way some hate the children of rape who also live behind the glass, after. But they exult in what they've done, how they've had the last laugh, how they've cheated their assailants of the final insult. I have seen them in the banks, at the ATMs, even at work, once. *Who's got the power now?* they shout at the children, and they laugh until they cry. Sometimes they only cry.

I fled her. I ran away—away from college, away from home, away from so much that had been my life before. Away from Tessa. A mandatory sentence of six years of persecution for one mistake, one accident, seemed like an eternity. She was almost the end of my future and my sanity.

And then, one day, it changed. One day I looked at her and she wasn't a punishment; she was my little girl, my Tessa with her long, silky blond curls and her shining blue eyes and her downy cheeks that must smell like roses, like apples. One day I was tired of hating, tired of running. One day I looked at her and I felt love.

Now they're taking my baby away.

No.

I find a phone booth. "Hello, Ms. Thayer? I'm sorry, something's come up. I can't go with you to the clinic today . . . Yes, this is Linda . . . No, really, you'll be all right. No one will bother you; it's against the law. And after, you'll handle it just fine . . . Sure, you will. I did."

"Hello, Mr. Beeton? This is Linda. I don't think I'll be in tomorrow . . . Yes, I know you can't give me two days off with pay. That's all right."

"Hello, Paula? Linda. Listen, there's a spare key with my neighbor, Mrs. Giancarlo. Feed Squeaker . . . No, just do it, I can't talk now. And for God's sake, don't let him hide in the closet. I have to go. Good-bye."

I am walking east. I realize that I am still holding the envelopes full of all the money the women need. Singly they are small sums, but put them all together . . . I could buy a lot of pretty things for Tessa with so much money. I could afford to keep her, if I were rich as Frances Hughes.

There are no mail boxes near the river. I'm letting them all down, all of them except for Frances Hughes and her husband. I'm so sorry. Maybe I should call Oralee—? No. She's a coward. I despise her. If I turn back to find a mailbox, I might turn back forever. Then I'll be a coward too. It's Tessa who's been so brave, so loving, so alone for so long, and still she smiles for me. Tessa is the only one that matters.

I lean against the railing and see another shore. Gulls keen and dip their wings above the river. Starveling trees claw the sky. The envelopes flutter from my hands, kissing the water. No one is near. I take off my shoes to help me step over the railing. The concrete is cold through my stockings.

There she is. I see her as I have always seen her, smiling up at me through the sleek, shining surface that keeps us apart. She is giggling as she reaches out for the envelopes. Oh, greedy little girl! You can't spend all that. Now that you're six, maybe Mama will give you an allowance, just like the big girls. After all, you're going to school tomorrow. But first, let Mama give you a kiss.

We fly into each other's arms. Oh, Tessa, your lips are so cool! Your laughter rushes against my ears. I breathe in, and you fill my heart.

Happy birthday, my darling.

A Pig's Tale

After he escaped from Alice's clutches, the first thing the piglet did was to rub that annoying baby bonnet off his head against the bole of a tree. Free at last, he clipped through the dark woodland as fast as four trim little trotters would carry him. He was not a very big piglet at first, but the Wonderland wood was as full of acorns and beech mast as any other, and the piglet had an inherent knack for knowing which mushrooms were good to eat and which were someone's idea of a joke.

Time means nothing to a pig, as the old rouser goes, so it was no wonder (even for Wonderland) that for this little piggie the years did not pass but the meals did. At length there came a time when acorns were at a premium, and the woodland did not seem either so dark or so cozy. This was disquieting, to be sure. The misshapen birds and uncanny cats who haunted the leaf-strewn forest alleyways seemed—to a pig's perception, at least—to be fewer and farther between and occasionally beside themselves. Not good.

It was all rather sad, really. Pigs are as subject to free-floating anxiety attacks as humans, and since this pig had been human once (or as human as one could get, considering his environment) one fine afternoon he found himself plunged into the murkiest depths of Byronic angst and melancholia.

Byron really should have been a pig. (Lady Caroline Lamb

said that he was, the minx.) It would have perked him up no end. For pigs possess a certain native intelligence and common sense by and large missing from our greater poets. When despair lays its clammy paws across their fevered porcine brows, they do not slump about composing sonnets; they take action.

The only action the pig could think of taking was to go home and see about things.

It was the first time in years he'd thought of Home and Hearth and Mother. He recalled the sounds of crashing crockery and clanging pots, the voices of women raised in strident quarrel.

Pigs lack the proper dentition to pronounce the word "dysfunctional," so he went home anyhow.

Home was gone.

The pig stood in a little clearing, gazing at the ruins of what must have been a fairly pleasant little cottage in its day. He snorted and stamped his hoof, much put out by the thoughtless nature of Circumstance, which had so dared to discommode him. Then he decided to investigate more closely. Snuffling and rooting around the ruins filled his snout with the lingering odor of wood smoke. Charred timbers protruding from a mishmash mess of broken furniture and other domestic effects were another surefire (indeed) indication that someone had not closed cover before striking.

Accidents happen. The pig was not unhappy, merely disappointed. It would have been nice to see his mother again, he fancied, for nice belonged to the same class of words as interesting and we'll be in touch and your child has great potential. It carries little meaning other than the vague sense that no one is going to be hit with anything heavy.

There being nothing else to do, he turned himself back into a boy.

It was in this state that the Mad Hatter found him. Or rather, he found the Hatter, who was, as ever, ensconced at the tea table.

"Have some tea!" that worthy cried when the boy stepped out of the bushes.

The pig in boy's form—if not boy's clothing—said, "I'd rather have some britches."

It was a good thing that the Mad Hatter also dealt in miscellaneous haberdashery on the side. This revelation might have boggled Alice, but the pig accepted it as Q.E. very D. How else to explain the neatly tailored accoutrements of Wonderland's ill-sorted mob of zanies, beast and human? It wants a job of custom tailoring to fit a rabbit with a waistcoat or a frog with footman's livery. Accidents happen; clothing does not. Some people just don't stop to think; they're too busy swallowing nightmares whole.

Before long, the Hatter had the pig turned out in a dapper schoolboy style that would be the envy of any Eton scholar. "There!" he said, tying the lad's tie. "Now you're ready to leave."

"Leave?" the pig echoed. "But I just got here."

"Then it's past time you got out," the Hatter replied. "Save yourself, lad! It's too late for me, but save yourself while you can."

"Save myself from what?" the pig asked. A vase sailed across the sitting room of his memory and smashed against the far wall.

"Times," said the Hatter ponderously, "change."

"Am I to save myself from times or from change?" the pig inquired.

"Neither," the Hatter replied. "Both. Though always keeping a bit of change on hand to buy the *Times* is never a bad notion. Oh, bother it, lad, don't you see? They're *here*."

The pig glanced up and down the length of the Hatter's tea table, taking in a panorama of stale cakes, crumbled crumpets, a shambles of old scones. "Roaches?" he suggested. "Ants?"

The Hatter clucked his tongue. "Don't waste your time talking, but listen." He then lapsed into silence.

No one practices patience better than a pig, but even so there are limits to the length of time one can sit at a cluttered tea table in company with an attested loony and listen to nothing. Pigs could not care less about Zen. The question needs must at last arise: "Listen to *what?*"

"To me, of course," said the Hatter.

"But you haven't said anything," the pig objected.

"Of course I've said *something,*" the Hatter countered.

The pig sighed and picked up the largest cake knife he could get his hands on. He held this to the Hatter's throat and said, "Mother used to complain about you. If this is going to turn into another one of those word-swaps where you go on to say that you have, in the past, said something, I'm not the one to put up with it."

"Children today," the Hatter grumbled. But he eyed the cake knife askance and added, "Fine. I'll speak plainly. But it's not going to endear either one of us to generations of children yet to come."

The pig merely snorted. Then he snorted again, put out no end to learn that a boy's nose is physically unable to produce as loud and satisfying a snort as a pig's snout.

"You said *they're* here," said the pig. "Tell me who *they* are and you won't have to whistle through your windpipe."

"Analysts," said the Hatter.

"What?" The cake knife insistently pressed the wattled skin just above the Hatter's high collar and cravat.

"Analysts," the Hatter repeated. "Diggers after meaning,

blast them all to an eternity of moldy jam and rancid butter. D'you remember Alice?"

"We met," the pig admitted.

"Well, she woke up, told tales out of school, bent the ear of a *mathematician*, no less. A nice young man, scared witless of women. He was devoted to the girl; most girls, until they reached the age of imperilment. Next thing anyone knew"— the Hatter shuddered—"text."

"I don't understand," said the pig, but he was courteous enough to set aside the cake knife and pour the Hatter a fresh cup of tea.

"I am a poet," the Hatter said, pressing a hand to his well-starched shirt bosom. "I don't get out much, nor keep up with any books other than the slim volume of verse I am even as we speak preparing for the printer's. But some folks rush their scribblings into print with indecent haste, as if they were brides already eight months gone with child. Alice's adventures were common fodder long before you took it into your head to walk on two legs again."

"You know who I am?" The pig cast a weather eye behind him, as best he was able, to see if perhaps his transformation had been incomplete. No corkscrew tail distorted the seat of his trousers. All was well.

It was the Hatter's turn to snort, and very well he did, too, even lacking a snout. "Of course I know, you clod! How could I avoid knowing?" He reached under a pile of dusty Banbury tarts and excavated a floury copy of Mr. Carroll's most beloved work.

"It's all in the book."

The pig helped himself to the relic, paging through Alice's dream with the proper mixture of reverence and resentment that he had not merited longer mention. While he consulted the text, the Hatter grumbled on.

"The havoc he's wrought! The simple, homespun pandemonium! Oh, it was fine, at first—a book for children, harmless, charming. But then—*meddlers!* Not enough to occupy them, turning over every rock in their heads to see what hideous crawlies haunt the undersides, no! They must invade the nursery bookshelf and read, and read into everything they find."

The pig looked up from the book. He didn't understand much of what the Hatter was saying, but he dismissed it as madness. After all—! No need to have recourse to the cake knife.

"Scone?" he suggested, passing the plate and pronouncing the word to almost rhyme with done.

"Yes, it is," said the Hatter, glancing at the plate. "Although I prefer to pronounce it so it rhymes more nearly with *alone,* which is what I have been ever since *they* invaded." He helped himself to sugar.

"The hare was the first to go," he told the swirling depths of his tea. "They called him a rampant pagan fertility symbol and he never got over it. So much to live up to, and he a Methodist bachelor! The dormouse, on the other hand, was a dream of the womb. How clearly I recall his words of farewell: 'When they can't tell Assam tea from amniotic fluid, it's time to move on,' he said."

"Have they all gone, then?" asked the pig. His gaze weighed the all-surrounding woodland. At the Hatter's words it seemed to have put on the bleak aspect of a deserted house, dust on the oak leaves, cobwebs veiling the bark of the walnut trees.

"The Queen of Hearts is still around," the Hatter said. "I see her sometimes when she stops by to drop off a platter of tarts and to ask me whether I've yet been able to find out what, precisely, a symbol of Woman as Castrating Bitch (capital w, capital c, capital b, no less) is supposed to *do* all day. *Noblesse oblige* and all that. She feels the responsibility. Responsibility for *what* remains the question. The King tells her it was just an idle compliment, but she's a stickler. The distraction has sweetened her temper no end. She's no fun anymore."

At least it doesn't seem to have affected you, the pig offered by way of consolation.

"That's because I may be mad, but I'm not a weathercock. I've steadfastly refused to let them make me *mean* anything at all. Oh, they tried to have at me, lad, don't doubt it for a moment!" He waved a teaspoon in the pig's face. "I've been called everything from an icon of the ultimate tragedy of the Industrial Revolution to a fragment of embedded Masonic code. Do you know what you get when you rearrange the letters in the words *'Mad Hatter'?*"

"Nnnnno," the pig admitted with some reluctance.

"You get *Rhatemtad,* which some idiot decided was the name of a heretical Egyptian pharaoh of the Old Kingdom who did odd, un-Christian things with trowels and whose monuments were therefore suppressed." The Hatter's head fell forward heavily. "Get out, boy. There's nothing left for anyone here. They've stripped the flesh from the bones, sucked the blood and licked out the marrow."

"But where shall I get out *to?*" the pig asked.

"Their world. What else is there?" The Hatter sipped his tea, morosely, then suddenly demanded, "Why is a raven like a writing desk?"

"Who cares?" the pig replied. "How do I get there from here?"

"With an answer like that, you're halfway there," said the Hatter. "Although the usual method of transportation is to wake up."

"Wake up? But I'm not even asleep," the pig said, pinching himself to make sure.

"Then *fall* asleep, you tollywug," the Hatter snapped. "And wake up in a better world than this. That's how the rest of 'em did it."

The pig thanked the Hatter and took his leave. "And whatever you do," the Hatter shouted after him, "don't mean more than you are!" He backed up this advice by flinging a teacup at the pig's head. This caused the pig to feel the prickle of nostalgic tears in the corner of one eye (the left one) and the rise of a lump in his throat that turned out to be a poorly chewed piece of scone (pronounced however you damn well like). He returned to the forest, retreated to the shade of an ancient sycamore, curled up at the roots, and went to sleep.

He awoke in the shade of an ancient sycamore, but that was as far as Coincidence was willing to carry him without a supplemental fare being paid. Wonderland had vanished. He was on the grounds of an impressive, imposing, implicitly British boys' school. Instead of the tender hand of an older sister to brush away the leaves that had fallen on his face while he drowsed, he met the stern gaze of a Master who instructed him to get his lazy carcase into chapel for Evensong or expect six of the best across his backside afterwards.

The years that followed there—and at Cambridge after—are of little interest to the general reader and less to the pig. No one on the faculty, staff, or student body at his first school ever remarked upon the fact that there was an extra mouth to feed, a new bed to be made up, a fresh face to be recognized. The bills were paid in timely fashion; that sufficed.

The pig went home with his friends during the school holidays, where he was duly presented to this or that brace of beaming parents as the son of a duchess. (True enough.) On the school records, he rejoiced in the name of Anthony Piperade, Lord DuCoeur. He grew up straight and tall and honest, with a healthy pink complexion and an appetite that made fond mothers admonish their own chicks to emulate him.

He did not get fat. He did not see anything wrong with eating bacon.

When he attained his majority, he was summoned to the Inns of Court where he was solemnly invested with full control over his inheritance. Documents were pushed back and forth across the table. Thus did young Lord Anthony learn that the Mad Hatter's mercury-induced insanity had not left him blind to the advantages of investing (heavily) in textile interests. A sealed letter was placed in the pig's hands. *It's too late for me, my boy,* it read. *They have brought up the big guns. By the time this reaches you, I will have succumbed to being an Orphic archetype. Madness and poetry supposedly sleep in one bed. Fools that they are, they willfully overlook the fact that some poets manage to earn a living at it. Adieu and toodles. Destroy this before reading.*

"There was also this," said the man of law, giving the pig a small pasteboard box. It held the fragments of a broken teacup.

The pig looked up. "Why is a raven like a writing desk?" he asked.

The man of law chuckled and said that his lordship was pleased to be jocular.

Now that the mystery had been removed from his finances, he was his own pig. It was a very good feeling. He read Law at Cambridge and came to be a barrister with rooms in town and a fine place in the country. He continued to keep up his public school and university friendships. He traveled abroad and was enriched without becoming unduly aesthetic.

One drizzly day he encountered his mother in a Paris sidewalk café. The Duchess was sipping absinthe and reading a copy of Virginia Woolf's *Orlando*. (Time had passed. It will, given half the chance.) "Mother?" the pig inquired.

The Duchess looked up from her reading. "Oh, it's you," she said in an affable manner. "Join me, won't you?"

The pig was rather nonplussed by his mother's casual attitude. After all, he'd thought her dead, and what she'd thought his fate had been—

Or had she given that matter any thought at all? Women who thrust their infants into the care of other children—total strangers—cannot possibly have more on their minds than whether they've left themselves enough time to get good seats at the theater.

So the pig ordered a glass of gin-and-bitters when the waiter came, and made small talk until the drink was brought, and in general made himself as agreeable a companion as his social reputation always painted him. ("Good old Tony! He's a safe guest to make up your dinner party, Mavis. Pleasant-looking, wellborn, rich, nowhere near as witty as me, eats what's put in front of him, and he goes with any decor.")

But eventually the demon of Meaning would have his day, and the pig heard himself telling the Duchess that she was looking quite well for someone who had ostensibly burned to death in a conflagration lo, these many years agone.

"Oh, that," said the Duchess. She snapped her fingers and the waiter brought her another absinthe, although the fashion for the drink of Decadents has passed with the turning of the century and the introduction of mustard gas victims to polite society.

"Yes, that," said the pig as his mother imbibed. "I found the ruins. What happened?"

"Dejaneira set fire to the place," the Duchess informed him. She drank more absinthe.

"I see." He nursed his gin. "And who is or was or might be Dejaneira?"

"Why, the Cook, of course!" The Duchess regarded her son as if he had dropped out from beneath the tail of a pig rather than merely being one. "What else could she do? We were the embodiment of a fiery Sapphic romance gone awry under the merciless strictures of Victorian society. Her servile status was a galling reminder that even though she was the dominant partner, I would still have to be the one giving the orders. No wonder she threw things. As for the pepper—"

"*Must* I know?" the pig pleaded.

"It's all part and parcel, and you *did* ask," the Duchess reminded him. "Considering the shape of the peppercorn, my darling Dejaneira was grinding up the withered testicles of our enemies every time she employed that condiment. I don't even want to think about what significance the pepper mill's shape conveys." She smiled happily and patted the pig's hand. "My dear boy, it's been eons since anyone's asked to know all that. You can't imagine what a treat it's been to be able to get it out in the open one more time."

The pig shifted in his chair. "Where *is* Cook?" he asked. "She's not—she won't—will she be joining us?"

The Duchess's smile collapsed upon itself. She sighed. "She won't. It's over between us. I blame this post-War morality. Raise the hems and anything can happen. Everyone's gone all Sapphic now, even in the best homes, the finest families. Even in print, no less!" She waggled *Orlando* high, which the waiter took to mean an order for more drinks. "One can't *épater le bourgeoisie* if *les bourgeois* are looking at you over their milk-white shoulders and waiting for you to catch up. Some days I don't know what to do with myself."

The pig rose from his seat and laid a hand on his mother's shoulder. "Whatever you are, don't do more than you mean," he told her. It was advice given with the kindest of intentions. It was also the last time he saw the Duchess under those circumstances.

The Depression left him undepressed and as happily bereft of meaning as ever. During the bombardment of London by the Nazi forces he opened the doors of his country seat, *Gadara*, to several shipments of East End youth. Nothing was filched or broken or made to smell worse than before, and the experience left him curiously attracted to the thought of fatherhood.

Unfortunately, the practicalities intruded. Every morning he studied his reflection in the mirror and tacitly accepted the fact that he had aged, but nowhere near enough to account for all the years he'd seen pass by. To marry implied the inclusion of a more observant, less objective witness than the looking glass. From what he knew of women, not one of them would not consider it a privilege to be wed to a partner whose looks remained essentially unchanged while her own were diligently nibbled away by the mice of the minutes, the weasels of the weeks, the stoats of the seasons, and so on, until he ran out of measures of time and metaphoric animals with which to couple them.

Therefore he himself remained uncoupled, although he did engage in love affairs. Knowing himself to be what he was, he took pains to please his partners. When the dawn of the Women's Movement found him, no lady could point the finger at him and justly name him swine. (For the same reason, he had avoided a career in law enforcement when he came to the States in the '60s.) He remained in the States until all his old school chums were tidily dead or so senile they assumed he was his own grandson. Here he safely built up and improved upon the Hatter's textile empire.

A century had come and gone since the first publication of *Alice's Adventures Underground*. There had been some moments of dread, among the fluttering years, when he came dangerously close to meaning something. For a time he feared that they might view his slow, almost imperceptible aging process as symbolic of Man's Dream of Eternal Youth. Then he read about the Peter Pan syndrome and breathed easier. That slot was already occupied by Barrie's bonnie flying boy. His own peculiar loitering on the shady side of forty meant nothing, in and of itself. It was merely the halo effect of having first seen the light in an immortal work of fiction, a Chernobyl of the spirit.

The pig sat behind his desk and gazed out over the towers of Manhattan. The polished rosewood surface was only broken by the leatherette ticket folder his secretary had handed him a minute since. A one-way passage, First Class, would convey him back to Britain in three days' time. It would be good to see the old homestead—now a tourist mecca famous for its topiary display, damn the Inland Revenue to hell.

His telephone buzzed. He pushed a button and asked his secretary what she desired. The woman was weeping. He could hear the great, shuddery sobs, could imagine how they must be shaking her slender body. Had she lost a loved one? Received some discouraging medical report? Merciful heavens, it sounded like the end of the world!

Which it was. Someone else had chosen to push a button not too long before the pig had taken similar action. The news was blaring through the streets even as the missiles were shrieking through the sky. He was able to cast one last, fond lingering look over his ticket-folder before the bowl of heaven shattered like a teacup against a wall of light.

For a time afterwards, he clung to life by threads of pain that twisted themselves into hawsers before finally fraying and letting him plummet into a pit of oblivion (as viewed from Survivor's Point). The panorama, like most, was breathtaking. This was unfortunate, since want of breath precludes a wail of heartsick pity getting any farther than the teeth.

Not blinded by the blast, the pig was forced to see what had become of other beings and all their scattered toys. For a time he did, until his intelligence told him he had the option of will—that basic I-don't-give-a-shit-about-you-I'm-doing-this-*my*-way attitude that is the principle of all survival outside of beehives and ant colonies and certain family reunions. He did not *have* to look at the devastation surrounding him if that was not his—wrong word, but still—pleasure. And if he did look, he did not have to *see*. As the few miserable remnants of humankind (How kind? How human? How dangerously close to the forced extraction of *meaning* it is to hold a word accountable for its syllables!) straggled their way back onto the burnt and gutted stage, the pig kept to himself and pretended they were not there.

In part, this was the meat and not the intellect at work. Even in human form, even with his flesh frizzled by the bomb, he knew he was still edible. Prudence preached retirement, both for the purposes of healing and survival. No matter what the speculative bards had sung about the tedium of immortality, the pig knew they plucked their tunes from a lute strung with sour grapevines. What the hell was wrong with living forever? Losing your loved ones all the time? It was just an Army brat's life writ large. You'd adjust. You'd make new friends, dear. If you're bored, you must be boring. Snap out of it.

The pig wanted to live. Maybe not like this, he thought,

casting a wary look over yet another scorched cityscape, but things would get better. Or if they didn't, he'd get used to them. He wanted to live.

And whether it was his faith or his philosophy or just the fact that the world grew weary of supporting so much evidence that her top-of-the-foodchain children couldn't be left alone for two cosmic blinks without someone clobbering someone else (*Don't make Me stop this universe, kids, I'm warning you!*), the Earth kissed the nuclear boo-boo and made it all better.

Trees returned. Rough chunks of pavement not scavenged for cottage walls were worn away by the roots of new green things. The cockroaches decided to try for a better press this time around and evolved shimmery, iridescent wings and a lilting song that left the flash-fried nightingale spinning in her sepulchre.

And there were children. Babies were born hale and well, with the old-fashioned number of fingers and toes. The pig didn't see too many of them all at once, but he had lived through a time of not seeing too many automobiles, either. He saw his first when he left his hovel and went down to the riverbank to fetch some water.

The child was not dirty or scabby, nor did it look like a hunted animal. Its long yellow hair was clubbed back and there was a distinct pong of sweat and grease wafting from it, but the pig knew he was no bed of vanished roses either. He had some food with him—a dry but filling cake he made from acorns—and he offered it as a lure. The child carried mushrooms in a pouch and declined the lure in favor of a trade.

They did not speak the same language, but gestures helped and pigs learn fast. It also helped that they did not have much to talk about, which let them come to grasp the basics of each other's tongues. The pig still spoke English as he recalled it, the child an evolved offshoot of the same. It was a language linked to the mother tongue in the same way English was blood-kin to the lingo of Beowulf. It also helped that the pig was willing to play the fool to win a child's heart and that the child still knew laughter.

So the pig returned into a world that had recaptured its laughter and its joy in childhood and its sense that occasionally there would be times of no sense (which is as different from *non*sense as chalk from most kinds of cheese except Romano). He had gone gray by this time, and wrinkly, although he still had most of his hair and teeth and a peeling leatherette case that held crisp, crumbly yellow scraps of magic. And he knew where to find the best acorns.

The tribe took him in and sat him down with the other old men and told them to keep an eye on the children. The children tumbled around in the sun when it shone and sopped up the rain when it fell and loudly told one another that the real meaning of life was that they were to keep an eye on the old men.

The pig heard the M-word and shuddered. *Even here?* he thought. *Even now?* And he touched his leatherette ticket-folder and dreamed of topiary clipped into the shape of March Hares and Mad Hatters, of frogs in footman's livery and strident queens.

And one day, he began to talk of such things in his sleep—a sleep that is an old man's dozing compromise between slumber and death. He murmured of riverbanks and rabbit holes, of luckless lizards named Bill and flamingos coerced into service as croquet mallets. Asleep, awake, eyes open or closed, he spoke of these solemn matters, and like a tribe of wary dormice the children crept near to listen.

He knew the story, start to end. How could he not? It was his essence more than any double helix or stately manor now drowned beneath the waves that had devoured distant England. He spoke it slowly, neglecting not a word, and the children who did not speak the language of his tale still gathered close and cocked their heads and listened to the melodies of enchantment.

Most of what he told them was a barrage of names like autumn leaves, fluttering about wildly, detached from the objects they had once defined. It had been ages since anyone touched a teacup, let alone tea. But how much of Alice's world ever did follow her back up the rabbit hole, and for how long did it linger in the rolling world of daylight, leisure suits, and bombs? Her story did not deal in artifacts, but in wonders. In lands where men of law never wore wigs and climes where Cheshire Cats were never seen except as supper, Alice endured.

There are always miracles where there are children, and fascination for any tale that opens their eyes to marvels, whether or not they are sensible marvels. Even a pig knows that.

Soon the children were speaking a language closer to his own, and repeating long selections of the story. Soon the other old men waxed envious of the pig's ascendancy and dredged up other tales their own grandsires had told them when age made ancients babble nonsense: sweet nonsense of wolves who dressed up in granny's clothing, and maidens whose taste for pomegranate seeds deprived the world of spring, and babies whose birth brought winged beings down from the heavens, riding the tail of a splendid star.

And no one ever thought to tack a shred of *meaning* to a single one of those tales. Not one of all.

When the pig saw that the yellow-haired child he'd first met by the river had grown to have children of her own, he knew the time had come for him to go his way. The old men's corner hummed with tales of many tellings, the old women joining in with stories of their own in the wintertimes. Some of the striplings had taken to the road with only a burden of stories on their backs and returned with tales garnered and traded and fresh-made from among the other peoples they encountered in their wanderings. The world-heart beat strong with the blood of *Once upon a time.*

Yes, it was time to go.

He made a last batch of acorn cake and crumbled the last of the first class airline tickets into the mix. "Well," he said, "I'm going." The other old men nodded. Sometimes a man preferred to meet his death where the leaves would look after his burial.

He was on his way out of the settlement when he heard a trip-trip-trip behind him, like the ghost of a piglet long gone but never dead. He turned and saw that he was being followed by the daughter of his first child-friend. Her name was nothing like Alice.

"What is it, my dear?" he asked as she caught up to him and solemnly took his hand. "You should go back. Your mother will be worried."

"You never told," she said.

"Told what?"

"Why *is* a raven like a writing desk?"

He smiled. "Have you ever seen a raven, child? Or a writing desk?"

To his surprise she replied, "Yes, I have."

"What? But where—?"

"Over there," she said, pointing with one hand as she used the other to smooth the wrinkles from her pinafore. "By the riverbank." She took his hand and said, "This way. Hurry. We're late."

He was dragged after her as easily as if he were made of

paper. Leaves were falling from the trees, riffling across his eyes, bewildering him with their flittering pips of black and red, diamonds and clubs, hearts and spades. A church bell sounded somewhere far away. The child ran faster, so fast that he cried out for her to have a care, she'd tear her stockings on the brambles shielding the mouth of the rabbit hole. She ducked her golden head and pulled him through. His pouch of traveler's fare spilled in the root-hung darkness. She waited impatiently for him to gather up the fallen acorn cakes while she tapped her paw and frequently consulted a large gold pocketwatch. The last cake he retrieved was adorned with the words "EAT ME" picked out in currants.

"No time!" she cried, clapping a furry paw on his forearm. "She'll be furious! We're late!"

Past roses white and dripping red they ran, past the Queen, who flailed at her hedgehog-ball with her flamingo-mallet, past an ocean of human tears where all manner of curiouser and curiouser creatures ran heedlessly round and round in circles on the strand. It meant everything. It meant nothing. The pig went stumbling on, after a white-furred dream-child.

He hardly recognized the clearing. The Hatter and the mad March Hare laughed and sang and hailed him merrily. He drank a cup of tea that tasted suspiciously of dormouse and reached for a crumpet that filled his mouth with memory.

"Ah, no!" the Hatter cautioned, raising a finger. "Don't you start that old business all over again, my lad. It's only a story, you know. The troubles come when they try to make it mean things."

"Doesn't it?" asked the pig. "Does none of it mean anything?"

"It's a story," said the Hare. "It's a dream."

"You know, speaking of that dream, if you rearrange the

letters in the words *Mad Hatter,* you do get something sensible," the pig said.

"And what do you do with that sensible thing after you've got it?" the Hatter asked. "Stick it in your writing desk? Leave it out for the ravens?"

The dormouse popped out of the teapot. "Whatever you mean," he said sleepily, "don't be more than you do."

"Here," said the Hatter. "This one should fit you." He pulled a tiny, white embroidered baby bonnet from his sleeve and tied it around the pig's head. It fit precisely.

The infant in his cradle screwed up his red, wrinkled face and cried. His mother picked him up herself and began to rock him, singing a lullaby while thunder scoured the heavens with a sound like kitchenware and crockery being flung by an irate Cook.

Some of *them* would say it was all a dream. Some of *them* would insist his crying meant an anguish for the womb's Wonderland lost. Some of them might have the presence of mind to check his diaper and see if what they found in there *meant* anything.

Only an eternal story. Only a glimmering dream.

Only a child.

And for some, through all the ages of uncounted lives that yearn for wonder more than meaning, that would always mean enough.

Love, Crystal and Stone

This is the *saeta*, the song they sing in shadow, of the lost poet of Granada, the city where the Red Citadel, the Alhambra stands, and where the ghosts of Moorish kings and queens walk beside the long pool outside the Hall of the Ambassadors. The little spirits of the night, the *duendes* know it, and they have taught it to the gypsies, and the toreadors, and any who long to fill their hearts with the weeping roses of a distant death. Listen.

The poet sits in the shaded refuge of his sister's house, sipping a little water blossomed red with pomegranate syrup. Outside the streets of Granada shiver in the twilight, burdened with swords and bulls. There is talk in the house, the lizards of low and urgent whispers scuttling up the walls, leaving trails of pollen and dust among the burnished flowerpots. The poet's sister is also the mayor's wife, the mayor is also a Socialist, a Socialist is also wood for the fire and blood for the knife of the Insurgent troops who swarm the city. In their tombs beneath the chapel floor, Ferdinand and Isabella dream of dead princes and Christ triumphant while above them the marble raft sails on. Severed heads perch on the brown spikes of Franco's harvest, a rippling field of polished leather cheeks and wool steeped in gun oil. The Moors have returned, good blackfaced sheep, their hearts left behind to feast the eagles of the Atlas Mountains.

In his solitude, the poet sighs and gives himself up to cigarettes and memories. Wisps of smoke curl up from the eye burning scarlet between his fingers. The shutters are snapped tight across the sightless gaze of the windows, blind men basking in the pity of the rising moon. The ticking of clocks and cicadas seeps over his hands, drawing the evening home in nets of rosemary.

August overlays the city, pressing breasts of heat and spikenard against the hills, the searching fingers of the roadways tainted and glorified with the city's shattered maidenhead. The poet sits on the old velvet divan in his sister's house and inhales a dream of women with the dust that wafts from the antique fabric. Mermaids rise singing from the green and azure swirls of carpet at his feet. In the kitchen he hears his sister and her husband kneading whispers into bread, a strident congress of crickets caged within smooth plaster walls. He closes his eyes and draws the smoke deeper into his lungs, imagining that it drinks the crimson salt of his blood and re-emerges tinted to the shade of an old maid's keepsake of pressed roses.

He feels the cigarette bite his knuckles with its dwindling flame and crushes out the last hungry spark in the alabaster moon at his elbow, a flower afloat upon a sea of time-yellowed lace. The sweetened water is gone from the glass, though he can not remember having drunk it. All that is left is a ring of red lees at the bottom and a scattering of tears trickling down the sides. He knows that if he harvests a single droplet on his fingertip and lays it to his tongue he will taste ash and salt. Knowing this to be so, there is no need to put it to the hard proof of science.

It is very close and still in his sister's house. He breathes the cool, dry air of a rock-hewn tomb. He hears the moon crying into her winding sheet, and gunshots, and the distant sound of a hundred gypsy horsemen riding beyond the reach of the knives.

Someone is knocking at the door. There are no servants to answer it. His sister has sent the housekeeper home to be with her family in these days of shattered glass and naked feet. He thinks: All women are so. They dream that the power of their eyes alone can make a crystal wall to hold back the swords, that if they are there in their black mantillas and their fringed shawls to witness what the soldiers do, then the steel edges will frill and fray into sprays of orange blossom and no blood will fall to the earth. Time and again the swords keep their edge, the bullets drink, and still the women believe. Still they stand by the crossroads and by the riddled walls where the earth reaches up to embrace the newly dead, and still they refuse to let a thousand proofs keep them from their belief.

The poet thinks of women. He thinks of women and he feels the ants and the tigers begin to nibble away at his ungovernable flesh. He knows that they mean to take his faith and his bones and remake him in a new image, a woman who can defy the moon, who can hold back all the blood of the night by pressing it pent between her thighs.

The knocking at the door is louder now. It scatters the fearful tigers who hasten to guard their nests behind the bookshelves. Only the ants, with hearts of bronze, stand faithful at their post, jaws of many changes working over what is soft and what is hard, a transformation conducted in the purest spirit of the academics, dead among their smashed pages, their tattered alembics.

He shoos away the ants before they have done their work and rises out of the swarming hill of ten thousand shining bodies, black and hard as fingernails on slate. The tigers moan and cough. They roar a challenge from their safe haven behind the ramparts of the dead scholars. The night has settled her skirts over the city, the snouts of the rifles rooting in the hidden flower of her shame. The night cries out to the poet. Someone is knocking at the door. He will be the one to answer.

The young soldiers stand outside with roses seeping from between their lips. An accusation of rifles lays down a pattern of whiplashes across the naked street. Granada lies bound beneath the tread of their patent leather boots, the maiden's bared backbone a strand of pearls that trickles away into the shielding modesty of the river. The young soldiers stand at attention in the moonlight, heat rising from their bodies until they burn blue-white as the knife blade in the forge and their fine uniforms fall away in a breath of blown cinders. Only the glitter of their patent leather boots binds their feet to the black ice of their purpose. Only the bewitching little caps on their heads conceal the imprint of God's finger on their brows, the mark that warns all men to love them.

The poet steps out into the street, drawn by the beauty of their naked skin, the lazy rise and fall of their three-clawed patent leather wings. Behind them in the shadows the bull waits, a crucifix of gold and cheap enamel promising to snap the tower of his neck, the heavy links of its chain and the dry eyes of a withered Christ clinging to his flesh with the eternal wisdom of embryos and ivy.

The young soldiers take hands smeared black by the gun butts and lay them on his breasts. Their touch burns the poet's newfound woman's flesh, leaving the empurpled marks of love-bites, the tiny incised half-moons where the blood wells up and weeps its ecstasy from the shuddering heart. He gives himself to them with the helpless surrender of the night and the tigers and the little knife he carries bound with linen strips between his breasts. Wherever they mean to take him, he will go.

Up the streets of Granada and down to the two rivers, down the streets of Granada and up to the Red Citadel they take him, boots chattering over the stones, shining wings filled with the fecund breath of the night wind. The rivers put on their festive dresses, their gypsy garments of red and green and blue, and follow after the poet and the soldiers and the bull with his cross. Their eyes are bright with fishes and little golden birds. Their throats swell with drowned children, and the beautiful bodies of young men turned from bread to ivory by the razor's enchanted touch.

The Red Citadel slumbers atop its peak, dreaming of love among the myrtles. The moon has cast away her ancient song and races wailing across the sky, a madwoman to herald what the bull and the soldiers bring up the slopes of the Alhambra. She throws herself down into the waters of the long pool before the Hall of Blessing and tears comets from her hair, rakes her cheeks until they bleed angels and carnations.

The King of the Moors and the *duendes* comes forth to see what all the commotion is about. He is as tall as seven men when his wives love him, as weak as a trodden beetle when they turn away their eyes of kohl and forbidden wine. He stands before the long pool that holds the prostrate moon and lifts hands heavy with the waters of a hundred buried cisterns. Emeralds and olives fall from his fingers. His wives scatter their rage and their laughter among the myrtles, playing at hide-and-find with their little sons.

Why have you come before us, O Moon of jasmine and lilies? Bishop's daughter in your robes of purity and your scarlet petticoat, why have you tumbled from the sky?

The moon hears the words of the King of the Moors and the *duendes* and lets her head droop over her breasts which she stole from the Virgin of Pilar. They are hard and white, and when she beats them with her little fists they shatter into storms of butterflies. The sons of the queens shriek and dash after them, crying out Mama, Mama, give me a crown of such beauty to wear and I will live forever! Their mothers send the *duendes* scampering after the princes in their silk robes, their peacock turbans. And in the long pool which drinks the honeycomb of the Hall of Blessing, the maddened moon howls over her shattered breasts.

The prince whose mother has given him doves' hearts to eat runs the fastest. In all the Granadas that ever were and ever will not be there is none so swift as he. He races three dawns ahead of twilight, and his feet have become falling stars. He chases after the moon's lost butterflies, hands outstretched, fingers plucking lovers' sighs and the extraordinary notions of tomcats from the air. His eyes are polished metal, verdigris and pewter, and his cries startle the ghosts of dead flowers awake in the gardens of the Generalife, but he cannot catch the butterflies of the moon. His sorrow rasps the bones of sleeping mice, his tears fill the nests of the screech owls with the bitter judgement of deserted temples. Heedless of his footing, he tumbles headlong from the heights of the Red Citadel into the dreams of men.

The *duende* who is his tutor and his wetnurse and his lover sees but can not follow. The sprite made of the unseen spikes of hedgehogs and the tribal laments of toads is barred from passing the gate of dreams. In vain it hurls a hundred spells against the portal. The gypsies have built it with their hammers of crystal, cut its planks from water using saws of stone. A mermaid swims behind the curtain of palm fronds and melting roses, mocking the poor *duende* where it stares and stamps its thorny feet and stands divided from its prince, its lord, its love.

He is mine now, little *duende*, she whispers, and the flicker of her finned tail churns the waters beyond the dreamgate into a cloud of skulls. He is mine to keep, you will never see him more, and when his mother the great queen sends to seek him she will only find the blue gem of his left eye and the green gem of his right. I will take them from him with my kisses, I will fill his sight with pearls. Go down to the river, little *duende,* to the forge of the brown man whose song is beautiful. I will leave the blue gem of his left eye in one pocket of the brown man's leather apron, I will leave the green gem of his right in the brown man's heart.

This is what the mermaid tells the *duende* before she swims away laughing, rolling up the gate of dreams behind her with a single flicker of her fringed tail.

The *duende* sobs, and all the tears of its chestnut eyes fall in a shower of dry salt, angular crystals tumbling down in an avalanche that buries its black feet in burning snow. It sees into the darkened heart of the queen who is the lost prince's mother and more salt shivers down. The great queen is the special favorite of the King of the Moors and the *duendes.* For her he has bidden the dawn to wake the nuns of a hundred convents with the cries of newborn infants in their barren beds, filling their slacks teats with milk that smells of oranges. For her he has called down the last death of the phoenix so that he might serve her a collop of its breast meat sauced with mint and cardamom. He has bid his daughter open her thighs to the lances of the cross because of a single ill-spoken word from the lips of the last Moorish king to sit within the Hall of the Ambassadors which displeased his ladylove. For the slaking of his own rage and to salve the poisonous outcry of his beloved queen, bereft of her child, what will he not do to the incautious *duende?*

Despair embraces the myrtles. The *duende* clasps its badger's paws to its breast and flees the shadow of the mermaid's laughter. It races down the slope of the Red Citadel, spreads owl's wings, and breaks the waves of the sky with its breastbone of timber steeped in salt. The cows in their fields raise heads heavy with olive trees to see it fly, and where its shadow falls over the crossroads the Insurgents' bullets patter to the ground, their sinews snap between the jaws of the ants.

The *duende*'s shadow falls across the moon's white shoulders, a talon to lay bare the bone. The moon lifts her voice in an agony of lilies, and the sound of it frightens the scattered princes back to their mothers' hennaed breasts. Only the great queen stands with empty arms awaiting wind and rain. She cries her son's name, and in the Court of the Lions the stone beasts shift their creaking shoulders beneath the basin, spilling out the night. She lifts her hands of cinnamon and fills them with the moon's own blood, then casts it against the walls of the Red Citadel, blanching these to the color of boiled almonds, but her son still lies beyond the gate of dreams and still he does not come.

And now the King of the Moors and the *duendes* takes his beloved queen to his bosom, which holds the sea and the Rock of Tariq and the troops of Morocco who swarm out of the south to lick the bull's tail. Her tears fall in threads of silk upon his breast, their tracks twining into a golden cord from which he weaves a noose to bind the moon. He takes the cord of empty arms and wombs scooped hollow by the rifles and with it he ties the moon to the highest tower of the Red Citadel.

O Moon, if you had been true to your place, you now could tell us where our son has gone, he says. If you had swallowed madness like a slice of apple, you would now be free. I have taken your madness and forged it into five silver nails. With these I will affix your hands and feet and heart to the points of a star and set it rolling across the heavens. There will be no rest for you, O Moon, no bed of almond blossom and saffron. The stars will chase after you, wailing, and their places in the firmament will be taken by the flashes of the guns.

And he takes up the hammer of crystal which the gypsies have given him and drives the first nail deep into the moon's trembling heart.

The poet hears the moon's Gethsemane in his place among the soldiers. He feels the little knife bound between his breasts become a shrew that sets its teeth against him. He stops in the middle of the street, balanced on the slippery cobbled skulls beneath his feet, and ignores the barking of the soldiers, the rasp of their patent leather wings against his cheeks. The bull comes near, thundering Christ, and the poet opens the ruined bosom of his shirt to show the bleeding book and to tell them that he will not go on with them any farther.

The bull lowers its horns at such insolence, and the dead toreadors stir in their graves, reaching for their capes and swords, finding worms and beetles between their fingerbones. Upon the highest tower of the Red Citadel, the King of the Moors and the *duendes* drives the second silver nail into the mad moon's outstretched palm. Her cry awakens the dead toreadors and they burst from the earth, they storm the churches, they take the Virgin of Pilar from Her shrine and carry Her before them up the slopes of the Alhambra, the Red Citadel, making Her a banner painted with sand and the blood of minotaurs. And always their song is the ever-living *Gloria!*, and always it pours from mouths all bone and glass, the power of the Virgin of Pilar with them to reclaim their lips, their flesh, their city.

The bull hears and trembles. The young soldiers hear and fold their patent leather wings around their naked bodies, hoping for the mercy of a shadow's throat to hide them. Upon the highest tower of the Red Citadel, the King of the Moors and the *duendes* drives home the third silver nail.

The poet takes the fierce shrew from its feast within his bosom and sets it to mount guard over the soldiers and the bull, then races up the slopes of the Alhambra to rescue his betrothed. The cats in their midnight councils break from his feet in panic, their lips sweetened by a slaughter of white butterflies. The cobbled skulls crumble into red dust that gives up the odor of crushed thyme. There is a razor in his hand, a smiling blade molded from the lost songs of the Jews who wander in the gardens, the hidden dances of the gypsies in their caverns, the sighs of spinsters mated to cold sheets and iron priests.

Behind him, the poet hears the bull's outraged bellow turn to a wolf's howl. The owl-winged shadow of a *duende* crosses his path, and he tumbles into the grave that is the gateway to the land of dreams. The yellow dust sifts down between the skulls, sighing into the stream of salt that flows down the mountain into the sea. The poet falls until the mermaid's arms enfold him, blue lips pressed to his eyes.

With his razor he touches her lightly on the lips and she darts back, fringed tail flailing pearls of air. You can not have me until I have rescued the moon, he tells her. Neither my man's body nor my woman's body nor my soul within the Red Citadel. If you hold me, the dead toreadors will come with their banners. If you detain me, the rivers will come with their tiered skirts. If you close your arms around me, the wings of owls will dip beneath the waves of the sea and steal me from you, and all the ships you keep beneath your pillow, and all the sailors you hold between your breasts. I must rescue the moon, who has gone mad with thinking of my death. And he shows her the razor of dreams.

The mermaid sobs her challenge and opens her arms to

the razor, trailing scarves of sunrise and the cheap perfume of waterfront whores. She twines her body close around his own, but he is armored in a gypsy's flayed skin, and in the carapace of a beetle, and in a cloak of owl's feathers. His tears trickle from his left eye to his right, down the length of the arm that holds the razor, and with it he frees the mermaid from her solitude of turtles. Her legs are long and made of jasper, they break from their gemmed chrysalis staining the water crimson. She dances and she drowns. The cats will find her body washed up along the shore that borders daybreak and give her a high funeral. Her body will learn the mysteries of the bones that dwell inside a drunkard's guitar. The rivers wade into the sea to gather up the bright fishes smashed to life from her discarded tail and sing a festival out of the desert.

The gypsies dance on the riverbank, beside the forge of the brown man, making bonfires of cedarwood, setting the fishes to gossip on the flames. The poet leaves the river which has flowed from the dreamgate and the open grave to listen to the tales the fishes tell among the embers. The gypsies part to let him pass, throwing their bodies upon the streams of crystal that run from the mountains of his hidden breasts, greedily taking the sacrament.

The poet heeds only the fishes, sizzling behind the eyelids of secrets. They have much to teach him. They teach him the song which the great queen sings to hold the love of the King of the Moors and the *duendes*. They teach him the *saeta* whose melody will bring the lost prince back into the world. In gratitude, he takes them from the flames and strings them for a necklace, using a hedgehog's spine for a needle and the iron filament of Isabella's shroud for a thread.

And now he lifts his eyes to where the King of the Moors and the *duendes* stands with one foot in the gardens of the

Generalife and one foot in a field far beyond the city. There is the glimmer of crystal, a star falls, and a silver nail pierces the left foot of the captive moon.

You must hurry, poet, the brown man says. He stands before him, leather skin and leather apron, leather breath and leather eyes. He takes the poet from the gypsies, though the young men sigh with desire and the maidens try to snare his feet with orange blossoms. There is fear in their eyes, because they have touched the crystal and the cards, because they love the poet, and because they know there is not one of their fine horses that can outrun the bull.

Within the brown man's forge, a child is curled asleep within a glass walnut shell upon the anvil. The brown man takes the razor from the poet's hand and steals the taste of the sea from its edge with bread. The poet takes the brown man's hammer and wraps the sound of the *saeta* around it, then brings it down on the anvil of Tariq's Rock. He smashes open the walnut shell, then bares his woman's breasts and suckles the child until he is old enough to taste the bread and the blood. The child devours the bread and the milk and the sea until he is grown to be a prince once more. He stands between the poet and the brown man, under the owl's hard shadow, and his shout of joy makes his father drop the last silver nail from his hand.

Queens and princes, Moors and *duendes* all rejoice, the Red Citadel rings with their triumph. The poet sings the *saeta* over the prince's eyes, and he feels his beetle's carapace begin to squeeze itself closed over his breasts. He dances the secret dance of the caves of Albaicin, and he feels his flayed gypsy's skin begin to dry and grow tight around his thighs. The king's other sons have found him out, they are frolicking about him, begging for white butterflies, but all that he can offer them is the plucking of his wings. They despoil him of the tawny feathers one by one and flee chattering back to their mothers' arms.

The poet casts aside what is left of the skin and the shell and the cloak of feathers. He stands with one foot in the gardens of the Generalife and the other in a field far beyond the city. In his hand he holds the last silver nail which has fallen from the king's grasp, and in his eyes he holds the bull and the moon.

But the moon is still nailed to the highest tower of the Red Citadel, her blood a blue snake that the lions of the courtyard sup in bowls of stone. Beloved of the king's wives and of the gypsies and of the owls, the poet rises taller than seven men, but he can no longer free the moon. He has given away his little knife, he has parted with his razor, and the silver nail in his hand has grown dull in a skin of tears. He weeps, and his sorrow pools in the hollows of the moon's shattered breasts.

Do not weep, O poet! cries the prince whom he has freed from the mermaid's dream of pearls and skulls. I will give you jasmine and pomegranates if you will not weep.

The prince in his satins rides the night between the wings of an owl-winged *duende* that laughs, he paints his desire across the sky with his mother's russet milk. The shining seeds of a sword-split pomegranate tumble from his hands, each wrapped in a stolen scale from the drowned mermaid's fringed tail.

The moon opens a hundred thirsty mouths to drink a healing for her madness from the pomegranate seeds, but they will not open for her. In their glimmering armor thick with lost seas they are virgins among the thorns. Only the poet's touch can free them. Crowned with white flowers, he cups his hands to fill them with the prince's gift. He lifts them to his lips, but once the steel buds open he lets the bright seeds fall into the mouths of the moon. Her face becomes a single eye, fringed with olive leaves, and the silver nails and the golden cord fold dark wings around themselves and sink into the tomb of the Catholic Kings in their leather coffins. She has put aside her madwoman's rags, she has become a great lady in her laces and her velvets. A child of bone and wine kneels to offer her the bridle of a bronze horse shoed with the brown man's smile, saddled with the poet's songs. It spurns the dust of the Red Citadel with its hooves, carrying her away until she is no bigger than a crystal walnut shell in the heavens.

What have you done, O poet? cries the great queen. What have you done, squandering my sweet son's gift on the madness of the moon? Her anger shivers all the streets of Granada to a silence among the guns. It cracks the earth into a hundred mouths to swallow the dead toreadors with their banners and the Virgin of Pilar.

There is a pain between the poet's breasts that is not love. He glances down and sees the teeth of the shrew cleaved to his flesh. He falls from the summit of the Red Citadel amid a flurry of patent leather wings. The earth whirls below him, the gardens of the Generalife cruel with roses, the earth of a distant field where gypsies bury dreams. He falls, and in his fall he clings to one last seed of the prince's pomegranate. He has but to peel it free of the mermaid's scale and place it beneath his tongue if he wills to live forever among the ghostly princes, the phantom queens. He has but to swallow one seed of bitterness and desire if he wishes to bow as subject to the King of the Moors and the *duendes*.

The night wind's razors peel him like an apple. He plunges through salt water and women's eyes and the scent of spikenard. He brings the last seed to his lips and blows it from him on the wailing notes of the *saeta*. He falls away from the tumbling seed, free of everything but his own songs, subject to nothing but his own soul. The crimson seed drops into the long pool before the Hall of Blessing, a mouth of lotus. From her crystal throne the lady moon looks down and lets fall the last silver nail, which the gypsies stole and which they gave to buy her love.

The silver nail pierces the seed. The bull's hoof brands the sands of the Red Citadel, though the body of Christ impaled has fallen from the golden crucifix around his neck. The gypsies come to steal away the ragged Jew from between the hooves of the bull, and to cover His shame with the black mantillas of the women. When He asks after the soul of the poet, they pretend not to understand His question, smiling and pointing to the vanishing petticoats of the moon.

In a distant field, bullets tear the sound of the *saeta* with a gorgon's kisses. Among the olive trees there is no sound but the weeping of a mermaid's ghost. The poet drinks earth, and earth drinks smoke and embers, and carnations stream red from beneath the tiered skirts of the wailing rivers. Among the olives, the Moors reload their rifles and turn their broad backs on the men with their shovels. One corpse is kin to all, one drop of water holds an ocean, one seed of the pomegranate's heart is brother to a thousand drops of blood. All the streams run into the great sea, which is silence.

The great queens of the Red Citadel hear the silence that has arisen from a grave that is no grave and know that it is a razor of stone eyes that the bull in his triumph lays across their throats. They gather their sons to their breasts, they weep for their ravished daughter. The King of the Moors and the *duendes* seeks to comfort them, but he can only beat his hands against the crystal prison of the women's eyes. The poet is dead, who wore a woman's breasts beneath a man's body, and in his soul's departing wake all the towers of the Red Citadel are emptied of every ghost. They rise up on the silver ropes and the golden ladders of angels, dreams that have lost their life, smoke that has lost its song.

And the brown man sings in his forge of dreams beside the river, while the dead poet lies content in the arms of his gypsies and his toreadors, drinking the seasons into his bones under the burning eye of the widowed moon.

For Federico García Lorca

In the Realm of Dragons

The bus from Philly to New York was hot as hell. The air conditioning had broken down thirty miles out of the city. Not the best turn of events on a late September day that felt more like high August. Ryan Lundberg sat back limp in his seat without so much as a silent curse to spare for the sweltering air or the stink of urine from the tiny onboard bathroom. He had strength to save, a calling to heed. His eyes closed, dragged down by a weight of scales.

The little clay dragon in his hand smoldered and pulsed with the heat. He held it to his heart and told it to lie cool and still. Time enough for fire when they found Uncle Graham's murderers. Plenty of time for fire then. He drowsed, lapped in thoughts of flame. He was not even a little startled when his head nodded forward and he felt the sting of spiny barbells as his chin touched his chest.

He had not brought the dragon with him on the bus—he knew that with the same certainty that he knew his own name—yet here it was. *Here.* Not where his hands had placed it, tucked away safe in his top drawer at school, keeping watch over photographs, condoms, dryer-orphaned socks he never got around to throwing away. He'd found it in his wasn't-it-empty pocket after the bus left the rest stop on the turnpike. He did not try to understand how it had come to be there; that was to invite madness.

"I just draw the castles," Uncle Graham used to say.

"People who ask me when they can move into them and if the rent includes unicorns, *they're* the ones who've got problems." And he would laugh.

Problems . . . The echo of the long-since spoken word faded into the far-and-far behind Ryan's eyes. *Yeah, Uncle Graham, there's more than a few of us around with problems now.* He flexed his hand and felt claws gouge deep chasms into the cheap plastic armrests. *Insanity is not what you see, but what you admit to seeing.* The litany he'd composed to hold onto some sliver of control warmed his mind. *Craziness is the compulsion to explain. The dragon that's suddenly, solidly here when I know I never brought it—Let it be here unchallenged. And what I feel closing over me . . . let that come for me unchallenged too. Just accept the apparitions and no one needs to question if I'm numbered among the sane.*

You must do more than accept, the thin, sharp voice hissed in his head. *If you would have the reward I've promised, you know you must do more.*

A reward? Ryan repeated, wasting irony on the echoes in his skull. *A world!*

The key to Uncle Graham's apartment was also in his pocket, but at least he knew there was no magic connected with its presence. He had taken it himself, stolen it from Mom's dressing table last night, while she and Dad lay sleeping, after he awoke from the dream. The key had arrived with Uncle Graham's body, in a small envelope entrusted to the funeral director's care by his uncle's landlady. Included with the key was a friendly note urging Ryan's mother to come to New York as soon as possible to see about the disposal of Uncle Graham's possessions. That was the word she used: *disposal.* When Ryan read it, he thought of a hungry hole in the universe, devouring even the memory of a life that had been—honestly, now—an inconvenience and an embarrassment to so many, even to those who owed it love.

Ryan leaned his head against the window, feeling a film of sweat form between flesh and glass. The black kid in the seat ahead of him lost another battle with the window catch and cursed it out with a fluency one of Uncle Graham's graybeard wizards might have envied, stolen, but never improved. Ryan sighed, a hot gust of breath that only added to the bus's burden of muggy air.

He hadn't known deceit could be so exhausting. His parents had no idea where he was, what he intended to do once he got there. They thought he was back at college. The day after Uncle Graham's funeral, back home in Clayborn, Ryan's father had put him on the bus almost before it was light. When it reached Philadelphia he had only stayed in the city long enough to get some things from his dorm and give his folks a call to tell them that he had arrived safely. Then he went right back to the terminal and took the next bus to New York.

What would they say if they knew? Mom would have a cat-fit, most likely, and Dad . . . Dad would look at him that way again. *Why does Uncle Graham matter so to you? He's dead now, safely dead, but you—Why, Ryan? Why care? You're not—?*

And the question, even in thought, would die away, withered by the chill fear Ryan saw in his father's eyes, the fear should his only son give him the answer he could not stand to hear.

No, Dad, Ryan responded to his father's phantom face as the heat drank him further into sleep. *I'm not, don't worry, I'm not like him. Remember last year, the time old man Pitt showed up on our porch, mad as hell, yelling for you to keep me off his daughter? God, I don't think I ever did anything in my life that made you happier, not even the scholarship. Just the hint that I was screwing a girl, some girl, any girl—!* He shifted his shoul-

145

ders against the rough fabric of the seat back. *So now is it okay with you if I care about Uncle Graham? If I'm not gay, is it safe for me to love him now that he's dead?*

In his cupped hands, the little clay dragon stretched out a single paw and dug into his flesh with the talons of dreams.

So you're Ryan. Graham's told me all about you.

Slim and dark and exotic looking, only just into the beauty of his twenties, Uncle Graham's lover offered a hand that closed around the little clay dragon and cupped it in transparent flesh long since returned to earth. Through the milky prison of those ghostly fingers, Ryan could still see the dragon swirled roundabout with Christmas snow.

Ryan patted the last handful of snow into the dragon's side and smoothed it down, embedding jagged holly leaves for teeth, clusters of the bright red berries for eyes. His hands were damp and cold, even through his mittens. Mom was on the porch, holding her sweater tight around her, calling him home. Uncle Graham stood beside her, laughing at what his eleven-year-old nephew had done.

You know, most kids make snowmen.

Ryan shrugged. *I like dragons.*

Uncle Graham put his arm around Ryan's shoulders. *Watch out, kid. If you're any good at it, you get to leave this town.*

Ryan grinned. Eleven years old, he was just waking up to the possibility that he might want to live out his life somewhere else besides Clayborn.

Christmas in Clayborn. Christmas in a place where there were still things like corner drugstores with real working soda fountains, and big autumn bonfires down by the lakeshore, and pep rallies, and church bake sales where everyone knew how each housewife's brownies were going to taste even before they bit into one. There were still such things as high school sweethearts here, and special pools of warm, sweet,

146

private darkness, down the shady orchard lanes, between the rolling Pennsylvania farmlands, where a boy could take his best girl and see how far she'd let him go.

And this was where Uncle Graham brought his New York lover. Even without people *knowing*, Bill would have drawn stares. On Christmas morning he sat right up close beside Uncle Graham, resting his chin on Uncle Graham's shoulder while the presents were unwrapped, softly exclaiming the proper oohs and aahs of wonder and feigned envy as each gift was brought to light.

Ryan watched, fascinated. Whatever Mom had said about Uncle Graham's way of life, the reality was infinitely stranger. He sat on the floor, like Uncle Graham and Bill, and felt as if he were peering through an overgrowth of jungle vines at bizarre creatures never before seen by the eyes of civilized man. Bill's low laugh sent peculiar chills coursing over Ryan's bones. His mind blew a glass bell jar over Uncle Graham's lover and held him there, safely sealed away for observation.

Outside there was snow, crusted over, hugging blue shadows to every curve of the slumbering land. It threw back the brilliant sunlight in harsh assaults of dazzling whiteness. Ryan sat at his father's feet and looked up to see a taut jawline, a gaze fixed and fastened on Uncle Graham and Bill. Ryan felt his father's hands come to rest on his shoulders many times that morning—more times than felt right, when right means usual. The sunlight struck a wall of darkness cast by the shadow of the wings that Ryan's father called up out of empty air to mantle over his son. *This is mine; you won't touch him* hung across the room like a fortified castle wall that Ryan's father made and maintained and walked guard on from that moment until the day Uncle Graham and his lover left to go back to the city.

Ryan's father was not invisible and Uncle Graham was not blind.

There were no letters from Uncle Graham the rest of the winter, no calls, no more news than if New York were really a cloud kingdom full of so many sweet, glorious pastimes and amusements that the souls lucky enough to live there lost all track of time as it was reckoned on the earth. No one said anything, not even when Ryan's birthday came and went without a card from Uncle Graham, without a word.

And then, in late November, the telephone shrilled. Ryan answered. "Hello?"

"Chessie?" The voice was broken, shattered, and around the shards it sobbed the nickname Uncle Graham had always used for his beloved sister.

"Uncle Graham?" Ryan's cheeks flamed. His voice was changing. It was a sharp humiliation every time someone mistook him for his mother on the telephone. "It's me, Ryan."

"For God's sakes, Ryan, get your mom!" Uncle Graham's words stumbled through tears, his breath rags of sound torn out of his chest.

"What's the matter?"

"Just get her. Please."

So Ryan did as he was told, and when his mother got over the surprise of hearing from her brother after so long, there was worse to come. "How are you?" was slashed off into, "Oh, my God! Oh, Graham, I'm so sorry! When did he—"

The little dragon shuddered in Ryan's hand, breaking the spell. His mother's face froze, then crackled into void, the shattering of ice over black water. Bill's death seized Ryan and roughly shoved him from the haven of his home, sending him lurching forward through the gateway of the hours, bright and dark. Bill's hand faded from ghostly essence to purest air, a cool breath across hot clay that shivered like an egg about to bring forth monsters, mysteries. Ryan's eyelids fluttered, but when he shifted his weight again, instead of the rasp of cheap seatcovering against his jeans he heard the genteel creak of fine leather as he settled onto the green couch in Uncle Graham's apartment.

Bill's funeral was over. Ryan didn't remember too much about it. Mostly he recalled the hot, angry eyes of hard-faced strangers in black. They scowled at him and Mom and Uncle Graham where the three of them stood huddled together on the far side of the open grave. He never found out who they were. The minister read through the service for the dead and Uncle Graham cried. Ryan saw one of the hot-eyed people— an old woman with blue-rinsed hair—writhe her red mouth around an ugly word before pressing a wadded lace handkerchief to her wrinkled lips and bursting into tears.

Mom drove Uncle Graham back to his place in Manhattan, a downtown loft in what had once been an old factory. It was like having one big room for everything— eating and sleeping and watching TV. The only fully cut-off spaces were the bathroom and the kitchen. There was also a space where Uncle Graham worked, a drafting board and an easel, the floor beneath both liberally freckled with paint. Some men left Clayborn on their wits, some on their brawn. Uncle Graham had soared free of the town on dreams of fantastic beings given life by brush and pen. The loft walls were hung with Uncle Graham's paintings, commissioned illustrations for books—wonderful, terrible, entrancing books, the kind of books that people back in Clayborn pronounced cute and bought, if they bought them at all, for their children.

The couch creaked again.

She's making tea.

Uncle Graham's ghost sat at the far end of the couch, head

cradled back against the butter-soft upholstery, arms out-flung, eyes fixed on the ceiling. He had his feet up on a coffee table that looked as if it had calved from a glacier.

"What?" Ryan's voice barely scaled above a whisper.

"I said your mother's in the kitchen, making tea." And Uncle Graham was suddenly no more a ghost than the twelve-year-old self through whose eyes Ryan now saw everything.

"Oh." Ryan rested his palms on the couch and felt perspiration seep between flesh and leather. They sat there that way for a long time. Ryan heard the shrilling of the kettle and the sound of traffic from outside and the familiar, comforting clanks and clinks of Mom fumbling about in a kitchen not her own. He knew she would sooner die than ask Uncle Graham where he kept things. Dad called it the female equivalent of how a man refuses to ask directions when he's lost on the road.

"Ryan?" Uncle Graham's voice came so loud, so abruptly, that Ryan jumped at the sound of his own name. "Come here, Ryan." Uncle Graham was sitting slumped forward now, his big hands linked and dangling between his knees. Ryan hesitated, fearing the great grief he saw in his uncle's eyes. Uncle Graham could see only that Ryan remained where he was. "Don't worry; I won't touch you," he said.

Ryan did not move.

"I'm clean, you know," Uncle Graham said. "Negative. Bill used to make fun of me, call me paranoid, but—" Some phantom sound escaped his chest, laugh or sob or cough quickly forced back down. "Anyway, like I said, I won't touch you. I promise. Your father wouldn't like that."

Suddenly Ryan wore his father's absence like horns. "Couldn't get off work to come up here with us for the fun'ral," he mumbled.

"Of course not." Uncle Graham was too done out, too indifferent to challenge the lie.

Ryan . . .

Ryan saw the green glow cupped in Uncle Graham's palm, the sheen of a perfectly applied glaze, the ripple of tiny, incised scales like feathers lying sleek on a bird's wing. He sidled nearer on the couch, the cushions squeaking and whispering under his thighs. He craned his neck to see what wonder his uncle held out as an offering.

"It's a dragon," Uncle Graham said, letting the small clay figurine tumble from his palm. Ryan's hands shot out automatically, catching it in midair. Uncle Graham laughed. "Nice fielding. You must be a star with the Little League."

A shrug was Ryan's answer. He was too busy rolling the dragon from hand to hand, feeling its weight, its slick finish, the cold beauty of its eyes.

"Hematite," Uncle Graham said, pointing out the gleaming shapes like silvered almonds imbedded beneath the creature's brow ridges. "It's supposed to center you, keep you calm, let you see all things with tranquility." He closed his eyes and passed one hand over his forehead, brushing away a flutter of black wings.

"It's beautiful," Ryan said. Here, alone with his uncle, he could say such things. At home, with Dad watching—so closely now, so carefully—he would have limited his comments to "Cool."

"It's yours. I made it for—I want you to have it." He opened his eyes and managed a weak smile. "Late birthday gift. Sorry I missed it."

" 'S okay." Ryan stroked the dragon's back. The beast was curled in around itself as if for sleep, wings folded back, forepaws demurely resting beneath the barbelled chin. The scaly lips were closed, except where the two most prominent fangs could not possibly be contained. But the eyes were open and saw all.

"Here we are!" Mom burst from the kitchen, triumphant, an assortment of steaming mugs on the tray she carried before her. She sandwiched Ryan in between herself and Uncle Graham, weaving her own spells of strength and militant normalcy from the clatter of teaspoons and the hush of sugar crystals cascading into tea. There were even some cookies on a plate.

"Mom, look what Uncle Graham gave me," Ryan said, holding out the dragon for inspection. "He made it himself."

"It's wonderful, Graham," Mom said sincerely. "Is this something new for you? Are you branching out from painting?"

"I am definitely making some changes," Uncle Graham said. They drank their tea. That was the last time Ryan saw his uncle alive.

That year at Christmastime Uncle Graham didn't come to visit. He never came to visit them again. There were no letters and no telephone calls, although once, on Ryan's thirteenth birthday, a flat, oblong package arrived for him from New York City.

It was a book, a book enclosed between boards embossed with swirling gold and silver letters that eddied over depths of royal blue and green. "*In the Realm of Dragons*," he read aloud, wondering why his uncle had sent him a picture book clearly meant for little kids. Then he saw the artist's byline and understood: Uncle Graham had done the illustrations. He let the book fall open in his lap.

Page after page of dragons mounted the purple skies of evening, beating wings of gold and green and scarlet. ("The dragon is a nocturnal beast. He loves the hours of darkness.")

152

Youngling dragons peeped from shattered eggshells, stripling worms engaged in mock battles to establish territory and dominion. ("The dragon when it is grown chooses its company with care.") Maidens wreathed with flowers were led forth from villages paved with mud and manure to be offered up to the magnificent beasts, only to be spurned, or simply overlooked. ("It is a false tale that claims dragons desire the flesh of fair maidens, for what mere mortal beauty could hope to equal their own?")

And in the end, there were the pictures of knights—so proud, so arrogant in armor—swords bloodied with the lives of dragons. Here a warrior lurked like the meanest footpad to slay a dragon when it came to drink at a twilight stream. There the severed heads of many worms dangled as obscene trophies from the rafters of a great hall where lords and ladies swilled wine and grew brutish in revelry. The unseeing eyes of the dead were mirrors that hung in silent judgment over their supposed conquerors, each silvery globe giving back an image of man to make the skin crawl and the soul weep. ("Men slay dragons because they fear them, or do not understand them, or because other men tell them that this is what men do. And some destroy them because of how they see themselves captured in the dragon's eyes.")

The last page was an enchantment of art. A single dragon's eye filled it, infusing mere paper with a silver splendor reflecting Ryan's awestruck face. The boy reached out, fingers hovering a hairsbreadth above the sheen that pulled him heartfirst into the dragon's all-knowing gaze.

That night he dreamed dragons.

He woke into dreams, rising naked from a pool of waters silvered by twin moons burning low in a verdant sky. Drops of water fell from his wingtips, trembled at the points of his claws. Far away, over the hills where golden grasses nodded and bent beneath the wind's kiss, came the sound of hoarse voices mangling music.

He climbed the hills, his wings dragging the ground behind him. The air was sweet, heavy as honey. He shook away the last vestiges of human thought and opened his dragon mind to a universe unfolding its most secret mysteries. That was when he knew at last that he could fly.

The air was his realm; he laid claim to it with the first surge of his emerald-keeled breastbone against the sky. Its warmth bore him up from beneath with the steady love of his father's hands. His great head swerved slowly from left to right, his breath glittering with frost in the higher atmospheres, showering the bosom of the land with diamonds.

Below him he saw them, the villagers with their mockery of musical instruments, their faces upturned like so many oxen startled by lightning. The maiden was among them. They had dressed her in white, though even from this height he could see the thin cloth of her gown dappled brown with mud at the hem. Her arms were smooth and bare, her golden hair almost obscured by roses.

He felt hunger burn the pit of his cavernous belly. He stooped to the earth, wings artfully angled to ride the edges of only those air currents that would bring him spiraling down to his waiting prize. His mouth gaped, and licks of flame caressed his scaly cheeks like the kiss of mist off the sea.

And then air before him turned from native element and ally to enemy. The crystalline road solidified, a giant's hands molding themselves from emptiness. He slammed into the immobile lattice of their interlaced fingers, and the impact exploded into a sheet of dazzling pain, an echoing wave of light that hurled him back down the sky, back into the waters of the lake, back into the shuddering boy's body waking in its bed to the dark and loneliness and loss.

All that was left was a whisper: *Not yet. I give you this power, but you must earn its reward.*

Ryan hugged the sheet and blanket to his chest, cold with sweat, and asked the shadows for meaning. Then he became aware of something more than sweat making his pajamas cling to the skin between his legs. In silence, face burning, he stripped them off and stuffed them down the laundry chute, some part of his mind pretending that the gaping black slide into the basement would really send them falling into oblivion.

He did not like to think of the dream after that. He took the book from Uncle Graham and put it away in the attic.

The pulldown ladder to the attic's trove of dust and willfully forgotten memory was springloaded tight. The dangling rope that raised and lowered the hatch, improperly released, closed with a bang to jerk Ryan awake in time to bark his shins against the packing-crate coffee table in a friend's dorm room. He was waiting for someone. He had nothing to do while he waited. He glanced down at the table and picked up a magazine.

He didn't notice that it was a gay men's magazine at first. It was folded open to a beer ad. He picked it up out of boredom and thumbed through it out of curiosity. Uncle Graham's name leaped to his eyes from a photo spread covering the most recent Gay Pride march in Manhattan.

It was not Uncle Graham. Not with that face paint, not with that gaunt, ferocious grin like a wolf's skull. He wore clothing that was ill-considered plumage, meant to startle. It only put Ryan in mind of how old whores were typed in older movies: spotty, papery, raddled skin beneath the monster's pathetic mask of carnival. Uncle Graham marched with arms around two other men, one in amateurish drag, the other sheathed in neon pink hotpants and a T-shirt cropped to leave his midriff bare. Across his forehead he had painted the letters H.I.V.

When Ryan went home for Christmas, he told Mom about the photograph. All she said was, "I know." She showed him the letters she'd written to her brother, every one returned unopened, refused. Only once had he sent her words back accompanied by his own, a piece of lined paper torn from a spiral-bound notebook and stuffed into a manila envelope with the rejected letter. *You never liked cemeteries, Chessie,* it said. *Why hang on the gate pretending you understand the business of the dead? You need magic to look through my eyes, and you were born fettered to the world. But there is magic, Chessie. It lives and walks at our backs, beautiful and deadly, and when it gets hungry it takes its sacrifice. If one of us had to make that payment, to have our heart betrayed, I'm glad it was me. Leave it so.*

Mom asked Ryan if he remembered Bill; he nodded. "He's trying to die," she said. "He's running after his own death. Even after what Bill did to him—How the hell do you argue with *that* kind of proof you've been cheated on?—even now he still loves him." Mom sighed. "If he finds what he's looking for, do you think he'd call to let us know? I can't bear the thought of him dying like that, without—!" She began to cry.

Her tears were for nothing and for everything.

The little clay dragon sighed in dreams, rumbled with ill-banked fires. The rumbling rose up, but by the time it reached Ryan's ears it had become the urgent ringing of a telephone.

He was only half awake when he answered it, a towel swaddling his waist, up at a godawful hour of the morning because he'd had to sign up for godawful-hour courses in this, his second year of study. The toothbrush was still dripping in his hand while he heard his father's voice telling him that Uncle Graham was dead. Uncle Graham's head was shattered on the pavement in front of the old factory where he lived. The cops had called Mom even earlier that morning with the news. There was more that the police had told Ryan's father because they didn't think Mom could stand to know the other things that had been done to her brother. He shared it all willingly with Ryan because he thought his son was man enough to know, and because it was too much horror for one man to bear knowing alone.

And maybe too he shared it as a warning.

The closed casket under its blanket of roses blocked most of the aisle on the bus. Everyone from church was there, saying over and over again how talented Graham was and how wonderful his paintings were and how sad, how very sad that he was dead so young. Mrs. Baumann from the drugstore perched on the armrest of the black kid's seat and told Mom that at least Graham was at peace now. Comfort cloyed the air worse than the mingled reek of all the flower arrangements people had sent. Everyone was there, saying all the right things, leaving all mention of murder outside, with the dogs.

The black kid finally managed to jimmy the window enough so that it dragged in its track but slid open. The in-rush of fresh air blew away Mrs. Baumann, the roses, the closed black box, blew Ryan all the way back into his old bed at home, the night after the funeral.

He lay there unsleeping, painting the ceiling with endless fantasies of should-have-told-thems. Drowsing at last, he rolled over onto his side and felt something jab him in the hip. He reached between the mattress and the box spring and pulled out Uncle Graham's book.

"I thought I put this away, up in the attic," he said aloud. The silver and gold letters on the cover glowed with their own light. Ryan licked his lips and tasted lake water. He opened the book and read it again, after all the years.

There was a page he found that might have slipped from memory, if memory could ever lose hold of images that clamored to be recalled. Two young men—squires, not knights—laid up a snare of marvelous cunning and cruelty outside a dragon's vine-hung lair. One peered from ambush, knotted club in hand, while the other stood at the cave mouth holding out a sapphire of untellable purity and fire. He was fair, the one who played the lure, his eyes the rival of the sapphire meant to cozen the venerable worm from sanctuary. Already a single green-scaled paw crept into the dappled sunlight. The lure smiled, cold and exquisite as a lord of elven. Behind a fall of rocks, his confederate readied the dragon's death.

Both their faces were plain to see. Not a line could be forgotten. Ryan closed his eyes, and still their faces were outlined against his sightlessness as if with wires burning white-hot. He threw the book across the room and bolted for his bedroom door.

He stepped from bare wood onto naked air. His wings snapped open without the need for any conscious command to reach them. His headlong fall became a naturally graceful glide that carried him down, down to the vast sea of forest and the piteous, defiant roars of a dying dragon and the face of a maiden, lovelier than any girl he had ever known, wreathed with roses.

I give you this power, but you must earn its reward.

He awoke knowing what he must do.

He awoke half choked by the stink of exhaust fumes as the bus pulled into the Port Authority terminal in New York.

Ryan did not have enough money for a cab so he took the bus downtown. He got off at the wrong stop, got lost, wandered in sullen pilgrimage through streets where crumpled newspapers blew like tumbleweeds. Finally he broke down and asked directions.

It was sunset when he found Uncle Graham's address. A flimsy strip of black-and-yellow tape flapped wearily from the hinges of the big entry door to Uncle Graham's building. Ryan's taloned paws moved grandly, daintily overstepping the dull red-brown stains spattering the threshold and the sidewalk before it. Silence sang a hymn of welcome as he entered the loft, the last of the sunlight adding its own wash of color to the row of paintings Uncle Graham had left behind.

The girl from upstairs came down to see what was going on, alerted by the noise of a slamming door. Ryan told her, "I'm here to dispose of my uncle's things." He showed her the key and told her enough about Uncle Graham to convince her of his legitimate right to be there.

She shrugged, thin shoulders sheathed in stretch jersey glimpsed through thin brown hair. "Save it, okay? I couldn't tell if you're making it up or not anyway. I hardly knew anything about the guy. I mean, sure, I knew he was, like, gay, and he painted. I was scared for a while after he got killed, but—"

"I really am his nephew," Ryan insisted, clutching the doorpost until he imagined he must have driven his talons inches deep into the wood.

"Hey, no argument. You got the key." Another shrug, welcoming him to help himself to the apartment and all found so long as he did not trespass on her well-cultivated indifference.

She wasn't pretty. She was what the fashion world would call a waif. Ryan was more attracted to girls whose breasts were larger than orange pips. Still he invited her in. At first she declined, but she called herself an artist too. She had never had the chance to study Uncle Graham's work up close before. She might have come downstairs anytime while Uncle Graham was still alive and asked to see his paintings; she

159

never did. She admitted to Ryan that the idea had never crossed her mind.

"Why not?" he asked.

Again that shifting of the shoulders to let a person slide safely out from beneath uncomfortable questions. "I didn't want to intrude. I thought, you know, what if he's got someone over?"

He found tea to serve her. She drank in short, dull slurps, her eyes forever darting sideways to keep him under surveillance. She wasn't pretty and she wasn't his type and he wasn't attracted to her at all.

What'samatter, Lundberg, doncha like girls?

He gave her all the charm he had, the way he'd done with Karen Pitt, the way he'd perfected with all the college girls he'd ever sweet-talked into bed, the way that proved to everyone who never asked for proof that he wasn't like his uncle. Before she left, he got to kiss her and buy back his peace.

Uncle Graham's bed was made of pale pine with a bowed headboard, the kind you order from L.L. Bean catalogs. One of great-grandma Ruth's handsewn quilts lay across it, a bearpaw design in red and blue. Ryan lay down on the bed, quilt and all, fully clothed, and rested the little clay dragon on his chest. He gazed into its silvery eyes until he felt the lake waters rolling off his flanks and the alien moons of the dragons' realm welcomed him home.

He circled the skybowl once, his scent marking air as his hunting ground and his alone. Below, he dreamed the peasants singing for him to descend and accept the sacrifice. *Later,* he thought, and the power of his mind rumbled across the sky like thunder. *When I have earned it.*

The thunder of his thoughts rolled back to overwhelm him, knocking him sideways into a spin. When he righted himself he saw that the green land had vanished, the crude songs of the rustics thinned into the braying of traffic, the shriek of sirens. The stone forest of the city stood stark against the moon. He dipped into the canyons, following a trail of vision.

It was easy hunting; he knew the prey. He found them with his mind, not with his eyes. They were in a bar, drinking beer, laughing and talking and sometimes trying to get the attention of the women. The lure was loudest, telling the women what he'd like to do to them, telling them how grateful they'd be, telling them they were frigid, bitches, bull-dykes when they turned away. The killer with the club only smiled, and sometimes one of the women would smile back. That made the lure scowl and call her a whore.

"Hey! What you starin' at?"

Ryan gasped with surprise as the lure's hand shot out and closed around the collar of his shirt, yanking him forward. Stale beer stank in his nostrils and sprayed saliva dotted his cheeks as the lure shouted, "What, you see something you *like*, faggot?"

"Get your fucking hands off me!" Teeth like steak knives ground against each other as Ryan smacked the lure's grip away. By chance one talon scored the skin of the lure's forearm, a long, shallow cut. Sapphire eyes widened in child-like awe to see the blood go trickling down.

"Shit, he pulled a knife on me!" he yelled.

"What knife? Where?" the killer drawled, glancing at Ryan's empty hands. "You're crazy, Ted, you know that?"

"Stinking fag *knifed* me," the lure insisted. "Goddamn it, this whole neighborhood's crawling with 'em, like roaches."

"Who are you calling a fag?" Ryan asked quietly. Being what he was, he did not need to raise his voice to make the menace heard.

161

The killer gave Ryan a slow and easy grin. "Don't pay attention to him. He's been drinking. He don't know what he's saying."

"No shit." Ryan readjusted the lay of his shirt, sounding so calm he astonished himself. He had no idea of how he had become real in this place, how these two, his quarry, had gone from being part of a dragon's vision to tangibility. He did not know why he felt the dragon's body on him so surely that he wanted to grab these men, shake them, and demand, *Can't you see what I am?*

"What the hell are you doing, talking to this guy?" the lure cried stridently, tugging at the killer's sleeve. "You see what he *did* to me?" He stuck his bloodied arm out for inspection.

"With *what?*" the dark one replied. He sounded bored. "A fuckin' fingernail? You see he don't got a knife, so with what? Jesus, grow up. You probably did it to yourself."

"With *what?*" the lure mimicked, spreading empty hands.

"Asshole," the other muttered and turned his back.

Ryan walked out of the bar. The air was cooler than it had been all day and there was the promise of rain. He walked to the corner to check the street signs. The bar was only two blocks away from Uncle Graham's apartment. *This is where it began,* he thought. He wondered which way they would walk when they finally left the bar. He hoped they would walk together at least part of the way. He needed them to be in the same place at the same time. Then, one fiery breath, one slash of his claws, one short snap of jaws that could sever the body of a full grown stag—

It is a well-known fact that dragons do not forget those they love. Their love is always loyal, sometimes blind. This is perhaps a failing.

He took to the sky again to scout his place of ambush. He

was fortunate: The area was rich in alleyways. He landed lightly on the roof of the building across the street from the bar, warm tar underfoot making his paws itch, his toes curl. He set his silver eyes high, telling the hours by the slow journey of the moon.

His prey emerged when midnight was two hours gone. A woman was with them, holding fast to the arm of the killer while the lure tagged along behind, head down, shoulders hunched forward. Her hair was the color of lemon-yellow paint and just as lifeless, her face crumpled with rude laughter. She clung to the killer's broad shoulders, her stumbling feet scraping the sidewalk. The lure stared at her, disgust very plain on his face.

The three of them wove their way across the street, tracing the pattern of the drunkards' pavane. High on his perch, the dragon could still snuff up the reek of beer, sour wine, sweat, and old perfume. He flapped his wings once to lift himself into flight, taking care to do it so that the sound remained as muffled as possible. He wondered whether the men intended to share the woman and whether the woman wanted that. He knew that if they desired it, her wants would be nothing.

He hovered over them as they walked, a shadow on the pavement in their wake, a dark shape gliding over rooftops, safe from detection in a city whose inhabitants so seldom raised their eyes to heaven. He watched them stop at street corners to laugh; he saw them stop in the middle of the street to argue.

"What the hell you doin', Ted?" The dark one glanced over his shoulder, the woman wrapped around him like a cape. "You still here? You wanna take a left back there on that last block if you wanna get home."

"I know how to get home." The lure's chin rose, daring his

companion to contradict him. "I thought maybe you could use some help with her. You know, in case she pukes all over you before you get her back to your place."

The killer laughed. "Okay, come on."

"I'm not gonna puke," the woman objected. Her eyes narrowed as she glared at the lure. "You're just pissed 'cause you couldn't find someone to go home with you."

"Like I'd want to screw what comes into that bar," the lure replied loftily.

"Yeah?" The woman looked canny. "What *kind* of bars do you like, baby?" She made it mean things.

"Shut up, bitch," he snapped. He would have hit her if his friend were not there. The dragon knew this. As it was, the woman turned to the dark one, squawking indignantly.

"Hey, baby, it's okay, that's just him, he's a little nuts, you know?" the killer said. "Don't push his buttons, okay? And don't go saying shit like that about my buddy." Something in his voice tightened by an almost imperceptible degree. Drunk as she was, the woman sensed it. The dragon saw her cringe.

"I didn't mean nothing," she said.

"Like hell," the lure snarled. " 'What *kind* of bars?' Like I don't know! Stupid damn—"

"She don't know you, Ted, that's all," the killer said. "If she did, she'd never even think of saying something like that about you." He showed his teeth, and the lure returned the gesture, a look too sharp to be just a smile. The dragon saw them exchange the secret of a crime in a single glance.

The dragon came to earth. By rights, the walls of the alley it chose should have been too narrow to accommodate its wingspan, yet they did. This place was perfect, only a few yards ahead on the prey's path, on a street whose emptiness was a gift. It waited. The argument was over. They would all continue down the street in this direction now. The dragon

164

had decided on fire. Fire was quick and clean, if indiscriminate. It was too bad about the woman.

Footsteps rang on the pavement. The dragon's eyelids, smooth as shell for all their scales, drew back until the darkness filled with the silver light of its eyes. He heard the woman say, "What the hell's that in there?" and the killer answer, "Who gives a—?"

Then he had them. No deer was ever so transfixed by the headlights' glare. The brilliance of his gaze washed over them, a stark light to shear away everything but the truth. He gathered his breath for the flame.

And in a distant room a dreamer held a book open to its last page, falling into the silver eye of a dragon and seeing only truth.

I can't.

The fire died in his throat. He felt the dragon's form, the dragon's power slip from him. The image of the rose-wreathed maiden blew away like dust. The splendor of his eyes dimmed and vanished, leaving the alley lit only by the spill of the streetlamp. Rain began to fall, mizzling, penetrating. He felt cold.

"Who's in there? Come out!" the killer shouted. The spell was broken. Ryan crept forward because he didn't know what else he could do. "It's the kid from the bar!" The dark one sounded genuinely surprised.

Not too surprised to seize Ryan's arm and squeeze it hard as he jerked him forward. "What d'you think you're doing, following us?" The fingers drove deeper into soft flesh. "You some kinda pervert?"

"I *told* you what he is!" the lure cried stridently. "I can *smell* 'em."

"Yeah, maybe you can," the killer muttered. His grip shifted to Ryan's shirtfront. "You were right the last time."

"Honey, let him go; he's just a kid," the woman pleaded.

"This kid—," he gave Ryan a shake to make his teeth clatter, "—was in the bar before, trying to start something. What d'you wanna start, *kid?*"

"Watch out for him; he's got a knife on him," the lure piped up.

"Big deal." The killer reached into the pocket of his jeans. "So do I."

The blade snicked silver in the shadows. Ryan saw the reflection of his eyes along the shining edge. He remembered all the things that had been done to Uncle Graham, the things the police told Dad, the things Dad only hinted at to him, shaking. These two had only smashed his uncle's skull after they had done everything else they wanted. He heard a plaintive voice inside him say, *They killed me without a moment's hesitation, Ryan. I know I was looking to die, but like that? As less than a man, less than an animal, just a toy for willful, sadistic children? They'll kill you without a single regret. It will shatter Chessie's heart. Why didn't you destroy them when you had the power?*

And Ryan's heart answered, *Because that would make me one of them.*

"Jesus, let him *go*," the woman whined. "You're not gonna cut him, are you?"

"You don't wanna see, close your eyes," the killer instructed her.

"Oh, shit, you're crazy too." With a shake of her head she tried to bolt, but the lure grabbed her and held her fast.

"You don't wanna go running for the cops, *do* you?" he hissed in her ear. "Nah, I bet you don't." He seized her straggly hair and punched her hard in the face before she could scream. She groaned and folded to the ground.

"Hey! What'd you do to the bitch?" The killer spoke with

the same heat reserved for street punks caught putting scratches on a new car.

"Ah, so what?" The lure shrugged. "Like you can't do what you want with her now?"

The knife rose, a straight line of cold blue across Ryan's sight. He shut his eyes. A fist slammed into his shoulder.

"Uh-uh, pervert," the killer told him. "*You* gotta see it coming. I wanna see you see. Open 'em." Another violent shake of Ryan's shirtfront. "*Open* 'em!"

So Ryan opened his eyes.

Screams.

Screams not his, screams that battered his ears as the pure white light flooded the alleyway again. They jarred him free of his captive body, throwing him skywards into the rain. He gasped to feel chill droplets pattering over skin still human, then turned in wingless mid-flight to look down at what this release had left behind.

He expected to see the two men staring up after him, mouths agape like the lowest wonderstruck peasant of the dragons' realm. Instead he saw them crouching in the alleyway, on their knees in filth, hands trembling before their faces. He realized that they were trying not to look, trying to shield their eyes from the assault of sight. He let go his tenuous hold on the air and touched the ground behind them, beside the fallen woman.

He saw the dragon's eyes.

It was a great beast, huge, splendid, grander by far than the youngling worm that once housed Ryan's soul. The alley walls strained, bricks and mortar crumbling under the pressure of containing it. It lay with paws folded under its jagged chin, its gleaming eyes regarding the two men almost casually, in afterthought. There was no intent of a killing in its attitude. It only looked at them, slumbrous, steadily.

They tried to look away and could not, tried to close their eyes and found the lids frozen wide, tried to make screens of their hands and knew a strange paralysis that withheld that mercy. They had to look. They had no choice but to see.

And some destroy them because of how they see themselves in the dragon's eyes.

In one eye's curved and shining surface, the killer crouched in a dark place, jabbing sticks at phantoms, wailing with fear. His naked body was covered with lesions, his limbs skeletal, his face all blades of bone beneath a patchwork of bare, purple-veined scalp and pitiful tufts of hair.

In the other eye, the lure clung to the killer's arm, pressed himself against that towering, healthy body. He let his mouth wander at will, his eyes holding all the ecstasy of long-deferred fulfillment. His hands were everywhere, touching, caressing, claiming all he desired for his own. *I want this,* his image mouthed in the monster's mirrored gaze. *I've always wanted this . . . I've always wanted you.*

The dragon raised his head and blinked once, shuttering away the vision. When he opened them again, he disappeared.

The two men turned to stare at each other, the rain running down their faces. The woman stirred and whimpered, waking. They did not hear her. Ryan stooped to murmur in her ear, "Get up. We've got to get out of here." She cursed and shoved him aside.

So he ran away. He ran alone, stumbling down the rainwashed street, wondering how far he would be allowed to go before the spell of the dragon's gaze broke, before the others came after him. He thought he could hear them behind him, coming up fast. His breath burned in his chest. He did not dare to look over his shoulder. His hunters were as certain a presence as the night. He could almost feel the icy breath of the knife on his flesh.

He ran harder, and the harder he ran, the thicker the air around him became. He needed to fight a passage through it. His feet were weights instead of wings. The wet pavement turned to tar, sucking him down, holding him back against his will, keeping him prisoner. There were more enchantments loose in this world than the magic of dragons. Dark things commanded more servants here than things of light. Ryan opened his mouth to scream for help and no sound came. Again and again he filled his lungs, again and again only black silence packed his chest and throat and mouth like wool. The tar hardened to stone, holding his feet; he could not move at all. He gathered his breath for a last cry before the hunters had him—

—and woke screaming in his uncle's bed.

He was sitting upright, stiff as a doll. His clothes stuck to his skin. The waterlight that came before the dawn whitened the windows. He swung his feet out of bed and heard a crunch underfoot when they touched the floor.

Beside the bed, the little clay dragon lay shattered. He picked up all the pieces, glad to see that they were fairly large. Some glue should fix it. He assembled it dry on the coffee table and studied the results. All that was missing was the eyes.

He made himself some instant coffee and locked up the apartment when he left. The street was damp and cool from the rain. Puddles of oil in the gutter gave back rainbows. He stood in the doorway, looking down. The threshold stains did not stand out at all now that the concrete was wet. Soon who would know what had happened here? He fingered the tattered end of black and yellow tape still caught in the door hinge and tore off as much of it as he could.

He wondered whether he should call the police when he reached Penn Station and give them an anonymous tip about who had killed his uncle and where to find them. He could describe them exactly, send the police to the bar that was their hangout—

—if the police would take the time to listen to a caller who refused to admit how he knew so much. And if he explained? They'd believe it when the sky between worlds split open. But he had to do something. This was all he could think of to do.

He decided that the first thing he should do, even before he made the call, was to go and see whether there really was a bar where his vision had placed it. He began to walk.

The police cars were there when he turned the corner. Two of them were pulled up at the curb in front of the alleyway, blue and red lights flashing. The ambulance was sandwiched in between them. It wouldn't be going anywhere in a hurry, but there was no need for speed. The stretcher slipping away into the back held a zippered bag.

The killer glowered and shouted obscenities at the yellow-haired woman talking to the cops. His hands were manacled behind his back, but there was nothing to stop his mouth. Passersby on their way to work or homeward bound from a life between sunset and dawn stopped to listen. The man did not care for the rights he had been read, it seemed. He was willing to tell the world what he'd done. He didn't think of it as a crime, but a service. He had cleansed, purified, rescued society from a monster. He was a hero, a knight, a slayer of unnatural horrors! How dare they call it murder; even when the victim had once been his friend?

"Honest, I don't know why," the yellow-haired woman was saying as the man was forced into one of the police cars. "We was all going along here, real late, and all of a sudden—"

She turned and saw Ryan. For an instant her bruised face flushed, then bloomed, its unmarred beauty embraced by roses.

Then the policeman said, "Ma'am?" She shuddered and shook off all seeming. She went back to telling the officer what she had witnessed.

Ryan stooped at the barricade of black-and-yellow tape. The rose was red without holding memories of blood or fire. It had no thorns. He breathed its fragrance all the way to the train station, all the way home.

Jesus at the Bat

Philip Roth had already written *The Great American Novel*; Victor Harris was screwed. If you're going to be successful with the writing thing you have to write about what you know, and the only thing Victor Harris really knew was baseball. (He thought he knew sex, but that's another story.) The only question remaining was: How much longer would he be able to keep up the sweet, unstressful position of sensitive, creative, Aspiring-Author/Househusband (without actually becoming *Published* Author/Househusband) before Barb, his wife, caught wise?

He kept a copy of Stephen King's *Playboy* interview prominently displayed in the small basement cubby that was his "office," the better to remind Barb of at least one loyal lady who'd held down a decidedly unfun job (Dunkin' Donuts) while hubby mud-wrestled with the Muse until he hit pay dirt. *Stand by your man,* it seemed to say, *and soon you shall limo beside him. Cast your sugar crullers upon the waters and they shall be returned to you a hundredfold as caviar.* But the interview was curling with age faster than Victor's first rejection slip (also prominently displayed: it was from the *New Yorker* and had the distinction of sporting an actual, human, handwritten note of comment scrawled in the margin, *viz.:* "Sorry." Whether this referred to the rejecting editor's regrets or the manuscript's quality was best left nebulous) and Barb was starting to get the hard-bitten, narrow look of a ten-year-old facing off against parents who persist in chirping about Santa. Not good.

So the King interview was a life-vest whose kapok molecules were rapidly metamorphosing into cesium. Victor told himself that many a good woman of Barb's generation would be grateful to have a fulfilling multiphase career as aesthetician by day, Amway rep by night, but Barb didn't see it that way. Why didn't she appreciate the stresses of the Art? Why must he cringe each time she demanded, "Haven't you sold anything yet?" or "Why don't you go down to Four Corners Used Cars and see if Jerry'll give you your old job back?" or "Why in hell did you ever major in *English?* Everyone around here speaks it already."

Useless to attempt explaining the creative nature to such a scrawny soul. Futile to preach the exquisitely painful yet glacial process of inspiration, motivation, and execution in *l'oeuvre* Harris to the heathen. None so blind as they who will not see themselves vacationing in Hawaii this year—*again!*— and the Millers next door have already gone *four times!*

Of the bricks of such marital differences are the divorce courts of this fair nation built. So, too, the occasional ax-murder-with-P.M.S.-defense case. On the surface it would seem that a miracle would be necessary to save Victor Harris' neck from the chop. That was where the Brothers' Meeting Little League came in.

No, really.

And that was why, with luck, there would forever be one less used car salesman at Four Corners and never a moment's peace for the Harris family at the Sharon Valley Regional Elementary School P.T.A. spring picnic.

"Barb, hon, you look just gorgeous!" Sally McClellan swept down on Barb like a tornado on a trailer park.

The McClellans and the Harrises didn't usually move in

173

the same circles. Victor Harris moved in circles pretty constantly, while Phil McClellan moved solely in a steep, straight line of ascent to the windswept heights of financial success whence he might safely piss on the upturned faces of those below.

However, when the first sweet shoots of spring green burst through the hard Sharón Valley earth, Phil McClellan graciously maintained temporary bladder control so far as Victor's face went. As he told The Little Woman, if kissing Victor Harris' skinny ass was called for to achieve your goals, then by God and Ted Turner Industries, Phil McClellan would take a back seat to no one when it came to posterior pucker-ups. The Little Woman conducted herself accordingly as regarded *Mrs.* Victor Harris' more shapely buns, indeed.

Barb was nobody's fool except Victor's and he'd had to marry her for that privilege. She knew just what Sally was after and she sat back on the picnic table bench with all the smirking superiority of a Renaissance prince contemplating where to insert his next dagger. "Sally, darling," she purred. Cheeks brushed. Kissy-kissy mwah-mwahs were uttered. "When are you gonna come around to the *La Belle* so I can get my hands on your hair?" (*La Belle* being the town aesthetorium where Barb currently aestheted.)

Sally gave a nervous little giggle and fluffed her golden pouf of curls with no apparent need. "Oh, I'll be around. I don't think I'm due for a trim just yet."

"Every six weeks." Relentless, that was Barb in the spring. "And I know, I haven't seen you since last September." Somewhere a ghostly poniard glittered. "I hear tell you've been going up to Pittsburgh to have it done." *Zzzip-zot,* a slender blade slipped in and out between Sally McClellan's spareribs without The Little Woman feeling anything but a draft tickling her pancreas.

Sally turned bright red. "Who told you that?"

"Marylynn Drummer." Barb's eyes were hooded and inscrutable, but she licked her lips to savor the taste of blood.

"Well, it's just a baldfaced *lie!*" Sally spat. "When did she say so?"

"Mmmm, hard to recall." Barb sucked a few last crimson drops off the tip of her index finger. "I see her so often. Every week she's in the *La Belle* for a shampoo and blow-dry at least. She's got a standing appointment." It was time for the *coup de grâce*, the mercy stroke to end the victim's misery but good. "Sometimes she even brings in little Bobby, and you would be amazed to see how that boy has grown. Why, just the other day Vic was saying to me, 'Barb, I'd like to see what Bobby Drummer could do if I gave him a chance to pitch, I really would.' "

It was all over except for where to ship the body.

Sally McClellan's face sank in on itself like an old helium balloon with a pinhole leak. "Isn't that interesting," she said through a smile so stiff it clattered. "But do you think it's wise? My Jason has always pitched for the Bobcats, and I assumed—"

Barb laughed. "It's not like Vic was breaking up a *winning* team set-up, sweetie. Who knows? If Vic gives Bobby a chance to pitch, maybe that'll turn the trick. And you should have seen Bobby's little face light up when I told him what Coach Vic was considering."

"Considering? Then it's not settled?" Sally's eyes flashed. She fingered her hair. "You know, it's so easy to let yourself go over the winter, don't you agree, Barb? Maybe I should take a lesson off Marylynn Drummer. You got room for another standing appointment on your calendar?"

"I'll see what I can do," Barb murmured. "Of course it is harder to fit things in these days. Did I tell you that Pauline

Fleck's having me host an Amway party at her family re-union?" Needless to say, Barb went on to rhapsodize over how much dear little Scott Fleck had grown this past winter and didn't Sally agree that the boy deserved a tryout as pitcher for the Bobcats, too?

That night, Victor didn't have to listen to Barb's barbs about where he was on the stairway to success and where he ought to be. Happily swamped with pleas for *La Belle* and Amway appointments (high tips and high sales guaranteed, you betcha), Barb had better things to do with her tongue than rag on the man whose chronic underemployment made his Little League coaching job possible. Yes, baseball season was upon them once more, and so long as Victor owned the power to say whose son played (and whether the boy's field position were somewhere in this time-zone), domestic bliss and Barb's own auburn-turfed diamond were his all his.

Nor did it matter a lick that the Brothers' Meeting Bobcats were a team so slack and poorly that a reputable publisher of dictionaries had asked them to pose as the illustration for *pathetic*.

No, it didn't matter to Coach Vic at all, but it mattered very much to Vic Junior.

Vic Junior loved baseball. He was one of those pure souls born with a vision of The Game untainted by the dross and illusion of this sorry world. To him, baseball spoke of Buddha-nature, not Lite Beer. (The *Tao* which can be named is not the *Tao*, but the *Tao* which has its batting stats printed on the back of a trading card is way awesome.) The smell of a newly oiled glove, the clean crack of bat hitting ball, the sight of so many strong, young lads tearing around the bases in those tight-fitting pants, all moved him in ways he could not yet hang a name on. It was a source of spiritual pain to him that his team so seldom won.

Jesus at the Bat

It was a pain less spiritual every time Jase McClellan knocked him down in the school yard and taunted him with the fact that he wouldn't be on the Bobcats team at all if not for the fact that his old man was the coach.

Vic Junior could have tattled on Jase, but he was what adults called a *good* child. In other words, there were sponges adorning the ocean floor who had more backbone than he. He went to church without a fuss and even listened to what his Sunday School teacher had to relate of Hell. He tithed his allowance not because his mother made him but in the sure and certain hope that he was making time payments on one colossal, outsize, super-mega-omniprayer of his own asking being answered some day. He wasn't sure what he was going to request when he finally submitted his sealed bid to Glory, but he knew it would be something *much* better than just asking God to burn Jase McClellan in the fiery pit until his eyeballs melted and his hair frizzled away and the skin on his face blackened and cracked and flaked from the charring bones and his dick fell off.

And then, one day, something happened. Who knows how these things get started? So much depends on serendipity. Pharaoh's daughter might have kept on walking when she heard that wailing in the bulrushes. "Just one of the sacred cats being devoured by one of the sacred crocodiles," she'd say with a shrug of her sweet brown shoulders, and Charlton Heston's resume would have been several pages shorter.

What serendipped in this case was Vic Junior came into *La Belle* to see his Mom and by some karmic radar happened to find the one copy of *Sports Illustrated* in the whole establishment. Like a crow among the lilies it reposed in dog-eared splendor amidst the issues of *Woman's Day* and *Mademoiselle* and *Good Housekeeping*. Last desperate refuge of the male compelled for whatever unholy cause to accompany his

177

woman into the lair of glamour, its well-thumbed antique pages gave moving testimony that a man will submerge himself in last year's sports "news" sooner than he will open a copy of *Cosmopolitan* to willingly read "Impotence: Things Are Looking Up."

"Mom!" Vic Junior cried, bursting in on his hardworking parent, waving the tattered magazine. "Mom, did you *see* this?"

Barb was giving Edna Newburgh a streak job. Mom couldn't see much of anything for all the ammonia fumes peeling her eyeballs raw. "Don't bother Mommy now, sweetheart," she said testily.

"But Mom, *look!* There's an article in here about how the American Little League champions got to go to Japan!" Vic Junior was insistent. Despite the noxious atmosphere he jiggled closer to Edna Newburgh's reeking head and thrust the magazine under his mother's nose.

"So what's that to you? *Champions* means *winners*. I said *not now!*" Barb snapped, flipping the open copy out of Vic Junior's hands with one jab of her elbow. (That she could do this at all was mute testimony to the worthiness of Vic Junior's team nickname, "Wimpgrip Harris.") Like some monstrous mutant butterfly, the magazine took wing and fluttered to the hair-strewn floor.

Giving his mother a cold you'll-be-sorry-when-I-grow-up-to-be-a-crossdresser eye, Vic Junior gathered up his treasure, brushed clots of brown, black, blonde, and red tresses from the slick pages, and retreated to his chair in the waiting area.

He didn't need her to tell him what *champions* meant. It was a fishbone of resentment lodged deep in his throat, proof against all psychological Heimlich maneuvers, that the Bobcats were the losingest team in the history of Little League, baseball, and American sport. The only time a group of kids ended up with that much public egg on their faces was during the Children's Crusade when hundreds of starry-eyed juvenile pilgrims to the Holy Land ended up in the slave pens of the East instead. But even some of those guys could hit better than the Bobcats.

For Vic Junior it was his mother's scorn that hurt more than losing *per se*. A man might rail against the sun's rising in the east as easily as against the Bobcats once again playing the part of the walked-on in the league's latest walk-over—such were the dull-eyed Facts of Life—but she didn't have to be so *mean* about it! Of course she wouldn't see it that way; *she'd* say she was only being realistic.

In his subconscious, Vic Junior understood as follows: *A man ought to be entitled to hold onto his dreams without some female always yawping at him about reality. Somewhere in the Constitution it should say that any woman apprehended in the act of trying to yank us back down to earth by the seat of our pants will be stood on her head in a pit of hog entrails and left for the buzzards, just to see how she likes* that *for reality!*

But a little above the subconscious, in his heart-of-hearts, all that Vic Junior said into the listening dark was: *Please, God, give us the way to win!*

It was a child's simple prayer: sincere, unadorned, pure as a baby dewdrop. On the cosmic scale of values it had clout, pizzazz, and buying power.

It worked.

"Excuse me, sir, but is this where the Little League tryouts are?"

Victor Harris looked down at the brat presumptuous enough to tug at his clipboard-toting arm. "Who are you?" he snapped. His mirrorshades filtered through the picture of a skinny twelve-year-old kid like many others on the team: dark hair, dark eyes, all arms and legs, a little more sun browned than most of the specimens currently blundering through warm-ups on the outfield. "Did you sign up at school?"

"No, sir," the kid replied, too respectful to be true. "I just got here." He tapped the brim of his cap so Victor could see the *Angels* logo.

Fine, good, *no problemo,* that explained it. Brothers' Meeting wasn't exactly your hub of suburban commerce, but it was close to Pittsburgh. You did get the occasional corporate family popping in from points unknown to settle down amongst the simple natives to swap beads 'n' trinkets until Daddy's company shipped the poor bastard somewhere else.

"L.A., huh? Nice tan. Okay, kid, what's your name?"

"Yeshua ben Jose."

Was that an accent? Accents made Victor nervous. So did names that sounded like they ought to be stuffed in a pita pocket instead of spread on Wonder Bread.

"Yeshu—what?"

"Yeshua ben Jose, sir." The kid pounded a fist into his glove. "Can I play?"

Victor thumbed back the brim of his cap. "You're not from L.A., are you, son?"

"No, sir." The boy didn't volunteer anything more. In another kid, you could put it down to obnoxiousness, but this one's face was empty of anything except a clear-burning eagerness to please. It wasn't natural and it made Victor's teeth curl.

"You wanna tell me where you *are* from?"

"Israel."

A big fat wrinkled *Uh-oh* tickertaped across Victor's face and stayed there until he heard the kid go on to say: "Last thing, I was in Jerusalem, but I was born in Bethlehem and—"

"Bethlehem?" It was like saying *Paris* to someone from

Kentucky. Notre Dame and *la Tour Eiffel* just didn't show up in the equation. "Oh, hey, fine, that's all right, then. My mother's people came from Bethlehem," Victor said. He clapped the boy on the shoulder. "So your father work in the steel mills before or what?"

For the first time, the boy looked doubtful. "My father works just about everywhere."

"No fooling. It's a pain, isn't it?" Victor was starting to feel sorry for the kid. Hard enough row to hoe, coming all the way from Israel where things kept going *kaboom!* Harder when your old man couldn't hold down a job and had to keep switching positions and places to live and even countries just to earn a living. At least the kid had been born in this country, but still, just wait until the other Bobcats found out he was Jewish! (Brothers' Meeting wasn't exactly world famous for its cosmopolitan attitude in matters of religion. Old Mrs. Russell, a devout Presbyterian, had disinherited her daughter for entering into a mixed marriage with a Lutheran.)

Maybe the kindest thing to do would be to send him out onto the field for the tryouts and let him fall on his face. That shouldn't take too long. Everyone knew for a fact—including Victor Harris, who had once owned a Sandy Koufax card— that Jews played even worse baseball than Bobcats.

Of course the kid was dynamite. Prayers for smiting your enemies don't get answered with your enemies just catching mild colds and missing a couple of days' work, oh no! It's the plague or nothing. The same and more goes for a child's prayer that the hand of the Omnipotent yank his Little League team out of the cellar. Yes sir, one look at how little Yeshua ben Jose (simpler to call him "Bennie" and be done with it) hit, pitched, fielded, and ran, and Coach Vic was left slack-jawed, poleaxed, and passionately in love at home plate.

"Porter Rickin'," he declared later that night while Barb cleared the dinner dishes. "That's got to be the only explanation."

"What has?" Barb asked, not really giving a damn.

"That new kid, Bennie. I mean, with a last name like *Jose?* I know he doesn't pronounce it Spanish, but still—I mean, there is no other way to account for how good he is and he's still Jewish. His folks might come from Israel, but somewhere back along the line they must've had a Porter Rickin' in the kibbutz woodpile. Or a Mexican at least. Now *they* can play ball!"

"Uh-huh, uh-huh, uh-huh, uh-huh," said Barb which was her little way of playing ball with her husband without having to endure the drag of actually listening to what he had to say.

"He's pretty good, isn't he, Dad?" Vic Junior asked brightly, proud of himself.

"Good? Why he's a fuckin' mira—!"

"*Vic*tor!" Barb's warning tone got drowned out by the shrilling of the telephone. Coach Vic was still going on about how he was going to play Bennie to best advantage when she went to answer it.

She returned a grimmer woman.

"That was Sally McClellan," she said, in the same way a medieval peasant might have returned from a visit to the local witch to announce *The* good *news is I've got the Black Death.* "She says you're not letting her Jason pitch this year."

"You bet your sweet ass, I'm not!" Victor beamed. "With someone like Bennie who can actually get the ball over the center of the plate ten out of ten, I should put in 'Twelve Thumbs' McClellan? What am I, crazy?"

"What you are," Barb said, "is stupid."

"Look, Barb, I know baseball, and I've been coaching this

team for five years, ever since Vic Junior was in Pee Wees and didn't know which end of the bat to hold. And five years is exactly how long it's been since I saw a *glimmer* of hope for the Bobcats winning even one damn game. I'm telling you, Bennie is *it!*"

"Is Bennie's mother going to take over the weekly appointment Sally McClellan just cancelled, and pay up all the ass-kissing big tips that went with it?" Barb shot back. "Is she going to buy all the Amway products that Sally McClellan just *happened* to discover were defective and wants to return for a refund? And if she'll do that, will she do the same when all the other mothers come after us with chainsaws because you dumped Jason as pitcher and didn't replace him with one of *their* brats? Oh no! *You* had to pick a newcomer, a foreigner, a *Jew!*" She stomped out of the house. The two Victors could hear her car tires gouging canyons in the gravel driveway as she roared off.

Barb's outburst was so shocking that it left her husband staring off agape into space. "Do you think I did the wrong thing, son?" Victor asked his boy. Normally he never asked Victor Junior anything except *Where did your mother hide the butter?* but these were special circumstances.

"I've got faith in you, Dad." Victor Junior reached across the table to pat his father's arm and got his elbow in the left-over mashed potatoes.

Faith can move mountains even if it's no good at getting mashed potatoes out of the way. In the next few days, Coach Vic had his faith sorely tested in the raging fires of angry mothers. At every practice, he found another of the ladies lurking for him, wearing flinty eyes and a deadly *ninja* combat brassiere that turned perfectly good ornamental boobs into twin symbols of outthrusting, nuclear warhead-tipped aggression.

The questions they inevitably shot at him were always the same:

"Who *is* that kid?"

"Why are you letting *him* pitch and not my [insert child's name here]?"

"Is something funny going on?"

"What, did his mother sleep with you or something?"

"Why didn't you tell *me* that was the way to do it?"

Coach Vic just as inevitably replied, "Bennie, because he's good, no, no," and "Well, it's too late for that to change anything *this* year because I've got the roster all set up but I bet by *next* season Bennie's folks will have moved somewhere else so see me then, honey."

Then the Bobcats met their first opponents of the season and it was a whole new ball game.

"We won."

It was uttered as a whisper, softer than a butterfly's tap-dance routine, on a dozen lips at once. No one dared to say it out loud, at first, for fear that they would wake up and discover it had all been just a Frank Capra movie.

Still, there were the Bobcats, for once getting to give the Good Sportsmanship cheer to the losing team. It was a simple "Two-four-six-eight, who do we appreciate?" holler, but there was a slight delay while Coach Vic taught his boys the never-used words they'd long since forgotten.

"We won."

Mothers turned to fathers, eyes meeting eyes in a climax of mutual awe and wonder better than what most of them had been having in the bedroom. Hands clasped hands, bosoms swelled, manly chests inflated, pulses raced. (There were more than a few damp spots left behind on the bleachers, but delicacy prevents any closer investigation into how they got there.)

"We fuck-u-lutely *won!*" Coach Vic shouted in the confines of his home, and got a dirty look from Barb that quickly melted when she recalled the ecstatic smiles of the other mothers. For once they had seen their manchildren taste the thrill of victory, and lo, it was savory to the max. Their maternal fibers exuded endorphins like crazy. They were *happy.* A happy mom is a beauty-shop-going, Amway-buying mom.

"You fuck-u-lutely said it!" Barb shouted back and threw her arms around her hubby's sweaty neck.

Well, there it was: They won. And there it was again the next week, and the next. Bennie's skills on the mound left other teams looking at a steady diet of three-up-three-down while his batting *savoir faire* was—

Hmmm. Honesty's best when speaking of matters pertaining to the divine or the IRS. Bennie could hit, but Bennie was only one skinny little kid. He got a homer every time he was up, then Coach Vic had to plod his hitless way through the team roster until Bennie's number came up again before the Bobcats could get another run on the board. They won, but never by much. It was galling.

Still, since Bennie's pitching disposed of the other team one-two-three and the other team's pitcher could do the same for every Bobcat save Bennie, the local Little League enjoyed a season of the shortest games on record. Parents with limited attention spans and only one six-pack in the cooler were grateful.

Ward Gibbon was not grateful.

Ward Gibbon was the father of Jim Gibbon of the Breezy Lake Lions, and up until this Bennie-kid showed up, Jim Gibbon looked fair to cut a major Bennie-like swath through the local opposition, hauling the Lions along with him to the Championship in true and veritable Bennie-style.

Now you've got to understand something about Ward Gibbon: He was a man embittered to the bone. It began when his loving parents named him after their favorite Golden Age television character. Naturally, once he hit school-age, he was dubbed Mental Ward by his juvenile cronies at Breezy Lake Elementary. (A few of the better educated children preferred to seize upon his last name as the means to make his life a living hell, following him around the school making hooting noises and pelting him with bananas.) Worse, creeping nostalgia for Golden Age TV struck his marriage a telling blow when the kittenish Mrs. Gibbon insisted on initiating intimacy by announcing coyly, "Ward, I'm worried about the beaver."

Ward bore his nominal cross grimly, but resolved that no son of his would suffer so. That was why he gave the boy a simple name: *Jim!* So crisp, so clean, so common! Let the infant rabble try to make mock of *that!*

Children love a challenge. Ward Gibbon heard with horror from his son how the other kids at school called him Jungle Jim and Jim Nastics and Jimbo-Bimbo. And there were still some kids around not wholly sunk in the Teenage Mutant Ninja Dorkocracy who knew what a gibbon was. Young Jim Gibbon came home with enough mashed banana in his hair to prove that.

Ward was not a man who gave up easily. If he could not save his son from the horrors of the nyah-nyah mob, he resolved to at least make him proof against all taunts. To this end, there was only one means: Excellence! And for this purpose, diamonds were also a boy's best friend.

Who mocked at Daryl Strawberry's juicy name? Who jeered and jiggled digits at Rollie Fingers? Who had ever been fool enough to make wiggling whisker-signs at Catfish Hunter? Once you climbed the mountain, few *hoi polloi* you

186

left behind had the nerve to toss insults at you, nor the arm to fling bananas to that Olympian height. Let Jim Gibbon triumph on the Little League field, and none would dare sneer at him off. So Ward Gibbon commenced to push his son harder than Mrs. Gibbon ever did in all her nineteen-and-a-half hours of hard labor, and do you know what—?

It worked. Isn't life strange? No operating manual accompanies the afterbirth, yet somehow, sometimes, natural-born humans do manage to stumble across one of the Answers To It All. For the Gibbons, *père et fils,* that Answer was baseball.

Or it was until they came up against Bennie.

Ward Gibbon sat on the top rung of the bleachers, his Sans-a-Belt slacks pressed into permanent horizontal ridges across his butt by the hot aluminum slats. With his 'nuff said *I'm With Stupid* cap pulled low over his eyes and his beaky red nose thrusting out from beneath the visor, he glowered over the ballfield like an avenging, alcoholic owl. He was pissed.

Most loyal dads will become pissed to a greater or lesser degree when their son's team is losing, but this went beyond mere *pro forma* pissitude. His son's team—his *son,* goddammit!—was losing to the *Bobcats!* Losing scorelessly, what's more. It was like being told you'd come in second to Lizzie Borden for the title of Daddy's Girl.

Ward Gibbon's eyes narrowed. He wouldn't know a gimlet unless you poured it into a cocktail glass, yet for all that he now fixed a steely gimlet eye on the one spectacular, incredible, patently obvious cause of it all: Bennie. There was something about that kid . . . Ward's mouth screwed up into a hard, bitter nut of sullen wrath that boded no good if cracked.

The Breezy Lake Lions lost the game, and with it all chance to go on to the Regionals. Jim Gibbon flung down his

glove and burst into tears. Ward Gibbon descended from the
bleachers with hate in his heart and cold-blooded, premeditated research on his mind.

"Disqualified?" Victor Harris bellowed into the telephone.
"What the fuck are you talking about?"

There was a pause while the party on the other end of the
call explained. From the motel bed, Barb watched her man go
whiter than a sheet washed in Amway detergent. He slammed
down the receiver hard enough to score several Loony Tunes
sight-gags by making the furniture jump.

"Honey, what's wrong?" she asked.

"Son of a walleyed *bitch*," he explained. This might have
been enough for other wives, but Barb was a Virgo. She demanded details.

Vic strode to the window and gazed out at the inspiring
panorama of Williamsport, PA, site of that cosmopolitan
Holy Grail, the Little League playoff Finals. The Brothers'
Meeting Bobcats had sheared through all intermediate opposition like a hot knife through a mugging victim. Somewhere
out there was a Taiwanese team who were about to get their
sorry asses kicked (in the spirit of international brotherhood
and good sportsmanship). To this peak of glory had Bennie's
prowess brought the team, and now—O ironic son of a
walleyed bitch!—from this peak of glory was Bennie about to
get them booted. Off. Of.

"You don't have any forms turned in for the kid?" Barb
skirled. "All this time he's been with the team and you never
got his papers in order?"

Vic did not like the way she was so lavishly using the second-person-singular. Voiced that way, the situation seemed
to be all *his* fault. He was quick to pivot the spotlight of blame
right back to where it truly belonged.

"Shit, those desk jockeys wouldn't't've even noticed Bennie's papers weren't in order if not for some asshole troublemaker coming in, nosing around, and making them get off their butts to look up the kid's records. You think all I've got time for is *paperwork?* The boys need me on the field, not stuck behind some desk shuffling bureaucratic crap. You think they'd have come this far on *paperwork?*"

"No," Barb said. She was a reasonable woman. "But if I know my bureaucrapheads, I'll bet no paperwork on Bennie equals no Finals for the Bobcats. Also disqualifications on all the games that brought them here. Also one hell of a shit storm for my *La Belle* and Amway profits when the team parents find out." She reached for the telephone. "Hello, Information? Brothers' Meeting, please. I'd like the number of Four Corners Used Cars."

Vic burst out of the room, his jawline a white, tight wedge of bone knifing through taut scarlet skin. He rolled out of the motel and down the street like a stormcloud. His years as a writer had taught him that there was always a way out: an eraser, a bottle of Wite-Out, a *delete* command, a hundred last-minute ways to drag the Cavalry over the hill to the rescue. He would lay his case before the Little League Powers That Be. He would cajole, he would reason, he would threaten, he would beg, he would cite patriotism and misrepresent the entire Brothers' Meeting Bobcats team as composed exclusively of spunky HIV-positive hemophiliac orphans if he had to, but one thing he would not do:

He would not go gentle into that Only-one-owner-creampuff good night.

The Taiwanese team was good, but as Vic Junior told Bennie, they were godless.

Bennie scratched his head and eyed the opposing dugout. "No, they're not."

"Yes, they are," Vic Junior maintained. "They don't believe in You, do they?"

"Well, maybe not specifically, but—"

"So that means they're godless, and *that* means they're all going to Hell, and that *really* means they can't win this ball game," he finished with satisfaction.

"Look, Vic, about Hell . . ."

"Yeah?" A keen, canny look came into Vic Junior's eye. Ever since Bennie had showed up and made his true self known (It's only good manners to inform the petitioner when the Answer to his prayers blows into town.), Vic Junior had peppered him with questions about the Afterlife. In particular, Vic Junior wanted to know what sort of gory, painful, humiliating eternal trials and punishments awaited bullies like Jase McClellan. Bennie remained closemouthed under direct inquiry, and even reprimanded Vic Junior quite sternly for prying too closely into matters Man Was Not Meant To Know (i.e. "Mind your own beeswax!"). But as long as Bennie himself had brought up the subject . . .

"Yeah, what *about* Hell?" Vic Junior demanded. Hey, the backdoor's better than no door!

Bennie sighed. "Never mind."

"Aw, *c'mon!*" Vic Junior whined. "I won't tell anyone. Is it really full of fire and brimstone and cool shit like that? Our Sunday School teacher told about how You went down into Hell to yank a whole bunch of guys out, so You oughta know. I mean, how hot *was* it?"

"Suffer the little children, suffer the little children, suffer the little children," Bennie muttered to himself, *mantra*-wise, eyes on the blue sky above. It was the perfect day for a ball game, cloudless yet cool and dry. He was jabbed out of his

190

reverie by Vic Junior's bony elbow and nasal bleat:

"Pleeeeeeeze?"

Bennie gave Vic Junior a look that would have sent a whole passel of Temple moneychangers scurrying for cover. It was a scowl of righteous wrath fit to turn innocent bystanders into pillars of salt or fig trees or divorce lawyers. Just so had artists through the ages portrayed Him enthroned in glory on Doomsday, running sinful Mankind across the celestial price-scanner to separate the metaphysical Brie from the pasteurized American-style-flavored cheese-food product. He opened His mouth to speak and Vic Junior heard a distant rumble of thunder, saw tiny lightnings flash behind Bennie's retainer.

"Aw, skip it," Vic Junior said. He knew when to quit. He was one of the Top Ten quitters of all time, but for once it was a good idea.

"Blessed are the peacemakers," said Bennie with a smile.

"Yeah," Vic Junior agreed. "Now let's kick butt."

The flags were raised, the anthems played, the cry of "Play ball!" rang out, and the teams streamed onto the field to the wild applause and cheers of the spectators. The Brothers' Meeting Bobcats' parents shouted encouragement to their youngsters and hardly any racial slurs worth mentioning at the Taiwanese team.

"Eat *sushi,* you heathen zipperheads!" Sally McClellan stood up and hollered.

"Sally, they're *not* Japanese!" Her husband Phil jerked her back down into her seat by the neck of her Brothers' Meeting Bobcats Booster jacket. "Now shut up. These assholes might have some stupid good-sportsmanship rule in effect. Do you want the boys to lose the game thanks to your big mouth?"

"No, dear," Sally replied meekly, then took advantage of the crowd's overwhelming roar to snarl, *sotto voce,* "Eat *me,* darling."

It was a game that would live forever in the annals of Little League and the casebooks of psychiatry. A play-by-play report would profit a man little who might strive to understand what happened that day on the grassy fields of Williamsport. Between Bennie and the Taiwanese pitcher it was a virtually scoreless game. The batting order prevented Vic Junior's visiting miracle from racking up more than one run every three innings, yet even so, it should have been sufficient.

It was not sufficient for some.

"Smite them, O Lord," Vic Junior said to Bennie in the dugout as they prepared to take their last turn at bat in the bottom of the seventh (this being Little League).

"Huh?" said Bennie.

"You know, *smite* them." Vic Junior gave his Savior a poke in the ribs. "Pour out Thy wrath. Drive them before Thee. Score us some more runs."

"We've got two runs and they don't have any. I'm up third. We'll have three runs and win the championship. What more do you want?"

"Winning it with *three* lousy runs? That's not a *man's* game." Vic Junior's sneer was much like his father's. "That's *pussy!*"

Bennie's face darkened. "Having enough to win isn't enough for you, huh? You want more runs. You don't *need* 'em, but you want 'em anyway. Is that all you *really* want?" It was asked in a tone of voice that should have set off whole carillons of alarm bells in Vic Junior's subconscious. It was the big bad brother of his Sunday School teacher's voice when she oh-so-sweetly inquired, *Do you really want to read that comic book instead of studying the Ten Commandments, Victor?*

It was a shame that Vic Junior's subconscious chose that moment to step out for a quick snack and a full-body massage, leaving his feckless conscious mind to eagerly reply, "You bet!"

"So be it." Bennie turned his eyes from Vic Junior's greed-glowing face to the scoreboard.

Numbers twinkled. Numbers crunched. Numbers skittered and fluttered like a yard full of chickens on speed. All the zeroes in the Brothers' Meeting Bobcats' Bennie-less innings mutated to tens and twenties and portions thereof. A murmur went up from the stands. The umpire, blind to anything save the play at hand, commanded that the Taiwanese pitcher stop gawking at the scoreboard and get on with it. The boy, badly unnerved by this Western mystery, actually lost control of his first pitch, leaving a startled Bobby Drummer to get a single.

"What are You doing?" Vic Junior seized Bennie by the sleeve.

"Just what you asked," Bennie replied. "I'm giving you more runs."

"Not that way!" Vic Junior moaned. "They're gonna think we dicked around with the scoreboard somehow and disqualify us!"

" 'Dicked around'?" Bennie repeated, the picture of (no surprise) innocence. "That's the first time I've ever heard anyone describe a miracle that way."

"Aw, Jeez, You know what I mean! I wanted us to get more runs on the board by earning them!"

"Oh." Bennie smiled and nodded.

The scoreboard winked one last time, then subsided. Its effect did not. Half of the Brothers' Meeting parents hooted, demanding that a higher score once posted ought to stay put. The other half shouted that it was all a ploy on the part of the visiting team to make it look like the Americans were cheating when everyone knew the computer system controlling the scoreboard was Made in Taiwan. Newsmen split and scattered throughout the stands, hoping to catch someone with unsportsmanlike foot in mouth, LIVE!

The coach of the Taiwanese team lost it. In the passion of the moment he forgot himself sufficiently to storm the Officials in their lair. The pitcher, stunned to see such behavior in a man he had previously thought of as less volatile than suet, let Jase McClellan connect for a double that placed a bewildered Bobby Drummer foursquare on third.

"I know what You're gonna do now," Vic Junior said, trembling. "You're gonna use this to teach me a moral lesson, like it's a parable or something. You let those guys get on base, and now You're gonna miss Your first two swings on purpose and You're gonna let it get down to the one last swing and if You think I repented enough for being a greedy prick, You'll get that last hit and bring Jase and Bobby home, but if You think I'm not sorry enough You'll strike out and we'll just win the championship by two lousy runs."

An awful afterthought ran him through like an icicle to the heart. "Or—or maybe You're really mad at me, and You're gonna make the scoreboard wipe out all our runs and we'll—we'll *lose!* After everything we went through to get here, You're gonna make us lose the championship! You're gonna smite us! You're gonna pour out Your wrath all over the Bobcats. That's what You're gonna do, right?"

"Who, Me?" Bennie touched the brim of his batting helmet in salute. "I'm just gonna play baseball." And he stepped up to the bat, leaving a white-lipped Vic Junior in the dugout behind him.

Maybe it's not a good notion to drop suggestions into certain Ears. When Nature comes up with new and improved ways to destroy big chunks of Mankind, perhaps She's been cribbing over Humanity's shoulder. Heaven knows, we've done *our* part toward getting those pesky human stains off the face of the earth.

Heaven knows.

In any case, Bennie swung at the first pitch and missed. You'd think it was a bigger miracle than all the times he'd swung and connected for a homer, judging by the gasps that arose from the stands.

Bennie grinned. The Force that (Pick one: created/allowed Evolution to create) the emu, the mandrill, and disco music has to have an ironic sense of humor. He whiffed the second one, too.

Watching from the dugout, Coach Vic felt a sharp pain in his chest. He looked down and realized he'd ripped out a fistful of hair through his shirt. Had he begged and beseeched and groveled before the Officials, wildly plea-bargaining for them to overlook the missing paperwork until post-game, for *this?* "Do it for *America!*" he'd implored. "Or I'll write up this whole incident and name names and send it in to *Reader's Digest.* You wanna be known as The Men Who Stole The Children's Dream for the rest of your lives?" The carpet burns on his knees still smarted.

What was it with Bennie? Sure, the Bobcats were set to win, but the kid's sudden attack of incompetence was no mere fluke. It felt more like a meaning-heavy omen, one that Vic wanted to see averted, and fast. The only hoodoo strong enough to do that would be seeing Jase and Bobby come home. Vic was too staunch a realist to believe that if his star struck out, anyone left in the batting order had the juice to do it, and he was sore afraid. He thought he heard the sound of much weeping and gnashing of teeth. He saw it was only Vic Junior having a conniption fit, babbling about Hell and wrath and smiting and Cooperstown. Coach Vic shook his head: That boy never did do well under pressure.

And then he heard a ghostly voice say unto him *Fear not.* He looked, and lo, there was Bennie giving him the thumbs-up sign. The boy hunkered down at the plate. He'd only been toying with the Taiwanese, yeah, that was it. Vic didn't know much, but he knew baseball, and he knew Bennie loved the game too much to let it down.

"Hold it right there!"

The man vaulted out of the stands, bullhorn in one hand, a piece of paper in the other. He surged across the field to home plate. The Taiwanese pitcher threw down ball and glove, folding up into the Lotus position until these crazy round-eyes could get it in gear and play the game. A security guard jumped the fence after the man. He caught him within arm's length of the umpire. The man calmly swacked the guard straight in the face with his bullhorn. The guard folded up into a less classical position than the Taiwanese pitcher.

"Who the hell are—?" the umpire began. The man drew back his bullhorn in a gesture of invitation to a coma. The umpire bolted. The Taiwanese catcher dropped over backward onto his hands and scuttled away crabwise. The other players remained where they were, frozen on the field.

Alone at the plate with Bennie, the man raised the bullhorn to his lips and bellowed, *"There's been a mistake! This whole series doesn't count! The Bobcats should have been disqualified long ago!"*

"Who the fuck asked you?" Sally McClellan didn't need a bullhorn to make herself heard. Phil tried to make her shut up. He got a surprise out of her pack of Crackerjacks that the manufacturer never put inside. *"Who the fuck* are *you?"* she added while Phil fumbled for a handkerchief to press to his bleeding nose.

"I'm Ward Gibbon, goddammit, and I refuse to see this game

destroyed by cheaters! Why don't you ask this kid who the fuck he is!" Ward pointed dramatically at Bennie.

From the dugout, Vic Junior stopped his hysterics, heart somewhere up around the soft palate. The black look Bennie had given him for his greed was nothing compared to the glare Ward Gibbon was now getting from the kid at the plate.

"My name is Yeshua ben Jose. Are you calling me a cheater, Mr. Gibbon?" Bennie sounded modest and respectful and toxic. No one seemed to think it odd that his voice carried as far and farther than Ward's and Sally's combined, though he wasn't shouting at all.

"I call 'em like I see 'em, and this paper calls for plenty!" Ward rattled the sheet in Bennie's face, then waved it from side to side overhead in Perry Mason style, as if the whole stadium could see what it said. *"I've smelled something fishy about this team for a long time, so I did some research. This is a permission slip! Every Little Leaguer's got to have one of these on file!"*

Sally McClellan told Ward Gibbon where he could file it. Two of the major networks turned cameras on her.

Ward was implacable. *"This slip is filled out for Yeshua ben Jose by his coach, Victor Harris, but this slip is not signed!"*

"Excuse me, sir." Bennie tugged at Ward's arm. "You mean that because that paper's not signed, I can't play?"

Ward lowered the bullhorn. "That's right, son." He didn't mean his smile for a minute.

"Can't Coach Vic sign it for me?"

" 'Fraid not. It's a parental permission slip. Only your father or mother can sign it."

"Yes, sir." Bennie nodded his head obediently. "Coach Vic told me about that, but he said it was all okay because he'd talked to the Commissioners and if I get it signed later on—"

Ward clapped the bullhorn to his mouth and bawled for

the benefit of the stands, *"And how much did your Coach Vic pay the Commissioners to overlook a FLAGRANT VIOLATION OF THE RULES? That's bribery we're talking about!"*

"You bastard!" Coach Vic was on his feet, shaking his fists at Gibbon. *"You're* the one who raised that stink over Bennie's papers!!" He lunged from the dugout, howling for Gibbon's blood. A quartet of loyal Bobcats flung themselves around his legs to save him from certain doom. Gibbon was big enough to snap their beloved Coach Vic into handy, bite-sized pieces one-handed, and he still had that bullhorn. Victor Harris got a good taste of diamond dirt when he went down. A helpful reporter was right there with a mike when he pushed himself up on his hands, spat dust, and shouted, *"I didn't bribe anyone!"*

"Well until you can prove that, that's all she wrote for playing this boy!" Gibbon countered. From the corner of his eye, he could see police streaming onto the field. They'd lock him up, but it would be worth it just to boot this miserable Jewboy's ass the hell out of the championship. "Sorry, son, you're history," he told Bennie.

"But I *love* baseball, sir. I really want to play." It was heart-rending, that look in Bennie's eyes. It carried the distilled essence of nearly two thousand years of great Christian artworks portraying Jesus' suffering for Mankind's sins, plus a hefty slug of the ever-popular crown-of-thorns-on-black-velvet portraits. Who could resist such an appeal?

One guess. Two words. First word sounds like "Lord." Second word likes bananas.

Ward Gibbon's lip curled into a wolfish leer of triumph. "Tough, kid. You can't always get what you want."

History grants Mick Jagger the credit for originating that phrase, but the smart money knows it was first uttered by an unfeeling *hôtelier* a couple of millennia ago when a weary

Nazarene carpenter knocked at Ye Olde Inne door in Bethlehem and said unto him, "My extremely great-with-child
wife and I want a room for the night." There's a lot that's
been written about what kids remember overhearing from
their time *in utero*. Believe it all, especially about this kid. He
remembered it, He didn't like it then, He liked it less now,
and this time He was on the outside and able to make His
anger felt.

"Sez you," He said. And lo, it came to pass.

The lightning bolt hit Ward Gibbon right up the bullhorn.
You never did see a man achieve such instant mastery of hip-
hop. Like that other famous Bush (the one that didn't need
readable lips to make itself heard), he burned and was not
consumed. Of course he yipped a lot.

But that was not all. This was no minor theological tan-
trum. No, this was a manifestation of the Divine displeasure,
and that required more stage dressing.

The heavens opened. Rays of limpid light unfurled from
the celestial heights, sending hosts of angels and gaggles of
cherubs skidding down the heavenly speed slides. They hit
the ground running and did beautiful springboard leaps to
get airborne, then soared for the scoreboard. The numbers
did that flicker thing again, this time mutating into letters
that spelled out REPENT YE NOW, although because there
were just nine spaces on the board it looked like
REPNTYNOW. Sally McClellan said she was sure it was a
city in Yugoslavia. The angels in their robes of glory sang ho-
sannas. The cherubs, bum-nekkid, set up a counterpoint of
"Take Me Out to the Ball Game." That's cherubs for you.

As the heavenly choirs perched upon the top of the scoreboard, legions of demons burst from the bosom of the earth.
Waving pitchforks and wearing regulation umpires' uniforms, they cavorted along the baselines with hellish glee. On

second, Jase McClellan covered his eyes and wet his pants. Bobby Drummer tried to crawl under third base. The Taiwanese infield all started shouting at the top of their lungs. Either it was an ancient Oriental stratagem for driving off demons or they were just scared spitless, no one ever found out which. The demons abandoned the field and swarmed into the stands, throwing complimentary bags of piping hot Gluttony™ brand popcorn to the crowd before they reached the top of the bleachers and vanished. It wasn't very good popcorn, but there was plenty of it.

As soon as the demons disappeared, Ward Gibbon stopped sizzling at home plate. He shook himself like a wet dog, astonished to discover he was still alive, though the bullhorn was past hope. He dropped the lump of slag and would have done so with the permission slip as well, only he could not stir hand nor foot. His sphincter was business as usual, though. Aghast, astonished, embarrassed, he stared at Bennie and in an awestruck whisper asked, "Who are you?"

"Who do you say I am?" Bennie replied.

"Ungh," was Ward's best comeback. The angels on the scoreboard held up placards reading 5.6, 5.8, 5.0, and so on. A cherub even jeered, "Throw the bum outta there!" Oh, those wacky cherubs!

Then, "Behold," said Bennie in a tone of awful majesty, and He did take His bat and lo, He did gesture therewith, and lo again, the object of his gesturing was the permission slip whereon were suddenly writ in characters of fire the four letters that are the Name of God.

That is, they might have been. There are no guarantees, and Lord knows, no hard evidence because, being characters of fire, they instantly reduced the permission slip to a smattering of ashes in Ward Gibbon's trembling hand.

"The slip's signed. The Bobcats' wins are legal. I'm going

home before I smite someone," Bennie said. And without further ado, He did.

Well, would *you* have tried to stop Him?

After the paramedics took Ward Gibbon away and the Officials conferred and the angels wandered off and both teams took a much-needed potty-break, a judgment call was made:

"There is nothing in the rule books against having God on your side. Play ball!"

Vic Junior went up to bat, hit a single off the frazzled Taiwanese pitcher, and brought his teammates home. Jase McClellan's cleats squished when he ran and he never teased Vic Junior again.

When it was over, both teams skipped victory/consolation outings to Disneyworld or Japan or even the nearest ice cream parlor in favor of a quick scamper into the nearest house of worship. The Taiwanese pitcher got separated from his group and couldn't find a church, but he did find something. Later he got credit for bringing *santeria* to Taipei, but that was about it as far as any repercussions worthy of the name.

Vic Senior wrote up the whole incident, couldn't sell it, and got that job at Four Corners Used Cars. When a story is an outright gift from God but the handwriting on the wall still reads *Mene, mene, tekel, does not suit our present needs,* the wise man finally admits it's time for a career change.

Barb wrote it up too, only she put in a lusty, long-legged, red-haired spitfire of a woman as the team coach. Later in the book she goes on to become the owner of a sprawling multibillion dollar sports equipment and cosmetics empire. Everyone knows that the infamous midnight "sushi sex" scene between Barb's heroine and the Taiwanese coach on the pitcher's mound was what sold the book and a heck of a lot of raw fish, besides.

After the divorce, Victor Harris went in for coaching Pop Warner football and tried to forget. And it worked, too, until the day at practice when he saw Vic Junior talking to a boy he'd never seen before. The stranger was about Vic Junior's height, three times as broad, four times as muscular, and sporting an uninhibited non-reg beard the color of a thunderhead. He'd brought his own helmet. He was clearly a Vikings fan.

The boy noticed Vic Senior staring at him and came over.

"Is this where the football tryouts are, sir? he asked politely. "A mutual acquaintance said you might like to have me on your team." He stuck out his hand. "I'm Thor."

"Wait'll you're married," Victor Harris sighed.

Chanoyu

Today she was still Kamiko because it pleased Matsukawa-*sama* to dress her in the old silk kimono that had been his grandmother's. The blue of the wave pattern matched the blue of her eyes, and the cranes with their glorious wings of gold and flame were the ideal foil to her matte white skin and cataract of midnight hair. When they met like this, outside of working hours, Matsukawa-*sama* forbade her to put her abundant tresses up in any sort of restricting style, although he had given her hair ornaments as gifts, pins of the finest Kamakura lacquerware starred with pearls from Lake Biwa, and thin tortoiseshell combs inlaid with slivers of gold and jade.

It was cold in the *yoritsuki*, the waiting room of the teahouse. Kamiko could feel the intimation of a chill pass over her skin like the trailing cobweb sleeves of a ghost. No sound of preparation reached her ears from the *mizu-ya*, where by rights her "host" should now be readying the utensils he would use in the performance of the *chanoyu*, the tea ceremony to which he had bidden her.

Matsukawa-*sama* had been delayed—an understandable occurrence given the demands of business, although one that would irk him. He was a man always concerned with the faces of things. Kamiko knew that his lateness to the ceremony would irritate him more than the fact that his performance of the *chanoyu* was flawed before it was begun. Other hands than

203

his had prepared the teahouse and the garden, bought hands
had readied whisk and ladle, tea bowl and the finely powdered *gyokuru* tea. The true tea master saw to all the prepara-
tions himself.

Most people would say that it was no insult at all for
Matsukawa-*sama* to leave Kamiko here, waiting for him; no
more than it would be an offense to allow the usual morning
hour for turning on the coffeemaker to pass. He alone would
view it otherwise, and his anger at himself would mar the serenity of the ritual. She did not wish this; not today.

For a few moments Kamiko considered leaving the
teahouse until after he did arrive, thus assuming to herself all
blame in the matter of the missed appointed hour. He would
save face, and she—Such things as face could not concern
her. All that mattered was that the master be at ease.

Her life was his, his contentment the purpose of her existence. It was an arrangement as exquisite as a poem traced on
a butterfly's wing, and as fragile. What she had done and
must soon tell him would shatter it to dust. Therefore let her
conserve for him the illusion of serenity for as many breaths
as might remain to it, to her. To think was to act. She was on
her feet and walking the garden paths almost before the last
Should I? took form behind the perfectly painted mask of her
face.

Cold sunlight striped the winding gravel pathways. Whip-
thin willows bowed to brush their famished branches across
the surface of the koi pond. The carved image of a tortoise,
half-hidden among reeds, met Kamiko's abstracted glance
with golden brown eyes and the ageless hauteur of moss-
flecked stone.

You are so thoughful tonight, Kamiko, so closed in on yourself.
Will you let me in? A soft hand stole out of memory to stroke
back one straying lock of Kamiko's thick black hair. Miyoko's

teasing smile once more cast its sweet radiance down upon her where she lay among the deliciously rumpled sheets of their bed.

It's nothing, Kamiko heard her memory-self reply as she pushed herself up and out of bed. Naked, she padded across the carpet to the dresser that served them as a bedroom bar. There was a real bar, fully stocked, out in the sitting area of the suite, but she'd convinced Miyoko that it was more convenient to keep drinks close at hand so that they would not be inconvenienced no matter which room they used. Miyoko didn't require much persuasion. Already her pearly skin was taking on the sallow cast of one who wasted too much time believing that drink could offer refuge from unpleasant realities.

With her back blocking Miyoko's view of the Baccarat highball glasses and the bottle of Chivas, Kamiko paused for a moment, considering whether this might not be the best time to flick the little yellow pellet out from under her fingernail and into her lover's drink. The blinds were drawn, the room was dark, but outside it was still afternoon. There was no need to rush; Miyoko had reserved the suite for the entire week. The only constraint on their time together was Kamiko's fabricated job as an O.L., and even that gave them some leeway. As Miyoko herself said, who would dare utter a word against an Office Lady's absence when everyone knew it was done to accommodate the daughter of the Chairman of the Board?

I was just thinking . . . Kamiko paused, one hand encircling the neck of the scotch bottle. *You told your father that you wanted me to help you with your shopping before you go back to Sapporo. Shouldn't we buy something?*

Are you worried he'll care enough to demand evidence of how we've spent our time? Miyoko laughed. *My father is too busy to bother himself over that. He won't ask to see the packages, darling, and his secretary handles the bills so he won't notice if there are a hundred receipts or none.* She swung her legs from the bed and walked up behind Kamiko. *And if he should ask, I'll tell him that it's my vacation, after all, and that I changed my mind about wasting it on a shopping binge. Instead I chose to spend the two weeks in Tokyo sightseeing, with your capable help. You know he's so traditional, he thinks it's a terrible shame that I never took an interest in our illustrious past. But with your guidance, my dearest one*—Her hands stole up under Kamiko's arms to close over flawless breasts, her thumbs persuasively stroking the nipples, and her next words were a warm murmur against the silk of Kamiko's neck—*instead of shopping, I've made offerings at the chief shrines and burned incense on the graves of all the forty-seven faithful samurai buried at Sengakuji temple.*

She laughed again, and tried to draw Kamiko back to the bed, but Kamiko resisted. *You must not speak of them so lightly,* she told Miyoko. There was just the slightest hint of reproof beneath the timidity in her voice, an artful touch entirely in keeping with the image of the beautiful but humble O.L. who had attracted the notice of the Chairman's daughter. *They were loyal to their lord, even to death.*

Miyoko made a face. *They were fools. Loyalty to their lord, wanting to avenge his death, very well, I can forgive them that. If I told you half the people I've wanted to pay back—But the forty-seven knew they'd have to pay for their revenge with their own lives, afterward. Couldn't they have contrived to act secretly and live?*

Kamiko bowed her head, the proper gesture. *That would have been dishonorable.*

Only by the rules as they stood then. But to change the rules—! To anticipate that the rules will *change, that they* must *change—!* Glee transformed Miyoko's face into a mocking demon's mask. *Times change, and rules, and we can choose whether to sit like old priests, staring at lines raked into sand, or be the ones to cut the new patterns.*

There was a shrill, disturbing note in the young woman's voice. *This one would make new patterns not with a rake, but with a sword,* thought Kamiko, and carefully set the thought aside as an observation that Matsukawa-*sama* might find of use (or perhaps merely of interest; his, always his to choose which) when he debriefed her at mission's end.

"As if she ever could have done so," Kamiko murmured to herself. Her *geta* crunched crisply into the gravel as she allowed the wandering garden paths to bring her where they would. "As if she ever truly held even the hope of a sword."

A soft sound made still softer by distance reached her ears, the muted hiss of a wooden door sliding open. Even here, so far from the teahouse, she could hear it and know that Matsukawa-*sama* had arrived and was noticing her absence. She had never been given any programming intended to simulate human imagination, yet what was imagination beyond memory, conjecture, and deduction? These three qualities she owned as surely as Matsukawa-*sama* owned her. Why should it still surprise her to realize that she had acquired the power to conceive possibilities? She found herself picturing his face as it went from vexation at his own unacceptably late arrival, to relief that there was none present to witness it, to renewed anger directed now at his undutiful slave.

Certainly Matsukawa-*sama* would not give any sign of his displeasure with her before the *chanoyu*. Preserving the tranquility vital to the proper performance of the tea ceremony was his paramount concern, even when his guest was also his property.

And when he hears my report? She turned her head away from the teahouse, her eyes resting on the scarlet leaves of a maple tree, a thousand papery little hands stretched out in supplication, imploring the fancied mercy of a waning sun. She attempted to engage her reasoning processes so that she might create a logical simulation of his rage when she confronted him, but every scenario that flickered behind her eyes seemed somehow inadequate.

It was time to turn back.

It was as she had foreseen: Matsukawa-*sama* greeted her with the gracious reserve and composure that usage dictated, making no reference to her absence from the *yoritsuki* on his arrival. Instead he chose to beg her pardon for the inadequacies of the ceremony which it would be his honor to perform for her.

Kamiko bowed and made a suitable reply. Words and gesture were no less perfect than they were automatic, her maker's legacy. *You can not create, but you will preserve, and for this alone you were created.* Shinoda-*san*'s lined face was still as sharp as ever among her archived visual memories, even though it was the first of them all and had come when she wore the aspect of the beautiful boy-child Goro. The old scientist had also been a lover of the ancestral arts, and had seen to the adorning of his creation with as many of these accomplishments as might not interfere with Goro-Ume-Natsuko-Tadao-Yuzo-Fumiko-Haruo-Kamiko's primary function programming. If he had owned any rights to his shining treasure, no doubt he would have kept it by him to sweeten the few remaining years of his life with poetry, music, *ikebana*, calligraphy and the rest.

Shinoda-*san* was dead, all of his creative genius diminished to ashes, exalted to memory. This too Kamiko preserved. Master to master, she had kept this one small place within herself apart, his image, his teachings, her shrine. And if she could not say why she still wandered with him there in all her changing guises, on inner paths of unchanging beauty, it did not matter: None knew that it was there, thus none had cause to ask her for reasons.

He was there now, in the sacred place within her, standing beside a stone lantern she had copied from the Toshogu shrine. She had taken her first memory of him, enhanced it, given it substance from a thousand other memories. Layer upon layer she had given it beauty, as the oyster formed the pearl. Layer upon layer she had lent it strength, as the master swordsmaker at his forge doubled and redoubled the steel of a warrior's blade. While the body she presently wore followed Matsukawa-*sama* through the rituals of the *chanoyu,* her self in Goro's seeming raced forward to greet Shinoda-*san* with a child's innocent abandon.

He frowned when he saw the pretty boy come running up to him, as was to be expected. *Is this how I taught you to behave? Is this how you shame me?*

It was the same reproof that always began their meetings. Kamiko would no more have it otherwise than she would care to see the rigid ritual of the *chanoyu* desecrated. And yet . . .

On a garden path where wisteria bloomed a beautiful boy fell to his knees and touched his forehead to the small white stones. *Lord, forgive me.*

This time. The old scientist allowed a smile to warm his eyes, though his lips remained downturned. *But you are too old for such childish behavior. You must learn.*

Yes. The boy touched his forehead to the stones once more, then sprang to his feet and bowed deeply. *Yes, honored teacher.*

Walk with me.

They walked through clouds of falling plum blossom and stands of snow-frosted pine, over paths of sand and gravel, earth and stone. The deep pink of summer lotus crowned the surface of cool black pools where white cranes waded, until crane and pool and lotus all whirled themselves away into the matchless bronze beauty of a single autumn chrysanthemum. The old man and the boy walked on, while all around them seasons swirled and bloomed and burst forth in their unnumbered glories, answering to no rule but loveliness.

At last they came to a bench in the shade of a young willow tree. Here the old man sat with that same vague look of pain that Goro remembered and Kamiko preserved.

These bones, he said, by way of apology and explanation. *These are old bones.* This time his smile brought up the corners of his mouth as well as kindling his eyes. *How I wish I were like you, child. You will never know the pain of age. Here, let me look at you.* And he did a thing which Shinoda-*san* had never done nor ever would have dreamed of doing while he lived: He cradled the boy's exquisite face in the palm of one wrinkled hand and held it as tenderly as if contemplating the priceless perfection of an antique teacup. *Ah. Other pains touch you, though, child. Still. Are they always there? Every time you visit me, you seem to bring fresh ones.*

I'm sorry, Lord.

You must not apologize for this. Go on. Tell me.

The boy hung his head. *This time you will hate me.*

The old man's hand came to rest on Goro's shoulder. *Can that word ever be spoken between us? You are my son, precious and beloved, all the children I will ever have, now. My death leaves only you behind, but you are enough, little son who carries all the sons and daughters of my dreams.*

Goro looked up, and in the teahouse Kamiko saw her first self's eyes like twin ghosts whose images rippled over the steam rising from Matsukawa-*sama*'s ladle as he scooped boiling water from the little iron pot. The water poured in a thin stream over the powdered tea, the whisk stood ready to beat it into green froth delicate and fragrant as the scented breath of heaven.

Goro slipped his small body from the bench beneath the willow tree and prostrated himself on the beaten earth of the garden path. *Lord, I have failed you, to my shame. As you gave me life, take it back again.*

Kamiko heard Shinoda-*san*'s measured, raspy breath flowing in and out of her head with a noise like a knotted string being drawn through cardboard. There was an empty teacup in her hand, a beautiful object. She gave it the admiration that the ceremony demanded, but her vision was consumed by the face of an old man, ashes in a shrine, the echo of whose living self was preserved only within the shell of metal and plastic that he had himself created.

If she died, he died.

Child . . . The word was spoken softly. *What have you done, to desire death so much?*

Lord, I do not desire death. My life is yours, I live so that you may live on in me.

I did not create you for that purpose. How did such an idea come to you?

Goro raised his face from the earth. Kamiko's hand reached up automatically to wipe from her own cheek a smear of tear-wet soil that wasn't there. Then she saw Matsukawa-*sama*'s critical eye upon her and remembered where she was.

Lord—Goro's voice was less than the whisper of a dream. *Lord, how could I not come to hold that thought when you created me to hold the seeds of it?*

A frown passed over Shinoda-*san*'s face. *You were made to contain and preserve viable germ plasm, to offer a favorable environment for fertilization, and in certain circumstances to incubate fertilized ova temporarily, until a human surrogate can be found. Have you failed in this?*

Goro lowered his eyes, beautiful, luminous, with lashes too long to be real because they were not. *In this purpose, Lord, I have succeeded too well.* He stressed the words just so, with deliberation.

What do you mean, child? The old man's eyes opened only a little wider. It was a true question. In Goro, in Kamiko, in all the other semblances Shinoda-*san*'s creation had assumed to satisfy the demands of each new assignment, Shinoda-*san* lived on as he had in life, a separate entity. He did not, as a matter of course, know all that Kamiko knew simply because she carried him within her. Such an arrangement would deprive him of the independent being she had struggled to create, would in turn deprive her of his unaffected counsel. Of what use would their conversations be if he were only an extension of herself? What new wisdom could come from such self-defeating encounters? It would be an effort as sterile as pouring water into water and imagining one had created something new in the world.

Lord . . . The boy Goro was young, and being young he lacked the confidence to go on. Therefore he changed from being Goro into the first new seeming he had ever assumed: the young woman Ume, a form and face that Shinoda-*san* had thought more appropriate for performing his creation's projected purpose. Ume was an adult. She had left Shinoda-*san*'s laboratory to take up what should have been her life's work in the fertility clinic. She had seen and done much, and was not afraid to speak frankly:

Lord, you also made me to obey.

Shinoda-*san*'s lips turned down once more, as they had when he reprimanded Goro. *What is this? Do you confess to disobedience? Impossible. You were not made so.* He words fell on her, short and sharp, like strokes of a bamboo cane.

No, Lord. Not by you. She wore a simple cotton *yukata,* a

212

garment of function without much beauty. Her hair was cut short and straight across like a schoolgirl's, making her round face look rounder. Everything about her from her placid gaze to the comfortable width of her hips was intended to promise desperate people sons.

She took his hand in hers. In the outer world where she was still Kamiko the fingers of her right hand gracefully received the cup of tea that Matsukawa-*sama* presented to her, balancing it with elegant perfection on the palm of her left. Between the time she began her bow of thanks to Matsukawa-*sama* and the time she straightened her back again, her Ume-self had communicated to Shinoda-*san* all that had been done to her since her purchase from the clinic. She had never seen the need to tell him such things until now.

Changes? The old scientist's face was as stiff as if some evil spirit of the snows had forced it into a mask of ice.

Modifications, Ume said softly. *That is what my new employer calls them. That and . . . improvements.* She could not meet Shinoda-*san*'s eyes when she said that.

She only looked up when she heard him murmur, *Better if I had taken you with me into the flames when I died. Better still if my Goro had lived. He would not have let anyone do this to you. He would have bought you back. If not that, then I know he would have found some way to use the law to prevent this . . . obscenity. He was a clever child. He would have been a great man.*

Ume's eyes shimmered with tears that were only thoughts. *Am I not your Goro?* She could hardly believe she had dared to speak those words.

Shinoda-*san*'s anger-hardened mask melted only a little way back into flesh. *He was the child of my body. You are the child of my mind, of my hands. I do not think you could ever come to know how deep a difference this—*

He is dead, Lord. Kamiko's anger shook Ume's body in the

inner garden where lingering memories tended the blossoms and wandering thoughts raked the paths. *Dead, gone, and little more than a child when he died. And I am here. I preserve you better than he ever would . . . or could. Why then do you exalt him over me? You call me your precious son, but only when I wear his seeming. Am I not dear to you as myself? Why do I see that hungry light in your eyes when you speak his name? I recognize it. I know it. I have seen its like too many times warming the faces of Matsukawa-sama's clients.*

For the first time before or since his death, Shinoda-*san*'s face revealed uncertainty when his creation was there to see it. *What do you mean, child?*

In the teahouse Kamiko's throat felt the trickle of tea. The documents that Matsukawa-*sama* owned concerning her capabilities stated that the android's senses were nowhere near fully human, yet some might argue the same for others born mortal. Without a finely developed sense of touch, she could not fulfill her purpose. If Matsukawa-*sama* ever learned that she could feel the tea on her lips, in her throat, it would not surprise him. If Matsukawa-*sama* ever learned what else she could feel, he would be too appalled to be surprised.

Child, Ume echoed. *You call me child, your child, but you could as readily call me table, turtle, stone. For you, for me, it is only a word. What good is another word to me? I have tried to honor you, to serve your memory as faithfully as my duty and my love demand. What I have done—the offering I have made to you—will destroy me. For what? I am less to you than a little container of bone chips and ashes you hold in your heart.*

How can you hope to understand? The old scientist shook his head. *What my son was to me—*

I, who have taken every pain to preserve you as you were, how can I not understand? Willow leaves shadowed Ume's eyes. *I who hold you within me, shelter you, cherish you as you are, when it would be so easy for me to remake you so that your love for me is perfect, how can I not understand what it is to love a child?*

It's not the same.

Oh, I agree. I have seen what it truly means to be a child of the body. It makes me rejoice that you are all the father and all the child I may ever have.

Shinoda-*san*'s face darkened. *You won't put me off with riddles, Ume,* he declared. *You will answer me. What has this man truly done to you? This goes beyond the "modifications" you've specified. You are no longer as I made you. Why?*

And Ume threw her head back, and laughed, and became Haruo, who was little more than sixteen, and who looked handsome the way a starving tiger on the prowl is handsome, and just a little dangerous.

Don't you mean how do I dare not be the kid you thought *you had?* he jeered at the old man. *Same as the rest of them. When I popped out between my mother's bloody thighs you thought you had it licked, didn't you?* Didn't you? Yeah. *A child of your body, that's right: A son to carry on your name, a daughter to carry on your blood. Only I wasn't born to give you what you expected, all that crap you thought was part of your* rights *as my father. What the fuck good was I if I'd only take your name so far down the path and then drop it in the dirt? Hey, Dad, I've got a* biiiig *surprise for you: Your little* boy *doesn't like little* girls. *And your little boy's the only kid you're ever gonna get out of Mom, and it doesn't matter how much money you're willing to pour out before the gods: The dynasty stops here.* He struck his chest hard with his fist. *End of the line, old man, end of the line.*

In the teahouse, Kamiko's face showed nothing but peace. Inside her head, her old Haruo mask strutted boldly before Shinoda-*san*'s horrified image, all black leather and tight bluejeans, crowing like a cockerel.

One time the boss took me out with him to a bar when I looked like this, Haruo said, eyes narrow and foxy-bright. *A test run, like I was a car. He wanted to see whether I'd been revamped good enough to attract his latest client's son. Attract? Ha!* It went way *past that the minute they saw me. Man, I* had *them: Every eye in the place right on me, right here.* This time he only tapped his chest, but he let his glance slip slyly down to his crotch so that it was impossible for Shinoda-*san* to mistake his meaning. *Those other times when my job was to snag one of the pots, I played it meek and pretty, but we knew that wouldn't do for Yamamura-*san*'s son. He liked them tough.* Not *too* tough, *though—he was a pussy underneath all that expensive leather Daddy's money bought him—just tough enough for him to pretend he had the balls to be a* real *bad boy. Want to know the "modifications" Matsukawa-*sama *had his trained monkeys put into me for* that *job? And there's more where those came from. As long as there's money to pay the monkeys and old men to pay Matsukawa-*sama*'s price for grandsons, there'll always be more.* Haruo's laugh was a crow's harsh cry.

The laughter faded away. Within herself Kamiko painted the image of a crow taking flight from a pine bough and winging off towards the garden's imagined horizon. On the stone bench, Shinoda-*san* sat with head bowed.

Why could you not have left me dead? he asked.

Haruo froze at the old man's voice, shook himself like a poorly tracked videotape, refocused as Tadao, still handsome but softer, gentler, wearing the pristine uniform of a schoolboy. He sat beside the old scientist and softly said, *Because I could not go on in that life alone. Because I needed you to be with me, a refuge. Because the thing I do now to serve the one who owns me is like acid in my skull, scouring away all memories but the worst, those that most trouble me.*

Memories? The old man's eyes caught once more the light of speculation. Tadao had still been Goro, Shinoda-*san* had still been alive the last time such a look had illuminated the scientist's face. A thousand doors opened, offering glimpses of a universe where all things were possible. *You have* trou-bling *memories?*

Tadao did not answer. His thoughts flew back to the clinic, to the time when all he had needed to be was Ume. Memories overwhelmed him, swarming with countless por-traits of human indignation, revulsion, even rage, all of these collected and focused on the ever-repeated moment when Ume's human colleague had explained to the child-hungry couples precisely what Miss Ume was and what she must do with both wife and husband if they wished to conceive. Ume sat placidly and heard herself called *unthinkable, revolting, monster, obscenity.* But in time they all calmed down and per-mitted her to do her job. There was nothing a human would not do to have a child of his or her own blood. Nothing.

What she had done to them, with them, was what she had been created to do. She had been surprised, at first, by how vi-olently the clients reacted when they learned exactly how she would give them what they craved. She had always owned the potential to shift shape, to modify her own size and sex and seeming as need demanded. Shinoda-*san* had given her that function to meet the specifications which the clinic considered necessary. Sometimes the wife was not to blame for failure to conceive; sometimes the husband's sperm was vigorous but he was not. A proper go-between must be employed, a transfer must be made, one which required Shinoda-*san*'s creation to gather seed as a woman, then to pass it on as a man. It was her duty, the harvesting of eggs, the gathering of sperm, the incu-bation until such time as a human surrogate could be found or, in cases where the trouble was not with the client's womb, until the mother might receive the transplanted embryo.

And they came back, the same people who had cursed and

cried out in disgust and called her an abomination. They came back with their fat, round-faced babies and gave her their blessings.

If you teach a child the same lesson over and over, time after time, even one of the slowest wit will retain it, Tadao said. *I was not created to lack intelligence. Once, when Matsukawa-sama brought me to an interview with an American, the man said that a chicken was just an egg's way of making another egg. He behaved as if he had said something very clever because it was something that Matsukawa-sama might not understand, and yet he would be forced to smile and nod as if he did. But I understood. The American's daughter did not desire men. She was the sole child of his body; he could have no more, because his wife was old, and he was used to her, and divorce would be more costly than hiring me. To seduce his daughter, I became Fumiko. The American girl was unpleasant to be with, harsh, evil-tempered, cruel; it was a blessing that she would never have children of her own to torment. I have often wondered, since then, how much of her ugly disposition came from knowing she had failed her parents by the very act of being born as she was.*

You . . . have wondered? Shinoda-*san* regarded Tadao closely. *Without being directed to do so? Is this another of your master's modifications?*

Tadao seemed not to hear the question, although that was impossible. He continued speaking as though Shinoda-*san* had said nothing at all: *After I had drugged her and removed enough eggs to ensure that at least one embryo would result, I came back to him to learn where I was to harvest the sperm that would give him the grandchild he demanded. He laughed and stripped away his clothes and showed me.* A chicken is just an egg's way of making another egg, *he said again while he grunted over me. It was then I first became aware that I would not be unhappy if his sperm was inadequate to the task, or if the implantation failed, or if his wife utterly refused to accept the child when it was placed before her for adoption, or if that child too grew up after the way of his daughter, for there are no guarantees that—*

What has this to do with memories? the old man broke in. *You were not made to think or to judge or to wonder, but to* do; *you were certainly not made to* question *what you do, nor to follow the path that confusion lays before your feet. Child, what has become of you?*

In the teahouse, the *chanoyu* was coming to an end. As she had been taught, Kamiko requested to examine the implements which Matsukawa-*sama* had used to prepare the tea. Suitable words of admiration for their beauty and simplicity came from her lips. Throughout her praises Matsukawa-*sama* retained a well-cultivated look of modesty.

I have become the child whose chosen way is bitterness to the one who gave me life, Tadao said. As he had done when he was Goro, now Tadao too crouched in the dust at Shinoda-*san*'s feet and pressed his forehead to the earth. *I regret to tell you that this is how I am, my teacher, my Lord. I do not know how this came to be, but I do not regret that it is so—only that it will displease you. For once I became aware of what I did, once the path of troubling thoughts lay before me, I followed it. It was paved with questions like stepping stones over swiftly rushing waters. I followed each to the next, though the way became more perilous. I gazed down into the waters and saw in them the racing images of those who had come to me because their hearts hungered for the children of love, but I also saw reflected there the faces of those old men whose only hunger was for their own immortality. How easy to see the difference! And what a true abomination that I, being what I am, should do so. I am not human: This difference should have meant nothing to me, but it did. It did, and because it did, I could not help but follow the path of the stones.*

Where has it brought you, child? Shinoda-*san* spoke as one who did not want to hear the answer but who could not refrain from asking the question.

To refusal. (In the darkened hotel bedroom Kamiko gazed down on Miyoko's drugged sleep. She had already brushed the young woman's abdomen with disinfectant, deployed the instruments, prepared herself to receive the eggs. What she had to do she had done many times before, at the behest of many clients, at her master's command. It was almost a sacrament, a ritual task whose steps were as clearly prescribed and defined as any tea ceremony.)

To death.

The *chanoyu* was over. Kamiko and her proprietor left the *sukiya* separately, only to meet again almost immediately outside. It was here that Matsukawa-*sama* at last asked her for her report.

"Is that all?" he asked when she was done.

Kamiko bowed. "I have failed you, my master. I did not complete my task." She kept her eyes fixed on the ground. "I could not."

"Ah." He nodded. "Come." And that was all he said. He started along the path that led away from the *sukiya*. Dutifully she followed, in silence and in fear.

What will he do with us? Tadao was Goro again. The little boy slipped his fingers into his creator's hand.

I do not know. Shinoda-*san* gave the plump fingers a tender squeeze, as if the gesture had the power to drive out demons. *Are you afraid?*

I do not fear my own death. I mourn yours. You did not choose this.

Shinoda-*san* smiled. *No more than I chose my birth. And do you now regret your path, your choice?*

Only for your sake, my Lord.

Why? My existence ended long ago. The world believes me dead. Only you know that I am here, within this place of your creation. What difference will it make if I depart?

The little boy looked away. *It will make a difference to me, Lord. I love you.*

Shinoda-*san* let go of Goro's hand and stroked the child's smooth cheek with his bony knuckles. *Do you know, little one, that there are wise scientists, men of learning and brilliance, who would tell me that it is impossible for one like you to love, or choose, or sense the difference between what you did in the clinic and what you can no longer do for your master?*

Yes. The child's lips trembled.

And do you now regret having chosen, having loved?

No.

Then regret nothing. Fear nothing. You are my child. I've heard your protests, how you insist that I hold you less dear than my lost son. Yet I tell you I do love you as well and as much as I ever loved him. Differently, yes, but with the difference that exists where a man has been blessed with two children to cherish instead of only one. And you are *my child: More than anything, I do not want you to be afraid.*

In the outer world, Kamiko got into her owner's car. Matsukawa-*sama* was saying something. Kamiko carefully recorded it for future review. He asked no questions, therefore he did not expect any reply from his property. Most likely he had had enough of her responses for a time. The sound of his words detached from any meaning was as restful to her ears as the whisper of water trickling over smooth stones. She hardly noticed the moment when the car reached its destination and he ordered her out.

As she walked behind him through the bright halls she found the slick, hard surfaces around her changing as she herself owned the power to change. Hurrying people in crisp white coats turned into unhurried rocks, wind-eaten, moss-grown. The ruler-straight path of shining black floors became the meandering gray and gold of sand combed into swirling patterns by a snub-toothed wooden rake.

Shinoda-*san* sat with her on a flat rock colored like a rain cloud. Because he had told her not to be afraid, she had become Kamiko for his eyes as well as for Matsukawa-*sama*'s. Even now she could not believe she had become someone as brave as Kamiko.

So now it ends, she said. *It can't be much longer. He's not taking me upstairs to his office. This part of the building holds the laboratories. He's brought me here to be destroyed.*

Shinoda-*san*'s face was calm, holding serenity as simply and easily as a cup held tea. *I don't think he will destroy you,* he said.

Why not? He can make another to take my place. He purchased your design specs when he acquired me.

He can. He might. But will he? You were not cheap to make, and I know that my former employers would not surrender the rights to my design without securing an impressive profit. Shinoda-*san* smiled. *You are an investment. Your owner doesn't destroy such things.*

But I've changed. I'm no longer the tool he needs. Why should he preserve the device that does not answer to its master's will?

Another question. Shinoda-*san* passed his hand over the patterned sand. The ripples moved, flowed, melted into water's living glass. The great rocks shattered, scattered themselves across the pool, stepping stones that failed to bridge the banks. Kamiko found herself alone, balanced precariously on the stone nearest shore. She could not explain how she'd come to be there any more than she could explain how she'd come to see the outer world through questioning eyes.

The rock beneath her feet was slick with rotted water weeds, arched like a turtle's back, but the distance between stone and land was too great for her to leap. If she tried, she would fall.

Where have your questions brought you, child? Shinoda-*san* called softly from the bank.

Too far, Kamiko whispered miserably, hugging herself tight.

When the traveller goes too far on his chosen path and turns back to face the way he has come, has he still gone too far or not far enough?

I—She could not find the words or the time to answer. Shinoda-*san*'s riddle reached her just as her foot touched a bloom of slime and skidded off the rock. She pitched forward, arms spread like a crane's wings, seeking to embrace the shore. The water fell up to meet her, a pool, a curtain, a ghost whose face was all the kindness she had ever known.

She landed in a shock of light that was the world, her thought-gardens torn away. She was in a small room with all manner of diagnostic tools ranged against one wall and a gurney with no mattress waiting against another. Matsukawa-*sama* was there, his face flanked by the faces of the white-coated demons. There were four of them, the number of death, all bespectacled, grave young men with lips so thin that Kamiko imagined a god cutting open the flesh of their faces with a razor's edge.

Matsukawa-*sama* was speaking. The words floated out to reach her: "—another try, afterwards" burst like fish-blown bubbles from the surface of a pool just as Kamiko sensed the intruding jab of the probe at the base of her skull, and then more than darkness.

Waking came back to her as a ceiling slashed with fluorescent lights. She was still Kamiko. She sat up on the worktable and saw the four young men waiting for her, one with a palmtop, one with a laptop, one tidying away the tools, one holding out a crisp blue-and-white *yukata* patterned with the company logo for her to wear.

"The tests have all run satisfactorily," he told her as she slipped her arms into the sleeves and tied the belt around her waist. He nodded to where a pair of *tabi* and sandals waited. "We have already informed Matsukawa-*sama* of this; he's pleased. He wants you in his office immediately for instructions."

Kamiko sat down on a cold metal chair to put on the thin socks, the straw-soled sandals. It was impossible for her to feel dizzy, and yet when she bent down to pull the *tabi* over her bare feet she almost tumbled out of the chair. The grim young man was there to catch her, his colleagues to make hasty notes. She met his concerned frown with a smile and was quick to get to her feet and out the door.

"I know the way," she said pleasantly, leaving them.

Matsukawa-*sama*'s office was beautiful, black and gray and gold. She lived there, when she was not working, in a place between the stand that held his swords and the brass and rosewood rod on which he hung his grandmother's kimono when he did not order her to wear it. The kimono was back there now, on display against the wall.

"I have just spoken with our client," was how Matsukawa-*sama* greeted her. "I begged for his forgiveness and promised him unconditional success this time. He has graciously consented to allow us a second chance. Of course this means you will have to travel to Sapporo. You leave tomorrow. I want you to change your appearance entirely—go younger, I think, but not *too* young. Keep nothing that might remind her of you as she knew you. Her father tells me that the girl went back home in a black mood. She wouldn't say why, but I think we know: You abandoned her without a word of goodbye, and she could find no trace of you in her father's office. A woman scorned, eh?" He smiled, pleased with himself, his world.

Kamiko bowed. "I will initiate the changing routines immediately," she said, and by the time she lifted her head again, her eyes were already brown instead of blue. Her hair shrank back into her head, began to go pale, ending as a sharp, short, hedgehog cut bleached white as bone. The underlying planes of her face shifted, carving deep hollows in her cheeks, giving her the feral, fascinating look of a female Haruo.

Matsukawa-*sama* frowned. "Too different. Work on something else." He waved her away, dismissing her to her niche in the wall. Soon he was on the telephone and she was forgotten.

While Kamiko played idly through all the changes of which her body was capable without recourse to the lab, her thoughts stole away joyfully to the garden. The willow tree stirred in the breeze and there was the scent of summer-ripe plums on the air. In this place she did not need the white-coated demons to help her alter her adult body to child size. She could become Goro at a thought. The little boy raced along the white path. He knew how strictly Shinoda-*san* would reprimand him for such uncontrolled behavior, but he didn't care: He was happy to be alive.

He called out the old man's name as he ran, feeling his cheeks grow red, his hair lift in the wind. *Lord! Lord, you were right, he* didn't *have me destroyed! Here I am! Here I am!* Down the white path he ran, calling, calling, laughing because everything was going to be all right after all.

And next time you refuse to do what your owner bids you? The question sounded hollow, words without a human voice, carrying the twang and echo of a machine.

The child stopped short at the sound. *Lord, where are you?*

Or have you determined to go back the way you came?

Lord? The boy was shivering now. He gazed around the garden. It was not as he recalled it. The foliage was the uniform green of a child's crayon drawing, the flowers were sharp-edged as if they had been etched by a sword. *Father?*

There was no answer; not even the voice of the machine.

In the alcove in Matsukawa-*sama*'s office Kamiko froze in mid-transformation, giving her face the aspect of a stroke victim's. Within herself the white paths crumbled, the willow's tender leaves curled to the brown husks of abandoned insect shells, and shadows came creeping out of all the empty places where he had once dwelled. She doubled over like a woman in the throes of miscarrying the child she already loved.

"Father!"

Matsukawa-*sama* glanced up from his work. "Did you say something?" He scowled when he saw her. "What are you up to? I hope that's not a joke, that face," he said, jerking his chin at her. "It's hideous, an abomination. Is something still wrong with you? The techs assured me that they'd removed a massive anomaly from your programming and that your normal behavioral routines should reintegrate themselves around the excision within hours. If you're exhibiting signs of humor, though, I doubt the excision was complete." His hand reached for the intercom. "I'll send you back to the laboratory at once. We can't risk a second failure. With the profits from this assignment, we'll finally have the assets to begin constructing—"

"No." She stepped out of the alcove and was across the room in a breath, her hand flashing between his own and the intercom so quickly that he jerked back out of reflex, taken by surprise. She looked so human that it was easy even for him to forget that she owned more than human strength, more than human speed. "Be assured: The excision was complete. He's gone."

" 'He'? What do you—?" Matsukawa-*sama*'s question withered on his tongue. He saw what she had plucked from the place beside her alcove even as she had raced across the room. He stared at her in horror, and his last breath braided with the whisper of the sword as it left its scabbard. She did not know what her face looked like as she drew back the blade, but she hoped that it would prepare his mind for hell.

In the shade of the great trees of Sengakuji Temple the graves of the forty-seven samurai sent up the twisting wraiths of burning incense. It was late in the day. The old man who tended the portal and who sold bundled incense to those who would honor the loyal dead was about to close up his gatehouse and go home when he saw the girl. She wore a simple blue-and-white *yukata,* and she was seated in an attitude of contemplation at the grave of the youngest of the forty-seven. He could not remember whether or not he had seen her come in.

He went up behind her and politely told her that it was time to leave. Her eyes stayed shut, her face a mask as young as a newly opened blossom, as peaceful as the moon. He spoke to her again, and again received no answer. When he dared to touch her shoulder, he found that she was cold.

It was only after the police arrived that anyone paid attention to the cloth-wrapped bundle lying before the place where she had been. It was a good thing that the police were the ones to open it.

Everyone asked who she was. No one knew what she was until later, and then no one knew how such a thing as she could ever die. And no one ever knew why the photograph of an old man and a little boy in a lost garden had been left there on the grave, wrapped within the bundle that held the face of neither one.

Ilion

"Troy," said the angel. "That's what it's like, I think."

I looked up from my mug of coffee, long cold on the counter. "Troy?" I echoed. The city echoed. There were holes torn all around us in those days, places of emptiness holding silence, cupping loss. I raised the cold mug to my lips. "No," I said in a little while. "Not Troy. They didn't even believe in angels at Troy. Gods, yes; angels, no."

"Well, excuse me," the angel said, "but I ought to know if it's like Troy or not. After all, I was there."

I didn't ask *There? Really?* He was an angel. He was at Troy; he was here. I drank my coffee until the thick, white cup was empty of everything but the gritty dregs of too much sugar. These past few days I'd been loading my cup with it to the point of turning ordinary coffee into syrup, but the bitterness stubbornly remained. There wasn't enough sugar in New York to take the taste of dust from my mouth. There wasn't enough sugar in the world.

"We won't argue about it," I told him. He shifted his wings, mantling the great white feathered pinions like a hawk settling onto its perch, and preened just a little. He was pleased with my concession, perhaps a little proud as well. *A pride of angels,* I thought, remembering Lucifer. Even here, in the little coffee shop that was my haunt whenever the word-demons of the night would not let me sleep; even now, when all the words that tumbled through my head screamed with pain and denial, with sorrow and a child's desire to close my eyes so that everything I'd seen would disappear; even here and now I could not keep from dealing with this life by wrapping it in words.

The angel finished his own cup of coffee and signaled the waitress for more. She was all the way at the other end of the counter, staring at a tiny television set. Either she didn't see his imperious gesture at all or else, if she did catch a glimpse of his shining hand out of the corner of her eye, she ignored it. The angel's mouth went flatline.

"This is awful service," he said. "Even for New York."

"Sorry. We're a little distracted today," I replied.

That was when I learned that angels have no use for irony.

"Do you think I don't know?" he snapped, and the flames behind his eyes were almost worse than the fires we had all been watching on our little silver screens. *It isn't right,* my voice told me, the voice that binds my heart's ache to my fingers, my fingers to these keys. *September fires should smell of crisp, bright mornings, fresh apples, frosted dew on grass. All that they should burn is leaves.*

"I *know,*" he went on. "I dwell where all things are known, where we have no choice *but* to know. Little one, don't tax me with your cleverness, trying to put me in my place. You couldn't bear to share what's on my shoulders for an instant. *Miss!*" His face, bright as the sun, turned sharply from me for a moment; his voice filled the small eatery. The waitress couldn't help but hear. "More coffee," he said, more softly. "Please."

She refilled our cups. I watched how skillfully her hand tilted the brown-handled glass bubble. Her lips were trembling, her eyes trickled tears, but her hand held steady. She had done this same small task uncounted thousands of times before.

Uncounted thousands.

"Did you see that?" I asked the angel. "She's shattered inside, her heart's breaking, but she never spilled a drop. That's New York for you: Holding on, keeping to the path, standing firm. Steady as a rock."

The angel sneered over the rim of his cup. "Clichés at this hour of the night? And you call yourself a writer."

"Sarcasm?" I shot back. "And you call yourself an—"

I didn't get the chance to finish what I meant to say, and he guessed wrong when he assumed I'd end with *angel*, not *illusion*. He sprang up from the poorly padded red vinyl stool where he'd been sitting and grabbed me by the shoulder, spinning me around to face away from the counter. The shadows beneath his wings were caverns where smoke billowed and men and women looked into hell.

"Do you think it's easy, what I've been brought here to do?" he demanded. I glimpsed the sword in his hand, flickering in and out of my vision like a tongue of lightning.

"I— I was only going to say—" I began.

He wouldn't listen. "Come."

The wings closed over me and we rose into open space that was suddenly all around us, the coffee shop no more than an eggshell, easily broken and fallen away, far beneath our feet. He held me to him and I imagined that I felt a heart beating beneath his robes, a human heart. But I knew that to be impossible, wrong.

And what are these days if not impossible? my voice whispered against the roaring of the wind in my ears as we soared up towers now made out of smoke, only smoke and ashes. *What is all this if not wholly, unutterably wrong?*

I closed my eyes and clenched my hands, feeling the angel's fingers digging deep into my arms as he lifted me ever higher. A small chill looped itself around my fingers and I opened my eyes to see that I was still holding onto my coffee mug, the last few drops tumbling to earth like rain. I held it even more tightly, then, folding my hands around it in fresh prayer.

The great wings shielding me from the upward rush of our passage opened, petals of a rose, and I saw the burning world beneath us. I thought of a child's building blocks scattered, toy cars and trucks overturned, the painted streets of a playmat swarming with ants in an abandoned nursery.

Then I heard the angel's mirthless laughter. "Why do you try to put a frame of words around it?" he asked. "And words that blunt what's happened into such a timeworn, battered shape? A nursery! Toys! The handiwork of a child! What do you think of children if you soil them with this, even in your mind?"

I didn't answer. He claimed he knew things; he must already know what I would say: That my words were clumsy, but that I was weak, bled out by sorrow. I did with them what I could—not my best, but the pain wouldn't let me wait for prettier ways to wash the poison from my eyes. The words become my lantern, letting me contain the fire, letting me turn it into light or die trying. And there must be light to cast away this darkness. Sooner or later, there must be light.

The words will save me, body, mind and soul.

I was right: He knew.

"Come," he said a second time, more kindly now. "If that's how it is with you, little one, then I am right to show you this."

"I've seen this," I said, gazing down heartstruck at what had been done. "I've seen this too long, too much, too often."

"No," he said. "*This* you have not yet seen."

And we were in the midst of many wings.

They were everywhere, the beings whose brightness our poor words name *angel*. But *angel* has a meaning that runs

231

deeper than the tinseled image of white robe, silver harp, gold halo, sword of flame.

"Messengers," he said, as we hovered in the tainted air. "That has always been our calling, our purpose, our very name. Look."

I did, and my eyes were filled with their presence. I could not let the fires of sorrow burn me barren inside without using words to contain them, trying to salve them into a shape my soul could encompass. So too my sight gave shape to things beyond the power of rational sight to see.

"Each has a purpose," the angel said, speaking of the multitude of his fellows swarming the air. "Each serves as he is told to serve, doing what he must."

"Death angels," I murmured. "So many . . ." My voice broke, seeing them ascending and descending through the core of fallen stone and twisted steel, their downward flight leaving trails of tears to mark their pathway, their hands filled with the gathered brilliance of hundreds of abruptly exiled lights as they rose up again. "I thought there was only one."

"Little one, you must come to understand: There is no death angel," my guide said. "Death *is;* an ending, not an angel. Those are the messengers of memory, sent to remind the soul that it still lives; only the body's time is finished."

More of the angels stood amid the rubble, holding out their arms to cradle the mortal hearts of heroes, giving strength while their fellow messengers drew swords and without mercy fought back the hissing spirits of despair. The ruins glowed like embers fast dying into ash, though not without the breath of an angel to blow them into light as the rescuers discovered, here or there, a life still able to be saved, a heart still beating, hope.

I looked to my messenger, my guide. "Where are the ones we need?" I asked him. "Where are the angels of vengeance?"

"They will come," he said. "But they are not the ones you need; simply the ones you desire. They are nearer than you think, waiting, coiled beneath the silver of a million mirrors, easily freed." And in his eyes I saw those mirrors shattering, shards of vengeance tearing apart an already bleeding world.

"Not vengeance, then, but justice," I said. "Where are they, those messengers?"

He lifted his gaze to stare beyond the crystal blue of sky. "They too will come," he said. "When it is time. For now, we are the ones given charge to watch over you. We have our jobs to do, each to each, and I have lingered too long, avoiding mine." And he sobbed, the grief of angels surpassing the grief of men because to him the dead were not a tally of numbers; because he dwelled where knowledge dwells, and he had no choice but to know each face, each life, each heart now lying still among the embers. His mouth was filled with all the acrid terror of their last moments, his ears with the names they had cried out before they died, his eyes with the image of their faces from the moment a mother had first seen them come squalling into the world until the moment it had all been snatched away.

"Why?" I asked. "What is your job? Have you too been sent here to gather up the dead?"

"No," he said, now holding me to his body with a fierce, protective strength. "Nothing as easy as that." He spread his wings to catch a different angle on the air and we were falling earthward again.

The force of our descent took the breath from my body, made my head spin, my sight go dark. I lost all sense of awareness, but I welcomed that, though I'd never been one to think of oblivion as a blessing. Not until now.

When I opened my eyes once more, I was back in the little coffee shop, alone. The mug between my hands was empty.

The waitress came by and noticed this. She brought me a refill without being asked. I blinked and shrugged and fidgeted in my seat, trying to cast off the nagging itch insisting that I was *supposed* to have an overly active imagination, that it wasn't my fault if it sometimes ran (or flew) away with me, that none of this was any reflection on my sanity. We dream. For better or for worse, we dream.

I was letting the sugar cascade into my cup when I saw him. He was there, an image shimmering on the surface of that small, dark pool. A smell that had no kinship whatsoever to coffee rose from the cup and hit me sharply between the eyes, the too-clean stab of bleach, of disinfectant, of hospital rooms.

I saw him standing by a woman's bedside while she wept, hugging her newborn baby to her breast. His lips brushed lightly past her ear as he whispered, "All is well. There is only darkness now because an outcast fool has tried to place himself between you and the light. But the darkness blows away like dust, the light endures. Weep to ease your heart, not to fill it. Find blessing. Know joy."

He held his wing out above their heads, and now there was nothing in the shadows that it cast but a homely fire's warmth, springtime dawns, summer roses, the gift of music, of poetry, fresh bread and a friend's shared laughter, mountains and dance and mankind leaping up to meet the stars. Life.

And while these shadows held them tight, he leaned in low to whisper in the infant's ear, "Be strong. Be always loved and loving. Be not afraid."

I saw him in a thousand places then, a thousand times a thousand, and more. I saw the terror-blinded eyes of children open to fresh sight as he whispered those same words for them alone to hear, not only in New York but in other places, other times, in Belfast and Jerusalem, Damascus and Chernobyl, in the instant before the bullet struck or the bomb exploded or the gas hissed into the waiting chamber. Always he was there for them, always with those words to banish fear, though his brother angels might be standing at his back all the while, waiting to bring the final message. Always they waited for him to finish before they took up their own task, messengers of memory to the soul.

"You see now?" he said. He was seated beside me, in the same place as before. The waitress brought him a fresh mug of coffee and gave me the green and white bill to pay for us both. "It was like this at Troy, too, lost Ilion, when death filled the streets, when the towers fell in flames. The children didn't understand. How could they? Grown men and women barely did. It didn't matter whether or not they believed in angels. *Angel* is only a word. There are some things, little one, that overthrow the despot's rule of words." He took a sip of coffee. "I take their terror from them, make them free. I steal all terror's power. I carry it away and leave them cleansed to greet whatever comes to them—death or life—unafraid."

And you call this task a burden? I wanted to ask. *To give hope, a burden?* But all my words had flown. They fluttered away, just out of reach, burnt pages on the updraft from a fire.

He finished his coffee and stood up from the counter, looking down at me, at the city, at a world that held too many demons and not enough angels. He had no need for any words from me: He knew. "A burden because I am only one," he said. "And I must reach them all."

He was gone.

I paid the bill and left the tip and went home to my apartment through streets where sirens wailed, where dust roiled down deserted roads, where the sound of engines overhead now made people dart fearful glances skyward. As I walked on, I met a father holding his little daughter by the hand. His eyes were filled with all the rage in his heart—not that this thing had happened, but at his helplessness, that he felt his hands were no longer strong enough to hold back the darkness from his precious child.

I saw her look to him, and in her eyes there were only questions: *Why are you so angry? What's wrong? What's happened? Why?*

How could he answer? How could I? And yet . . . and yet . . . I think I meant to try.

I turned where I stood, to call them back or just to watch them walk away—I no longer know which it was—but they were gone. A curtain of ash had fallen between us, a twilight gritty gray that fell and fell and seemed as though it never would stop falling, a cataract of dust. *This can't be!* I protested silently. *We're miles away from the place, and there's nothing left to fall!* but still the ashes tumbled down like rain.

I threw my arm across my eyes, covered my mouth and curled myself up small. The south wind blew, sweeping the dust around me. It filled my eyes, damming up my tears; my ears, keeping out the voice of angels; my throat, choking back every cry, every prayer.

And then it was over, done. I lowered my arm, opened my eyes, stood up in the stillness and saw that I stood among trees that grew out of the dunes of dust. My tears returned, and I caught them in my cupped hands, let them fall in a stream through my fingers, turning dust to clay.

I knelt and gave the clay the body of a child.

I marked her forehead with the proper signs. I watched as she took life from desolate earth and ash-laden air. I set her on her feet and whispered in her ear the angel's words of comfort before I sent her on her way. Let her find the other children, give them the words like gifts, save them from the darkness.

Then I let my tears stream down again and made another. *I am only one,* he'd said, my vanished angel. I knelt in ashes and made children into whose ears I whispered his words of hope, of strength, of light. I worked until my arms ached and my hands were raw and my voice was a broken thing, yet even as I rasped the angel's words into those countless shells, I felt his grief. This, even this would not be enough. The carrion birds would come in the angels' wake. They would swoop down to snatch away the bones, to call out in the marketplace that they had skulls for sale, to grow fat from living on the splintered relics of the dead.

"Don't be afraid." An arm embraced me, a breath stirred in my ear: "They'll only *try* to blind us, turning our sorrows into souvenirs. They won't succeed. We'll keep the true memories. If we don't guard the freedom of the living, we'll never keep faith with the dead."

I looked up, ready to welcome back an angel. Instead I only saw the face of another human being like myself. He stood and helped me to my feet. I only dropped his hand to dry my eyes with my fingertips.

"Whoa, what are you trying to do there?" he asked. "If you wanted to clean yourself up, you didn't quite do the job. In fact, you kind of smeared your face up pretty bad. Wait, I'll get it." He smiled and wiped my cheeks gently with his handkerchief.

"Yeah, that's better," he said. "You know, you look like I feel. Come on; I'll buy you a cup of coffee."

We walked into the daylight, he and I. We talked about where we had been when it all happened, words turning fears into words, shadows into shapes that we could see and grasp and fight and conquer. We spoke with pride of heroes. We stood together, fragile human flesh and blood and bone, ready to face down dragons. We laughed, because our hearts told us how deeply demons feared the sound.

And all around us the darkness blew away like dust, ashes scattered on the wings of angels.

How to Make Unicorn Pie

I live in the town of Bowman's Ridge, Vermont, founded 1746, the same year if not the same universe as Princeton University. But where Princeton has employed the intervening centuries to pour forth a bounteous-if-bombastic stream of English majors, Bowman's Ridge has employed the same time to produce people who are actually, well, employable.

Bowman's Ridge is populated exclusively by three major ethnic groups, the two most numerous of which are Natives and Transients. I've lived here for twenty-five years, in one of the smaller authentic Colonial Era houses on Main Street. It has white clapboard siding, conservatively painted dark green shutters, the original eighteenth-century well, a floral clock, a flourishing herb garden, a rockery, and a paid-up mortgage. Local tradition claims that Ethan Allen once threw up here.

I'm still just a Transient. That's how the Natives would have it, anyway. On the other hand, at least I'm a Transient that they can trust, or perhaps the word I want is *tolerate*. Just as long as I don't bring up the unfortunate subject of how I earn my living, everything is roses.

You see, (and here I ought to turn my face aside and drop my voice to the requisite hoarse whisper reserved for all such disgraceful confessions) I . . . write.

UNCLEAN! UNCLEAN!

Someone get a firm hold on the carriage horses lest they stampede and make sure that no pregnant women cross my path. I wouldn't like to be held responsible for the consequences.

No, I am not taking on unnecessarily. I've seen the looks I get on the street and in the stores. I've heard the whispers: "There goes Babs Barclay. She *writes*." (Uttered in the same deliciously scandalized tone once applied to prim old maids with a secret addiction to overdosing on Lydia Pinkham's elixir, cooking sherry, vanilla extract, and hair tonic.)

To the good folk of Bowman's Ridge, having a writer in their midst is rather like having a toothless, declawed cat in the chicken coop. The beastie may look harmless, logic may insist that in its present state *sans* fang and talon it is by *fiat* harmless, but the biddies still huddle together, clucking nervously, because . . . *You never know.*

I know what they are afraid of. It's the same fear that's always plagued small towns condemned to harbor the Pen Pushers from Planet Verbiage. It's the ultimate terror, which I first saw voiced by a secondary character in one of the *Anne of Green Gables* books when the heroine began to garner some small success as an author: *What if she puts us in one of her stories?* Not a direct quote, but it'll do.

Forget what you think you know about fame. Not everyone wants his or her allotted fifteen minutes' worth. The people of Bowman's Ridge want it even less than the people of Avonlea, or Peyton Place, or any other small town which had the poor judgment to allow writers to burrow into the wainscotting and nest for the winter. They are simple, honest, hardworking folk, who will take a simple, honest tire iron to your head if you so much as hint that you're going to make the outside world aware of their existence. (I think that the surplus of deferred fame-bites gets funneled into an off-

240

shore account where Donald Trump's ego, Michael Jackson's manhood, and Madonna's uterus spend much too much time making withdrawals. I could be wrong.)

It doesn't do me a lick of good to explain to my friends and neighbors that their fears are for nought. I write romances. *Historical* romances. Books with titles like *Druid's Desire* and *Millard Filmore, My Love.* The only way I'd write about anyone from Bowman's Ridge is if they were romantic, famous, and dead. Why, they could no more get into one of my books than a taxman into heaven, a linebacker into leotards, or a small, sharp sliver of unicorn horn into a nice big slice of Greta Marie Bowman's apple pie.

"Ow!"

It was a snoozy afternoon in mid-November and I was seated at the counter in the coffee shop when it happened. The coffee shop in Bowman's Ridge is the nexus for all manner of social interaction, from personal to political. I'm afraid my Transient heart doesn't get all revved up over the Planning and Zoning Commission's latest bureaucratic brouhahaha or the Women's Club's plans for yet another authentic Colonial weekend to honor the memory of our own Captain James Resurrection Bowman (1717–1778). I go there because the coffee is good but the apple pie is downright fabulous.

Or so I thought, until I found the figurative needle in the Northern Spies.

Carefully I put three fingers into my mouth and drew out the thing that had stung me, tongue and palate. I pulled it between my lips to clean off any adhering fragments of cooked apple and flaky crust. I have no idea why I went to the trouble. Would it make any difference to my throbbing mouth if I got the barb clean before seeing what it was?

I might as well have saved myself the effort and simply spit it out. Even clean and wiped dry on a paper napkin, it was nothing I could put a name to. About as long as the first joint of my little finger and one-quarter as wide, it caught the light from the coffee shop overheads and shimmered like the inside of an abalone shell.

"Something wrong, dear?" Muriel's shadow fell over the object of my attention.

Muriel and her husband Hal own and run the Bowman's Ridge coffee shop. I like to think that they belong to some mystic fraternal order of interior decorators—the Harmonic Knights of the Cosmic Balance, Fabric Swatch and Chowder Society—for the way they keep the place charming without being cloying. Anyone who's dallied in small town Vermont knows how easy it is for an eatery to sink into the La Brea Cute Pits. Either the management heaps on the *prêt-à-porter* antiques, or wallows in frills and dimity, or worst of all, beats it with the Quaint stick until it catches a case of Terminal Rusticity from the knotty-pine paneling and dies.

Hal and Muriel just serve good food, never patch the vinyl counter stools with duct tape, adorn the place suitably for holidays, and periodically change the basic decor according to the grand, universal imperative of We Felt Like It. Oh! And they never shop at *Everything Guernseys*, thanks be to God, Jesus, Ben and Jerry.

Muriel has never treated me like a Transient and she sees to it that all the waitresses know how I take my coffee (black, two sugars) without my having to tell them every time. She even awarded me the supreme accolade, posting a Happy Birthday, Babs message on the whiteboard where they display the daily Specials. This privilege is as good as telling the world that I might not be a Bowman's Ridge Native, but I was one of the Transients they could take out of the attic on visiting days to show the neighbors. I like Muriel a lot.

So of course I lied to her. "Nuh-uh," I said, hastily clapping my hand over the extracted sliver. "Nothing's wrong, not a thing, great pie."

Muriel gave me a searching look, but all she said was, "Yes, Greta Marie said she's gotten some superior apples this season." Then one of the waitresses came up to tell her she was wanted in the kitchen and she was gone.

Left to myself once more, I uncovered the sliver and picked it up delicately between thumb and forefinger. It twinkled with all the hues of prism-shattered light, but it was made of no substance I could name. The man on the stool next to me cast a curious glance at it, but promptly went back to reading his newspaper. People in this town don't pry. Why bother, when every scrap of local news scoots around faster than a ferret on amphetamines? Sooner or later, everyone knows everything about everyone else.

Well, I thought, *it's very attractive whatever it is. I'll bring it home: maybe Rachel can make something out of it.* Rachel is my teenaged daughter. She has discovered the Meaning of Life, which is to make jewelry out of any object you find lying around the house, yard, or municipal dump, and pierce another part of your body to hang it from. At least this object was pretty, and I always say that a good soak in Clorox will clean anything, up to and including Original Sin.

I was so fascinated by the way the light played off my little bit of found art that I didn't notice Muriel's return until I heard her say, "Uh-huh. Thought so."

Caught in the act, I tried to cover up my sorry attempt at willful misdirection by dropping the sliver onto the open pages of the magazine I'd brought into the coffee shop with me and slamming the glossy pages shut on it. Slapping my hand over the bare-chested male model on the cover, I gave

Muriel a sickly smile. "Dropped a contact," I said. "I don't want it to fall on the floor."

No dice. You can't fake out a woman who can tell good tuna salad from bad at fifty paces. "Honey, who are you trying to protect?" she said. "Greta Marie? You don't even know her."

That was true. Greta Marie Bowman belonged to the third and smallest segment of Bowman's Ridge society: Eccentrics. As my dear mother would say, an eccentric is what you call a lunatic who's got money. Mom was speaking from the jaded, materialistic perspective of big city life, however. In places like Bowman's Ridge, we realize that money doesn't excuse abnormal behavior. You don't have to be rich and crazy to be classed as an eccentric; you can be poor and crazy, so long as you're also the scion of one of the town's oldest families. Or in Greta Marie Bowman's case, the scionette.

Yes, she was the descendant of *that* Bowman. And yes, she was living in what the Victorians referred to as genteel poverty. Whatever mite of income she derived from her ancestors' surviving investments needs must be eked out by the sale of apple pies to the coffee shop. This was one of those cold, hard facts that everyone knew and no one mentioned. A Mafia don brought up to follow the steel-jacketed code of silence, *omerta,* is a harebrained blabbermouth next to a resident of Bowman's Ridge who's got something *not* to say.

"Look, it's nothing," I said. "I may not know her, but I certainly don't want to get her in—"

"Trouble?" Muriel finished for me. She sighed. "Babs, you want to know the meaning of the word? That thing you just found in your pie, what do you think would've happened if someone else had found it?"

"Not much. Everyone around here knows Greta Marie and no one would say anything that would—"

"Think that goes for the Summer People?"

Na-na-na-naaaaah. Cue the sinister chords on the pipe organ. The only critters lower on the Bowman's Ridge food chain than Transients are Summer People. I don't know why the Natives despise them so. They are the single best thing to happen to the local economy since maple-leaf-shaped anything. They swarm up here every June, July and August, with a recurring infection come leaf-peeping time, and pay top dollar to stay in spare rooms that would otherwise be mold sanctuaries. They attend church bazaars and rummage sales, fighting to the death to buy the nameless tin and wicker doohickeys that the Natives clean out of Aunt Hattie's attic. (Aunt Hattie could never tell what the hell that bug-ugly *objet d'*awful was either.) And of course if you've got any piece of house-trash, no matter how old, no matter how dilapidated, all you have to do is stencil a pig or a sunflower or a black-and-white cow on it and it's outahere, courtesy of the Summer People.

On the other hand, serve them a slice of pie that's packing a concealed shiv and they'll bring the Board of Health down on your head faster than you can sell them a busted butter churn.

"I see what you mean, " I said. "But the season's over, the Summer People are all gone, and—"

"Skiers," Muriel reminded me. "Snowmobilers."

"Oh." I'd forgotten that, like weasels, when winter came the Summer People changed their coats and returned to our little town in swarms.

"It really would be a kindness to tell her." Muriel patted my hand in a motherly way. "Won't you please?"

"Ummmm. Why don't you?"

"Oh, I couldn't!" She laid her hands to her bosom. "She'd just simply fold up and die if I did. She doesn't take criticism too well, poor child." Only Muriel would refer to a spinster pushing fifty-five as *poor child*, bless her. "She'd stop baking pies for us altogether. She needs the money, though she'd never admit it. What would become of her then? It'd be plain awful."

In my heart I agreed with Muriel, though more out of my love for the pies than any concern for the pie-maker's welfare. "But if she doesn't take criticism well, how could I say—?" I began.

Muriel pish-tushed me like a champion. "But it's different if it comes from you, Babs."

I didn't need to ask why. Wasn't it obvious? I was a Transient. My cautionary words concerning unidentified opalescent objects in the pastry wouldn't shame Greta Marie the way a Native's would. In fact, if I were to go to Greta Marie's place and accuse her of using the fat of unborn goats for pie-crust shortening, she could live it down.

So I went.

Greta Marie lived out on the Old Toll Road. This was a stretch of highway so narrow, frost-heaved and godforsaken that the fact that someone had once collected real American money from travellers to allow them the privilege of breaking their axles in the ruts and potholes was a testimony to Yankee ingenuity, to say nothing of Yankee gall. There was hardly enough room for two cars to pass, unless one climbed up onto the shoulder at a forty-five degree angle, bumping over the gnarled roots of pine trees flanking the way. Luckily, the Old Toll Road had gone from being a throughway leading to Montpelier to a dead end leading to nowhere when the bridge over Bowman's Gorge collapsed in 1957. The town decided it would be a waste of money to rebuild it, since by then everyone took the State highway anyway, and that pretty much put an end to the two-way traffic problem.

That is, it did unless you happened to be heading *up* the road at the same time that Greta Marie Bowman was headed *down* it. She drove an old Rambler the color of mud with a crumpled fender and enough dings in the sides to make it look like the only car on the road suffering from cellulite. Wonderful to relate, she could actually get that bundle of battered tin up to considerable speeds, even over the humps and hollows of the Old Toll Road.

Wonderful to relate if you're safely out of the way, terrifying to tell if you're driving the car that's right in her path. Like a deer caught in the headlights, I spied the glitter of Greta Marie's Coke-bottle glasses and I froze. My hands spasmed tight to the steering wheel, my foot refused to move from the accelerator, and the only thing I could think was: *Dear Lord, if I die, what the hell body part will Rachel pierce to commemorate the funeral?*

I felt like a complete idiot when Greta Marie brought her vehicle to a ladylike stop with room to spare and nary the smallest squeal of brakes to be heard. She peered over the steering wheel like a marmot testing the first sniff of spring air, then dropped from sight behind the dashboard.

One hefty car door swung wide and she was walking towards me, all smiles. I lowered the window to greet her and was nearly bowled into the next county by her preferred scent, Eau de Mothballs, but in the name of preserving the honor of all Transients, I managed to dig up a smile of my own and paste it to my face.

"You're that writer-person!" was how Greta Marie Bowman chose to say hello.

"Um, yes, I am."

"Oh, I knew you'd come! Really I did!" She clapped her hands together with girlish glee.

"You did?" This was news to me. I wasn't sure whether it

was good news. In her oversized, out-at-elbows black cardigan, with her steel gray hair anchored to the top of her head with at least three pairs of knitting needles, Greta Marie Bowman put me in mind of a large, amiable spider.

"My gracious, and when I think that we almost missed each other entirely—!" She spoke in the chirpy, lockjawed accents of a young Katharine Hepburn. "Now you just follow me up to the house and we'll talk."

And then, as God is my witness, she gave me a roguish wink, went back to her car, and backed up *at speed* all the way to the ancestral Bowman property, which lay a good quarter mile or more up the Old Toll Road.

From what I had gathered in my quarter century of Bowman's Ridge residence, the Bowmans had always been farmers, but they made a better living selling off the land than tilling it. The hard soil of their property let a diligent man grow him a bumper crop of rocks, though only if he was willing to work for it.

The last male Bowman to inhabit the place had been Greta Marie's grandfather, dead lo these many years. By the time he was under his native soil, he'd sold most of it. The only exceptions were the ancestral apple orchard, a swampy meadow beyond that, and the homestead plot. This latter supported a meager vegetable garden, a dilapidated chicken coop and poultry yard, the half of the old barn that was still standing, and the Bowman house proper. All of these flashed before my eyes as Greta Marie hauled me out of my car and into the front parlor where she assaulted me with tea.

"Now the important family papers are mostly safe in the attic," she said, pouring out some Oolong strong enough to strip paint from metal. "I can let you have those today, but the best sources are Caroline Elspeth's notebooks, and they're over in Brattleboro at Cousin Victoria's house. She said she was going to do something with them, but everyone knows how far that got. Vicky never finished anything in her entire life except her husbands."

I took a sip of tea, set the cup aside, and stammered, "I—I beg your pardon?"

Greta Marie slapped a wrinkled hand over her mouth and, as God is my witness, tittered like a chipmunk. "Oh mercy, there I go again. I forgot: You're not from around here. You wouldn't know about Vicky." And with that, she proceeded to bring me up to speed on Cousin Victoria Bowman Randall Smith Chasen, her antecedents and her heirs. It was a lengthy recitation that left me knowing more about the Bowman family and any related Native families—which is to say everyone in town—than I'd ever wanted or needed to know.

When she was done, I gazed down at my now-frigid cuppa and murmured, "That was . . . very interesting, Miss Bowman, but I don't see—"

"—how you can use all that for your book? Well, of course you can't use all of it," Greta Marie reassured me. "After all, I wouldn't be very bright if I gave away *everything*. I simply must reserve some of it for my own book as well. I'm sure you won't begrudge me that much? Mine won't be nearly as fascinating as yours, but then you've had so much more experience, you have connections, and as Daddy always used to say, when you've got connections, who needs talent?" Another giggle, this one ending in a snort. "All I want to write about is the branch of the family that settled near Brattleboro, old Zerusha Bowman's boys and that Martin woman—you know, she swore she came from Boston, but everyone here just knew she was from *New York*." Pronounced *Sodom*.

It was then that the diaphanous phantom of Understanding tiptoed up and tapped me gently on the cranium with an iron mallet. To this day I couldn't tell you whether my subsequent spate of blather was more of an apology for *not* having come to use the generations of Bowmans past as raw material for my next book, or an explanation for why I *had* come.

"Oh," said Greta Marie, regarding the shining sliver I held out to her in my cupped hand. "I see." If she were at all disappointed, she bore it well and swallowed it whole. "That certainly was careless of me. Thank you so much for bringing it to my attention." She stood up from behind the tea things, which I assumed was my cue to scurry back into the Transient woodwork, duty done.

As it happened, I was wrong. No sooner had I risen to my feet, stammering some social pleasantry about having to go home now, I'd left the children on the stove, but Greta Marie raised one briary brow and inquired, "Then you'd prefer to come back another time to see the unicorns?"

Three minutes later, to the tick, I was outside the Bowman house with Greta Marie, leaning my elbows on the top of a drunken split-rail fence that marked the boundaries of the meadow. And there, prancing and pawing the spongy ground and bounding hither and yon in matchless beauty at the slightest provocation, were the unicorns. There were three of them, all a luminous white so pure as to be almost ice-blue, with flossy manes the color of smoke glimpsed by moonlight. Even without the time-honored single horn in the middle of the forehead, it would be impossible to confuse these entrancing beasts with the most thistledown-footed thoroughbred.

Which was a good thing, because . . .

"Their *horns*," I gasped. "Where are their *horns?*" I leaned farther over the fence, staring at the three dancing shapes in the meadow. "All they've got are these . . . *lumps.*"

"Lumps?" Greta Marie shaded her eyes, as if that gesture

could hope to counteract a truly heroic case of myopia. She sighed. "Oh dear. It's happened again. Wait here." She left me teetering on the gateway to Wonderland as she trudged off to a nearby toolshed, to return with a small, bright hacksaw in hand. Setting two fingers to her lips, she blew a piercing whistle.

The unicorns heard and the effect was galvanic. They paused in their frolic, heads up, ears pricked forward, a pose of frozen loveliness so exquisite that it hurt my heart to see it. Then they broke from a standstill to a gallop, three clouds of lightning racing across the meadow. For an instant I was afraid that they meant to charge right through the fence— God knows, it didn't look strong enough to halt a stampede of bunny rabbits—but I needn't have worried. Dainty cloven hooves planted themselves hard and decidedly in the earth just a handspan from the fence, bright garnet eyes twinkling with amusement. I could have sworn that the critters were laughing at me.

Just so I wouldn't make that mistake in future, the largest of the three curled his lips back from a double row of nastily pointed teeth and *did* laugh at me. It was a sound birthed at the junction of a horse's whinny, a stag's belled challenge, and a diva's scorn. He did it loudly and at length, giving me more than enough time to study him.

His eyes were, as I've mentioned, a deep, gem-like crimson, very large, highly intelligent, and possessed of an almost human capacity for malice. And yes, there in the place where tradition dictates the horn must be, there sprouted a pearly lump. Small as it was, I could see that it wasn't to grow into the sleek pool-cue object some folks fancied, nor was it the twisty narwhal tusk others preferred their unicorns to sport. It was multi-sided, multi-edged, and the edges thereof fuzzy with the added menace of minute, vicious serrations, almost barbs. At full growth it would be deadly, and not an easy death either. Just looking at it made my skin go cold.

The unicorn cocked his head at me as if to say, *Seen enough, rube? Take a picture; it lasts longer.* Then he swung his muzzle away to plant a long, snuffly kiss on Greta Marie's withered jowl.

"There's a good boy, there's a fine fellow." Greta Marie stroked the slab of silky white cheek. "Now just hold still, this won't hurt a bit." Placing one hand on the unicorn's nose, she used the other to ply the hacksaw. The steel blade bit into the base of the resurgent horn, which made a frightful screeching as it was severed. The unicorn submitted to the operation with that air of gallant indifference popularized by the better class of 18th century highwaymen about to swing at Tyburn Tree. Greta Marie worked quickly. There was a dull plop as the horn-nub hit the dirt.

"There," said Greta Marie. She fluffed up a little fur to cover the newly raw spot on the unicorn's forehead and announced, "Next!"

I watched with a combination of fascination and revulsion as she proceeded to treat the two remaining miracles as if they were parlor cats getting their claws clipped. When the third shining stub fell to earth, she sighed with satisfaction, then shouted, "Shoo!" Spooked like a flock of buff Orpingtons, the unicorns took off for the far end of the meadow, the place where boggy grassland melted into a small patch of wildwood. They flickered under the shadows of the leafless branches, then turned to fog and were gone from sight.

"Well, we won't be seeing any more of them today," Greta Marie declared, stooping to gather the fallen nubbins. Still dumbfounded, I followed her back into the house where I watched her set the horn-nubs on a butcher's block cutting board and whack them to flinders with a cleaver. Using the flat of the blade, she scraped the resulting pile of iridescent toothpicks into an old stoneware crock marked *Garlic*.

"You . . . *save* them?" I asked. She gave me a look that as good as accused me of Wastefulness, chief among the Seven Deadly Sins of Transients.

"I *use* them," she replied.

"Er, how?" Visions of an alchemist's lab hidden in the old Bowman root cellar taunted me. I pictured Greta Marie huddled over her bubbling alembics, a stuffed corkindrill suspended above her head while she added a pinch of unicorn's horn to her latest batch of hellbroth.

"Why, I simply—Never mind, it would be easier to show you. Do you have a minute to spare? Several?" And with that she opened a cabinet and donned not the wizard's pointed hat, but the cook's muslin apron. Still without waiting for my yea or nay, she favored me with the privilege of witnessing the process by which Greta Marie Bowman took plain apples, sugar, spice, and pastry, and confected them into the food of the gods.

When at last she dropped the top crust into place over the mounded fruit filling and fluted the edges, she turned to me and commanded, "Watch." From the *Garlic* cannister she took one splinter of unicorn's horn and with five deft jabs opened steam slits in the piecrust. "There. *That's* how I use them."

She cleaned off the sliver and dropped it into a jelly jar on the windowsill above her sink before popping the pie into the oven. "You can get about three perfect pies out of each one," she informed me. "After that they crumble into dust—the horns, not the pies. But the dust makes a wonderful scouring powder—gets out every stain you can think of and a few you can't—so I don't feel too bad about getting so little use out of them. And the critters are always growing new ones."

She removed her apron and folded it over the back of a kitchen chair. "I can't imagine where my mind was when I let that splinter you found slip into the pie. Oh wait, yes I can. That must've been the day I was in such a terrible hurry, and it seemed like every time I turned around, the phone was ringing itself off the hook. No wonder I got all muddled, between trying to get the Congregational Church bazaar organized and all that baking and *baking*—! Ed Franklin had come by that week to bring me three extra bushels of Cortlands— he's had a bumper crop this year. I know he meant it to be kind, but I had my own apples to use and I knew that if I didn't get his Cortlands baked up they were going to go bad on me. Not that it matters any more—I could use rotten apples in my pies and the horn would turn them to nectar, just nectar—but old habits do die hard. My mother raised me to bake a decent apple pie and I can't do any less." She finally paused for breath, plucked the kettle from the stove, and beamed at me. "More tea?"

I left her house about an hour later, burdened with the apple pie, the Bowman family papers, the promise to at least *try* to write *Jim Bowman's Woman,* and a vow of silence: Under no circumstances was I to tell a single, living soul about the presence of the unicorns on the Bowman property. As Greta Marie herself told me, the only reason she went to all the trouble of sawing off the creatures' telltale horns was so that unexpected callers who caught sight of them would assume they were only horses.

"But if you want to keep them a secret, why did you show them to me?" I'd asked.

"Oh, you're different," Greta Marie reassured me. "It doesn't matter if *you* know about them."

Right. *Sic semper Transientis,* or however you'd say *Transients Don't Count* in Latin.

I went back to the coffee shop to make my Mission Accomplished report to Muriel. I was promptly rewarded with a cup of coffee, a glazed donut, and the question: "So which one of the unicorns is your favorite?"

"*Nurk?*" I replied, mouth stuffed with a chunk of donut that bid fair to wedge itself in my throat if I let shock get the better of me. I chewed vigorously, swallowed, then leaned across the counter like a comic strip anarchist to whisper, "You *know?*"

Muriel chuckled. "Bless your heart, Babs, *everyone* knows. Only no one says anything. You know, I can't say we were at all surprised when the first one showed up, oh, maybe ten, twelve years ago. It was the middle of winter, long about Christmas time, when we have the Pinecone Handcrafts Fair at the firehouse; *you* know. Greta Marie's car was in the shop so Sally Norton and her boy Ron offered to drive up the Old Toll Road to fetch Greta Marie there and back. They pulled up into her yard and that's when they saw her and it. She'd already sawed the creature's horn clean off, but even so, even in the nighttime with no more light to see by than the spill off that old kerosene lantern she leaves burning near the gatepost, there was no way a sighted person could ever believe that was a horse! Of course Sally and Ron never said *that* to Greta Marie."

"Of course not," I mumbled.

"And if you ask me, it was that natural when the other two joined the first one. Frankly I'm kind of puzzled that there aren't *more* than three haunting the Bowman place. Maybe three unicorns are all that's left in this part of the state, and it's no wonder they've all come to roost with Greta Marie."

"It is?"

"Of course it is! Lord love you, Babs, don't tell me that an educated city woman like you doesn't know what it takes to attract a unicorn?"

City woman? Twenty-five years ago, maybe. Which translates into Bowman's Ridge-ese as *yesterday*.

And I *did* know what it takes to attract a unicorn.

"Oh, come on, Muriel!" I protested. "Don't you stand there and try to tell me that Greta Marie is the one and only virgin in this whole town!"

Muriel's eyes twinkled. "All right, I won't. Wouldn't be true, anyhow. But how long does your average virgin last, these days? Sixteen, seventeen years at most, and that's like an eyeblink of time to a unicorn. They're immortal, you know," she confided. "I may belong to a different generation, but I'm not blind or stupid. We all know what goes on with our young people, especially since the government's been making them go to that regional high school at Miller's Falls." Pronounced *Sodom* again, and no matter that the government redistricting edict was handed down in 1953, when even Vegas was wholesome.

"You see," Muriel went on, "it's not just that Greta Marie's a virgin, it's that she's so damn *good* at it. Pardon my French."

"So everyone knows and no one objects?" I asked.

"Why should they? She's a respectable member of this town and if she wants to raise mythical beasts on her own property that's her own business . . . as long as she keeps them under proper control at all times and they pose no threat to the community."

"That's comforting to know," I said with a merry chuckle that didn't become me at all. (The glazed donut had gone straight to my brain and the sugar rush convinced me I could try my hand at wit.) "You see, I found this darling little dragon's egg on my lawn last Easter and I was worried that if I hatched it, people would talk."

Muriel stared at me blankly for the count of three, then

said, "You writers," and took off as if the kitchen had caught fire.

I was left alone at the counter, Dorothy Parker *manqué,* with nothing to hide my blushes save my coffee cup and my copy of *With Pen and Passion.* The cup being empty, I chose to go to ground behind the cover of the very magazine between whose pages I had dropped the original sliver of unicorn horn.

This might be the best place to mention that *With Pen and Passion* is one of the many fine periodicals to which I subscribe as part of my career as a romance writer. *WiPP,* as we in the trade call it, is a slick monthly whose chief allure is the book review column. That is to say, whose chief allure *had been* the book review column.

As long as we're opening narrative parentheses, let the worst now be revealed: His name was Wellcome Fisher and he was my own damned fault.

I'd met him at a romance writers' convention in New York City about ten years ago. He was an aspiring author, scion of a proud old New England family, almost attractive in a tweedier-than-thou kind of way, well-bred, well-read, pumped full of the Wisdom of the Ancients at the ivy-covered tit of Mother Princeton, rarin' to put pen to word processor and make his genius known to the fortunate masses. There was just one little thing standing in the way of his brilliant career: He couldn't write for toffee.

Of course I didn't know this from the start. He seemed like such a nice man. Many successful romance writers *are* male, you know. They all write under female pseudonyms unless they're Fabio or churning out mainstream lunchblowers like *The Bridges of Madison County.* He introduced himself, said how much he admired my work, and asked me if he could buy me a drink.

He bought me several. It was all strictly professional. We had a lovely, long chat about the importance of research in writing historical romance. He told me that he was always extremely punctilious about his research, and he didn't understand why the one book he had managed to sell was doing so poorly.

"I don't merely say 'Gwendolyn stood before her mirror wearing a velvet gown'," he told me. "I put in *details*." And he gave me an autographed copy of *Lady Gwendolyn's Gallant* so that I could see for myself.

I did, once I got it home. Wellcome had done his research, all right. His book gave me a painfully thorough education about the provenance of food, clothing, furniture, music, and transportation in Regency England. It told me who ate what and how much of it, who slept where and for how long, and who used which finger to excavate whose nostril. In fact, it told me everything except an entertaining story.

We had exchanged telephone numbers, so when the inevitable happened and he called to ask my opinion of his work, I found myself in a bit of a quandary. I don't like to lie, I just do it for a living. However, neither do I like to tell someone that his book, his effort, his hardbound baby, stinks like a gopher's armpit. For one thing, it's cruel. For another, it's dangerous. Alas for the world, we now no longer know which eager young writer will take constructive criticism as an invitation to assassination.

So I hedged. I evaded all direct questions about the book itself. I chattered and gabbled and blithered about a plethora of other subjects in an attempt to divert Wellcome Fisher from the original aim of his call.

Unfortunately, one of the subjects on which I blithered was the fact that *WiPP* was looking for a few good book reviewers. Wellcome heard, applied, and the rest was history, much like the *Hindenberg,* the *Titanic,* and the Reagan Years. From the moment he got the job, he announced that he would now devote his fair young life to the aesthetic improvement of the Romance genre. It was a noble aim, in theory.

In practice he appeared to have slapped on a pair of six-shooters and gone out gunning for authors whose work had committed the unpardonable sin of having a better track record than his. (Which is to say, everybody and Cain's dog.) He implemented this game plan by reducing any book he reviewed to a pitiful clutch of *execrables, derivatives, pathetics,* and *don't bothers.*

Any book, including mine. Though we remained on social terms, Wellcome was quick to inform me that he would not let our acquaintanceship sway his critical judgment, and he proved this by a scathing review of *Raleigh, Truly* (Sixth in my ever-popular Elizabethan series.). Furthermore, said he, I ought to be grateful. He was only being honest. I, in turn, informed him that I thought his critical judgment consisted entirely of bloodyminded revenge on writers who, unlike himself, had managed to create something people wanted to read. What was more, he might call it honesty, but anyone with half a glass eye could see that he had more axes to grind than Paul Bunyan. The rest of our interview is clouded in my mind, but I believe that a condescending remark on his part, a bowl of extra-chunky salsa on mine, and a dry cleaning bill for a man's suit figure in it somewhere.

If only the chunks had been larger! Wellcome sustained no permanent injuries from the episode. He wrote on, his pen unblunted and his bile unmitigated, an Alexander Woollcott wannabe in full flower (Deadly nightshade, since you asked.). As a matter of fact, the very issue of *WiPP* into which I had slipped the odd finding from my apple pie likewise contained

Wellcome's review of my latest novel, *Beloved Babylonian*. I'd been waiting to read it until I was sure we were all out of razors.

Why did I let his reviews *do* this to me? Even though I knew he trashed everyone's books equally, even though I knew he wrote solely out of envy and spleen, his words still had the power to wound, or at least to give me the stray twinge in the coccyx. When he wrote romances, he bludgeoned whole chapters to death with a stack of research books as high as it was dry, but when he wrote reviews, he was the undefeated master of a myriad barbed bitcheries. We writers claim to be indifferent to any voice save that of our Muse, but we writers lie.

Living among the stoic folk of Bowman's Ridge for twenty-five years had not helped to harden my skin or toughen my ego. However, it had taught me the simple, rock-ribbed lesson most hardscrabble folk learn early: Get the worst out of the way first. I decided to read Wellcome's review, swallow his abuse, question his masculinity, and curse his name, all so that I'd be able to enjoy the rest of the magazine in peace afterwards.

> Fans of Barbara Barclay's stunning Elizabethan series will rejoice to learn that the justly praised First Lady of the Torrid Quill is now also the Queen of Sizzling Cuneiform.
>
> *Beloved Babylonian* takes you on a breathless, breakneck, no-holds-barred roller coaster ride of ecstasy through the reign of that hottest of historic hunks, Hammurabi himself. No wonder they called it the Fertile Crescent!
>
> If you want to read the best and the brightest that this field has to offer, then I urge you to run, don't

walk, to your local prosemonger and buy your copy now! If these books don't fly off the shelves, they'll set them on fire.

"Babs? Babs, honey?" Muriel shook me gently by the shoulder. "You've just been sitting here for the past ten minutes staring off at nothing. You all right?"

"Uhhhh, sure," I said, and clutching my copy of *WiPP* to my heaving bosom, I fled. I didn't stop fleeing until I was safe at home, up in my office, with the door shut and the cat banished. I didn't like doing the latter. Like many another writer's cat, my gray tabby Gorbaduc has aided my career immeasurably by critiquing all my manuscripts with her asshole. It was the only thing that she and Wellcome Fisher ever had in common.

Until now. I read the other reviews. Each was as glowing and brimming with bouquets as the love-feast he'd laid out for *Beloved Babylonian*. I put down the magazine, unable to move, unable to speak, and more than a little inclined to scream. I'm a flexible sort, but to accept the fact that Wellcome Fisher would ever write an all-rave review column required my mind to acquire the elasticity of a boneless belly dancer. Wellcome's abandonment of acrimony was the apocalyptic harbinger that St. John missed, the Unlisted Number of the Beast. I don't like it when my whole world pitches itself tush over titties without a word of warning. It frightens me.

"What's happened to that man?" I mused aloud. "Is he sick? Is he insane? He couldn't have gone nice on us spontaneously. What could put him in a charitable mood? Oh God. Oh no. Oh please don't let it be that he's actually gone and sold another of his books! Even vanity presses couldn't be that unprincipled. No, it can't be that. It's too horrible to contemplate. He must be up to something else, and it's something big and nasty or he wouldn't be trying to put us off guard with a few kind words."

I re-read his review column and my hands went damp and cold. "Jesus, to counterbalance something like this it's going to have to be something really big, and really, *really* nasty." I shuddered to think what that something might be. Wellcome Fisher had little talent, but like the Spanish Inquisition's primo torturer he was a man of bottomless invention, mostly vindictive. This was not going to be pretty.

Existential fear is one thing, dinner's another. Every writer is allowed only so much time to wallow in the great trough of emotional resonance, with all-day privileges extended solely to those of us foresighted enough to be born male and to have obtained that handy labor-saving device, a wife. This was not the case for me, and while my husband is a dear who "helps with the housework" (Translation: "Where do we keep the butter? Where's the frying pan? Are you sure we have a potato peeler?") he was out of town on another of his ever-recurring business trips. (Alas, the darling of my heart is in Sales, and I am left forlorn. Not all single parents are divorced or unmarried, you know.) A glance at my desk clock told me that time and frozen fish-sticks wait for no man and so, using that wonderful human survival skill called *If I stop thinking about it, it will go away,* I purposely put Wellcome Fisher's aberrant reviews from my mind and hied myself downstairs to the kitchen.

The plates were on the table, Grace was said, and Rachel had just informed me that squash was Politically Incorrect (and gross), when the telephone rang. I scowled—first at the phone, then at Rachel—and announced, "If that's one of your friends, they know very well that it's the dinner hour and I'm going to tell them they can just call back later." This said, I picked up the receiver.

"What is the meaning of this flagrant violation of my Constitutionally guaranteed freedom of expression, you pandering troll?" a voice boomed in my ear.

"Oh. Hello, Wellcome," I replied.

"You can tell *your* friend to call back later, too, Mom!" Rachel called out joyously. (When did any daughter of mine develop such a provoking smirk, I'd like to know?)

"It's all right, dear, it's no friend of mine; it's a critic," I replied, not bothering to cover the mouthpiece.

"Eeeuuuwww." Rachel made a face even more contorted by revulsion than when I'd served her squash. Truly I had raised her well.

I returned my attention to my caller: "All right, Fisher, what are you yapping about?"

"You know damned well that to which I refer, Barbara Barclay, you sorry hack. I call your attention to the December issue of *With Pen and Passion*, my review column in particular."

"I've seen it," I told him. "Really, Wellcome, you were much too kind. Much."

I could almost see the apoplectic color rising in his face when he spluttered out, "You're damned well right I was much too kind! If I weren't so fornicating kind, you'd be getting this call from my lawyer!"

"Of course I would," I replied serenely. At last I had my answer: He was insane. Multiple personality disorder at the very least. He must've written those reviews under the brief influence of the Good Wellcome Fisher, and now that Evil Wellcome had reasserted sovereignty, he wanted to shift the blame.

"Don't condescend to me, jade. And don't try to convince me that this is none of your doing. I know exactly what I wrote about that hideous mound of toxic verbiage you call

Beloved Babylonian, and this review is not it! Nor are any of the others printed therewith the work of my pen. Oh, you'll pay for this effrontery, Barbara. *J'accuse!*"

It had been ages since Rachel was a bratty two-year-old, but it was remarkable how quickly I recovered the patient, measured tone of voice necessary for dealing with tantrums. "Wellcome, dear, before I put in a long-distance call to the wacko-wagon down in your neck of the woods, would you mind telling me *how* you think I managed to change your precious spew—I mean, reviews?"

"Ha! As if you didn't know. Thanks to a barbarous mob of so-called readers whose vulgar tastes are directly responsible for the imminent fall of Western Civilization, you are an author who is—who is not without—" Something was sticking in his craw, but he made the effort and horked up: "*—who is not without some influence in the publishing world.*"

Ah, so he'd built his palace of paranoia on *that* little patch of quicksand. I was a Name in the field of Romance, therefore I could prevail upon the publishers of *WiPP* to delete Wellcome's real reviews and insert some of my own creation. Sure, I could. Now that I saw whither his twisted thoughts tended, I didn't know whether to laugh out loud or pity the naiveté that believed genre authors could influence anything except their editors' drinking problems.

"Look, Wellcome, I'm telling you that I didn't have anything to do with—" I began. Then a stray thought struck me. "Could you hold the line a sec?"

Without waiting for his answer, I put down the phone and fetched my copy of *WiPP*, opening it to the reviews. Something was nagging at me, worrying the corners of my mind. It was a scrap of legendary lore that I'd acquired years ago, back in college, when *Lord of the Rings* held all the secrets of the Universe and my holiest desire was to get an elf greased up, buck naked, and ready to rock 'n' roll. But when I wasn't dreaming of more unorthodox uses for pointed ears, I read a lot, everything from trilogies to treatises on myth and folklore. After all, when you just *know* you're going to be the Queen of Elfland (or at least the Love-Slave) you don't want to make the gaffe of addressing a troll as if he were a dwarf, or calling a boggart a bogle.

From out of the mists of those damned embarrassing memories, a graceful white creature stepped. It printed the grass of an emerald meadow with its cloven hooves and knelt beside a tainted fountain. It touched the poisoned waters once with its horn. Once was all it took. The waters bubbled up bright and clean, free of all contamination.

Carefully I ran my fingers along the inner spine of the magazine until they encountered the faint trace of stickiness I had been half expecting. No matter how carefully you lick a batter spoon clean, some residual goo will cling to it until it's properly washed, and no matter how painstaking you are about getting all the apple filling off a sliver of unicorn's horn before you drop it between the pages of your magazine . . .

"Wellcome," I said wearily, picking up the phone again, "I confess. I did it. I used my amazing professional influence to force the publishers of *With Pen and Passion* to drop your original reviews and substitute mine, but it wasn't supposed to happen until the April issue, as a prank. I'll be happy to contact them ASAP with a full retraction. Good enough? Good boy. Good bye."

I didn't wait for him to answer. I hung up the phone but it took a while before I could unclench my hand from the receiver. I stood there for some time, silently cursing the incredible-but-true reason behind the metamorphosis Wellcome's vitriolic rants had undergone along with the promise of confidentiality I'd made to Greta Marie.

As if you needed to be sworn to secrecy! I thought. *Outside of Bowman's Ridge, who the hell would believe you if you did talk about the unicorns?*

I finally got a grip on my emotions and sat down to dinner. I was pleased to see that Rachel had cleaned her plate while I'd been on the phone with Wellcome. It wasn't until she'd scooted upstairs to do her homework that I noticed a double heap of mashed squash covering my fish sticks. I molded a tiny little voodoo doll of Wellcome Fisher out of the surplus squash, drove a fish stick through its heart, and enjoyed my dinner in peace.

Peace is precious because, like chocolate, it never lasts long enough to suit me. Wellcome Fisher took the next bus to Montpelier, rented a car, and showed up at my house the following afternoon, without benefit of invitation. I would have set the dogs on him, but we don't have any dogs and Gorbaduc wasn't in the mood.

His first words to me when he stepped out of the car were, "I don't believe you, you shameless Machiavellian magsman!"

"Fine, thanks, and you?" I muttered. I have nothing against reality save the fact that there is no way—short of small arms fire, a Doberman, or a dimensional trapdoor— that you can hang up on a face-to-face encounter with a pettyminded twit like Wellcome.

"I have here in my hand certain documents—" he began, wagging a clutch of papers at me as he advanced like grim Pedantry "—that prove beyond a shadow of a doubt that your confession is as full of holes as your plots. Behold the galleys of those same reviews which you *claim* to have removed and replaced! They are precisely identical to the versions published."

I frowned. "So what's the problem? Of course they'd be

identical. That's how galleys work, you know. Who gave you those?"

"They were given to me by the editor of *With Pen and Passion* approximately three months ago, as is the usual procedure for production of all of my columns. According to my wont, I faxed back the typographical errors and kept the galleys themselves for my library. The *problem,* as you so infelicitously put it—" (Here a needle-toothed leer spread itself over Wellcome's face, a grimace for a dyspeptic possum to envy.) "The *problem* is that when I filed these galleys they were my reviews as originally written, but when I took them out for inspection yesterday, after our delightful conversation, they had somehow become *yours.*"

(The unicorn bends his head over the polluted stream and touches it once with his horn. The magical powers of purification act immediately, but they can't distinguish one drop of water from another. Unicorns don't do partial cures or managed care. It's all or nothing.)

"Tell me the truth, Barbara," Wellcome was saying. "Tell me how you managed to accomplish this, short of hiring catburglars to infiltrate my domicile."

"I can't tell you."

"Then perhaps you can tell my attorney."

"You wouldn't believe me and neither would he."

"Faugh!" (The man actually said *Faugh!*)

"It's a long story and parts of it are pretty far-fetched."

"You're not scaring me, Barbara; I've read your Elizabethan series."

I held onto my temper by counting the bristly ginger hairs springing from Wellcome's ears, then said, "If it were up to me, I'd tell you straight out, devil take the hindmost. It's not. It involves someone else, a respected and respectable person who lives in this town. I'd like to keep living in this town too, so I'm not going to tell you dick without this other person's permission, and I don't care if you sue my ass off."

"And if this person gives consent?" Wellcome's pudgy lips drew themselves into a *moue* of anticipation.

"Then I'll tell you everything."

"Hmph. Very well. Let us be on our way." He pivoted on one battered loafer and headed for his rental car. When I neglected to come bounding after, he paused and in tones of the highest snittery commanded, "Well, get *in*. You say the person you must consult likewise lives in this dainty suburb of Ultima Thule? Fine. You shall play Virgil to my Dante and bring about a meeting without delay."

I decided that some battles aren't worth fighting: Lie down with dogs, get up with fleas, and that includes getting down to word wrestling with this pedigreed s.o.b. I got into the car and directed him back to the center of town where I led him straight into the coffee shop.

"And what do we call *this* fallen temple of Epicurus?" Wellcome inquired loudly as we walked through the door. It was past the breakfast rush and before the lunchtime crowd, a few minutes short of eleven, for which I gave thanks. The only witnesses to my mortification were the three waitresses, two young mothers preoccupied with keeping their toddlers from shoving toast into each others' ears, and Muriel.

"We don't need to call it anything; it's the town coffee shop," I gritted.

"Ah. How delightfully self-referential. And what unspeakable offense against human society have I committed that entails even temporary incarceration here as my punishment?"

"That's what I've always admired about you, Wellcome," I said. "Your simple yet elegant style. I brought you here because this is where we've got the best chance of meeting the person we're after. Now can I buy you a cup of coffee?"

"I'm assuming a decent cappucino is out of the question. I'll settle for a clean cup." He sniffed, wrinkled up his nose dramatically, and made a great business out of whisking off the immaculate surface of one of the counter stools with his handkerchief. Muriel saw him do this, her expression unreadable. I performed the usual pantomime of those forced to keep company with chowderheads: Sickly smile, shrug of shoulders, silent mouthing of It's-not-my-fault. Muriel pressed her lips together and went into the kitchen. While I writhed, our waitress came over and Wellcome asked her what was the ptomaine *du jour* in a voice so carrying that even the young mothers took note of us.

Oh, for a cloak of invisibility! Or even just an Acme anvil to fall from the ceiling and squoosh Wellcome into clodbutter. I placed my order, though I had precious little appetite for anything except a certain critic's head on a platter.

It was while Wellcome was ingratiating himself with the waitress by staring at her breasts that Greta Marie arrived. My sense of timing had been impeccable: She always made her delivery at around eleven o'clock. She backed in through the door, an apple pie balanced on either hand, a look of intense concentration on her face. I hailed her by name and she startled like a duchess dry-gulched by a whoopee cushion, then recovered and smiled.

It took me a while before I realized that she wasn't smiling at me.

"*You're* Wellcome Fisher!" she gasped, rushing forward, still bearing pies. I couldn't say whether her bosom was heaving with the strain of unbridled passion, but the front of her tatty old Navy pea coat was imitating a bellows pretty well. "The flyleaf photo just *doesn't* do you justice. Oh my! Babs never told me that *you* were one of her writer-friends.

This is such an honor! I simply adored *Lady Gewndolyn's Gallant!* So rich! So detailed! So—"

Forty minutes later, I walked myself back home. If Wellcome noticed me leave, he made no demur, and as for Greta Marie, she'd scarcely noticed my presence to begin with. I left the two of them seated at the counter, gazing deeply into each other's eyes, Greta Marie telling Wellcome how wonderful his book was and Wellcome telling Greta Marie that she was so very, very right.

That was the last I heard of Wellcome Fisher for weeks thereafter. *WiPP* made no inquiry into the unique eruption of sweetness and light in Wellcome's reviews, and the man himself seemed to have dropped the matter. He also seemed to have become a regular fixture in Bowman's Ridge, motoring up whenever he had the time, just to be with Greta Marie. Townsfolk saw them walking hand-in-hand down Main Street, a public display of affection that was the Bowman's Ridge equivalent of indulging in the love that dare not bleat its name on the church lawn. Eyebrows lifted, tongues clicked, and whoever coined the phrase "No fool like an old fool" must've been raking in the residuals for all the times the good Natives muttered those very words under their collective breath. If Greta Marie overheard, she didn't care. She was happy.

I suppose I should've been happy too. I suppose that as a Romance writer I should've sat back and enjoyed such a picturebook-perfect ending, cue violins and soft-focus fadeout. Unfortunately, just because I write the stuff doesn't mean I believe it. My outlook on life would be so much serener if I did. It's impossible to enjoy a front row seat for Happily Ever After when you're waiting for the other shoe to drop, and if I knew Wellcome, it was going to be a brogan.

So I waited, and Thanksgiving came and went. I waited,

and the Christmas decorations went up all over town. I waited, and Bobo Riley stuffed two pillows down the front of his old red union suit, slapped on a cotton batting beard, and passed out candy canes to all the kids who came into his hardware store with their folks. But as for Greta Marie and Wellcome—? Nothing. Not even a rumor of trouble in paradise. It was just too good to be true.

Muriel agreed. "I don't know what's gotten into the girl," she said to me. (In this town you're a girl until you become the charge of your husband or the undertaker.) "She's all atwitter, can't find her head using both hands and a roadmap, most days, and irresponsible—? I don't like to say how many days she's skipped bringing in the pies, and when she does, the quality's fallen off something terrible. When I think how good those pies used to be, I could just weep. Not that *I'd* ever mention it to her. Poor child would die. On the other hand, she really ought to know. I don't suppose you'd consider—?"

Which is how I came to be driving up the Old Toll Road to the Bowman place in the snow. I'd taken the precaution of calling ahead. No way was I going to risk my neck jouncing over ice-filled ruts for nothing. Greta Marie told me how much she'd be looking forward to my visit, and then:

"Dear Babs,

So sorry I missed you. Got a call from the postmaster that there's a registered letter for me down town from my Wellcome. Let's make it another time.

Very truly yours,
Miss Greta Marie Bowman"

I tore the note off the front door and stuffed it in my

pocket, then went stomping back to the car, thinking bloody red thoughts. Just as my gloved hand touched the handle, I heard a loud trumpeting sound, the singular, strange, fascinating cry of the unicorn. I looked back at the house and saw one come walking around the corner in stately beauty.

It was the largest of the three, the one who'd given me that contemptuous stare the first time I saw the critters. He'd changed; his horn was back, grown almost to full length. It shone with its own pale phosphorescence, a flickerlng blue-green flame. The beast held his head high and seemed to be in the best of spirits. Maybe animals can't smile, as we humans understand the grimace, but they do have their ways of letting the world know they're happy, and this was definitely one happy unicorn.

Was, that is, until he saw it was only me. I could mark the exact moment when recognition struck him right where the horn grew. His feathery tail, once flaunted high as a battle-flag, now drooped with disappointment. His whole demeanor seemed to say, *I was expecting someone else.* A spark of anger kindled from dashed hopes turned his eyes a dangerous scarlet. How dare I be anyone but the woman he was waiting for? He lowered that long, razor-edged horn in a manner that made my heart do a drumroll of dread. I'd seen how fast he could run and I knew that there was no chance of my getting inside the car before he reached me. I wondered whether it was going to hurt when he skewered me for the heinous crime of not being Greta Marie.

Then his head bent even lower, so low that the tip of his horn came within an inch of the ground. A dull gray film obscured its glorious fire. Sorrow had conquered anger. He let out a little whicker of misery that wrung my heart with pity.

I went up to him and threw my arms around his neck,

crooning words of comfort. Yes, I talked to him as if he were a despondent collie pup. Yes, I voluntarily brought myself within easy stabbing distance of the horn. Yes, I'm an idiot, I admit it, it says so on my driver's license.

If you want proof-positive of my stupidity then consider the fact that I went into writing because I wanted a high-paying, glamorous job where everyone respected me and internecine mudslinging just wasn't the Done Thing. But I couldn't turn my back on the poor creature.

"There, there," I said, running my hands through his flossy mane. "She'll be back, you'll see. It's just that she's a little soppy now. Love makes you temporarily brain-dead."

The unicorn looked me in the eye, his gaze eloquent. *Don't sugar-coat it, my lady,* he seemed to say. *You and I both know what love leads to. She may be back, but she won't be the same, and where are we going to find another virgin at this time of year? Those Christmas parties are hell on maidenheads.*

"You mean that Greta Marie and Wellcome have—?" Curse my imagination! The very thought of Wellcome *al fresco* and taking care of business was enough to purge a cat-fish. My conscious mind immediately tacked up wall-to-wall signs reading *Don't Go There, Girlfriend. Don't Buy the Ticket. Don't Even Ask to See the Full-Color Brochures.*

The unicorn flared his nostrils, scorning the whole hideous idea. Ah, true, true: Would he still be hanging around the property if Greta Marie had done the dire deed with Wellcome already? But to judge by his hangdog expression, he figured it was only a matter of time.

"Look, I'm sorry, but what can I do about it?" I told him. "Greta Marie's happy. I realize she's been neglecting you, but—"

The unicorn snorted again and tossed his head, casting off my paltry attempts at consolation. I watched as he picked his way across the farmyard, heading towards the straggle of apple trees. I thought I glimpsed the images of his two companions in the distance, under the spindly shadow of the branches, but that might have been a trick of light on snow.

I cupped my hands to my mouth. "Don't give up!" I called. "Please don't just walk away! Even if she and Wellcome Fisher *do* get nasty, it's never going to last. Greta Marie's not stupid and she's not desperate: One day she'll see him for the ego-leech he is, unless he slaps her in the face with it first. That's when she'll really need you. She's been good to you for God knows how many years; you owe it to her to stick around. *Nice* unicorns. *Good* unicorns. Sit! Stay!"

I was babbling, but it got their attention. Three shimmery streaks of marine light lifted beneath the barren orchard boughs, three pairs of glowing garnet eyes winked at me once before vanishing.

I drove back to town alone.

Greta Marie was in the coffee shop, seated on one of the stools at the counter nearest the big display window up front, reading her registered letter over a steaming cup of Muriel's best brew. It was a wonder she could make out the words for all the stars in her eyes. When she saw me come in, she broke from covert in a whir of bliss.

"Babs, it's so wonderful! I do hope you forgive me for not being at home when you called, but it was such a good thing I came to town and got this letter. Darling Wellcome! I know he meant to give me a few days' notice, but when one is as significant a figure in the field of *belles lettres* as he, sometimes it's simply impossible to take time for personal matters until the demands of one's career have been met."

Belles lettres? Wellcome? The only demand ever attached to his career was "Please, please, please, don't write another book!" As I seated myself on the stool beside hers, I did a rapid mental translation of Greta Marie's words, allowing for drift, wind resistance, drag, and converting from the Stupid-in-Love scale.

"There's something vitally important in there and he didn't bother mailing it until the last minute?" I presumed, nodding at the letter. Muriel brought me my own cup of coffee, glanced at Greta Marie, then looked at me and raised her eyebrows in a manner that said *Lost Cause*.

"Oh, I don't mind," Greta Marie chirped, pressing the unfolded sheets of spiral notebook paper to her heart. Wellcome might waste words but never stationery. "He says he's coming up today, and that I'm to meet him here because there's no sense in him driving all the way out to my place and then all the way back into town to the *travel agent*."

She pronounced those last two words as if they'd been the *Holy Grail*, fraught and freighted with a deeper meaning than was given mere mortals like me to know.

"Planning a little trip, hm?" I asked, striving to keep it casual.

"A very *special* sort of trip, Babs dear." She blushed. "I do think he's coming up to ask me . . . to ask me if I would consent to become . . . if I would consent to become his—"

"*There* you are!" Wellcome Fisher burst into the coffee shop with the élan of a juggernaut. He shouldered his way between us, nearly shoving me off my stool without so much as a word of greeting. Usually it is a fair treat to be ignored by Wellcome Fisher, but not when it means you've been relegated to the role of superfluous stage-dressing. I was miffed. I got up and moved, taking my cup with me.

Wellcome slithered onto the stool I had vacated. He looked Greta Marie up and down, his gaze severe and judgmental. "You're *not* prepared," he accused.

"Prepared, dear?" It was sickening to see the way Greta

Marie went into mouse-mode at the sound of her master's voice. "But—but I'm here. You did say to meet you here, didn't y—?"

"Ye gods, and was that *all* I said?"

Greta Marie cringed, but she summoned up the gumption to reply, "Well . . . yes. That and the part about going to the travel agent." She extended the letter for his inspection and added, "See, darling?"

He rolled his eyes, playing the martyr so broadly that I wondered whether he had a pack of stick-on stigmata hidden in the pocket of his anorak. "Merciful powers above, you're a supposedly intelligent wench: Do I have to spell out *everything* for you, chapter and verse? Are you *that* literal-minded? Are you incapable of basic *inference?*" He paused, striking a toplofty pose, apparently waiting for the applause of the multitude.

Now mind you, the hour of Wellcome's self-styled Calvary was lunchtime and the coffee shop was packed to the gussets with the usual Natives, all of whom knew and respected Greta Marie Bowman. It was out of this selfsame respect that they went deaf, dumb and blind by common consent. They understood that she had fallen in with this acerbic yahoo of her own free will, they realized that she had brought all her sufferings down upon her own head voluntarily, they were firm in the belief that she should have known better, but damned if they were going to underwrite her humiliation, deserved or not. No one present reacted to Wellcome's words with so much as a glance in his general direction. In fact, as far as the good folk of Bowman's Ridge were concerned, Wellcome wasn't even there. They didn't just ignore him, they nullified him.

Gadfly that he was, Wellcome did not take kindly to being overlooked. The Natives' lack of cooperation irked him. He took a deep breath and brought his fist down on the countertop just as he bellowed, "You peruse, but you do not *read*. Have you no grasp of *subtext?*"

Poor Greta Marie. I could see her lips begin to tremble, her eyes to shine with tears that didn't spring from joy. "I'm—I'm sorry, dear," she said, her voice all quavery. "I—I suppose you mean I ought to be prepared for—for our trip, yes?"

Wellcome slapped his brow and let his celluloid smile glide across the room. "Finally!" he informed the audience. They gave no sign that he had spoken. "At the very least, I expected you to be packed."

"Packed? But—but how could I? I wouldn't know what to bring. We haven't even discussed where we'll be going."

His shoulders sagged. Now he was both martyr and victim. "I thought you *listened* to me," he complained, wounded to the marrow. "Haven't I said time and time again how the winter weather affects my artistic spirit? Haven't I spoken of my very deep, very basic need to follow the sun?"

"You did mention something about visiting your aunt in Tampa every year, but—"

"Well, my dear Auntie Clarice has just written to say that *she* is going off on a holiday cruise this coming week and that *we* may have the use of the condo in her absence, with her blessing." He beamed at her as if he'd just laid the crown jewels of Zanzibar at her feet.

Greta Marie turned pale. "Oh no," she said, hands fluttering before her face. "This *coming* week? Oh no, it's much too soon. I couldn't possibly make all the arrangements. Reverend Fenster is too taken up with the Christmas season, and we Bowmans have always been married from the Congregational Church. Besides, there's simply nowhere we could book a large enough hall for the reception, let alone arrange for refreshments, and what about the blood test and the license and my gown and—"

Wellcome's brows rose and came together until he was glaring at Greta Marie from beneath the shelter of a hairy circumflex. "What the devil are you jawing about?" he demanded. "Since when does one need a blood test to go to Tampa?"

"Oh," said Greta Marie softly. She folded her hands above her bosom and repeated, "Oh." Her head bowed like a flower on a broken stalk. "I thought you meant we were going to be—" she began, then sank into silence.

"What? To be what?" Wellcome was mystified. For one fleeting moment he seemed rapt by words that were not his own as he attempted to solve this present conundrum. "Do you imply—? That marriage twaddle you were spouting about your ancestors and the First Congregational Church— Surely you weren't serious?" Without waiting for her reply, he dismissed the very possibility with a brief wave of his hand. "No, no, you couldn't have been; something else must be nibbling your liver. Spit it out, woman! I don't indulge in telepathy."

Greta Marie set her hands firmly on the edge of the counter. I swear that I could see the ranks of Bowmans long gone form up in ghostly phalanx behind her and then, one by one, add their ectoplasmic mite to the stiffening of her backbone. By degrees she sat up taller, straighter, prouder, looked Wellcome in the eye and coldly said, "I thought you were a *gentleman*."

There could be no greater condemnation uttered by a woman of Greta Marie's age and station. For all his failings, Wellcome was not slow on the uptake; the penny dropped, the "marriage twaddle" that he had dismissed as ridiculous returned to leer at him, nose to nose. I saw the flickering play of emotions over his countenance: shock, comprehension, a smidgen of shame, and then the urgent realization that if he didn't act fast, he was in peril of losing face before the one earthly creature he loved above all others.

If you think the creature in question was Greta Marie, you haven't been paying attention.

Frost crackled at the corners of his mouth as he smiled thinly and said, "Well. Here's a surprise. Don't tell me that you still cherish orange blossom dreams at your age?"

Greta Marie jerked her head back as if she'd been slapped. His words jarred her to the core, that much was plain to see, but the old blood bred hardy souls. She drew her mouth into a tight little line and refused to give him the satisfaction of a reply.

This sat ill with Wellcome, who would have preferred more concrete evidence that his words had hit the mark. "And I thought we understood each other," he said, reloading his figurative blowpipe with a freshly venomed dart. "What a sorry disappointment you are. I expected more of you. I believed that you were different, that you were a woman of perception, a woman of spirit, one to whom the petty constraints and empty rituals of society mean nothing so long as she can serve Art."

That did it. That was my limit. "Art my *ass*," I blurted out. "You just want to get *laid*."

Wellcome curled his lip at me. "Enter the white knight," he drawled. "And what concern of yours is this? Barbara Barclay, champion of Romance! I should think you'd want to encourage your friend to seize the golden opportunity I'm offering her. Do you honestly believe she'll get many more like it on this side of the grave? *If* she ever got any before."

"I don't have to sit here and listen to this!" Greta Marie

stood up and started for the door, but Wellcome blocked her escape.

"I urge you to reconsider," he counselled her. "I've always been passably fond of you, you know, especially your good sense. Certainly a woman like you, wise enough to perceive the rich aesthetic contributions of my work to world literature, must also see that I have only your best interests at heart in proposing *cette petite affaire.* Tampa is lovely at this time of year. Do you want to end your days as a hollow husk, a topshelf virgin whose life will be forever incomplete without so much as the memory of a man's attentions? I'll spare you that horrible fate, but you're going to have to be a good girl and—"

Greta Marie just gave him a *look;* a look that plugged his chatter snugger than jamming a badger in a bunghole; a disinterested, calculating look such as a farmer might give a stubborn tree stump, mentally debating which was the best crack into which to jam the dynamite.

"My ancestor, Captain James Resurrection Bowman, received a grant of land in this town as reward for his heroism in the Revolutionary War," she said. "A friend of his received a similar grant, except his was much smaller and located on Manhattan Island. He offered to swap, Captain James chose to decline. In retrospect it was a stupid choice, but it was his own. All my life I have followed Captain James' example; I have always made my own choices. If I remain a virgin until I marry, it will not be for lack of such . . . generous offers as yours, but because that is my decision to make and no one else's."

"Talk about stupid choices," Wellcome snarled.

Still calm and collected, Greta Marie gave him one short, sharp, effective slap across the face, and it wasn't a figurative one either, no, sirree. And with the echoes of flesh-to-flesh impact still hanging in the air she said, "The only stupid choice I made was loving you."

The incredible happened: The denizens of the coffee shop, to a man, rose to their feet and gave that slap a standing ovation. Bobo Riley from the hardware store was even heard to let out an exultant Yankee whoop that would have put a Rebel yell to shame.

That should have been Wellcome's cue to leave, making as gracious an exit as he might hope for in the circumstances. Alas, Wellcome had never been a man to read the signs or take the hint. If you told him his writing clunked like a freight train off the rails, he took this to mean that it had the power of a runaway freight instead.

He seized Greta Marie's hands. "So you do love me," he exclaimed triumphantly. "Ah, I see your little scheme: You're playing hard to get. You've read far too many of the shoddier sort of Romance novels, those dreadful bodice-rippers—" (Here he looked meaningfully in my direction.) "—and you want a rough wooing. So be it!"

He was more athletic than his nascent paunch and pasty skin might lead you to believe, fully capable of sweeping a grown woman of Greta Marie's size off her feet and out the door before any of us could react. She shrieked in shock, not fear, but she didn't struggle as he made off with her. Maybe she thought she'd already made enough of a scene in the coffee shop to last Bowman's Ridge well into the next century.

I was the first to address the situation. "Hey! Aren't we going to *do* something?" I demanded of my fellow townsmen.

No one answered. Most of them went back to eating lunch. Bobo Riley looked as if he wanted to take action, but something was holding him back.

"Babs . . ." Muriel jerked her head, indicating I was to sit back down at the counter. Dumbly I obeyed in time to hear her whisper, "It not our place to interfere in other folks' domestic quarrels."

"This is an abduction, not a family spat," I hissed. "If I know Wellcome, he won't stop until he's stuffed Greta Marie into his rental car and *driven* her all the way to Tampa! And then what? She hasn't got enough cash to come back on her own hook, and would she ever *dream* of calling anyone up here to send her the busfare home?"

Muriel didn't say a word. We both knew the answer: Greta Marie would sooner become a beachcomber or—the horror!—give Wellcome his wicked way with her before she'd ask a fellow Native to lend her some money. On the other hand, her fellow Natives would sooner allow a thrice-cursed outlander like Wellcome Fisher to make off with the last living Bowman than they'd ever dream of interfering directly in someone else's personal matters.

"Well, I don't care what the rest of you do, *I'm* not going to put up with this!" I announced and started for the door. A large, work-hardened hand darted in front of me to hold it open. I looked up into Bobo Riley's kind blue eyes.

"Mind if I walk with you down street a bit, Mrs. Barclay?" he asked. "I just happen to be going your way."

Within two minutes I found myself transformed into the most popular woman in Bowman's Ridge. Simply everyone in the coffee shop was suddenly seized with the simultaneous urge to pay their checks and join me for a little stroll down Main Street. Even Hal abandoned his kitchen and Muriel her place behind the counter, leaving the waitresses and a few stragglers behind to hold down the fort. We weren't going to deliberately *interfere* in anything, perish forbid. We were just going to exercise our Constitutional right to take, well, a constitutional.

We followed the faint sound of Greta Marie's fists beating

a muffled tattoo on Wellcome's chest. They hadn't gotten far. Wellcome had parked his rental about a block away, down by the old war memorial on the green. Our itinerant Town Meeting caught up with him as he was trying to dig out the car keys without letting go of his prize.

When he saw us coming his eyes went wide as a constipated owl's. He forgot all about the "rough wooing" underway and dropped Greta Marie smack on the town green, then took to his heels. At first I thought that he was running away in fear for his life, that he intended to beat feet all the way to Montpelier, but it turned out that I underestimated him. He fled only as far as the war memorial—a truncated obelisk, its sides inscribed with the names of the Bowman's Ridge men who'd died in both World Wars, Korea, and Vietnam, its flat top crowned with an urn that the Women's Club filled with flowers on appropriate occasions. Spry as a springtime cockroach, he clambered up the monument and perched there, holding onto the lip of the empty urn.

"A lynch mob," he sneered down at us from his perch. "How typical of the rustic mind. Haven't you forgotten something? Pitchforks? Torches? You cracker barrel cretins, how dare you harass me? A plague on your pitiful frog-fart of a town! And *you*—*!*"

His glittering eyes zeroed in on Greta Marie. Bobo Riley had fallen behind the rest of us in order to help the lady up and now squired her on his arm. "This is all your fault, you squalid excuse for a hicktown Hypatia! You pathetic pricktease, I'll wager you fancy yourself quite the bargain basement Mata Hari, don't you? *Don't you?*"

"Oh!" Greta Marie covered her face with her hands and shuddered. Wellcome's sharp tongue had finally drawn blood. She was crying, and in public, too! Bobo Riley folded his big arms protectively around her and glowered up at the treed critic, growling threats that failed to stem Wellcome's spate of vengeful poison.

"Don't cry, darling," Wellcome crooned sarcastically. "There's nothing wrong with you that a good upcountry rogering wouldn't cure. So sad that you'll never get it now. Thank God I came to my senses in time. You contemptible dirtfarm Delilah, how a man of my breeding could have ever been mad enough even to *consider* the sensual enrichment of your dusty, backshelf, remaindered life—!"

Greta Marie threw her head back and howled her misery to the skies.

They were on him in the time it takes to blink. We never saw them come; they were simply there, all three of them, eyes hollyberry bright, horns blazing in the thin winter sunlight. The largest of the three, the one I'd comforted earlier that same day, was the first to reach him. It set its forefeet on the pediment of the war memorial, paused for an instant to look Wellcome in the eye, then jabbed him straight through the center of the chest with its horn. He fell to the snow-covered green and lay there unmoving.

The other two unicorns took it in turns to sniff the body and to snort their disdain. They did not depart as abruptly as they had arrived. The three of them turned as one and trotted up Main Street, tails swishing, in the direction of the town library. One of them paused to munch on a swag of Christmas greenery decking the front of the florist's. No one made the slightest move to stay them, and Greta Marie, still weeping in Bobo Riley's arms, never once tried to call them back.

Wellcome Fisher was dead. We had no illusions of anyone being able to survive a direct thrust to the heart with something as sharp and pointed and long as a unicorn's horn, but we only thought we had all the answers until Hal bent over the body and exclaimed, "Hey! There's no hole."

Everyone swarmed around. Hal was right: There was no hole. Not a puncture, not a piercing, not a scratch. No blood stained the snow. There wasn't even the teensiest rip in Wellcome's clothing. The crowd buzzed.

I stood apart. I knew what had happened, but darned if I was going to tell my neighbors. They already thought I was weird enough, and if I started explaining about the rules that govern unicorns—!

The unicorn is not a monstrous beast; it doesn't kill for sport or spite, it lives to heal, not harm. It bears upon its brow a horn whose touch has the power to purge all poisons and make what is polluted sweet and wholesome once more. The unicorn hadn't been trying to kill Wellcome, merely to cure him. It had touched his heart with its magical horn, intending to remove only the taint of malice and envy, leaving behind all that was good and selfless and decent in the man. No one was more surprised than the unicorn by what actually happened.

Let's just put it this way: It was going to be one hell of an autopsy, one of the starring organs gone without an external clue to explain its vanishment. Oh well, the medical examiner would probably call it a coronary anyway, heart or no heart. Old Doc Barnett hates to make waves.

It took a goodly while to sort things out on the green. By the time Chief Dowd and the rest of the local authorities finished taking statements ("Dunno. He just sorta keeled over. Not a mark on him, see?") and viewing the body, it was getting dark. I looked around for Greta Marie. I figured she shouldn't try to drive herself home after all she'd been through today.

I'd been anticipated. When I found her, she told me that Bobo Riley had already offered to drive her home and she'd accepted. Despite the fact that several other Natives were within earshot, Bobo went on to say that he'd pick her up at her place come morning and take her back to town so she could recover her car next day. Then he asked her if she'd like to help him down at the hardware store by dressing up as Mrs. Claus and giving the kids candy. This was the Bowman's Ridge equivalent of him clasping her to his manly chest, raining kisses upon her upturned face, and telling her that he desired her above all women with a raw, unbridled passion that knew no bounds. I don't know if Greta Marie felt all the earth-heaving thrills and collywobbles I put into my books, but her eyes were shining with that special To Be Continued light.

I went home. Rachel was waiting for me by the front gate. Something was clearly wrong. Instead of her usual air of carefully cultivated angst and ennui, she was bouncing like a Labrador puppy.

"Mom! Mom! This is so cool, you've got to see this! I don't think he belongs to anyone, and he is soooo gorgeous. I'll take care of him myself, I promise, and if there's some kind of problem with the zoning geeks I'll pay for his board out of my own allowance, honest. Can I keep him? Can I? Can I? Pleeeeease?"

"Keep—?"

The unicorn stepped out of the lengthening shadows, rested his heavy head on my daughter's shoulder, and—one Transient to another—grinned.

This story is respectfully dedicated to the memory of Clifton Webb.

Death and the Librarian

In an October dusk that smelled of smoke and apples, a lady in a black duster coat and a broad-brimmed hat, heavily veiled, called at Rainey's Emporium in Foster's Glen, New York. She descended from the driver's seat of a black Packard, drawing the eye of every man who lounged on the wooden steps of the crossroads store and attracting a second murmuring throng of idlers from Alvin Vernier's barber shop across the way. The men of Foster's Glen had seen a Packard automobile only in the illustrated weeklies, but to see a woman driving such a dream-chariot—!

However, by the time the lady reached the steps of Rainey's and said, "I beg your pardon; I am seeking the home of Miss Louisa Foster," she had become a middle-aged man in a plain black broadcloth suit, a drummer with sample case in hand and a gleaming derby perched on his head, so that was all right.

"Miss Foster?" Jim Patton raised one eyebrow and tipped back his straw hat as he rubbed his right temple. "Say, you wouldn't be a Pinkerton, now would you?" And the other men on Rainey's steps all laughed, because Jim was reckoned a wit as wits went in Foster's Glen, New York.

The gentleman in black smiled politely, and a trim moustache sprouted across his upper lip to give him a more dapper, roguish air. (This at the expense of his drummer's case, which vanished.) "Yes, she's in trouble with the law again," he replied, turning the jape back to its source and stealing Jim's audience along with his thunder. "Lolling on the throne of an opium empire, I'm told, or was it a straight-forward charge of breaking and entering?" He patted the pockets of his vest. "I'm useless without my notes." The idlers laughed louder, leaving poor Jim no hope but to drop the cap-and-bells and try the knight's helm on for size instead.

"That's a scandalous thing to say about a lady!" Jim snapped. "And about a lady like Miss Foster—! I can't begin to tell you all she's done hereabouts: church work, the Ladies' Aid, visiting the sick . . . Why, she's even turned the east wing of the judge's house into a library for the town!"

"Is that so?" The stranger shot his crisp celluloid cuffs and adjusted a fat ring, pearl and silver, on his lefthand littlest finger. It twinkled into diamond and gold.

His remark was only a remark, but Jim Patton took it for a challenge to his honesty. "Yes, that's *so*," he blustered. "And she's even set aside the money to make the judge's house over to the town for use as a library entire after she's gone."

"What does the judge have to say to all this?"

"What does—?" Jim gaped. "Why, you scoundrel, old Judge Foster's been dead these twenty years! What's your business with his daughter but mischief if you don't even know that much about the family?"

"That would be business that concerns only Miss Foster and me," the stranger replied, and he grew a little in height and breadth of chest so that when Jim Patton stood up to face him they were an even match.

Still, Jim bellowed, "I'll make it my business to know!" and offered fists the size of small pumpkins for inspection. He was farm-bred and raised, born to a father fresh and legless returned from Gettysburg. Caleb Patton knew the value of begetting muscular sons to follow the plow he could no longer master, and Jim was his sire's pride.

The stranger only smiled and let his own muscles double in size until his right hand could cup Jim Patton's skull without too much strain on the fingers. But all he said was, "I am a friend of the family and I have been away." And then he was an old man, dressed in a rusty uniform of the Grand Old Army of the Republic, even though by rights the thick cloth should have been deep navy blue instead of black as the abyss.

The Packard snorted and became a plump, slightly frowsty looking pony hitched to a dogcart. It took a few mincing steps forward, sending the Emporium idlers into a panic to seize its bridle and hold it steady until the gaffer could retake his seat and the reins. Most solicitous of all was Jim Patton, who helped the doddering veteran into the cart and even begged the privilege of leading him to Miss Foster's gate personally.

"That's mighty kind of you, sonny," the old man in black wheezed. "But I think I can find my way there right enough now."

"No trouble, sir; none at all," Jim pressed. "When your business with Miss Foster's done, I'd be honored if you'd ask the way to our farm after. My daddy'd be happy to meet up with a fellow soldier and talk over old times. Were you at Antietam?"

The old man's tears were lost in the twilight. "Son, I was there too." And he became a maiden wrapped in sables against the nipping air. She leaned over the edge of the dog-cart to give Jim a kiss that was frost and lilacs. "Tell Davey to hug the earth of the Somme and he'll come home," she said. She drove off leaving Jim entranced and bewildered, for his Davey was a toddler sleeping in his trundle-bed at home and the Somme was as meaningless to his world of crops and live-stock as the Milky Way.

The lady drove her pony hard, following the directions Jim and the rest had given. Her sable wraps whipped out behind her in the icy wind of her passage. The breath of a thousand stars sheared them to tattered wings that streamed from her shoulders like smoke. Her pony ran at a pace to burst the barrels of the finest English thoroughbreds, and his hooves carved the dirt road with prints like the smiling cut of a sword. They raced over distance and beyond, driving time before them with a buggywhip, hastening the moon toward the highpoint of the heavens and the appointed hour.

At length the road Jim Patton had shown her ended at the iron gates of a mansion at the westernmost edge of the town. By the standards of Boston or New York it was only a very fine house, but in this rural setting it was a palace to hold a princess. Within and without the grounds trees shielded it from any harm, even to the insinuating dagger of curious whispers. The judge himself had ordered the building of this fortification on the borders of his good name, and the strain of shoring up his innumerable proprieties had aged wood and stone and slate before their time.

The maiden stepped out of the dogcart and shook out her silvery hair. The black kitten mewed where the pony had stood and sniffed the small leather portmanteau that was the only tiding or trace of the dogcart.

The elderly woman gathered up portmanteau and kitten, pressing both to the soft fastness of her black alpaca-sheathed bosom with the karakul muff that warmed her hands. She glanced through the fence's tormented iron curlicues and her bright eyes met only darkened windows. She had ridden into town with the twilight, but now she stood on the hour before the clocks called up a new day.

"None awake? Well, I am not in the least surprised," she commented to the kitten. "At her age, quite a few of them grow tired at this hour. It's almost midnight. Let us try to conclude our business before then. I have a horror of cheap dramatics."

Then she caught sight of a glimmer of lamplight from a window on the eastern side of the house. "Ah!" she exclaimed, and her breath swung back the iron gates as she sailed through them and up the long white gravel drive.

The front doors with their glass lillies deferred to her without the hint of a squeak from latch or hinges. She took a moment in the entryway to arrange herself more presentably. Her black-plumed hat she left on a porcelain peg beside a far more modest confection of gray felt and ivory veils, then studied her reflection in the oak-framed glass the hat-pegs adorned.

"Mmmmmm." She laid soft pink fingers to her lips, evaluating the dimpled, dumpling face and all its studied benevolence. "Mmmmno," she concluded, and the black kitten mewed once more as the handsome young man in gallant's garb took final stock of every black-clad, splendid inch of his romantic immanence. He opened the portmanteau out upon itself, and it turned into an onyx orb. He felt that when a woman spent so much of her life circumscribed by domesticity and filial attentiveness, she at least deserved to depart in more dashing company than that of a fuddy-duddy refugee from a church bazaar. He sighed over the glowing orb before he knelt to touch the kitten's tail. Was that a purr he heard from the heart of the black sword he raised in the silent hall?

He passed through corridors where clutter reigned but dust was chastened out of existence. His gaze swept the house for life and saw the cook snoring in her room below the rooftree, the maids more decorously asleep in their narrow iron beds. A proper housecat patrolled the kitchen, the pantry and the cellar, hunting heedless mice, dreaming oceans of cream. He noted each of them and sent his whispers into minds that slept or wakened:

"If you love him, tell him not to leave the farm for that factory job in New York City or the machines will have him."

"She must be born in the hospital, no matter how loudly your mother claims that hospitals are only for the dying, or she's as good as never born at all."

"Let the silly bird fly across the road; don't chase it there! The delivery man cannot rein back a motor-driven van in time and he does not know that you are a queen."

In certain times, in certain cases, he was allowed this much discretion: he might give them the means to forestall him, if they only had the wit to heed. Would he call it kindness? Ah, but in the end there were no whispered cautions that would avail. He could not change the fact he embodied, merely the time of its fruition. The grand black swan's wings he called into being as a final touch were neither grand nor black enough to hide him from the inevitability of himself.

Still, he thought she would appreciate the wings, and the way he made the black sword shine and sing. He came to the east wing, to the door past which the library lay. He knew the room beyond. Every wall of it was armored with bookshelves, except for the interruption of a massively manteled fireplace and where a pair of heavy French doors framed a view of the hill sloping down to the town. He had entered that room twenty years ago, wearing somber juridical robes and a bulldog's grim, resigned expression as he informed Judge Foster of the verdict *sans* appeal. Then his hands had been blunt as the words he had spoken. Now his fingers were long and pale as he touched the orb to the doorknob and let himself in.

She looked up from the book she was reading. "Hello,"

she said, closing the buff-colored volume and laying it aside on the great desk of rosewood and brass. A snowy wealth of hair crowned her finely featured face. Lamplight overlaid with a dappled pattern of roses shone on the fair hands she folded in the lap of her moire dress, a gown so lapped in shades and meanings of black that it left his own dark livery looking shabby by comparison. Her expression held recognition without fear.

"Were you expecting me?" he asked, rather taken aback by the calm she wore draped so gracefully around her.

"Eventually," she replied. Her smile still had the power to devastate. "Isn't that the way it is supposed to be?" She rose from the high-backed chair and the bottle-green leather moaned softly to give her up from its embrace. "Father always told me I'd go to Hell, though he'd beat me black and blue if I so much as pronounced the word. Now that I've said it, I assume that's my destination." Her eyes twinkled, and in the air before them fluttered the ghost of a long-vanished fan. "Is it?"

The swan's wings slumped, then trickled away entirely. The gallant's costume diminished to the weedy suiting of a country parson. The sword lingered only long enough for him to realize it was still in his hands, an embarrassment. It shrank posthaste to become a raven that hopped onto the parson's shoulder and croaked its outrage at being transformed into so inappropriate an accessory. At least the orb had possessed the good taste to become a well-thumbed copy of Scripture.

"I—ah—do not discuss destinations."

"Not even to tell me whether it will be all that much of a change from Foster's Glen?" She owned the miraculous ability to be arch without descending to kittenishness.

"I am—er—I am not at liberty to say," he replied, polishing the lozenges of his pince-nez with a decidedly unclerical red kerchief he yanked from a trouser pocket.

"What are you at liberty to do, then?" she asked. "Collect the dead?"

"Er—ah—souls, yes. In specific, souls." He settled the lenses back on the bridge of his nose. "One does one's duty."

"One does it poorly, then," she said, and there was a great deal of bite to the lady's words.

Her vehemence startled him so that he did a little jump in place and bleated, "Eh?"

She was happy to explain. "If souls are what you gather, I said you do a shoddy job of work. You could have had mine twenty-five years ago. I had no further use for it. But to come now—! Hmph." Her small nose twitched with a disdainful sniff that had once broken aspiring hearts.

"Twenty-five years a—?" He made the pages of his Bible flutter as he searched them with a whirlwind's speed. His eyes remained blank as he looked up again and inquired, "I *am* addressing Miss Louisa Foster?"

The lady sighed and moved toward the nearest wall. From floor to ceiling it was a single, continuous tidal wave of books. The musty smell of aging ink and paper, the peculiarly enchanting blend of scents from cloth and leather bindings, sewn spines and the telltale traces of all the human hands that had turned those pages enveloped her like a sacred cloud of incense as she took a single volume down.

"So it is true," she said, looking at the text in her hands instead of at him. "Death does mistake himself sometimes."

"But you are—?" he insisted.

"Yes, yes, of course I am!" She waved away his queries impatiently. "Louisa Jane Foster, Judge Theophilus Foster's only child, sure to make a brilliant marriage or Father would know the reason why. A brilliant marriage or none. Father gave me as few choices as you do."

She replaced the book and took down a second one, a cuckoo among the flock of fine leather-fledged falcons. It was only bound in yellowing pasteboards, but when she opened it a scattering of scentless flower petals sprinkled the library carpet. The laugh she managed as she paged through the crumbling leaves trembled almost as much as her smile.

"Have you ever heard of a man named Asher Weiss? More than just in the way of business, I mean. Did you know he was a poet?" She did not look disappointed when her caller admitted he did not. "I didn't think so." Her eyes blinked rapidly. "And the rest of the world is now as ignorant as you.

"There is a poem in here called 'For L.'," she said. "I don't think seven people alive today ever read it. But I was one who did. He wrote it and I followed a trail of words into his heart, like Gretel seeking a way out of the darkling wood by following trails of pebbles and breadcrumbs." She stooped to gather up the petals in her palm and slip them back between the pages. "Not very brilliant, as matches go; nothing his faith or mine would willingly consecrate, so we made do without consecration. We two—we three soon learned how hard it is to live on pebbles and breadcrumbs." She slid the booklet back onto the shelf.

"May I?" He helped himself to the poet's pasteboard gravestone and read the dead man's name. "But this man died more than twenty-five years since!" he protested.

"And did I ever protest when you took him?" she countered. "At least you left me . . . the other." Her mouth hardened. She snatched the booklet from him and jammed it back between its more reputable kin. "A consolation, I imagined; living proof that God did not solely listen to Father's thundered threats. For a while I dreamed I saw the face of a god of love, not retribution, every time I looked down into his laughing eyes, so like his father's. Oh, what a fine joke!" She plucked a random volume from the shelf and flipped it open so that when she spoke, she seemed to take her words from the printed lines before her. "With all the best jokes, timing is everything."

She held the timorous parson's gaze without mercy. "Is sickness your purview too? Is hunger? Is fever? Or are you only there to settle their affairs in the end? That time—crouching by the bed, holding his hand—I wanted it to be me you took, not him. God knows how he would have gotten on without me—maybe Father's heart would have softened to an orphan's plight . . ." Her smile was bitter as she shook her head. "No. I only read fairy tales. It is for the children to believe in them."

She looked up. "Do you like children, Death?"

Before he could answer, she folded the book shut. "I know," she said. "Ask no questions. Bow your head. Accept." She jabbed the book at the judge's portrait above the fireplace and her voice plunged to a baritone roar: *"Your choices will be made for you, girl! When I want your opinion, I'll give it to you!"* She clapped the book between her hands and laughed. "You would think I would have learned my lessons better than that by now, living with the voice of God Almighty. Almighty . . . whose word remakes the world according to his desires. You know, I never had a Jewish lover, never had a bastard child. When I did not return with Father from New York City, all those years that I was gone from Foster's Glen, I was studying music abroad, living with a maiden aunt in Paris. So I was told. The townsfolk still think I am a lady."

"But you are!" he exclaimed, and the raven sprang from his shoulder to flit beneath the plaster sunbursts on the ceiling.

"You are as happily gulled as they, I see." She extended her hand and the bird came to rest upon it. "I am sorry," she told it. "We have no bust of Pallas for your comfort here, birdie. Father viewed all pagan art as disgraceful, because like my Asher, so few of its subjects seemed able to afford a decent suit of clothes."

"Well, ah—" The parson took a breath and let it out after he had comfortably become a gentleman in evening dress, offering her his arm and the tribute of a rose. "Shall we go?"

"No." The lady laughed and kissed the bird's gleaming plumage. "Not yet."

"Not—? But I thought—?" He cleared his throat and adjusted the starched bosom of his shirt. "From the warmth of your initial greeting, Miss Foster, I assumed you were quite willing to accept me as your escort tonight."

"How gallant," she said, her words dry as those ancient petals. "And at my age, how can I refuse so fine an offer? I cannot. I only wish to defer it."

"So do they all," he responded. "But this is the appointed time."

She ignored his summons, moving with a smooth, elegant carriage to the portrait above the mantel. She aped the judge's somber look to the last droop of jowl and beetling of brow as she thundered, *"Where is the blasted girl? Will these women never learn to be on time?"* She rested her free hand on the cool marble as she gazed up into the judge's painted scowl. "How long did you wait for me in the lobby of our hotel, Father, before you realized I had flown?" She looked back at her caller. "If I found the courage to keep him waiting, I have little to fear from baiting Death."

The stranger coughed discreetly into a black-gloved hand. "I am afraid that I really must insist you come with me now."

"Why should I come to you when you would not come to me?" Her eyes blazed blacker than the raven's feathers, blacker than the curl of downy hair encased in gold and crystal at the neck of her high-collared gown. "I called you and you would not come. Why? Couldn't you hear me? Was the rain falling too hard on the tiny box, or was the echo from the hole they'd dug for him too loud? I doubt it. They never dig the holes too deep in Potter's Field. Or was it the rumbling of the carriage wheels that drowned out my voice when *dear* Cousin Althea came to fetch me home again? Ah, no, I think perhaps it might have been impossible to hear my cries to you above the fuss she raised because she was so overjoyed to have 'found' me at last."

She slammed the book down on the mantel. "Of course it was impossible for her to have found me earlier, when all she had was my address on any of a dozen letters; letters I sent her pleading for money, for medicine, for the slightest hint of compassion . . ." She sank down suddenly on the hearthstone, frightening the raven to flight.

He knelt beside her and took her in his arms. Her tears were strong reality against his form of smoke and whispers.

"You have waited so long," she murmured, her breath in his ear warm and alive. "Can't you wait a little longer?"

"How much longer?" He smelled the lavender water that she used after her bath and felt the weary softness of her old woman's skin, her old woman's hair.

"Only until I finish reading." She laid her hands on his shoulders and nodded toward the desk where the buff-covered book still lay.

"Is that all you ask? Not days, not months, only until—?"

"That is all." Her hands clasped his. "Please."

He consented, only half comprehending what he had granted her. All she had said was true: His was the discretion that had assumed there was no truth behind a woman's pleas. So many of them cried out *Let me die!* who thought better of it later. Only when he was compelled to greet them below the railing of a bridge or with the apothecary bottle still in hand was he assured of their sincerity, and Miss Louisa Foster had not sought either of those paths after her cousin Althea fetched her home. *Hysterical* and *She'll get over it* tapped him on the shoulder, leering. He did have memories.

Still dressed for dancing, he helped her to her feet. She returned to her place in the green leather chair and took up the buff-covered book again. "To think I don't need spectacles at my age. Isn't it wonderful?" she said to him. And then: "You must promise not to frighten them."

He nodded obediently, although he had not the faintest idea of what she meant. He recreated himself as a lady of her own age and bearing, a tangle of dark tatting in her hands, a woolly black lapdog at her feet, the image of the poor relative whose bit of bread and hearthfire is earned with silence and invisibility.

The coach clock on the mantelpiece struck midnight.

The French doors creaked as a little hand shyly pushed them open. A dark head peered around the edge of the door. *Mother?* the wind sighed.

She did not look up from the open book as the child blew across the carpet and settled into her shadow. The small head rested itself against her knees and thin, milky fingers that should have been pink and plump and scented with powder instead of mold reached up to close around her hand.

Read to me.

"Why, Danny, I am surprised at you," she said softly. "You know we can't begin without your friends."

The wind blew more phantoms through the open doors, gusts and wracks and tumbling clouds of children. They swept into the darkened library, whirling in eddies like the bright autumn leaves outside, catching in snug corners, in favorite chairs before the breath of their advent died away and left them all sitting in attentive order around Miss Louisa Foster's chair.

The stranger felt a tiny hand creep into hers, a hand whose damp clasp she had last disengaged as gently as she could from the breast of the young, despairing mother fated to survive the plunge the child did not. It was not the stranger's place to ask what became of her charges after she called for them. The child tugged insistently at her hand, then clambered up into her lap uninvited. She settled her head against the lady's shawled shoulder with a contented sigh, having found someone she knew. Her feet were bare and her golden hair smelled of factory smoke and river water.

"Now, shall we begin?" Miss Foster asked, beaming over the edge of the open book. Smiles answered her. "I think that if you are all very good, tonight we shall be finished with Tom Sawyer's adventures, and then—" Her voice caught, but she had been raised with what Judge Foster liked to call "breeding." She carried on. "—and then you shall rest."

She raised her eyes to the patient caller in the other chair. "You see how it is? Someone has to do this for them now. They were lost too young for anyone to share the stories with them—the old fairy tales, and Mother Goose, and *Kim,* and the legends of King Arthur, and *The Count of Monte Cristo,* and—and—oh! How can children be sent to sleep without stories? So I try."

"When—?" The lady with the lapdog wet her lips, so suddenly dry. "When did they first come to you?" The child leaning against her shoulder shifted, then pounced on the tangled tatting in her lap and sat happily creating a nest of Gordian knots as complex and as simple as the world.

"They came soon after I made over this room to be the town's library, after Father was dead. I scoured the shelves of his law books and filled them with all the tales of wonder and adventure and mischief and laughter they could hold. I was seated right here one midnight, reading aloud to myself from Asher's book of poetry, when the first one came." She leaned forward and fondly ruffled the hair of a little boy whose pinched face was still streaked with coal dust. "I never guessed until then that it was possible to hunger for something you have never known."

Then she bent and scooped up the child who held so tightly to her skirts. She set him on her lap and pressed his head to the high-necked, extremely proper sleekness of her dress front. The little ghost's black hair curled around the brooch that held his single strayed curl.

"One night, he was here with the rest. Come all the way from New York City, can you imagine that? And the roads so cold." Her lips brushed the white forehead. "So cold." She set him down again among the rest and gave the stranger a smile of forced brightness. "I've found that children sleep more peaceably after a story, haven't you?" Before her caller could reply, she added, "Please forgive me, but I don't like to keep them waiting."

Miss Foster began to read the last of Tom Sawyer's adventures. The oil lamp smoothed away the marks of fever and hunger and more violent death from the faces of the children who listened. As she read, the words slipped beneath the skin, brought a glow of delight to ravening eyes. In her own chair, Miss Foster's caller became conscious of a strange power filling the room. The ghosts were casting off their ghosts, old bleaknesses and sorrows, lingering memories of pain and dread. All that remained were the children, and the wonder.

At last, Miss Foster closed the book. "The. End," she announced, still from behind the stiffness of her smile. The children looked at her expectantly. "That was the end, children,"

301

she said gently. "I'm afraid that's all." The small ghosts' eyes dimmed. By ones and twos they drifted reluctantly from the lamplight, back toward the moonlit cold.

"Wait."

The stranger stood, still holding the little girl to his chest. He was dressed as a road-worn peddler, with his goods on his back and a keen black hound at his heels. He dropped his dusty rucksack on the rosewood desk and plunged his arm inside. "Here's *Huckleberry Finn*," he said. "You'll have to read them that after they've heard *Tom Sawyer*." He dug more books from the depths of the bag, piling each on each. "Oh, and *The Three Musketeers. Uncle Tom's Cabin. Little Lord Fauntleroy* . . . well, it takes all kinds. And *David Copperfield, Treasure Island, Anne of Green Gables, 20,000 Leagues Under the Sea, Sarah Crewe*—" He stared at the tower of books he had erected and gave a long, low whistle. "I reckon you'll have the wit to find more."

She seized his wrist, her voice urgent as she asked, "Is this a trick? Another joke that Father's own personal god wants to play on me?"

"No trick," he said. "I shall come back, I promise you that, Miss Louisa. I'll come back because I must, and you know I must."

She touched the mourning brooch at her throat. "When?"

"When I promised." His eyes met hers. "When you've finished reading."

He placed the girl-child in her lap, then lifted up her own lost son; together they were no more burden than the empty air. Her arms instinctively crept around to embrace them both and he placed an open book in her hands to seal the circle. "Or when you will."

"I don't—" she began.

"Read."

He shouldered his rucksack and whistled up his hound. The ghostly throng of children gazed at him as he passed through their midst to the French doors. Outside there was still smoke and apples on the air, and a thousand tales yet to be told. He paused on the threshold and turned to see her still sitting there in the lamplight, staring at him.

"Give them their stories, Louisa," he said, his face now aged by winds and rains and summer days uncountable. "Give them back their dreams."

"Once—" She faltered. The children drew in nearer, faces lifted like flowers to the rain. "Once upon a time . . ."

He watched as the words took them all beyond his reach, and he willingly let them go. He bowed his head beneath the moon's silver scythe blade and took a new road, the black dog trotting beside him all the way.